Discover why everyone's talking about
Charlotte Betts

Praise for *The Apothecary's Daughter*

'A colourful story with a richly drawn
backdrop of London in the grip of the plague.
A wonderful debut novel' Carole Matthews

'Romantic, engaging and hugely satisfying.
This is one of those novels that makes you feel like
you've travelled back in time' Katie Fforde

'A vivid tale of love in a time of plague
and prejudice' Katherine Webb

'If you are looking for a cracking good story and
to be transported to another age, you really
can't beat this' Deborah Swift

'A thoroughly enjoyable read which will
keep you enthralled until the very
last page' Jean Fullerton

Charlotte Betts began her working life as a fashion designer in London. A career followed in interior design, property management and lettings. Always a bookworm, Charlotte discovered her passion for writing after her three children and two step-children had grown up.

Her debut novel, *The Apothecary's Daughter*, won the YouWriteOn Book of the Year Award in 2010 and, the Joan Hessayon Award for New Writers. It was shortlisted for the Best Historical Read at the Festival of Romance in 2011 and won the coveted Romantic Novelists' Association's Historical Romantic Novel RoNA award in 2013. Her second novel, *The Painter's Apprentice*, was also shortlisted for Best Historical Read at the Festival of Romance in 2012 and the RoNA award in 2014. *The Spice Merchant's Wife* won the Festival of Romance's Best Historical Read award in 2013 and was shortlisted for the Romantic Novelists' Association's Historical Romantic Novel RoNA award in 2015.

Charlotte lives with her husband in a cottage in the woods on the Hampshire/Berkshire border.

Visit her website at www.charlottebetts.com and follow her on twitter at www.twitter.com/CharlotteBetts1

Also by Charlotte Betts:

The Apothecary's Daughter
The Painter's Apprentice
The Spice Merchant's Wife
The Milliner's Daughter (e only)
The Chateau by the Lake
Christmas at Quill Court (e only)

The House in Quill Court

Charlotte Betts

piatkus

PIATKUS

First published in Great Britain in 2016 by Piatkus
This paperback edition published in 2016 by Piatkus

1 3 5 7 9 10 8 6 4 2

A CIP catalogue record for this book
is available from the British Library.

ISBN 978-0-349-40453-0

Printed and bound in Great Britain by
Clays Ltd, St Ives plc

Papers used by Piatkus are from well-managed forests
and other responsible sources.

MIX
Paper from
responsible sources
FSC® C104740

Piatkus
An imprint of
Little, Brown Book Group
Carmelite House
50 Victoria Embankment
London EC4Y 0DZ

An Hachette UK Company
www.hachette.co.uk

www.piatkus.co.uk

For Sophia

Acknowledgements

Much like giving birth to a baby, producing a new novel is an exciting, emotional and sometimes uncomfortable experience. Now that the hard work is finished I hope that you, Dear Reader, will enjoy the fruits of my labours. This book will not truly live until you enter the world I have created.

My thanks go to everyone who helped me to bring this story into being: to all the team at Piatkus but especially my lovely editor Lucy Malagoni; to my wonderfully supportive agent, Heather Holden-Brown: and to the best-ever writers' group, WordWatchers, who encouraged me with helpful comments and cake.

Most of all, thank you to my family who have uncomplainingly accepted that my thoughts are often in another century, and especially to my husband Simon for bringing me endless cups of tea and not saying a word if the dinner is late.

Chapter 1

Kent

November 1813

Venetia skittered down the lane, her feet slithering over cobbles glistening from a recent shower. She pushed through the gate on to the tussocky cliff top where a blast of icy wind snatched at her blonde hair and pinched colour into her cheeks. The tide was out and the sun sinking. She'd have to be quick.

The narrow steps cut into the cliff side were as familiar to her as her own face as she'd climbed up and down them almost every day since she could remember. She stopped midway to catch her breath, clinging on to a cushion of thrift growing in a crevice. Salty wind tugged at her skirt, flapping it about her legs as she scrambled down, a basket clutched in one hand.

There'd been another landslip and clumps of chalk littered the ground at the base of the cliffs. Head down into the wind, she strode across the shifting sand. She scanned the water's edge where the ceaseless waves frothed on to the sand. There! Hurrying forward, she picked up a handful of bright green sea lettuce. Father would be home again soon and he always said that her sea lettuce soup was the best he'd ever tasted.

She gathered seaweed until her basket was full. The soothing suck and hiss of the sea whispered in her ears, as intimately known to her as the beat of her heart. Above, the wide dome of the sky was a gauzy pearl grey, melding with the water at the horizon so that it was impossible to distinguish where they met. The sun, bright white with a hazy halo, was reflected in a shimmering path, inviting her to cross the water. What would it be like to take the path over the horizon and enter that shining, radiant world? Suddenly seawater foamed around her boots and then shrank away again, halting such flights of fancy. The tide was turning. Time to go.

As she walked back to the chalky cliffs she picked up a whelk shell, partly encrusted with barnacles. She rubbed off the gritty sand with her skirt. The colour of thick cream, the shell was as big as a baby's fist and spiralled to a point. Inside it was shaded blush pink. A beautiful thing. Smooth under her fingers but with regular ridges and an intricate pattern of hair-thin crosshatching, it felt like the finely woven linen Father had ordered from Ireland for the sitting-room curtains.

She caught sight of a man on a chestnut horse cantering towards her along the sand, his cloak flying out behind. She squinted into the dying light as the thundering hooves drew closer and her heart lifted.

'Father!' she shouted, waving her arm.

Dante came to a standstill a few feet away, tossing his mane.

Her father, thick white hair blowing around his head, slid down from the saddle and caught her up in a hug. 'There you are, my darling girl! I came at once to find you.'

Venetia smiled and held up her basket. 'Sea lettuce for your soup.'

His green eyes smiled back at her. 'We'd better be away home,' he said, mounting Dante again.

She climbed up behind him and they trotted along the water's edge while the sun dropped into the sea.

Father looked over his shoulder. 'Hold tight!' he said.

Venetia wrapped her arms around his broad waist and rested her cheek against his solid back. His cloak smelled the way Father always did, a comforting mixture of leather, Eau de Cologne and tobacco.

Dante gathered speed and Father shouted in exhilaration as the wind buffeted their faces. The tide was out far enough for them to canter across the sand and round to the neighbouring bay. At last he pulled on the reins and guided Dante into a sedate trot towards the steep lane leading up to the town.

They clip-clopped over the cobbles and turned into a lane running parallel with the sea until they came to the higgledy-piggledy row of cottages set on the side of the hill. Lights glimmered in the windows.

Kitty opened the front door, her trim figure silhouetted against the light. She tucked a dark curl back into her cap and gave Father a welcoming smile.

'There's a smugglers' moon tonight,' he said, handing her his cloak. 'Isn't that right, Kitty?'

'If you say so, sir,' she replied, looking at him from under sweeping eyelashes.

A fire crackled in the parlour hearth and Mama, looking absurdly young for her forty-two years, sat beside it with her fair hair confined by a blue velvet ribbon that matched her eyes.

The black pug that had been lying curled in front of the fire leaped up and ran to greet them.

'Down, Caesar!' Father laughed as the dog jumped up at him, trying to lick his face.

'Caesar? That's not the first time you've called him that,' said Venetia.

'He looks like a Caesar. Sorry, Nero, old chap.' Father fondled the little creature's ears and then rubbed his hands together. 'Well, isn't this cosy?' As always, his solid figure looked too large for the neat little parlour. He peered at the fireplace. 'What's this I see? You've marbled the fireplace, Venetia?'

She nodded and held her breath while he ran one finger over the painted finish.

'You have a sure hand,' he said. 'It's quite as good as work produced by any of my painters' apprentices.'

She basked in the warmth of his smile.

'We had no fire for three days,' said Mama, 'and were obliged to sit in the kitchen to keep warm. But I will admit that I'm pleased with the result.'

'Mama, where's Raffie?' asked Venetia.

'He went to White Place Farm to see George.'

'Didn't you tell him he must be back by dark?'

'He'll be home soon.' Mama smiled at Father, her face glowing with love for him. 'You look tired, Theo. Now tell me what's been happening while you were away.'

Venetia peered between the curtains into the darkness outside. 'I'll go and look for him.'

'Raffie's seventeen and more able to look after himself in the dark than you are,' said Mama. 'He'll be going away to university next year.'

Venetia sighed and arranged the curtains into neat folds again, while unease whispered in her mind.

'Now, Fanny, my love,' said Father, 'have you been practising your pianoforte?'

Mama clasped her hands together. 'I have something new for us to sing.'

Venetia slipped out of the room. They'd be entirely wrapped up in each other for hours.

The kitchen was full of steam and a rotund little figure enveloped in a clean apron leaned over a simmering pan. 'I've put the leg of mutton on to boil, Miss Venetia,' said Mrs Allnut.

4

Kitty sat at the table peeling turnips.

From the parlour came the sound of the pianoforte and then Mama's clear voice singing 'The Last Rose of Summer'.

The back door opened abruptly, letting in a cold draught.

'Raffie!' said Venetia. 'I was worried.'

Her brother came forward into the light.

A gasp caught in her throat. There was blood on his cheek and his coat was muddy and torn.

'What happened?' she asked.

'I bet George I could stay on the back of one of his father's bullocks for three minutes.'

'And did you?' asked Kitty, her hazel eyes gleaming with suppressed laughter.

The boy thrust a hand into his pocket and grinned as he showed her a silver coin.

'You risked your life for half a crown?' Concern made Venetia's voice sharp.

'Don't fuss!' said Raffie.

'Sit down so I can clean you up before Mama sees.'

Sighing heavily, Raffie sat.

After supper, Father bellowed with laughter at the tale and clapped Raffie on the shoulder, calling him a chip off the old block. The family played whist by the fireside. Eventually Mama yawned and retired to bed, soon to be followed upstairs by Raffie.

Father stirred the embers with the poker and smiled at Venetia. 'I have something to show you.' He delved inside his saddlebag and pulled out a roll of thick paper, which he laid over the table. It was decorated in pretty shades of cream and French green, the ground imitating drapery with delicate pink rosebuds ascending in stripes.

Venetia laughed with pleasure. The rosebuds brought back to her those languorous days of summer she'd spent painting in the garden. To see the design she'd produced made into a paper hanging was a source of great excitement to her.

'I've called it "Venetia's Rose",' said Father. 'Soon it will make its debut in a Mrs Beresford's bedroom and then on the guest-room walls of a smart townhouse in Hanover Square. Furthermore, I've shown your sketches for the "Feather and Leaf" design to some other clients, who've expressed an interest.'

'And I've been working on more designs,' said Venetia. Full of enthusiasm, she opened her sketchbook to show him. 'I found a beautiful whelk shell today and I'll use that as inspiration for another design.'

Father put on his gold-framed spectacles and studied the drawings closely. 'The one with the garlands is delightful. I like this with the medallions and ribbon swags … it's perfect for grand staircases … but I'd like to see more pastel florals and stripes for bedrooms and also something bold for reception rooms.' He looked up at her and smiled. 'You've done well, my love.'

Venetia's heart swelled. When Father praised her she felt as if she could do anything.

He leaned back in his chair.

'If you turn a few pages you'll see my latest ideas for our imaginary shop,' Venetia said.

Father peered at the sketches. 'Here it is, just as I pictured it!'

'The wall panelling would be painted in cream with touches of gold so as not to compete with all the colours of the fabric samples,' she said. 'A shelf would run around the walls above head-height to display decorative items, and the furniture pattern books would be laid out on satinwood counters for customers to stand and look at them. There'd be sample carpets on the floor.' She held her breath, eyes fixed on her father's face while he studied her drawings. He looked tired and older than his fifty years tonight.

Nero jumped up on to his knee and settled down to doze.

6

At last Father put the book down. 'You have a gift for this, my darling. You should be working with me, Venetia.'

'Then why can't I? I can make as many designs for paper hangings and curtain and upholstery fabrics as you like.'

Father coughed and pressed a hand to his chest. 'Perhaps it might be possible. I doubt Raffie will follow me into the business. He hasn't the feel for it.' He closed his eyes and leaned back against the chair again, his fingers stroking Nero's silky coat.

Venetia frowned. 'Father, are you quite well?'

He opened his eyes and gave her a tight little smile. 'I'm tired after the travelling and my heart flutters a little. But it's so good to be at Spindrift Cottage again with my family. Nothing matters in this world except family, does it?'

'You need a drop of brandy.' Feeling suddenly anxious, she fetched the brandy and poured him a generous measure.

He held the bottle up to the firelight. 'Nearly finished. I'll have to speak to my fisherman friends to see when another consignment is expected. I have some curtain silk on order, too.'

Venetia's pulse steadied as the colour flowed back into Father's face. Just for a moment she'd been frightened.

'You know, I've been thinking a great deal lately about my old friend John Chamberlaine,' he said, staring into the fire.

'The one who died when you were travelling back from Italy?' She sat down on the rug at her father's feet and leaned against his knees. She'd heard the story before.

'After university,' he said, 'we spent two years on our Grand Tour. We planned to start up a business together afterwards. In Italy we bought antiques, paintings and artefacts, and sourced the best silks, paper hangings and furniture. Had 'em all shipped home. John acquired a wife, too. But then he developed a putrid inflammation of the lungs and it carried him off. Poor Clarissa! She was completely undone.'

'What happened to her?'

7

'She died, too, later on.'

'Of a broken heart?'

'Perhaps.' Father sighed deeply. 'John and I were only twenty-three and had everything to look forward to. It never occurred to us that we wouldn't live for ever.' He reached out and stroked her hair. 'We should all live each day as if it were our last because we never know when life may be snatched away from us.'

Venetia shivered. This wasn't at all like Father's usual blithe manner and she didn't like it. 'I wish you'd let me help you with the business. I'm sure I could learn.'

He dropped a kiss on top of her head. 'I know you could. But there are difficulties.' He sighed. 'So many obstacles to overcome.'

'Because I'm a woman?'

He shrugged. 'Once clients came to know you, I don't believe that would signify.'

'Lovell and Daughter. Don't you like the sound of that?'

Father laughed. 'I do.'

'Well, then?'

'I'm tired of travelling all over the country and must face up to the fact that I can't go on doing this alone. I've set a plan in motion but it's too soon to discuss things with you.'

'What plan?' Venetia laughed. 'You're being very mysterious.'

'You'll just have to wait and see. Now I think it's time for bed.'

❦

Kitty waited until the household settled before creeping downstairs, boots in hand. As she crossed the hall there was a movement in the shadows.

'Kitty?' The master was standing right in front of her.

She clutched her shawl to her throat. What did the old man think he was doing, creeping up on a body like that?

'I didn't mean to frighten you,' he murmured. 'Are you going to the cove?'

She nodded.

'I have some blue silk damask on order. Will you tell Tom Scott I need another bottle of brandy, too?'

'Yes, sir,' she whispered. Thank God, he wasn't going to punish her. But then, in his own way, he was as guilty as she was.

'Don't let me keep you.'

She bobbed a curtsey.

'And, Kitty?'

She turned, wary again.

'I'll leave the key under the mat.'

She closed the back door quietly and slipped on her boots. Tom was waiting for her at the bottom of the cliffs, with her pa and some of the other fishermen.

'All right, Kitty?' asked Pa, his hands in his pockets and shoulders hunched against the wind.

She nodded. 'And Ma and the little ones?'

He shrugged. 'Tired. Your ma's always tired.'

Tom took Kitty's hand and pulled her out of the wind into the narrow opening of one of the caves. His eyes gleamed in the moonlight as he planted a quick kiss on her mouth. 'Soon now,' he said, nodding towards the sea.

Shivering, she stared into the dark, waiting. Five hours was all it took in calm weather for twelve men to row the forty-foot-long galley from France, laden with brandy, silk shawls and kid gloves. Even with a headwind the boats were faster than any preventative officer's sailing vessel. 'Guinea boats' they called them. Tom had told her that upwards of thirty thousand pounds' worth of golden guineas couriered from London could be carried to Gravelines or Dunkirk on one trip in payment for the contraband goods that were then smuggled in. Thirty thousand pounds!

Kitty shifted her feet, not liking to think too hard about those guineas being used by Napoleon to feed his army. Sometimes she lay awake, imagining she could hear the sound of Boney's troops marching up from the beach to invade the town, and felt guilty for her own small part in the trade. But, as Pa said, free trade gave the fishermen a far better living to feed their families on than they could earn from the sea. God knows, they needed it.

Tom pulled her close and blew on her hands to warm them. 'Better?' he whispered.

She nodded, even though her fingers were cracked and bleeding from the day's washing and scrubbing. Tom only let her come and help on unloading nights. The other times were too dangerous, he said. When the guineas arrived from London they were brought under guard. Rough men armed with knives and pistols would line the beach and make sure the cargo wasn't interfered with, and that any preventative officers who dared show their faces were outnumbered and afraid.

Once, she'd hidden in one of the caves to watch. There'd been a big man in a caped greatcoat standing on the sand, counting the boxes of gold as they were lifted into the galleys. As he'd turned to look up the beach she'd frozen at the sight of his face, with its long nose and hooded eyes that seemed to bore straight into her, but he'd turned away without observing her, leaving Kitty shaky and sweating. They called him King Midas, she knew. He always travelled with armed bodyguards and she felt sick when she saw the moonlight glinting on their firearms. Since poor Jim Staycote had been shot in the face and killed by them, no one had dared cross King Midas.

'Look!' whispered Tom.

A low black shape was moving rapidly towards them over the sea; it was soon followed by another. Then, over the sighing of the waves, came the scrape of timber against shingle.

Men swarmed out of the shadows and ran towards the water's edge.

'Stay here!' hissed Tom, and set off to join them.

The bitter wind, damp with sea spray, wormed its way inside

Kitty's clothes, right under her shift. The last thing she needed tonight was to be freezing her innards on a beach. She yawned widely. Burning the candle at both ends, that was the trouble. Up at four to set the washing to soak and light the fires while the rest of the household snored away like pigs, and now she'd be late to bed because of the shipment. Still, she'd be a handful of coins richer when the night was out, a handful of coins closer to being able to leave this god-forsaken village and start a new life in London, where they said the streets were paved with gold.

Women's voices murmured from the cave to her left; a horse, yoked to a cart in the lee of the cliff, whinnied. Chewing at a broken nail, Kitty anxiously scanned her surroundings for preventative officers. She wasn't sure which scared her the most: the riding officers or the men from London.

Then Tom was back again and thrusting an armful of damp, canvas-wrapped parcels at her. 'Ma's waiting for you,' he said.

Kitty wrapped half the parcels in her shawl, tied it over her back, and lifted the rest in her arms. Several other women carrying similar burdens trudged past her over the sand. Silvery moonlight lit the way as she climbed the cliff steps. Their uneven risers and the weight of her bundle made Kitty's legs ache. Stopping halfway, she looked down at the cove and saw that the horse and laden cart were being led away and the men were busy rolling barrels and boxes into the caves. There was a narrow passage leading from them to the cellar of the Admiral's Arms.

A loose stone rattled over the rocks below. Her belly lurched. A preventative officer? Kitty froze, the bundle in her arms as heavy as a dead child. Nowhere to hide and a sharp stone in her back when she pressed herself against the cliff face. A dark figure lumbered into view. God help me! she prayed. But it was only Danny Hall, breath rasping in his throat as he struggled under the weight of two barrels strapped to his back. She started to climb again, dragging one foot after the other. A stitch bored into her side like a red-hot knitting needle and she didn't have a hand free to rub it. Jesus God! Would she ever reach the top? Then a gust of wind nearly blasted her off her feet as she emerged on to the summit of the cliff.

Ten minutes later she knocked softly on the back door of Tom's cottage. Mrs Scott must have been waiting on the step for her because the door opened so quickly Kitty almost fell into the kitchen. Together they rolled back the threadbare rag rug and lifted the trapdoor to the cellar.

Upstairs a child cried and Tom's ma stood motionless, listening. She was as thin as a lath, her hair drab and lifeless. The child wailed again. 'I'd better go,' she sighed. 'I'll send Jimmy down.'

Suddenly exhausted, Kitty sank on to the bench and laid her arms on the kitchen table. The scrubbed surface was rough under her cracked fingertips, covered in the thousand cuts and dents inflicted upon it by a family of eleven.

Wet clothes were draped over the rickety clothes-horse standing before the meagre fire. Torn and patched, they were in all sizes, from a baby's nightgown to Tom's oiled fishing sweater. Just like Kitty's own ma, Mrs Scott had produced a baby a year before her husband had drowned in a sudden squall a few months ago. And now Tom, the eldest, was responsible for the whole family.

Kitty fingered one of the canvas-wrapped parcels, imagining the silken shawls inside and wondering what it would be like to feel that slippery softness against her naked skin. Would anyone notice if she filched one out of the parcel and hid it under her shift? But she knew what had happened to others who'd thought like that. Besides, it wasn't her lot in life to own even a silk handkerchief, only to wash them for those she worked for.

Fourteen-year-old Jimmy came into the kitchen, nodded to her and climbed down the ladder into the cellar.

Silently, she passed the bundles down.

A few moments later Kitty was outside in the cold night air again, hurrying back to the cove. There were two or three more loads yet and weariness made it hard for her to set one foot in front of the other. She was eighteen years old and already half worn out. Tom, with his warm hands and urgent lips, wanted to marry her. Perhaps she loved him, she wasn't sure, but the thought of living in that cramped cottage with his ma and all his brothers and sisters made Kitty want to cry. Their childhood days of running barefoot over the sand and falling about with laughter as they splashed in the surf seemed a very long time ago.

Wiping her nose on the back of her hand, she set her mind resolutely to the task in hand.

Chapter 2

Kitty thumped the buckets on the frozen ground and knocked the ice off the pump handle. Wrapping her hand in her apron against the biting cold of the iron, she grasped the handle and resentfully worked it up and down. The pump gurgled and spewed a dribble of water into the bucket while her breath clouded the air like Mr Lovell's tobacco smoke.

Heaving the buckets along the path, she shouldered through the scullery door where a heap of muddy boots and the dubbin pot awaited her attention.

'Kitty!' Mrs Allnut's voice called from the kitchen. 'There's coal wanted in the parlour before you peel the carrots.'

She rolled her eyes to the ceiling and huffed. Was there no let up? What with Christmas coming in a few days, there'd be a goose to pluck, silver to polish and tablecloths to starch. Mr Lovell would be home again on Christmas Eve bringing his washing and his exuberant presence to disturb the smooth running of the household, not to mention the shaving water to be carried upstairs and extra stinking chamber pots to be carried down.

In the fuggy warmth of the parlour Nero snored gently on the hearthrug. Miss Venetia was scribbling in her sketchbook again while the missus lay on the chaise-longue, reading. Neither of them lifted their eyes to look at Kitty as she picked up the coal scuttle. There was something very wrong with the world when some people could laze about all day while others worked their fingers to the bone, she thought. She hurried outside again, the coal scuttle banging against her knee and leaving black smudges on her skirt.

Prising apart frozen lumps of coal with the shovel, she started when a man dressed in black appeared silently beside her. Lifting up the coal shovel, Kitty turned towards him. 'What are you doing in our garden?' If she hadn't been so uneasy, she'd have giggled to see the way that he jumped.

'I beg your pardon,' he said, leaning heavily on his ebony cane. 'I wonder if your mistress is at home?'

'You could have knocked at the door like everyone else.' Her voice sounded tart, too tart to use with a visitor, especially such a handsome one, but he'd made her uneasy.

'I wasn't sure if this was the right house,' he said. His hair was black as soot but his eyes were the blue of the sea on a summer's day. He smiled and it was like the sun coming out. 'You can put that down now, I'm not going to hurt you.'

Kitty realised that she was still holding the coal shovel aloft as if ready to batter his brains out. 'You're wanting to see Mrs Lovell then?' Keeping her back ramrod straight, she led him to the front door. 'I'll go round and let you in.'

Scurrying back to the kitchen, she called out 'Visitor!' to Mrs Allnut, then dragged off her coat and dropped it on the hook before walking briskly through the hall to open the front door.

She took the caller's coat and hat as if this were the first time they'd met. 'Who shall I say is calling?'

'Major Chamberlaine,' he said, pushing his unruly curls into some semblance of order as he spoke.

15

She opened the parlour door.

Nero opened one eye and growled and the missus put down her book and looked up expectantly. She got bored very easily, did the missus, and was always pleased to have a visitor, even if it was only the curate. 'Who is it, Kitty?'

'Major Chamberlaine.'

The book slid off the missus's knee and hit the floor with a thump. She turned as white as a sheet and her eyes were wide open as she stared out through the door into the hall.

The visitor paused in the doorway, his gaze fixed on Miss Venetia. His shoulders sagged. 'So it's true,' he murmured.

Then he was in the room and Kitty was on the other side of the closed door.

'Who was it?' asked Mrs Allnut as Kitty returned to the kitchen.

Kitty shrugged. 'Just a man. Nice-looking, though.'

'Not your place to comment, Kitty. Did they ask for tea?'

'Not yet.'

Mrs Allnut sighed. 'There's only stale pound cake and I'm not baking until this afternoon. Did you bank the fire?'

Kitty clamped a hand to her mouth. 'I left the coal scuttle outside.'

'Then go and fetch it, sharpish.' Mrs Allnut opened the larder door and surveyed the shelves. 'Let's hope he isn't staying to dinner,' she muttered.

Kitty braved the cold and brought the coal scuttle back indoors. What had the visitor meant by, 'So it's true'? Her hand was on the parlour door when she heard a shriek from inside the room. Alarmed, she hesitated and then turned the handle quietly and peeped through the gap. She needn't have worried; no one was looking at her.

The missus was wailing and throwing herself about on the chaise-longue, with Miss Venetia bent over her.

The gentleman, nearly as tall as the low ceiling, stood there in his black velvet coat watching them, with his mouth all pursed up like a cat's bottom.

At last the missus subsided into sobs with her head resting on Miss Venetia's shoulder.

Venetia looked up at the gentleman. 'Please, sir, will you explain more fully what happened?' Her face was as bleached as new-washed linen.

Major Chamberlaine lifted up his coat tails and perched on the edge of a chair. 'He was set upon by intruders ...'

'Oh, tell me they didn't beat him!' begged the missus, her hands clasped over her breast.

Major Chamberlaine chewed at his lip. 'They threatened him. When I found him he was pale and his lips were blue. He said his arm hurt. Afterwards, the doctor said that his heart could not withstand the shock of the attack.'

'But where is he?' The missus struggled to her feet. 'I must go to him!'

'It's too late, Madam,' said the gentleman. 'The snow made road conditions so bad I couldn't travel immediately and a two-day journey has taken four. We were obliged to bury Mr Lovell before I was able to bring you the news.'

Kitty pressed her knuckles against her mouth. Jesus God! There'd be some changes now and no mistake. She backed silently away, leaving the coal scuttle in the hall, and ran to the kitchen.

'Whatever is it?' asked Mrs Allnut. 'Did you spill the coal?' She lifted the big soup tureen off the dresser. 'Well?'

Kitty shook her head. 'It's poor Mr Lovell. He's dead.'

The crash as the tureen hit the stone flags reverberated around the kitchen. Shards of china skittered across the floor, spinning under the dresser and into the pantry.

Slowly, Kitty bent to pick up one of the largest fragments and then another. She ran her thumb over the delicate gold brushwork that curled over the painted surface and pressed the sharp edges together.

But some things can never be mended.

'I beg your pardon, Major Chamberlaine,' Venetia said formally, 'we haven't offered you any refreshment after your journey.' Uttering vacuous social pleasantries was a great deal easier than acknowledging the anguish that made it so hard for her to breathe.

Mama's weeping subsided into hiccoughing sobs while the stranger watched them intently with cool blue eyes.

'The news is naturally a great shock to us,' said Venetia. 'Do you ... did you know my father well, Major Chamberlaine?'

He stood up so abruptly that the chair scraped noisily across the floor. 'Your father's lawyer, Mr Tyndall, is outside. We hired a post-chaise for the journey and I asked him to wait until I'd broken the news to you. I'll fetch him.'

Venetia followed him into the hall and watched him limp down the front steps before she retreated inside. She gripped the newel post while she fought to steady herself then walked with dragging steps to the kitchen.

'Have you seen Raffie?' she asked.

Mutely, Mrs Allnut and Kitty shook their heads.

'Can you bring tea? Four cups, please, since we expect another visitor.'

'Yes, Miss Venetia.' Kitty bobbed a curtsey, her pretty face unusually sombre.

'And if Raffie returns, will you send him in straight away?'

Mama waited for her in the parlour, hunched over on the chaise-longue, her sodden handkerchief balled in one fist. 'I always knew this day would come, your dear father being ten years older than myself ...' She drew in a ragged breath. 'But I never expected it would be so soon.'

18

A moment later Major Chamberlaine and a stout man dressed in sober brown entered the parlour.

'Miss Venetia Lovell, I presume?' A few strands of greying hair were carefully brushed forward over the shiny pink dome of Mr Tyndall's head.

She nodded. 'And this is my mother.'

Mr Tyndall bowed to Mrs Lovell. 'I regret the unfortunate circumstances of our meeting, Madam.'

Venetia glanced at Major Chamberlaine. His face was expressionless but his clasped hands clenched and unclenched on the head of his cane as if he were nervous. 'Will you tell us more about what happened, Mr Tyndall?' she requested.

'I met Mr Lovell a week or two before his unfortunate demise, when he came to me to revise his will.' The lawyer looked at and frowned. 'He imparted to me certain ... delicate information.'

'Delicate?' queried Venetia.

Mr Tyndall glanced at Mama, who sobbed and looked away.

Venetia addressed Major Chamberlaine. 'As this is a family matter perhaps we might ask you to be kind enough to wait in the study?'

Mr Tyndall smiled thinly. 'This is indeed a private family matter, Miss Lovell, which is why Major Chamberlaine must be present.'

'Please explain.' Something nagged at the back of Venetia's memory. Sitting here in this very room there was something Father had said ...

'The chain of events Mr Lovell described to me began in 1787,' Mr Tyndall began. 'He was travelling back from Italy with his friend, John Chamberlaine ...'

'Oh!' said Venetia as realisation dawned. She turned to Major Chamberlaine. 'Are you related to my father's friend John Chamberlaine?'

'My father.' There was a brief flash of blue as he glanced at her, before fixing his gaze steadily on the beautifully polished leather of his top boots.

'As I was saying, they were travelling abroad when John Chamberlaine passed away. Before his friend died, Mr Lovell promised to take care of his friend's bride.'

'Clarissa,' said Venetia. 'Father mentioned her.'

'Your father spoke of her to *you*?' said Mama, her voice suddenly shrill.

'Perhaps what he didn't tell you,' said Major Chamberlaine, in equally sharp tones, 'was that Mr Lovell married Clarissa when it became apparent that she was expecting his friend's child. Myself, in fact.'

'*Married* her?' Venetia looked at Mama. 'You never told me that Father was a widower when he married you.'

Mama dabbed her eyes and moaned softly.

Mr Tyndall cleared his throat. 'It's my duty, Miss Lovell, to apprise you of a certain situation.' His mouth folded into a prim line but there was an anticipatory gleam in his eyes that made a tremor of alarm shiver up Venetia's spine.

'What is it?'

'I have to inform you that Mrs Lovell, Mrs *Clarissa* Lovell, that is, unfortunately passed away eighteen months ago.'

Venetia stared at him. 'You've made a mistake. My mother and father have been married for twenty-three years. Clarissa must have died twenty-four years ago.'

Major Chamberlaine stood up abruptly. 'I assure you, she did not. Mother and I lived together with my stepfather, Theodore Lovell, until her untimely death the summer before last.'

Venetia shook her head. There must be some confusion. 'Father lived here at Spindrift Cottage with my mother, my brother and myself.'

'For the avoidance of any doubt,' said Mr Tyndall, 'your father may have *visited* you here but his home was in Islington, a village near London. He remained married to Clarissa until the day she passed away.'

Venetia clenched her fists. Who did these people think they were, barging into her home and telling such lies? Had they no shame about coming to upset them when they'd just heard that Father was dead, killed in some kind of attack?

In the hall, the front door slammed.

Stony-faced, the two men watched her, while Mama sobbed into her handkerchief.

'Mama?' A tremor of alarm ran through Venetia. Why didn't her mother say anything?

The door burst open and Raffie sauntered in, his flaxen hair windblown and the scent of sea air on his clothes. He stopped when he saw the visitors and gave them his angelic smile.

'Mr Tyndall, Major Chamberlaine,' said Venetia, 'this is Rafaele Lovell, my brother.' Her stomach turned over with dread. She'd have to tell him straight away about Father. 'Raffie dear,' she said, 'will you sit down a moment?'

'Is Kitty bringing tea, Mama? I'm starving.' Clods of mud fell off Raffie's boots on to the rug and he picked up the largest piece and threw it in the fire.

'Raffie, these gentlemen have brought very bad news,' said Venetia. She took a deep breath to counteract a sudden wave of nausea.

Raffie looked at her, uncertain why she seemed so serious. 'What?'

She swallowed the bile that had risen in her throat. 'Father was attacked.'

'Is he all right?

Venetia shook her head. 'The shock of it ...'

Raffie became very still. 'Is he dead?'

Slowly, Venetia nodded.

The fresh pink drained away from his cheeks.

Major Chamberlaine cleared his throat. 'I found him after the attack. Your father wasn't in terrible pain. His heart simply stopped.'

Raffie swallowed, his eyes glistening.

Mr Tyndall cleared his throat. 'If I may continue? The situation is that Mr Lovell had two homes and two families ...'

Raffie reared to his feet. 'What nonsense is this?'

Mr Tyndall quelled him with a look. 'As I was saying, Mr Lovell's marriage to Clarissa twenty-five years ago provided him with a step-son, Jack,' he inclined his head to Major Chamberlaine, 'and fifteen years ago, a daughter, Florence.'

Venetia gasped. Father had another daughter! Anger and distress flooded through her. How could he? *She* was his daughter, his special girl. A sob escaped her. He'd *always* called her that.

Mr Tyndall addressed Mama. 'Mr Lovell bigamously married you, Madam, Frances Laetitia Wynne, some twenty-three years ago.'

There was a long silence.

'Mama?' said Venetia.

Then Raffie erupted from his chair again and stared at them, wild-eyed. 'So Venetia and I are bastards?'

'Raffie!' Venetia put a restraining hand on his arm but he shook her off. 'Is that it, Mama?'

'No!' She looked up at him imploringly, her eyes red from weeping. 'Your father and I were properly married last year, after Clarissa passed away.'

'But we're still bastards, aren't we?' Raffie kicked the brass fender and strode out of the room, slamming the door so hard flakes of plaster drifted down from the ceiling.

Major Chamberlaine raised his eyebrows.

A moment later the front door banged shut.

Silence hung thick in the air.

A shaking Venetia wondered where the tea had got to.

'Now that the facts are established we may consider practical matters,' said Mr Tyndall. 'Mr Lovell divulged to me that it was no longer possible for him to maintain separate households. Since his

22

first wife had passed away and he'd remarried,' Mr Tyndall inclined his head to Mama, 'his intention was to combine both families under one roof.'

'But there's no room at Spindrift Cottage for anyone else!' said Mama.

Mr Tyndall smiled thinly. 'Mr Lovell had intended to discuss this with you on his next visit. He had already given notice to your landlord before he came to see me. You will leave here in January to live in his London house.'

'London?' asked Mama.

'Your late husband invested heavily in a business venture and there are no savings left for you to draw upon. He intended you all to work together to furnish the income necessary to support yourselves.'

'Live together? Support ourselves!' Mama clapped one hand to her breast. 'We can't! It's monstrous!'

'Madam, I can only agree,' said Major Chamberlaine, his lips curling in distaste at the prospect.

The door opened and Kitty carried in the rattling tea tray and placed it on the table. 'Will there be anything else, Miss Venetia?' she murmured.

Venetia caught, and held, Kitty's sideways glance. The maid's cheeks blossomed rose pink but her eyes were full of pity. There were never any secrets from the servants. 'No. Thank you, Kitty. There's nothing you can do.'

Chapter 3

January 1814

Venetia was bone weary, an exhaustion wrought from grief and fear. The fortnight since Mr Tyndall and Major Chamberlaine had made their terrible disclosures had been unbearably painful. She wasn't sure which was worse, Mama's continual weeping or Raffie's silences broken only by sudden outbursts of temper. He'd gone very quiet, however, when Venetia had told him that they hadn't a feather to fly with and it was impossible in the present circumstances to find the funds for him to go to university.

Whatever had made Father imagine bringing his two families together could possibly work? All these years she'd believed there was a special closeness between them, that she knew him inside out, but he'd lied to her and betrayed them all. How could she live with this half-sister, Florence, the cuckoo in the nest? And what future was there for Venetia herself now? No man would marry a love-child without a fortune.

'It was always me your father loved,' said Mama, her soft mouth quivering. 'He married Clarissa out of pity and then, when we met, he knew he'd made a terrible mistake.'

'But, Mama, you must have known he already had a wife?'

'I didn't! He used to call at my father's draper's shop with samples of brocade and spread out all those luxurious pieces of silk for me to choose from.' Mama sighed. 'Oh, Venetia, he had such a charming way about him and made me laugh so with all his stories. I fell in love with him straight away.'

'But Father deceived you about Clarissa?'

Mama's eyes were bright with tears. 'You mustn't judge him, Venetia. He never loved Clarissa but he'd promised John to look after her.'

'But he still asked you to marry him.'

'I *begged* him to marry me when ...' Mama flushed and looked away.

'When what?'

'When I knew I was expecting you.'

Venetia gasped.

Mama lifted her chin defiantly. 'We loved each other. When I told him I was expecting a child, he didn't hesitate. He had no wish to see me disgraced. It wasn't until years later that I found out about Clarissa. Our wedding after she died made our marriage legal but we'd *always* felt that ours was the true union.'

Venetia rubbed her temples. Raffie was right. There was no escaping the fact that they were illegitimate. And now, they were about to lose their home.

She went to the window and rested her forehead against the glass. Rain dripped steadily from a leaden sky and the sea was obscured by mist. 'We cannot delay any longer telling the servants we're moving to London,' she said.

'But, Venetia, I can't possibly ...'

'Then I suppose I must.'

She hovered outside the kitchen while she planned how to break the news.

Kitty erupted into the passage with her arms full of freshly ironed linen.

'I must speak to you and Mr and Mrs Allnut,' said Venetia.

Old Mr Allnut was at the kitchen table, polishing the silver. He struggled to his feet, clattering the sauceboats together in his haste.

Mrs Allnut came out of the pantry with a bowl of eggs in her hand.

They arranged themselves awkwardly around the table and Mr Allnut replaced the half lemon into the bowl of salt he'd been using to scour the silver.

'It is with no pleasure at all that I must tell you the Lovell family is to leave Spindrift Cottage,' announced Venetia.

Mrs Allnut glanced fearfully at her husband and he reached out with one knobbly old hand to grip her wrist.

'Since our situation has changed, we're obliged to remove to London,' Venetia continued miserably.

'Are we to be turned off?' asked Kitty.

'If you wish to come with us, I'll see if it can be arranged.'

Kitty's hazel eyes lit up with excitement, which she quickly concealed by dropping her gaze to the half-polished silver.

Mr Allnut cleared his throat. 'Mrs Allnut and myself couldn't consider London at our time of life.'

'I quite understand,' said Venetia. 'And I'm sorry it has come to this.'

'I want to go to London.' Kitty's voice was high and quick.

'But all your family are here, Kitty!' The girl had no idea how lonely she might be, far away from everything she'd ever known.

'I've been saving up to go there.' Kitty's eyes burned with eagerness. 'There're opportunities.'

'Well, if you're sure ...'

Kitty nodded her head vigorously.

'Then I'll write to Major Chamberlaine.'

❧

Ten days later, after she'd gone through the painful business of saying goodbye to her family, Kitty hurried down to the beach, trying to forget how little Jamie had clung to her legs, screaming and begging her to stay.

Tom sat on an upturned rowing boat mending his nets. He didn't look at her as she sat down beside him, shoulder to shoulder, and studied him from under her eyelashes. Light reflected from the sea glinted off the blond stubble on his cheeks but he continued to focus his eyes on his blunt fingers, busy amongst the torn net draped over his knees.

'Tom?'

He didn't answer her.

'Tom, I'm leaving in the morning and I don't want us to part on bad terms.'

His fingers stilled while the sea breeze ruffled his hair.

'Tom Scott,' Kitty scolded him, 'we've known each other since we were knee-high to a lobster pot and I want a smile to remember you by.'

Slowly, he turned to face her and she wasn't sure if it was the wind that had raised tears in his sea-grey eyes. 'I'll ask you again, Kitty. Will you marry me?' He waited, his face taut.

'I cannot,' she whispered. It was like a marlinspike in her breast to hurt him but she knew she couldn't move into that tiny cottage with all those children and his mother. And if she married him, before long there'd be more little ones and she'd be trapped for ever.

Tom stared out at the endless, restless sea; the sea that gave them a meagre living but had stolen his father. He lifted his head to the rain-filled sky as a gull soared overhead. 'King Midas owes us money. When he's paid, perhaps I'll be able to rent us a cottage of our own. Or perhaps there's money to be made in London.'

Kitty stroked his cheek, his pain affecting her, too. 'Your mother and the children need you here.'

He grasped her hand so tightly that she winced. 'But I need *you*,' he said, his voice fierce as he gathered her in his arms.

27

She almost succumbed. He was home and familiarity. But then she pushed him gently away. 'I'm leaving in the morning, Tom.' She kissed his cheek, the sharp bristles grazing her lips, and hurried away before she weakened.

Great black clouds rolled across the sky and rain from the sudden squall needled her face as she climbed the cliff steps. She looked out over the sea and saw a figure walking along the water's edge: Miss Venetia. Her arms were wrapped tightly around her chest and her face was lifted to the sky. The wind and rain tore at her skirt and whipped her hair into rat's tails. Miss Venetia was finding it hard to say goodbye, too.

Kitty woke early the following morning, her heart thumping. She dressed quickly, stripped the bed and then looked around the attic room that had been her home for the last three years. Ignoring a pang of regret, she lugged her box down the stairs.

There was a flurry of activity and in no time at all the Lovells' travelling bags and Kitty's box stood on the front doorstep.

Mrs Allnut remained to clean the house and oversee the loading of the cart that was to take the family's goods and chattels up to London the following day; Mr Allnut walked with them into the town, carrying Mrs Lovell's bag. Miss Venetia, waxen-faced with misery, escorted Nero on his lead. He insisted on lifting his leg at every gatepost.

Kitty struggled along behind, the box containing all her worldly goods weighing her down.

Master Raffie glanced at her over his shoulder and waited for her to catch up. 'Let me take one of the handles,' he offered.

The courtyard of the Coach and Horses was bustling. Mrs Lovell, Miss Venetia and Master Raffie were quickly settled inside the coach along with Nero and the other inside passengers. Porters strapped luggage to the roof and the outside passengers climbed up to take their perches beside it.

Kitty looked up in dismay. Even if she could climb there without displaying her knees to all and sundry, how would she manage to stop herself from falling off?

'Don't worry, Kitty,' said Mr Allnut, smiling at her so widely that she could see his empty pink gums.

A net was slung between the back wheels, half-full of luggage. Mr Allnut hoisted her box into it. 'Sit there and watch the world go by,' he advised.

Gingerly, she climbed in and arranged herself with her feet hanging over the edge. 'I hope you settle in all right with your sister,' she told him.

'She'll be glad of the company, now that she's widowed. And it was time for us to retire.' He cleared his throat. 'Mrs Allnut and I will miss you.'

Suddenly there was a lump in her throat and she reached out to touch his arm, something she'd never dared to do before.

The coach jerked forward and Kitty clasped the edge of the net. Excitement made her want to visit the privy again but then the wheels began to turn.

And they were off!

As they gathered speed she watched Mr Allnut dwindle in size and finally shrink and disappear.

Chapter 4

Kitty's fingers were numb and she was too cold to unhook them from the edge of the luggage net and blow warmth back into them. Her feet were frozen too as they dangled over the grey slush covering the road that unfolded before her as she travelled backwards through the countryside. Mud and chips of ice continually splattered up from between the coach's wheels. She doubted she'd ever get her stockings clean again.

The three-day journey had been a torment of jolting potholes and being soaked by the wake of passing coaches. She hadn't trusted herself to say anything when the missus, tucked up all day inside the coach with a blanket and a hot brick, complained of the cold. She'd no idea what cold was really like! After the first day, when there'd been a blizzard that encased Kitty in snow, she'd withdrawn into a trance where she couldn't think any more but only endure, like a hibernating hedgehog curled up under leaves in midwinter. Not dead but not quite alive neither.

Something bounced on to her lap.

'Hey, sleepyhead!'

She looked up at the grinning faces of two men travelling on top of the coach as another piece of orange peel flew past her ear.

'I'm not asleep,' Kitty called back, 'just frozen solid.'

The man, barely more than a youth, nudged his travelling companion. 'We'll warm you up!' He drew a flask from inside his coat and took a swig.

'Don't be impertinent,' she said, trying not to smile.

'We'll be in London soon,' shouted the other youth, wiping his nose on his cuff.

'If we haven't turned into icicles by then.'

The road became choked with carriages and waggons. Horsemen overtook them constantly and pedestrians carrying backpacks trudged wearily along the verges.

Over to her left in the distance was the river, thickly covered with a forest of masts as boats waited to make their way towards the wharves. The coach swayed and creaked its way past a brewery and Kitty wrinkled her nose at its sickly smell. An acrid stench rose from the tanneries that lined the road, too, and over it all lay the stink of river mud, thick with rotting vegetation, tar, and decay. If the stink was this strong in winter, whatever would it be like in summer?

'The Tower,' shouted one of the youths on the roof.

Kitty peered over her shoulder but it was impossible for her to see anything in front of the coach, only what lay behind.

After a few minutes her eyes widened as the vast bulk of the Tower of London loomed into view on the opposite bank of the Thames. High as the chalk cliffs at home, it was surrounded by impenetrable walls of grey stone with a tower at each corner. It fair gave her the creeps when she thought of all the important people who'd had their heads cut off there.

A milling flock of sheep brought the coach to a standstill and the coachman blew his horn, sending the flock scattering in all directions before the vehicle lurched off again. There were fewer open fields and more buildings now, and before long the road was lined with houses.

The coach turned on to the bridge over the Thames. Kitty's bones felt as if they had been shaken to pieces by all the ruts and potholes but she sat up straighter, revived by excitement. Any moment now they would reach the city. A nose-to-tail stream of traffic passed by, iron-trimmed wheels grinding on the cobbles and sending up a spray of slush. With a glance over the side of the bridge she saw that the Thames was almost entirely frozen over; only a narrow channel of water remained to allow the river traffic to pass.

On the roof the two young men began to sing a bawdy song, leaning down and waving their arms to encourage Kitty to join in. She didn't accompany them, in case the Lovells heard her, but her heart was singing. The city of her dreams was only minutes away.

Raffie opened the coach's window to lean out and see what was causing the delay.

Nero stood up on Venetia's knee, ears pricked as a dog barked outside.

'What's happening?' she asked. The icy draught from the open window carried with it the ammoniac smell of horse dung.

'There's an argument going on between the driver of a dust cart and someone with a waggon load of furniture.'

The altercation reached their ears over the shouts of coster-mongers, horses whinnying and coach horns braying, while the passengers on top of the coach sang raucously, drumming their heels on the roof.

The elderly woman sitting opposite, with her bony knees pressed hard against Venetia's, raised a handkerchief to her nose.

Mama, huddled in a corner seat, slumbered on. She'd barely slept for the previous twenty-four hours, fretted to death by fleas in her bed at the inn last night.

The coach began to roll forwards again.

Venetia gazed listlessly out of the window at the tall, flat-fronted houses, so different from the characterful cottage she was used to, with its beamed ceilings, sloping floors and sway-backed roof.

'We must be nearly there now,' said Raffie.

Venetia sighed. Unhappiness lodged like an indigestible lump of dough in her stomach but, as uncomfortable as the journey had been, she dreaded their arrival even more and the prospect of having to face Major Chamberlaine with his frosty blue eyes. And then there was the girl, Florence. Her half-sister. She'd be sure to resent their intrusion into her home quite as much as Jack Chamberlaine did. Father had put them all in an untenable position. A flash of anger with him almost made Venetia forget her misery.

The coach turned into the courtyard of the Crosse Keys and there was a flurry of activity as the passengers gathered their belongings. The door was flung open and one by one the passengers descended, stretching out cramped limbs.

Mama clung unsteadily to Venetia who felt as if the ground still swayed under her feet, so used had she become to the motion of the coach.

Kitty, filthy with road spray but with her eyes shining with anticipation, lugged her box out of the net. A fleshy woman, dressed in a purple pelisse and jaunty feathered hat, went to help her.

Stable lads released the sweating horses and led them away, hooves clopping on the cobbles. All around was clamour and motion as passengers greeted relatives and friends. A swarm of ragged children darted amongst them, as noisy as seagulls when a catch came in, pulling at their clothing and begging a penny to carry their bags.

Suddenly Kitty shouted a warning.

Raffie yelled, 'Stop, thief!' He chased after a boy in a cap and a moment later caught him by his sleeve.

Pandemonium broke out as the other children shrieked and set upon Raffie, while he gripped the squirming boy.

Nero yapped furiously at the miscreants, tangling his lead around Venetia's legs as he darted backwards and forwards.

A young man appeared from nowhere. He grasped the villain's arm and sent the other children flying with a swipe of his arm. 'Get away, you little ruffians!' He retrieved Raffie's handkerchief from inside the boy's tattered coat. 'If I catch you again you'll be gallows meat.' He boxed the cringing boy's ears and sent him off on the toe of his boot. Turning to Raffie, he bowed and held out the handkerchief. 'Yours, sir?'

Raffie took it from him. 'I'm in your debt,' he said, feeling in his pocket.

'New to London?' The man shook his head at the proffered coin.

'Indeed we are. Thank you for assisting us,' said Venetia. Although clearly not a gentleman, their benefactor wore a smart blue velvet coat and clean necktie.

'Nathaniel Griggs, at your service.' He gave a gap-toothed smile and his dark eyes gleamed with amusement. 'I do believe the guttersnipes can smell a new arrival. Come far?'

'Kent. We're to live in Quill Court,' said Raffie.

'That's only a step from here.' Griggs nodded at the street children watching them from a distance. 'Poor little blighters, they're half starving. What say you give 'em a penny to carry your bags and I'll keep an eye out to make sure they don't run away with 'em?'

A few minutes later a procession of children, each with a bag on one shoulder, set off out of the courtyard, closely followed by the Lovells. Griggs shook his head at the woman in the purple pelisse as she spoke to Kitty and hoisted the maid's box up on his own shoulder.

Griggs was as good as his word. He guided the party along the busy thoroughfare that was Gracechurch Street before turning into a narrow lane leading to Quill Court.

'Here we are then!' He waved expansively at the imposing four-storey brick houses set around a courtyard with an oak tree in the centre.

Venetia handed him some coins. 'For the children, Mr Griggs.'

'My pleasure, miss.' He bowed to her, then to Mama, and shook hands with Raffie. 'Should you need any little service, you being new to London and all, you can leave me a note at the Crosse Keys.' He nodded to them and left. Venetia wasn't sure but she thought he might have winked at Kitty.

Quill Court was quiet after the hustle and bustle of Gracechurch Street. A path had been cleared through the snow to the steps leading to each front door. Venetia looked up at number five. A great lion's head doorknocker gleamed on the black-painted door. It was odd to imagine that for Father this grand house had been a home quite as much as Spindrift Cottage had.

Mama's hand slid into Venetia's.

Raffie gave them a wavering smile. 'Together we stand!'

Venetia nodded. There was no going back. However anxious and uncomfortable they were about the situation, it was what Father had wanted. And perhaps Jack Chamberlaine might prove to be more pleasant upon further acquaintance?

Raffie raised the heavy brass ring held in the lion's mouth and let it fall twice against the door.

Nero lifted his leg against the boot scraper and Venetia was mortified to see the yellow trail left in the snow. Still, better there than inside.

A young maid in a clean apron opened the door. She wore a black armband.

'I am Mrs Lovell,' said Mama.

The girl stood back. 'Please come in, Madam. Your maid can go down the area steps and wait for me there.'

Venetia glanced at Kitty as she began to lug her box down the steps. The poor creature looked half frozen. Later, Venetia decided, she would make sure their maid was comfortably settled.

They trooped into the hall and began to divest themselves of their coats.

It was a narrow space with a high ceiling and a stone floor inset with black marble diamonds. Stairs with a mahogany handrail led up to the first floor. There was a lingering smell of fresh paint and London smog, so different from Spindrift Cottage, where the scent of pot-pourri mixed with briny sea air permeated the rooms.

Venetia couldn't help noticing the elegant striped paper hanging in pale grey and white, finished with a richly decorated gold and purple border of garlands ornamented with pearls and rosettes. Father had brought samples of it for her approval some months before, telling her he was decorating the hall of a London townhouse. She could never have imagined the samples were for a house she would live in herself. But however smart it was, it wasn't home to her.

Taking off her bonnet, she placed it on a gilded console table. She peered into the mirror hanging above and tucked a blonde curl back into her topknot. Her face was wan and she definitely didn't look her best. She sighed. She'd just have to face Major Chamberlaine as she was and hope that Florence wouldn't be as antagonistic as she feared.

'You're expected in the drawing room,' said the maid.

'Will you take our dog to the kitchen?' asked Venetia.

The maid took Nero's lead and opened the drawing-room door.

Mama's face was as pale as Venetia's when they linked arms to enter. They stepped over the threshold together with Raffie close behind.

It was a graceful room with pea green walls and lofty ceiling with a decorative cornice. A French rug in soft shades of cream, gold and peach lay on the polished boards. Venetia's eye was immediately drawn to a painting of Venice at sunset hanging above the white marble fireplace. Father's touch was present wherever she looked and it made her want to weep.

A dark-haired child, no, a girl, sat on the sofa by the fire, dressed in deep mourning. She sprang to her feet. 'At last!' she said. 'I'm Florence.'

Venetia caught her breath in surprise. The girl, although her hair was dark, bore an uncanny resemblance to herself. Her eyes were blue and, like Venetia's own, had the same unusual ring of green around the iris.

'The snow made the roads near impassable,' said Mama.

'Well, you're here now. Jack has gone out again but, in any case, he hardly speaks to me at all these days. He was always so full of merry quips before he came back from the war. Now he has nothing to say, it seems. We've both been so sad since Father died.' Florence's full bottom lip began to tremble and her eyes filled with tears.

'It's a sad time for all of us,' said Venetia, the familiar pain sharp in her breast.

'It's not long since Mother passed away and now we've moved to this house and left my friends and my governess behind and I've been so very lonely.' Tears overflowed in a river down Florence's face.

A lump rose up in Venetia's throat. The poor child had lost both her parents in such a short space of time. Feeling helpless, she patted the girl's shoulder. Unexpectedly, her animosity towards Florence drained away. It was impossible not to be moved by her misery.

Mama handed the girl a clean handkerchief. 'You shan't be lonely any more, my dear.'

Florence dried her eyes. 'But nothing will ever be the same without Father, will it?'

'No, my dear, I'm afraid it won't.'

Raffie, hands clasped behind his back as he looked out of the window, said, 'I thought you sent Nero to the kitchen, Venetia.'

'I did.'

'Well, he's trotting across the courtyard with Major Chamberlaine.'

'Oh, is Jack coming at last?' said Florence. 'He went to the shooting range.' She bit her lip. 'I'm afraid he isn't very happy about Father's plan.'

Venetia was sure that Major Chamberlaine wasn't at all happy about it. 'It's an awkward situation for us all,' she said.

Booted footsteps clipped across the hall and then the drawing-room door burst open. Major Chamberlaine stood in the doorway, leaning on his cane, snow still visible on his top boots.

'So you've arrived,' he said. He had no time to say any more as a growling black pug pushed past him, hackles raised.

'Quiet, sir!' snapped Major Chamberlaine.

'Nero!' Venetia leaped to her feet. 'Come here at once, you bad dog!'

The dog let out a volley of barks and fastened his jaws around her ankle.

Mama screamed and Raffie and Major Chamberlaine hurried to pull him away, catching hold of the dog by the scruff of his neck. He was deposited outside the door. 'Are you hurt, Miss Lovell?' asked Major Chamberlaine.

Shocked, Venetia pulled up the hem of her skirt a fraction to look at her ankle. 'It's only a graze ... but I don't understand. Nero is the gentlest of creatures.'

'Nero?' said Florence. 'But that's Caesar. Father gave him to me when Mother died.'

Venetia stared at her. 'Father gave Nero to me a year and a half ago.'

Major Chamberlaine strode out of the room and returned a few moments later with a squirming black pug under each arm. He placed them on the rug where they circled and sniffed at each other. 'It would appear that your father bought litter mates for his daughters.'

'Oh, look!' said Florence, a delighted smile on her face.

The two little dogs began to chase each other around the room, yipping with excitement.

'And Father, no doubt, named them both,' said Venetia. 'Roman emperors, I believe? He always had a penchant for Italy.' She understood now why he had so often called Nero by the name of Caesar.

'It seemed he extended that penchant as far as his children's names, too ... Florence, Venetia and Rafaele,' said Major Chamberlaine.

'All except for you, Jack,' said Florence.

'He wanted to christen me Leonardo but Mother put her foot down and insisted I took my father's name,' he said, sitting down next to Venetia. 'I trust you have instructed your maid, as I requested,' he said in an undertone, 'to be discreet about the circumstances in which we find ourselves?'

'Kitty has proved to be a loyal servant to us,' said Venetia. 'Furthermore, she's aware that her continuing position in this household is entirely dependent upon that discretion.'

'Dorcas is a new maid to this household,' said Major Chamberlaine, 'and I have told Annunziata that your father married your mother a short while prior to his death. Since we have not yet made the acquaintance of our neighbours I sincerely hope, if only for Florence's sake, that we may avoid a scandal.'

Venetia chewed her lip and tried to think of something conciliatory to say while he stared resolutely at his boots.

The drawing-room door opened and the maid carried in the tea tray. She hesitated a moment, glancing first at Florence and then at Mama.

'Thank you, Dorcas,' said Florence. 'Mrs Lovell will pour.'

Mama smiled and made herself busy with the tea, asking Florence to pass around the Madeira cake.

Afterwards, Raffie and Florence laughed together as they fed crumbs of cake to the pugs, encouraging them to beg prettily.

Venetia's tense muscles relaxed a little. Perhaps this wouldn't be as hard as she'd expected.

Major Chamberlaine leaned towards her. 'What a cosy scene.'

'Isn't it?' she said, attempting a friendly smile.

39

He placed his cup carefully on a side table. 'But I tell you,' he said in an undertone, 'I'm not at all happy that Florence and I are obliged to share our home with a family of gold-diggers. She's young and impressionable, still grieving for her parents. You should know that I'm very protective of her and if anyone, anyone at all, should give her cause for unhappiness, they will have me to deal with.' He gave Venetia a steely-eyed stare. 'And it won't be pleasant. Do I make myself clear?'

A scarlet flush of anger raced up Venetia's throat. 'Perfectly,' she said.

'Good.' He stood and picked up his cane. 'If you will excuse me, I have business to attend to.' He limped from the room.

'Oh!' said Florence. 'What a shame Jack had to go, just when we're all getting on so splendidly.'

The back door to the area opened and Kitty and the other maid looked at each other.

'I'm Dorcas,' said the London girl. 'I suppose you're Kitty?' She pursed her lips. 'You're very dirty.'

'So would you be if you'd spent three days sitting between the back wheels of a coach,' said Kitty.

'Annunziata is waiting to see you.'

'Annun ...' Kitty frowned. 'What kind of a name is that?'

'Italian. She was the mistress's maid ... that is, the first Mrs Lovell's maid ... even before Major Chamberlaine was born. She was his nurse, and then Miss Florence's, and now she's the cook-housekeeper.'

'What's she like?'

Dorcas shrugged. 'Old, but she could turn the scrag end of goat into a dish fit for a king. Oh, and she has a moustache.'

Kitty laughed. 'Not really?' She followed Dorcas into the warmth of the basement kitchen.

40

A little woman sitting in a rocking chair by the fire looked up at them with beady black eyes. She stood up, hands planted on her broad hips.

'Kitty,' said Dorcas.

The cook barely reached Kitty's shoulder. She looked up at her with a fierce stare. 'I am Annunziata and I am the queen in my kitchen. Don't you forget it or there will be trouble.' Her tone was severe but there was a hint of a smile on her swarthy face.

'No, Annunziata,' said Kitty meekly. What Dorcas had said was true though; the housekeeper did have the shadow of a moustache.

'*Santo cielo!* Look at you, dropping dirt in my kitchen!' Annunziata clicked her tongue. 'You must change immediately.' She shouted through the half-open scullery door, 'James, hot water, *pronto*. And carry Kitty's box upstairs.'

A gangly youth, with a mop of ginger curls and ears that stuck out like open carriage doors, hurried into the kitchen.

Annunziata bustled to a tall cupboard and thumbed through a pile of folded linen, while James filled a ewer with water from a pan keeping warm on the trivet. 'Dress, towel and washcloth. When you have changed, bring down your dirty clothes,' the housekeeper ordered.

'Yes, Annunziata.' Kitty took the proffered linen and the ewer.

James collected her trunk and heaved it up the stairs.

Kitty followed him for several flights. She'd never been in a house so grand or with so many stairs and heaved a sigh at the thought. It'd probably fall to her lot to sweep them all.

James booted open a door in the attic and thumped the box down beside one of the narrow beds.

Kitty placed the ewer on the washstand. 'Thank you, James.'

Blushing a fiery red, he retreated.

Kitty sank down on the bed and the straw mattress rustled beneath her. It was hard with frozen fingers to unlace her boots and the little room was icy cold. She peeled off her mud-caked stockings and then the rest of her clothes and dropped them on the floor. Even her shift was dirty. Teeth chattering, she filled the washbowl and wriggled her fingers in the warm water. They began to itch painfully as they thawed. The dress she'd been given was too big but the apron tied over the top pulled it in. At the last moment she remembered to put on the black armband again.

Rubbing away frost flowers from the inside of the window, she saw it was a long way down to the garden below, which was blanketed in snow. There were tall houses as far as she could see, all with chimneys belching out thick smoke. Several church spires pointed up to heaven.

Kitty breathed a deep sigh of contentment. Now she was in London she'd really start living. A whole city full of delights awaited her. Already she'd seen so many fine carriages and ladies in beautiful clothes her eyes had well-nigh fallen out of her head. And somewhere out there was Nathaniel Griggs, the friendly young man who'd carried her box and whispered that he'd call by for her at the kitchen door one day. Oh, yes, Kitty's life was certainly about to take a turn for the better.

Chapter 5

Light crept through the cracks in the shutters and Venetia stirred and stretched in the half dark. Her head ached and her eyes felt gritty. There was a dark shape in the corner that wasn't usually there. Something was wrong. And then she remembered. She wasn't in Spindrift Cottage. This was Father's house in Quill Court.

Father. Squeezing her eyes shut again she summoned up his image: his burly figure, thick white hair and laughing green eyes. She'd loved him but he'd betrayed them all. A sudden stab of anguish made it impossible for her to lie still. Throwing back the bedclothes, she padded to the window to open the shutters.

There'd been another snowfall during the night and Quill Court and the bare oak tree were blanketed in white, already dusted with city smuts. A sharp longing for home made her want to weep. This place could never be home. Home was where you belonged, where you fitted into the curve of the landscape; the place where layer upon layer of memories enfolded you whenever you opened the front door.

The previous afternoon Florence had brought her to this room, opening the door and pulling her inside by the hand.

'Isn't it pretty?' she'd said. 'Father said this was a special paper hanging, designed by someone whose work will one day become famous.' Then Florence's eyes had opened wide as Venetia's face crumpled in distress. 'Oh! I thought you'd love it as much as I do,' she'd said.

Venetia's Rose. She traced with her finger the petals of a pink rosebud on the wall, remembering that summer afternoon in the garden at Spindrift Cottage, contentedly painting in the sunshine with the seagulls crying overhead. She'd had no idea then of the terrible turn that life would soon take. And Father must have decorated this room, planning it as a sop for her, knowing that soon she'd be forced to leave her beloved home.

There was a soft knock at the door and Kitty entered carrying a jug of hot water.

Venetia forced herself to smile. The poor girl was probably homesick, too. 'Are you comfortably settled, Kitty?'

'Yes, thank you, Miss Venetia. Except …' The maid stared down at her shoes. 'It's very cold and my blanket is so thin …'

'I shall speak to Annunziata about that and come to inspect your quarters later.'

'Thank you, Miss Venetia.'

'I don't like to think of you so far away from your family. You will come and talk to me if you feel too homesick, won't you?'

Kitty smiled. 'Why, thank you, Miss Venetia. But I'm looking forward to exploring the city on my afternoon off.'

'This house is very different from Spindrift Cottage, isn't it?'

Kitty laid out Venetia's clothes. 'I thought I might get lost on the way from my bedroom to the kitchen this morning.'

'It's very smart.' Venetia sighed. Despite that, she'd prefer to be back in cosy, crooked Spindrift Cottage.

'You've come up in the world, Miss. Shall I help you dress now?'

Venetia stripped off her nightgown and washed quickly. Despite the fire that had been lit while she slept, the room was chilly. Taking the towel Kitty held out to her, she briskly rubbed herself dry to bring the warmth back to her goose-pimpled flesh.

Kitty slipped a clean chemise over Venetia's head and then laced the short stays over the top, adjusting her breasts until all fitted comfortably. Stockings, a quilted petticoat and a black crepe dress followed.

'I'd better have the new black shawl, too, Kitty.' Venetia closed her eyes while the maid brushed her hair and wound it into a topknot, pulling a few curls free around her face. She hadn't slept well, not only because she was unsettled but because of the unaccustomed street noise, so different from the night-time peace that blanketed Spindrift Cottage. When at last the barking dogs, carriage wheels, drunken shouts and laughter had faded away and she'd begun to drift off, she'd heard a man shouting out in terror. She'd jumped up with her heart hammering, certain that the noise came from within the house, and hurried barefoot to Raffie's bedroom. Not a glimmer of light showed under his door and all was quiet. Then, just as she began to doze again, cart wheels began to trundle past towards Leadenhall Market and the costermongers' calls began.

'Will you have a ribbon today, Miss Venetia?'

'The wide black one, please, Kitty.'

The maid deftly threaded the ribbon through her mistress's hair and tied it in a bow.

'I shall need my black pelisse and bonnet this morning. After breakfast we plan to visit my father's grave.'

'Very good, Miss Venetia. I'll go now and see if Mrs Lovell is awake.'

Venetia warmed her hands by the fire, delaying the moment she must face Jack Chamberlaine. Her pulse began to throb with anger at the memory of the warning he'd given her about Florence. In agitation she stood up and paced the floor. Gold-diggers! Well, she wouldn't tolerate any more comments like that about her family.

Wrapping her shawl more closely around her shoulders, she stood by the window. A movement below caught her eye. Raffie chased the two black pugs around the snowy courtyard, throwing snowballs at them while they yapped with excitement. She watched with a half smile as he began to build a snowman. He may be almost a man but at times he still appeared to be the little boy she had always loved and fiercely protected.

There was a tap at her door. 'May I come in?' Florence didn't wait for an answer but slipped inside and sat on the bed. 'Did you sleep well?'

'I'm not used to so much noise at night,' said Venetia.

'I found that at first,' said Florence. 'We came from a village, too.'

'When did you move here?' asked Venetia, curious.

'Two months ago. I didn't want to come but Father wanted to leave the sadness of the past behind and look to the future in new surroundings.' Florence smiled. 'Now that you've come, I understand what he meant.'

'He must have been planning this for some time,' said Venetia, half to herself.

'Jack explained it to me after Father died.' Florence twisted her fingers in her lap. 'What I don't understand,' she said, 'is that if Father really loved Mother, as Jack said he did, why did he marry *your* mother?' She looked up at Venetia, her eyes brimming.

'Men look at things differently from women,' said Venetia slowly. How could she say to this unhappy girl that she didn't believe their father had ever loved her mother but had merely fulfilled a promise to his dead friend? Or could he have truly loved Clarissa? 'A woman can love more than one child so perhaps a man can love more than one wife. There are countries where they take several, you know.'

Florence looked thoughtful. 'I've read about that in the Bible.' She took Venetia's hand and pulled her towards the dressing table. 'Look!'

46

Two heart-shaped faces looked back at them.

'My hair is dark like Mother's,' said Florence, 'and yours is fair, but our eyes are just the same!'

'Father always said my eyes were the colours of the sea.' Venetia held back a sob as she pictured him smiling lovingly, and, as it turned out, traitorously, at her while he said it.

'He said mine were the colours of the sky and the fields near our village,' said Florence tremulously.

'I'm afraid your brother is very angry we've been forced to come here,' said Venetia.

'Jack's very angry about everything these days.' The corners of Florence's mouth turned down.

'Perhaps he's still grieving for your mother?' said Venetia. It wouldn't do to let her natural dislike of the man spoil this blossoming friendship with her half-sister.

'Mother was often unwell with her nerves and it irritated Jack. He was always closer to Father, who treated him as if Jack were his own son.' Florence sighed. 'He barely spoke a word when first he came home from the war with his bad leg. All his life he'd wanted to be a soldier but since his injury he's had to give up any thought of a career in the army. That was bad enough but he's been horridly bad-tempered ever since Father died.' Florence grasped Venetia's hand. 'He's not at all his usual self.'

'What was he like before, then?'

'Happy-go-lucky, like Father. He always found something to smile about, no matter what.'

Venetia nodded, her throat closing up as she blinked away tears. It was true; Father could always be relied upon to find the humour in any situation. Until near the end anyway, when he'd been so tired. Perhaps that wasn't surprising since he was facing up to telling his second family they were to lose their home and that he had another family in London.

'Shall we go down now?' said Florence.

Major Chamberlaine was drinking coffee in the dining room. He stood up as they entered and his stick clattered to the floor.

'Please, don't disturb yourself on my account,' said Venetia.

'I hope I am not so ill mannered as that.'

Florence picked up his stick and kissed his cheek. 'Good morning, Jack.'

His expression softened. 'Shall I pour you some chocolate, Florence? Will you take coffee or chocolate, Miss Lovell?' His tone to her was coldly polite.

'Coffee, thank you.'

A moment later the door opened again and Mama came in. Her eyes were darkly shadowed and red-rimmed from weeping.

Jack Chamberlaine stood up again, his face expressionless. 'Good morning, Mrs Lovell.'

'Good morning, Major Chamberlaine.' Mama smiled listlessly at Florence and sat beside Venetia.

The door burst open and a pink-cheeked Raffie strode in with the two pugs at his heels. 'Not too late for breakfast, am I?' He slumped down on a chair next to Jack and stretched out for the chocolate pot.

'You'd better hurry,' said Florence, 'because we're leaving for the churchyard shortly.'

Raffie paused in the act of pouring his chocolate. 'I'd forgotten,' he said.

'I can only say,' said Major Chamberlaine, 'that your casual attitude to your father's death does you no credit at all.'

'I didn't mean …' Raffie's face blanched and his eyes glistened. He stared down at the table.

'Theodore Lovell was as good as any father to me and I always held him in the highest esteem,' said Major Chamberlaine. 'But this preposterous idea of bringing his unlawful family to live with us is beyond belief. I can only presume that, near the end, he must have lost his wits.'

Venetia didn't trust herself to speak. This was going to be impossible. How could they ever hope to meld into one family when Jack Chamberlaine was so antagonistic? Anger made her hand tremble so much that her cup rattled against the saucer.

Two bright spots of colour flared in Mama's ashen cheeks.

'Father has gone, Jack,' said Florence, 'and we must follow his last wishes. It won't do any good for you to sulk.'

Jack pushed his cup away so rapidly that coffee spilled on the starched tablecloth. 'You're still a child, Florence, and don't understand the ways of the world.' He glowered at her. 'And you're still young enough for me to carry you screaming upstairs to your room if need be, until you learn not to be insolent to your elders and betters.'

Florence's eyes flashed with fury. 'Since you're the one behaving like a spoiled child, Jack, you'd do well to retire to your room and ponder upon your own behaviour.'

Jack reared to his feet, his face drained of colour. 'That's quite enough, miss! Leave the table at once!'

'I will not!' Florence pushed back her chair and stood up to face him. 'I know you're unhappy but such rudeness is not fitting behaviour for a gentleman.'

Venetia held her breath while they glared at each other and Mama's grip on her wrist tightened. Perhaps Florence wasn't as much of a child as she had supposed.

Then Florence's shoulders sagged and she reached out to her brother. 'You're the one who said we must follow Father's dying wish, and you can see Venetia, Raffie and our stepmother are grieving just as much as you and I are.'

Venetia decided it was time to step into the fray. 'Major Chamberlaine,' she said, 'despite your fears, we did not come here with any intention of cheating you or Florence in any way. The situation in which we find ourselves is as abhorrent to us as it is to you.'

Mama cleared her throat. 'Indeed, we would have much preferred to stay at Spindrift Cottage.'

There was a long silence and then, slowly, Jack Chamberlaine reached out to embrace his sister. 'I suppose I must apologise,' he said, kissing the top of her head.

Florence was all smiles again. 'Then we shall all be more comfortable.'

Venetia's gaze met Jack's cool stare over Florence's shoulder. He didn't look even remotely contrite. So, it was to be armed neutrality then. At least she knew where she stood and would take great care not to step into any bear traps.

They set off from Quill Court a short while later, Jack Chamberlaine leading with Florence while Venetia and Raffie walked either side of Mama. The snow had turned to slush and before long the hem of Venetia's pelisse was sodden.

St Peter's Church was at the north end of Gracechurch Street, opposite Leadenhall Market, neatly tucked in between a silversmith's premises and a pastry shop.

In the East Churchyard Venetia looked about her in dismay. 'Everything is hidden under the snow. Where is Father's grave?'

'There's no headstone yet,' said Major Chamberlaine. He picked his way between the snow-covered gravestones and stopped in front of a low mound.

We look like a flock of crows, thought Venetia as they formed a circle around it, their black mourning clothes in stark contrast to the snow. Mama trembled against her arm and Raffie pressed himself against her. No one spoke, each alone with their sad thoughts.

Snow began to drift down from the leaden sky and Venetia studied a snowflake as it landed upon her black-clad arm. The delicate pattern would make a beautiful design for a wall hanging. Angrily, she brushed the flake away. How could she even think of such a thing at a time like this?

She stared at the ground. Father had always been at his happiest while laughing and joking in the centre of a crowd and she couldn't bear to think of him alone in the frozen earth below. Somehow, until this moment, she'd been half expecting that he'd saunter through the door, but suddenly she felt sick and hollow with the certain knowledge that she'd never see him again. Tears stung her eyes. However angry she was with him, she'd have done anything to have him back.

Major Chamberlaine's closed face was unreadable.

Mama wept behind her black veil and Venetia slipped an arm around her waist. Raffie stared silently at the ground but tears dripped from his chin.

The snow was coming thick and fast now, a light wind whirling the flakes around them. 'We should go,' said Venetia softly. 'We'll come again but we don't want to catch our . . . to catch cold.'

Silently, they filed out of the churchyard.

Chapter 6

'If this cold weather persists, Venetia, I shall need some black sarcenet to line my second-best pelisse,' said Mama. 'And, Florence dear, you cannot go on wearing that same dress every day. Do you not have another?'

Florence shook her head. 'Jack bought me this one because I'd outgrown all my mourning clothes from when Mother died.'

'A man has no idea of what a girl needs.' Mama's eyes sparkled with sudden enthusiasm. 'We'll stop moping about indoors and go shopping. It's bad enough that a girl must spend a year in black without even a change for Sundays.'

'A new dress, for me?' Florence's face lit up. 'I mean no disrespect to Father but I can't believe it would have made him happy to see me look so dreary.'

'Of course it wouldn't!' said Mama. 'Venetia, will you come with us?'

She shook her head. 'I have all I need for the present.'

The door opened and Raffie came in, accompanied by a lanky youth.

'Mama, this is Freddie Crawford.'

Freddie, expensively dressed in a tightly fitting coat over buckskin breeches, bowed to Mama but his gaze was fixed on Florence. He swallowed and his Adam's apple bobbed up and down.

'How do you do, Mr Crawford?' said Mama. 'And may I present Miss Lovell and Miss Florence?'

'Enchanting,' said Freddie, still staring at Florence. 'I mean, enchanted to meet you.'

Florence smiled sweetly but with mirth in her eyes.

'And where are you going, Raffie?' asked Venetia.

'Or we could stay here and talk to your sisters,' said Freddie, hopefully.

Raffie gave him a withering look.

'In any case,' said Florence, 'Mrs Lovell and I have shopping to do.'

'Don't wait dinner for me,' said Raffie nonchalantly. 'I may be late.'

After they'd all gone Venetia closed her book and sighed. In the two weeks since they'd arrived they hadn't left Quill Court except to go to church. Their trunks and boxes of personal possessions had arrived on the hired cart, which had served to remind them that they'd never return to Spindrift Cottage. She closed her eyes and imagined herself striding along the beach with the salty wind in her hair and the wide sky overhead.

At least Jack Chamberlaine had resisted making any more sharp comments but sometimes she noticed his watchful blue eyes staring at her. He spent most of his time in the study. Now that the others were out, it was time she bearded the lion in his den.

She knocked on the door, wishing she were somewhere else.

'Enter!'

He was standing with his back to her, looking out of the window.

When he turned around she was taken aback by the bleakness of his expression. She hesitated, not wanting to intrude upon his apparent misery.

Gesturing to a chair, he limped back to his desk.

'My mother has taken Florence shopping,' said Venetia. 'She needs clothes.'

'She has a wardrobe full of clothes.'

'But only one mourning dress. There will be other essentials and household accounts to settle before long. Major Chamberlaine, we need to talk about money.'

He regarded her with a cynical smile. 'I assumed you'd bring up the subject sooner or later.'

She clenched her hands so tightly that her fingernails bit into the palms. 'I haven't come begging.'

He raised one eyebrow.

She fought to keep her tone of voice level. 'My father would most certainly have wished to provide for us, that is not in question. However, Mr Tyndall said that Father wished us to work together to provide ourselves with an income.'

'And how do you propose we do that? Are you experienced in matters of business?'

'You know that I am not. However, Father had received two commissions for new decorating projects using one of my paper hanging designs just before he died. Perhaps we could undertake the work?'

'One of your designs?' Major Chamberlaine frowned. 'What do you mean?'

'Venetia's Rose. He took one of my paintings and had it made into a paper hanging. It's the one on the walls of my new bedroom.'

'The room upstairs?'

She nodded. It gave her a great deal of satisfaction to see him look so discomfited. 'He took several of my designs to be made into a new collection and wanted me to work with him in his business.'

'Did he actually say that?' Major Chamberlaine's expression was incredulous.

'He did. But he also said that there were some difficulties to overcome first. I took that to mean that I was a daughter and not a son, but now I can see that even then Father had plans to bring us all together under one roof, while he was alive.'

Major Chamberlaine drummed his fingers on the desk.

Venetia waited.

'There's something I suppose you ought to see,' he said. 'Will you make yourself ready to go out?'

She inclined her head but resisted the temptation to ask him where they were going. 'Five minutes should suffice,' she said.

A short while later they walked up Gracechurch Street, turning into Lombard Street before they reached the Crosse Keys. They walked in silence and Venetia, noticing how badly her companion limped and how slippery the ice was, only just forbore from asking him if he'd prefer to take a hackney carriage. He was quite capable of suggesting that himself.

She looked about her with interest as they walked. Despite the cold, the streets were thronged with pedestrians, carriages and costermongers. The noise and bustle were unceasing. Horses whinnied, beggars in the gutters held up their hands for alms, dogs barked and street children plucked at the sleeves of passers-by.

They passed Mercers' Hall and the street became a stream of smartly dressed men and elegant ladies flowing in either direction. Venetia had never seen so many fascinating shops and would have liked to pause to look into the windows of the glove and fan makers, drapers, silversmiths and furriers, but Major Chamberlaine carried on striding ahead, looking neither right nor left.

At last he stopped outside a substantial four-storey building. Bow windows, empty of merchandise and with shutters firmly closed to the rear, were placed either side of a six-panelled door. He extracted a key from his greatcoat.

'Wait here,' he said, 'while I open the shutters.'

Venetia followed him in, stamping the snow off her boots. It was quite as cold inside as in the street. She took a step and broken glass crunched underfoot.

'Stay there!' he warned. He folded back the shutters, allowing light to flood in.

Venetia blinked. They were in a sizeable shop with glazed doors admitting daylight at the opposite end. A long satinwood counter ran down each side. She caught her breath when she saw that the cream-painted walls were violated with great splatters of scarlet paint. Empty shelves ran around the walls at head-height but the polished wooden floor was littered with broken glass and china. She bent to pick up a porcelain figurine, a shepherdess guessed Venetia, since the figurine held a crook in her delicately painted hand. Part of her frilled pink and yellow skirt was missing. Placing the fragments on the counter, Venetia stepped over a swathe of silk damask lying like a blue pool on the floor.

Blue silk damask. She gathered it into her arms and lifted it to her cheek, remembering. It smelled slightly of dust, as if it had settled there after its long journey from the continent by pack mule and smuggler's boat. Everywhere she looked there were more lengths of material: woven brocades, in all the colours of the rainbow, tossed over small side tables and chairs, pools of fine silk on the floor and richly embroidered Indian cottons crumpled underfoot. Many of the lengths had been slashed into ribbons. Outrage began to mount in her breast as she realised the significance of this place.

She glanced back at Major Chamberlaine, who leaned against one of the counters, his face pale.

A furniture pattern book had been ripped to pieces and the leaves scattered about; a painting of Venice hung askew over the marbled fireplace. Several delicate chairs were smashed, their satinwood remains scattered over a beautiful French carpet that was ruined by a puddle of red paint in the centre. And then she saw a length of unrolled paper hanging stretched out over the table. Venetia's Rose.

She turned to Major Chamberlaine. 'I know what this place is,' she said.

He stared at her. 'How can you?'

She held out the trailing bundle of blue silk damask and the roll of paper hanging. 'Because this is the silk Father bought from the smugglers who land their merchandise in the cove below Spindrift Cottage and this is my paper hanging, Venetia's Rose. And I know what this place is because it's the shop Father and I daydreamed about.'

'What do you mean?'

'I chose the colour of the walls and suggested the shelf for the vases and decorative objects. I sketched how we'd display the fabrics and the pattern books and furniture samples. This is the imaginary shop that we talked about for years made real. Who did this?' she demanded, waving a hand at the scene of destruction.

'The men who killed your father,' said Major Chamberlaine. He slumped down on a sofa, the velvet slashed so that the horsehair spilled out. 'They came here and demanded money from him even before the shop opened. He refused and they pushed him around and he had to watch them tear it apart. The shock of it killed him.' He wiped one palm over his face.

'Father died here?' Venetia sank down on the sofa, her knees folding with shock.

'I found him after they'd gone. He begged me not to fetch a doctor; he said there wasn't time. It was then that he told me about your mother and you and Rafaele. I'd loved him as a true father all my life and it felt as if he was throwing away all the love and respect I'd ever given him. He'd been false to Mother, Florence and me all those years! He made me promise him I'd come and find you and bring you to Quill Court as he'd planned. I argued with him but he said we hadn't any choice because he'd spent all his savings on this shop.' Major Chamberlaine swallowed to clear his throat.

Venetia saw the tears clinging to his black eyelashes and for the first time felt sympathy for him.

'I held him in my arms until he died and I haven't been back here since.'

'And the authorities don't have any idea who did this?'

Major Chamberlaine shrugged. 'I reported it to the parish constable but the city is so full of thieves he had no idea where to start looking.'

Venetia wiped away her tears. She walked to the rear of the shop, stepping over splintered furniture and tattered brocade. She picked up a pale green vase with a frieze of Greek figures dancing around the base. From one side it looked perfect but there was a large piece missing from the other. A length of crumpled yellow brocade lay on the central table. She smoothed it out. One end was slashed but the undamaged part was large enough to make a beautiful cushion.

A piece of pale green pottery lying on the floor caught her eye. Her heart leaped. Gathering up the damaged Greek vase, she slid the smaller section into the hole. A perfect fit.

'Major Chamberlaine,' she said, carrying the vase over to him, 'look! Perhaps we can repair it?'

He sighed. 'To what purpose?'

'I don't mean just the vase. Father wanted us to work together as a family to continue the business, didn't he? He believed we could do it.' Her heart had begun to beat very fast and she spoke quickly before she could change her mind. 'There's a lot of work to do but we could make this showroom beautiful again. And surely we can find out if there are outstanding projects and complete them? Father must have left a record of his suppliers and craftsmen.'

Major Chamberlaine stared at her. 'Are you completely deranged? We can't simply pick up where he left off.'

Venetia stood her ground. 'Why can't we? We're bound to make mistakes but it must be worth a try.'

He slammed the shutters closed.

Anger seethed in her breast. 'So that's it, is it? You're just going to give up?'

He whirled round to face her. 'Miss Lovell, I'm a soldier and not

58

the remotest bit interested in upholstery fabric and curtain trimmings.'

Her anger boiled over. 'Then why aren't you out soldiering? You need to face the fact that your injuries may now prevent that.'

He clenched his fists and his chest heaved as he sought to control himself. 'How *dare* you presume to tell me what to do?' The skin around his mouth was white.

For one frightening moment she glimpsed murder in his eyes but she stood her ground. 'Well, do you have any other means of earning a living? Or a private income perhaps?' She stood right in front of him so that he couldn't escape unless he pushed past her. 'Please, do tell me how you intend to support Florence once we've run through the meagre remains of Father's savings?'

'Move out of my way!'

'You may not care what happens to yourself or your sister but I care very much for the welfare of my mother and brother. And Florence, too, as it happens. At one stroke I've lost my father, my home and my means of support. I shan't now be able to provide for my family's future by making a good marriage since all such hopes have flown. Through no fault of my own I am damaged goods. No man will want a penniless love-child.'

'You shame us all by mentioning that.'

'But it's the truth, isn't it? If you have any better ideas other than trying to revive Father's business, do tell me. Somehow or other we need to earn our keep or we'll end up in the workhouse.' The echoes of her outburst rang in Venetia's ears in the ensuing silence. She was shocked by her own behaviour; she never shouted.

After a long silence the fury faded from Major Chamberlaine's eyes. He cleared his throat. 'I don't know anything about furniture or carpets or curtain materials.'

'Can you add up?'

He bristled. 'Of course.'

'Good. Then find Father's account books and make yourself

useful by seeing if you can discover the financial position of the business. And I'll come back here tomorrow with Raffie to clear up this mess.'

Major Chamberlaine shook his head. 'Who would have thought that easy-going Theodore Lovell could have fathered such a virago?'

Venetia, her head held high, swept out of the shop, slammed the door behind her and set off, alone, for Quill Court.

Kitty's fingers were rubbed raw from scrubbing a burned pan with sand. She dumped the pan upside-down on the drainer and sucked grit out of a split chilblain. This wasn't at all how she'd imagined it would be if she lived in London. The new house was much larger than Spindrift Cottage and she was up and down stairs all day as lady's maid to Miss Venetia and the missus, but still expected to carry out a scullery maid's duties and help Dorcas strip the beds and dust the drawing room.

A knock on the basement window made her start. 'Jesus God, Nathaniel Griggs!' She pressed a hand to the front of her apron and then pushed up the window sash. 'Where did you come from?'

A grin spread over Nat's narrow face. 'Aren't you pleased to see me?'

'You keep turning up when I least expect you, like a mouse in the wainscot.' He'd appeared in the back yard when she was returning from the privy and had jumped out at her in the area when she went to fill the coal scuttle.

'Then come out with me.'

'I only have an afternoon off a month.'

'The river's frozen and there's a Frost Fair,' said Nat. 'The ice might not last if there's a thaw.' He smiled winningly. 'There's an ox roast and yesterday they walked an elephant over the river at Blackfriars.'

'An elephant?' Kitty's eyes were round with wonder. Oh, how

she would like to see such a sight! 'I'm going with Miss Venetia to Cheapside later on today. I suppose I might be able to slip away.'

'Cheapside?' Nat chewed a fingernail with his chipped tooth. 'Tell you what, I'll wait for you at the Saracen's Head until half-past two. It's on Friday Street, just off Cheapside.' Suddenly, he glanced over her shoulder and ducked out of sight.

'Kitty?' Dorcas appeared at her side. 'Who were you speaking to?'

Kitty opened her eyes very wide. 'Just singing to myself as I scrubbed.'

'Miss Venetia's asking for you. She's ready to leave and said to bring a broom with you. What does she mean?'

'I'm to go with her to Cheapside, where Mr Lovell had his shop. Thieves broke in and we're to tidy up the mess.'

'So that means I'll have to dust the drawing room on my own?'

'I'm only doing as I'm told, Dorcas.'

Kitty went into the kitchen. 'Annunziata, have you any errands for me while I'm out?'

'Fetch another loaf of bread,' she said, stirring a simmering pan of pig's trotters. 'James and Master Rafaele empty the larder more quickly than I can fill it. How those boys eat!'

Venetia was waiting for Kitty in the hall. 'Raffie was going to help but he's gone out again without telling me.'

Kitty had seen him sliding out of the back door earlier that morning, just as she'd seen him creeping in late last night with ale on his breath. She guessed he'd found himself some new drinking companions but she wasn't going to tell Miss Venetia that.

They set off to Cheapside and Kitty stared at the beautiful shops as they passed, imagining what it would be like to buy all the rose-trimmed bonnets, kid gloves and silk shawls she wanted. She kept her eyes open for Friday Street and tingled with excitement when she found it.

It was noon when they reached the shop. It stood between an

old-fashioned bookshop and a business displaying the prettiest fans, lace collars and shoe rosettes.

Miss Venetia unlocked the door and opened the shutters.

Kitty gasped as she looked around. 'Oh, what a terrible waste!'

Miss Venetia's eyes welled with tears. 'The shock of this ransacking killed my father.'

Kitty leaned on her broom and surveyed the mess. 'Wherever do we begin?'

Miss Venetia stared at the broken china underfoot, her chin quivering as she tried in vain to hold back the tears. 'I don't know *where* to begin. Everything's ruined, my father's dead and my family disgraced. And Major Chamberlaine looks at me with those cold eyes as if he expects me to run off with the silver.'

Overcome with pity, Kitty tentatively touched her arm. Venetia had always seemed so capable but really she was nothing but a girl.

'My family are relying on me to find a way to support us all but however can I make this right again?'

'You can't do it all at once,' said Kitty, 'or by yourself. You'll have to find ways the rest of them can help.' She bent to pick up a length of pale green silk and ran it through her fingers. One end had been shredded but the other was untouched. 'Can you use this for something? It's so pretty.'

Venetia gathered up another piece of silk. 'Perhaps it might make a cushion cover.'

'It'd be a start. You're good at organising things, Miss Venetia. It was always you who remembered to order the coal in time or to take the shoes to the cobbler. You painted the fireplace so beautifully in the parlour at Spindrift Cottage, I had to touch it to be sure it wasn't real marble. If anyone can make this right again, it's you.'

Venetia wiped away her tears and gave Kitty a wavering smile. 'It is overwhelming but you're right, Kitty. It must be done bit by bit and the whole family must help.'

Kitty smiled back. 'So what shall we do first?'

Venetia took a deep breath. 'We'll decide which pieces of silk are large enough to make into a cushion cover or a small curtain. Then we'll sweep up the broken glass and china, saving anything we can repair.'

They worked steadily for two hours, while Kitty wondered how soon she dared make her excuses. The heap of damaged goods grew larger but there was also a neat pile of salvaged silk, linen and brocade. A few intact items of china and glass were placed on the shelves for safekeeping, together with those it might be possible to mend.

'I promised Annunziata I'd fetch bread,' said Kitty, as the church clock struck the quarter hour. If she didn't meet Nat in the next fifteen minutes it'd be too late. 'She'll be cross if I'm away too long but perhaps I can come again tomorrow?'

'Run along then,' said Miss Venetia. 'I'll carry on until it's too dark to see. Tomorrow I'll bring candles. And Kitty ...'

'Yes, Miss Venetia?'

'Thank you for your kindness earlier on.'

Kitty smiled and scrambled into her coat. Free! She hurried down the street as fast as she could without slipping on the icy ground, until she came to Friday Street. A few minutes later she saw the signboard for the Saracen's Head.

She went into the fuggy warmth of the taproom and peered through the drifts of tobacco smoke. Excitement began to be replaced by uncertainty when several men looked at her with interest. Should she go back? She didn't really know Nat, even though he seemed so pleasant. But then she saw him rising from a settle by the fire. Once again he wore his blue velvet coat with the two rows of shiny brass buttons and looked quite the gentleman. She wished she'd had something pretty to wear and hoped her face wasn't smudged with dust.

'See, I knew you'd get away.' Nat smiled at her, his dark eyes laughing.

63

'Only for a little while,' said Kitty.

'Best stir our stumps then,' he said.

His arm was reassuringly warm against her side as they slipped and slid their way downhill, crossed over Fish Street and, at the lower end of Bread Street Hill, turned into Upper Thames Street.

'We'll go on to the river at Three Cranes stairs and work our way up to London Bridge. Then you won't be too far from Quill Court when you have to go,' said Nat.

Greasy smoke perfumed with the scent of roasting meat drifted on the air and Kitty sniffed, suddenly hungry.

A chattering crowd queued at Three Cranes wharf and in the distance was the sound of lively music.

'The watermen and lightermen can't work while the river's frozen,' said Nat, 'so for generations they've charged the public to visit the ice fair.'

Kitty stood on tip-toe so she could peer over the crowd. The music was making her foot tap.

At last it was their turn and Nat paid the waterman and guided her down the steps. 'Hold tight,' he warned. 'It's slippery.'

Kitty could hardly believe her eyes. The wide expanse of the river was frozen solid as far as she could see. A bitter wind blew over the ice, nipping at her cheeks, but she didn't care. A village of stalls selling gingerbread and pies, and rickety tents made from boat sails draped over oars, were clustered around a leaping fire with a whole ox roasting upon it. There were booths selling roasted apples, slices of meat labelled 'Lapland Mutton', and any number of other delicacies. Children threw snowballs and slid about squealing with delight.

'Let's have a warmer,' said Nat.

She took a step and her feet slid away. Just as she thought she'd fall headlong, Nat snatched her up against his chest. 'Careful!' He grinned and wrapped his arm around her waist and together they made their way to one of the tents. If it hadn't been for the ice Kitty might have felt obliged to slap his hand away.

A man, singing out of tune, staggered out of one of the tents and fell in a snowdrift.

Kitty laughed at his comical expression.

'That's why they call them fuddling tents,' said Nat. 'He's well in his cups.'

Inside the tent, men huddled together laughing and chatting. Nat bought two pieces of gingerbread and handed Kitty a tin cup. 'Here you are, sweetheart. A nip of gin will warm the cockles of your heart.'

She sipped the gin and choked as it burned the back of her throat but a moment later a delicious heat spread through her body. The gingerbread was sweet and spicy and she ate it ravenously.

Nat smiled as he watched her. 'Good?'

She nodded, licking crumbs from her mouth as he drained his cup.

Nat glanced over her shoulder and waved. 'There's Billy and Black Sal,' he said.

Billy was a great shambling bear of a man with a broad face and a broken nose. The girl had skin the colour of coffee with a drop of milk in it and her hair was a curly black halo. Kitty couldn't stop staring. She'd heard of black people, of course, but she'd never seen one. When the girl smiled her teeth were very white against her dark skin.

'Nat, my old cock robin,' said Billy, clapping him on the shoulder. 'Who's your friend?'

'Kitty. Up from Kent to make her fortune in the Big Smoke.'

'What are you up to, Kitty?' asked Sal.

'I'm a maid.'

Sal laughed. 'You'll not make your fortune like that.' She winked. 'Well, not unless you catch your master's eye. Ain't that right, Billy?'

'The master died,' said Kitty, 'that's why we came to London. What do you do, then, Sal?'

'I'm a wrestler.' She laughed at Kitty's amazed expression.

'If you haven't seen Sal in action you've a treat in store, Kitty,' said Billy. 'Ain't she, Nat?'

Nat handed round tin mugs. 'Always put my money on Sal.'

Kitty sipped the gin. She'd have preferred another slice of gingerbread.

Someone began to sing and Nat and Billy joined in. The verses became bawdy and Kitty fidgeted with embarrassment. Sal was enjoying herself, though, waving her mug in the air in time to the music.

'Kitty's gotta get back before dark,' said Nat when the song ended.

They set off along what Billy called 'City Road', an icy thoroughfare between the tents and stalls. Hawkers of ballads and pedlars of brandy balls and all kinds of fairings pestered them at every turn. Nat treated them all to a go on the swing boats and Billy bought them a slice of roasted ox in a chunk of bread. Kitty thought it was the most delicious thing she'd ever eaten, even though her fingers were so cold she could hardly hold it. Sal dropped hers and shrieked with fury when a dog nipped in between them and snapped up the prize.

Arm in arm, singing as they went, they made their way towards London Bridge.

Kitty felt so alive, as if she'd been waiting for this outing and these new friends all her life. Tom's rugged face flashed through her mind, his hair tousled by the wind off the sea, and a sharp pain ran through her breast. But it was no good thinking of Tom. Her future was in London now.

Nat squeezed her arm. 'Enjoying yourself, sweetheart?'

She nodded and smiled widely to cover the momentary homesickness.

They followed the music and watched a small and boisterous crowd jigging on the ice.

'Fancy a dance?' said Nat.

Kitty glanced up at the sky. She'd been enjoying herself so much that she hadn't noticed how the light was fading. She was suddenly panic-stricken. 'Miss Venetia'll be back before me and I still have to buy bread.'

They said a hasty goodbye to Sal and Billy. Nat took her arm and they hurried towards the bridge. As they climbed the steps Kitty looked regretfully over her shoulder at the river. The stalls, prettily lit with lamps, glowed in the gathering gloom.

They scurried up Fish Hill, calling into a baker's shop, and then on to Gracechurch Street. At the passage leading to Quill Court they stopped.

'I'll never forget today,' said Kitty.

Nat kissed the tip of her nose. 'I'm pleased you enjoyed yourself, sweetheart.'

'I don't want the afternoon to end.'

He laughed. 'Go on then, before you get into trouble. I'll come and see you again, if you like?'

Happiness bubbled up into her smile. She waved and ran down the alley.

Chapter 7

'And in the back office I found a cupboard full of new cushion pads,' said Venetia.

Mama lifted up a piece of canary yellow silk. 'You're going to be far too busy refurbishing the shop to make cushions.'

'We must have something to sell before we can reopen.'

Florence smoothed out a length of pink brocade. 'I can sew,' she said. 'We can make them together, can't we?'

'I do believe we can.' Mama smiled.

Venetia ran her finger over the pile of folded silk, calculating how many cushions could be made.

Florence draped the brocade around her like a shawl and danced around the drawing room. 'We'll become famous for our cushions, just you wait and see!'

'It'll take a lot more than selling a few cushions to pay our household bills,' said a voice.

Venetia spun around and saw Major Chamberlaine standing in the doorway.

'Especially if you keep buying new clothes,' he continued.

'But at least we'll be doing something useful,' said Florence.

68

'Major Chamberlaine, I'm going to the shop again,' said Venetia. 'I'd be grateful if you could tear yourself away from your study for an hour or two to accompany me.'

A muscle clenched in his jaw but he inclined his head. 'I'm calling in at the shooting range later this morning but until then I am at your service.'

Half an hour later, when they arrived at the shop, Major Chamberlaine allowed his gaze to roam over the carefully swept floor, the neatly folded piles of curtain material and the half dozen satinwood chairs that hadn't been damaged. 'You've made a difference,' he said, at last. 'Though the red paint splattered on the walls is still very much in evidence.'

Venetia bit her tongue. She must find a way to work with him, however arduous it might be. 'It won't wash off but it makes me feel better to see everything tidy,' she said. 'I'm under no illusion that we're anywhere near being able to open for business, however.'

'I'm pleased to hear it,' he said, dryly.

'Did you look in Father's office?' she asked.

Major Chamberlaine shook his head. 'Only enough to bring the ledgers back to Quill Court to study them at leisure.'

'Have you taken a look at them yet?'

'They're not fully up to date and it's time-consuming matching the entries with the invoices and orders. For example, there's a record of the purchase of twenty Italian paintings and a number of valuable historical artefacts, bronze statuettes, marble urns and obelisks. I've no record of any of these being sold but they aren't in the shop.'

'Could they be in Quill Court?' asked Venetia.

'I've not found them.'

'I want to show you something,' she said.

He limped after her as she hurried to the back of the shop, where she opened the glazed doors to another spacious room. Two windows overlooked a walled yard and a staircase to their right curved up to another floor. The ceiling was double-height with tall windows.

'The light here is wonderful,' said Venetia. 'We must think of a way to use this space.' Her mind bubbled with possibilities. Another showroom for antiquities or somewhere to serve tea to customers while they were choosing their curtain fabrics, perhaps? Major Chamberlaine, of course, simply looked at her with a sceptical half-smile.

'We can't afford enough, or indeed any, stock to fill all this space,' he said.

'Not at present,' she said, evenly. 'But there are two floors and an attic above that we aren't currently using. We need some storage space but I wondered if we could rent out the other rooms?'

'I suppose that would bring in an income,' said Major Chamberlaine, reluctantly, 'but there isn't a separate staircase.'

Venetia opened the door to the office. There was a partners' desk, two chairs and a bookcase. Opening the bookcase, she took down several volumes and laid them on the desk.

'These are style books from furniture manufacturers,' she said. 'And there are pattern books with cuttings of different materials and curtain trimmings and carpet illustrations. I want us to visit the local wholesalers and factories to meet the suppliers.'

'To what purpose?'

'To persuade them to lend us samples. We can't afford to buy much ...'

'Hardly anything at all.'

'But no one will buy goods or our design services if we can't show them the quality of the workmanship first. Then there are the tradesmen and artisans. Father kept a book containing their names and addresses and we must visit them, too. They'll take more heed of me if I'm accompanied by a man.' Major Chamberlaine nodded thoughtfully and she experienced a flicker of relief. Perhaps she could bring him around after all. 'And the showroom must be redecorated before we can open.'

'We can't afford that.'

'We can't open for business until everything is put right again.'

'And what then?' The light of battle was in his eyes. 'Are you going to serve in the showroom everyday?'

'What alternative is there? And Mama and Florence, too, if necessary.'

'Florence is a child!

'She's not too young to help. Mama assisted her father in his draper's shop from the time she was eight or nine. And there's no reason you and Raffie can't help either.' She daren't meet his eyes as she spoke.

He turned away. 'I'm late. Despite your telling me I'm no use as a soldier any more, I intend to keep up with my shooting practice.'

'That isn't at all what I said!' But it was a waste of time arguing since he was already heading for the door.

Venetia sat down at her father's desk while she considered the next steps. The enormity of the task ahead gave her a tight feeling in her chest, as if she'd swallowed a knotted rope. When she'd said to Father that she'd like to help him with the showroom, she'd meant just that, help, not run it alone. Major Chamberlaine was right; she hadn't the first idea about business and, even if he hadn't been hampered by his injury, he certainly didn't appear as if he was going to put himself out a great deal to assist. Anger at his resentment of her family made Venetia clench her fists. But then she remembered the tears in his eyes as he'd told her how Father had died in his arms. He must have loved his stepfather.

Fear for the future, never very far away, overwhelmed her again. Mama, like Father, was always over-optimistic and assumed that, somehow, everything would turn out all right. Raffie hadn't grasped the seriousness of the situation at all. In fact, he seemed to revel in their arrival in London since he'd taken up with Freddie Crawford. He'd been creeping out at night to do Heaven knew what. She hadn't had the energy to confront him about that yet.

71

He needed a father's firm hand and it was all more than she could cope with. She was tired of always being the responsible one in the family.

Listlessly, she opened the cupboard doors and began to sort through the manufacturers' pattern books, order books and loose invoices, laying aside anything that needed further investigation. The bookshelves held a number of leather-bound and illustrated tomes on art and architecture.

She pulled out Palladio's *Four Books on Architecture*, translated by Giacomo Leoni, and carefully leafed through the pages. How Father had loved everything Italian! Then she took down the first of the four volumes of *Vitruvius Britannicus*. Everything she knew about architecture she had learned at Father's side while he showed her the drawings in these books and enthused about how the plans brought into being elegant buildings made of brick and stone. The books had taught her how to look at a building and read its bones, and she loved them.

She returned the book to the shelf but something prevented it from sliding back into place. Standing on tip-toe, she reached into the gap between the adjacent volumes and extracted a large sealed envelope bearing the words, *To be opened in the event of my death*. Father's familiar signature appeared underneath. She stared at it for a moment, her knees all at once as wobbly as calf's foot jelly.

She slid a shaking finger under the wax seal and five sealed papers slid out on to the desk. She placed them neatly in a row in front of her, turning them so that the names written on them were uppermost: Fanny, Jack, Florence, Rafaele and Venetia.

Very slowly, she picked up the letter with her name on it and broke the seal.

My darling girl,
If you are reading this, I fear the worst has happened and my poor old heart has failed before I had the chance to explain why

I wanted to bring all my loved ones together under the same roof. I love you all so dearly and, although I understand that it may be difficult for you at first, I truly believe it is possible for you to become one family. If you embrace the idea you will find strength in it.

No doubt you are running around like a mother hen, trying to keep together your brood of thoughtless chicks, believing that I lost my senses. I do not excuse my behaviour in marrying your mama but hope that, eventually, you will come to understand that, in the circumstances, I took the steps necessary to protect those I love as well as I could. Your dear mother did eventually forgive me and I hope that you will, too. I beg you to make the effort to forge bonds with Jack and Florence, however difficult that may be.

I have been so tired of late and the constant travelling between two homes and from one end of the country to the other to supervise clients' work has become an intolerable burden. It is for this reason that I shall very soon open the shop we have so often talked about. I have every confidence, since so many smart new houses are being built in London at present, that there will be a great influx of new clients. The shop will be an irresistible emporium.

You have great talent, Venetia, and a natural eye for what makes a house into a beautiful home. This talent must not be denied. I'd hoped to be granted the time to introduce you to the business but as you are reading this letter it seems this was not to be. Despite that, I urge you to take on the challenge, bringing fresh ideas and your youthful vigour with you. This will not only lead to your personal fulfilment but will provide you and the others with all necessary income.

I hope you find it in your heart to forgive me and always remember how much I loved you.

Be strong, my darling girl,

Father

73

Reading the letter, she heard his voice so clearly in her mind that it made her ache to have him beside her again. She pictured that last time they'd raced Dante along the beach with the wind in their hair while Father shouted with the pure joy of it. Now, misery engulfed her. She let out a cry of desolation and buried her face in her hands, weeping hot tears of sorrow for the loss of him.

At last her tears were spent. She must pick herself up and forge the future. If the family were to be able to earn a living from Father's business, she must find out everything she could about it. Taking a bracing breath, she opened his address book.

Some time later she replaced the book in the desk drawer. Father had used the services of Wallis and Greene, painters and varnishers. Venetia stood up and smoothed down her skirt. Time to pay them a visit and to meet the other neighbours.

Out in the street, she peered through the window into the adjacent bookshop and circulating library before pushing the door open. Books lined the walls, the highest shelves being reached by a library ladder. Two lady customers leafed silently through a small stack of books on the counter.

A portly old gentleman attired in a velvet coat tip-toed forward to greet her. He wore a beautifully starched and tied cravat and his thinning hair was neatly combed. 'May I help you?' He spoke in a hushed undertone.

'I am Miss Lovell,' she said, holding out her hand. 'My father, before his untimely death, had the shop next door.'

The elderly gentleman's eyelids flickered with surprise. 'Edwin Murchison.' He shook her hand. 'Do come and meet my brother Charles.'

Venetia followed him to the back of the bookshop, where another elderly man sat behind the counter. He stood up and she blinked. At first glance the two brothers looked identical but then she realised that Edwin was a little taller than Charles and his velvet coat was dark blue instead of brown.

'Miss Lovell,' he murmured, 'may I present my brother, Charles Murchison? Charles, Miss Lovell is Theodore Lovell's daughter.'

Gravely, Charles shook Venetia's hand. 'We were extremely sorry to hear of your father's premature passing.' He spoke in the same muted tones as Edwin.

'Thank you for your condolences.'

'It was a shock to us all. Your father, although new to the shop-keeping fraternity here, was well liked. He was a sound fellow, if a little impetuous.'

Edwin nodded in agreement. 'A sound fellow.'

'I intend to refurbish the shop and reopen it as soon as possible.'

Charles's neatly groomed eyebrows rose. '*You* will take over your father's business?'

'That is my intention.' Venetia drew herself up to her full height. Perhaps if she said it often enough she would believe it herself.

'We hear there was significant damage?'

'Most of the stock was ruined and the premises must be redecorated. I've been clearing up the broken items. Now, if you'll excuse me,' said Venetia, 'I have business to attend to.'

'Do call again one afternoon when we aren't so busy,' said Edwin.

Venetia glanced at the two ladies quietly perusing the books.

'We shall take tea,' said Charles. 'The baker's shop makes excellent custard tarts.'

The Murchison brothers bowed in unison and she left, finding a measure of comfort in her new acquaintanceship.

It was late afternoon by the time Venetia returned to Quill Court. After she'd taken off her pelisse, she went into the drawing room where Mama and Florence sat by the fire, heads bent over their sewing.

Florence looked up as Venetia entered the room.

'I've asked Kitty to light the candles,' said Mama, 'it's too dark to sew any longer. Warm yourself by the fire until dinner.'

'Have you had a good day?' asked Venetia.

'It's been very comfortable, chatting while we sew,' said Florence. 'I count myself fortunate to have such a congenial stepmama.'

'We've finished several cushion covers and Florence's work is very neat,' said Mama, smiling fondly at her.

Venetia picked up the small pile of covers and examined them closely. The stitches were tiny and she couldn't differentiate at all between Mama's and Florence's sewing. A small spike of jealousy pricked her. Mama appeared to have very readily accepted Florence as another daughter.

'There are a great many small pieces of leftover silk,' said Florence. 'We could make them into rosettes for the cushions.'

Her eager young face was entirely without guile and all thoughts of sibling jealousy evaporated. Venetia smiled. 'An excellent idea.'

Kitty came to tell them that dinner was ready. 'Master Rafaele has returned and Major Chamberlaine is already seated.'

Mama put aside her sewing. 'Then we mustn't keep him waiting.'

In the dining room Major Chamberlaine remained monosyllabic while Florence and Mama chattered about their day.

Raffie, hair unbrushed, appeared in the doorway and slid into his place.

'You look pale, Raffie,' said Venetia. 'Are you quite well?'

'Perfectly.' He crumbled a piece of bread over his plate.

'You have black circles under your eyes.'

'Stop fussing! I'm not a child, Venetia.'

'Then don't act like one,' snapped Major Chamberlaine. 'You owe your sister a little courtesy and you will apologise.'

Raffie stared at him, his cheeks flaring scarlet.

Venetia bit her lip, trying not to let her hurt and surprise show.

'Well?' demanded Major Chamberlaine.

'I apologise,' muttered Raffie.

'Perhaps I was fussing,' Venetia said, 'but I'm concerned for you.'

He sighed. 'You seem to forget, I'm grown up.'

76

'Perhaps I do.' Distracted, she put down her soup spoon. 'And now university is out of question we must decide what path you will follow in life. Will you work in Father's business?'

'Good God, no!' Raffie's expression was appalled. 'Father knew I didn't want that.'

'Maybe not,' said Venetia, 'but I need you to help until the business is settled. This afternoon I've been to visit the decorators. I'll start to repaint the showroom this week.'

'You're going to paint it yourself?' Major Chamberlaine laughed disbelievingly.

Venetia lifted her chin. 'Since there's been a noticeable lack of offers of help from the male members of this so-called family, I see little option. I'll need help with grinding the pigment but I'm perfectly capable of mixing and applying paint.'

'Venetia painted Spindrift Cottage,' explained Mama. 'Why, she even marbled the sitting-room mantelpiece.'

Major Chamberlaine pursed his lips. 'And how do you intend to pay for this paint?'

'I proposed an arrangement to Mr Wallis and he has agreed.'

'An arrangement?'

'Once the showroom is open, I shall recommend that our clients use Wallis and Greene's services. They'll allow us a commission for each project completed until the paint has been paid for.' Venetia had to suppress a self-satisfied smile at the stunned expression on Jack Chamberlaine's handsome face.

He looked down at his soup. 'Credit where it's due, that was a clever piece of business.'

Taken aback, all she could say was, 'Thank you.'

Mama glanced at her and raised her eyebrows.

'However,' Venetia continued, 'I had an unfortunate encounter with a Mr Bennet, whose shop is near Wallis and Greene's premises. He supplied Father with high-quality brocades and upholstery fabrics. He was so affronted that I, a mere female, should attempt to negotiate with him that he ordered his clerk to show me the door.'

'How humiliating!' said Mama.

'It was.' Venetia sighed at the memory. 'He also said that Father had unsettled accounts with him and asks that we attend to them immediately.'

'I see,' said Major Chamberlaine. 'Following on from our discussion this morning, I believe it prudent that we visit the remaining suppliers together, don't you?'

'Tomorrow morning, perhaps?'

'Very well.'

He turned his attention back to his soup.

Venetia ate some bread and reflected. So Jack Chamberlaine could be civil after all. 'There's something else,' she said. 'Sifting through the papers in Father's office, I found a letter from him to each one of us.'

Everyone stopped eating and all four faces turned to look at her.

'A letter?' Mama's face brightened. 'A letter for me from Theo?'

Venetia nodded. 'I opened mine. It appears he was anxious about his health and wrote the letters in case ...' She swallowed. It wouldn't do to cry over the dinner table. 'In case he didn't survive long enough to bring us all together in Quill Court as he planned.'

'Where are the letters?' demanded Raffie.

'I imagined you'd want to read them in private,' said Venetia, 'so I slipped them under your bedroom doors.'

'I've finished my supper,' said Florence. 'May I leave the table?'

'Of course,' said Mama, standing up. 'I'm sure we'll all want to read our letters straight away.'

One by one, the family filed out of the dining room. Venetia took her letter from her pocket and began to read it again.

Chapter 8

Kitty crept through the sleeping house and down to the scullery. Earlier, she'd greased the back-door bolts with lard and they slid back noiselessly but the key, taken from its hook in the larder, made a loud click when she turned it. She froze. Not a peep came from within but outside carriage wheels and horses still clattered by and the sound of a drunken argument drifted through the night.

Slipping out, she hid the key in the coalhole. Hardly daring to breathe, she climbed the area steps to street level and pushed the iron gate but it was locked. She pulled up her skirts and began to clamber over the top. Her foot got stuck when she was halfway over and she teetered backwards and forwards while she tried to pull her boot free. She gasped as hands caught hold of her.

'Don't struggle!' whispered Nat. He kicked the toe of her boot backwards, dislodging it from between the bars, and then lifted her to the ground. He dropped a kiss on her mouth and pulled her after him.

They ran without stopping until they reached Bishopsgate Street. Breathless and laughing, they strode on, arm in arm.

'I hope Dorcas doesn't wake up,' said Kitty. 'I stuffed all my clothes under the blanket so she'd think I was asleep underneath.'

'Would she tell on you if she caught you going out?'

Kitty made a face. 'She reads the Bible every night until we blow out the candle and then she prays aloud for at least ten minutes.'

In the distance a church clock rang the midnight hour. The last time Kitty had been out this late she'd been struggling up the cliff steps with arms full of smuggled silk, while the wind off the sea nigh froze her to death. Tonight was a different kettle of fish. Tonight she was out to have fun.

Nat ducked into a network of reeking lanes and alleys. A couple of men skulked past with their faces turned to the wall and somewhere a cat yowled. The moonlight barely penetrated the narrow passages and Kitty clung to her companion's arm as she fumbled her way through the darkness, thankful he knew where he was going. She let out a squeal as her foot slid in something unpleasantly slippery, and gasped when a rat scurried past. As they turned a corner, a welcome light glowed ahead.

They reached the lighted window where a girl wearing nothing but a shift sat on the sill, swinging her bare foot outside.

'Show you a good time, sir?' she called out.

'Get away with you, Peggy,' Nat laughed. 'It's me. Can't you see I'm with my best girl now?'

'No harm in trying, dearie. Business is slack.'

Nat pulled Kitty up beside him. 'It's cold tonight, Peggy,' he said over his shoulder. 'You'll catch your death.'

'Comes to us all, one way or the other.'

'You know her?' asked Kitty, suddenly consumed with jealousy. She knew about that type of girl, a light skirt who'd take a man's wages and lead him into ruin.

'Pay no mind to Peggy,' he said. 'We grew up together at Ma Slattery's.'

'Who's Ma Slattery?'

'She takes in orphans.'

'You're an orphan, then? Ma Slattery must be a very good kind of person.'

Nat snorted with laughter. 'She gave me a start in life, that's for sure.'

He took a sharp turn into another alley and light and laughter spilled out of an open door ahead.

The Goat and Compass was heaving. Nat held Kitty's hand as they forced their way through the noisily chattering crowd. Sawdust was gritty underfoot and the air clouded with tobacco smoke that made her cough. Men slapped Nat on the back and nodded at Kitty, eyeing her up and down.

At the bar Nat bought a tankard of ale and thrust a glass of gin into Kitty's hand. 'Drink up, sweetheart, and get some warmth in your bones.'

She sipped her drink as she took in the low, smoke-blackened ceiling and oak settles. Flickering tallow candles and a blazing fire cast a welcoming glow. The gin began to radiate its warmth through her body and she took another sip. Perhaps she ought to keep a bottle under her pillow to make her warm at night.

'Got you a present,' said Nat. He delved into his pocket and brought out the prettiest handkerchief Kitty had ever seen.

'For me?' she asked, delighted.

''Course it's for you! You're my best girl, aintcha?'

She stroked the soft white silk and examined the pink embroidered rosebuds. 'I've never seen anything so lovely,' she said, reaching up to kiss his cheek.

'Sal's fighting tonight,' he said, pointing to a bill on the wall.

Kitty moved closer to read the announcement:

TONIGHT!

WRESTLING FOR A PURSE OF GOLD

BIG BESSIE

THE BONE CRUSHER OF BERMONSDEY

VS

BLACK SAL

THE AFRICAN PRINCESS
FROM THE DARK CONTINENT

'Sal's a princess?' Kitty asked breathlessly.

Nat laughed. 'Her pa was a sailor from West Africa.' He waved across the room.

Kitty spied Billy and he came over to greet them, a wide smile on his broad face. 'Sal'll be pleased you're here to cheer her on,' he said.

'What's the competition?' asked Nat, grinning. 'Best to know the odds before I place my bet.'

'She's big all right, that Bessie,' said Billy, 'but the bigger they are, the heavier they fall. She's new to this game and my Sal's nippy so I'm not worried. Got a lot riding on this bout, myself.'

Nat laughed. 'Is that why you're sweating?'

Billy smiled sheepishly and wiped his shiny forehead. 'You know me, Nat. I allus get nervous afore a fight.'

'D'you still wrestle?' asked Kitty, looking at his broken nose.

'Nah! Too old. I train Sal and arrange her fights.'

'Where is she?'

Billy glanced over her shoulder. 'Out the back. I'd better go and

82

see if she wants anything.' He shambled away through the press of people.

'Come and meet the others.' Nat pulled Kitty over to a group who all turned to face them. The names came thick and fast, Tommy, Ben, Mary, Lennie, Ruth, John …

Kitty smiled, trying not to look bewildered. Lordy, would she ever remember them all?

The innkeeper rang a bell hanging above the bar and the crowd let out a cheer.

'Drink up!' Nat drained his tankard and snatched Kitty's glass as others made a stampede for the bar, too.

A few moments later the innkeeper's daughter collected their money as they jostled their way out of the back door and into a crowded yard lit by flaming torches. Men clambered up to sit on the walls or to stand on top of barrels so as to see over the heads of those in front as far as a central, straw-strewn platform.

A man in a tattered and stained soldier's uniform began to bang a drum and a bookmaker wormed his way through the throng.

Kitty hopped up and down, the drumbeat fuelling her excitement. Lennie, small and dark, stood beside her, his arm around Ruth's shoulders.

She smiled. 'Ever been to a fight before?'

Kitty shook her head, liking the look of the other girl's freckled face and chestnut curls.

'Don't take no notice if it seems they get hurt,' Ruth advised. 'It's only a game.'

The innkeeper chivvied the crowd to stand back.

A moment later the soldier began to bang furiously on his drum and a man in a high-crowned hat climbed into the ring. He strode across the platform, swirling his cloak and testing the strength of the ropes. Satisfied, he rang a bell and raised his hand for quiet.

'Welcome, gentlemen and ladies, to the wrestling match of the century! Tonight our two brave contenders will be fighting to win a purse of ten golden guineas.'

A collective gasp went up from the crowd and Kitty caught her breath. *Ten guineas!* Twice what she earned in a year. She could hardly imagine such riches.

The drummer began to beat his drum even faster and the master of ceremonies held up his hand again. 'It's my very great pleasure to introduce to you the pride of Bermondsey.' His voice rose to a shout. 'I give you ... Big Bessie the Bone Crusher!'

The storeroom door burst open and a sturdy woman ran towards the platform, waving her arms above her head. Her wiry ginger hair was tied in a thick plait running down her back and she wore a short green petticoat and a sleeveless bodice laced over her plump bosom. She strode to the corner where her second awaited her.

The crowd whistled and stamped their feet.

'And now, please welcome, Black Sal the African princess!'

There was a drumroll and Kitty caught her breath as Sal vaulted on to the stage. Her scarlet bodice and knee-length skirt were embroidered with gold and her oiled brown limbs gleamed in the torchlight. A scarlet turban adorned with a bunch of pheasant's feathers gave her extra height. She looked magnificent.

Billy stood in Sal's corner and whispered last-minute advice to her.

'Ready, ladies?' asked the master of ceremonies. 'No gouging or you're out. On the bell ...'

The crowd fell quiet.

The bell rang and the two women shot out of their corners and faced each other in the centre of the ring.

Big Bessie bared her teeth, most of them blackened, and hissed loudly.

Sal prodded Bessie's mountainous breasts.

Bessie roared and launched herself at Sal, clamping her mighty arms around her neck.

The crowd shouted approval, screaming in glee as Sal suddenly twisted her upper body, flinging off her opponent. Bessie landed with a bone-shaking crash and Sal jumped on her chest. Bessie groaned while her legs flailed and thumped the floor.

'Go to it, Sal!' yelled Nat.

Bessie squirmed in her captor's grip and a moment later their positions were reversed.

Kitty winced as Bessie's petticoat rode up around her waist and she bounced up and down on Sal's pelvis while the crowd whistled and shrieked obscene comments. Kitty cried out as Bessie gripped Sal's wrists above her head, forcing them to the floor.

Bessie rolled Sal on to her side and wrapped her monumental thighs, encased in Holland drawers, around Sal's waist and squeezed until the other woman screamed. They grappled together, rolling across the ring, pale freckled limbs entangled with darkly gleaming ones. Bessie's pigtail had come loose and her coarse ginger hair made a tattered curtain over her face. Grunting and sweating, she looked like a Bedlamite.

Ruth pulled at Kitty's sleeve. 'Enjoying yourself?' she asked.

'I hope Sal's all right. Bessie's so much bigger.'

'It's going to be hard,' said Ruth, groaning as Bessie let out a shriek of anger. 'Go on, Sal!' she yelled.

Kitty had never seen anything like it. Her eyes widened as, to the delight of the crowd, Bessie's bounteous breasts fell out of her bodice. The noise was deafening. She glanced at Nat, who was laughing and slapping his thigh. It wasn't decent. Both women's petticoats had rucked up and their legs were on display. Despite this, Kitty was carried away by the screaming and jeering all around and found herself joining in.

Then a strange thing happened. Nat suddenly gripped Kitty's arm and the crowd grew silent. All she could hear was the grunting of the two contestants and the slap of flesh on flesh. All heads had turned to watch a tall man in a caped greatcoat stride into the yard. His starched cravat was tied so high that he was forced to look down his crooked nose, which was silhouetted by the flaming torch behind him. Four burly men, as solid as oaks, surrounded him, watching the assembly.

Kitty stared at the man, an ice-cold shiver running down her back, just as if she'd turned over a stone and found a poisonous snake underneath. She recognised his hooded eyes and the bullyboys at his side, and broke out into a cold sweat. The last time she'd seen him it had been by moonlight on a windswept beach as he watched the guineas for Napoleon being loaded into the galleys. King Midas.

Then Sal, oblivious to the crowd's silence, let out a screech, breaking the spell. She landed, sprawling, on the floor.

Someone whistled, a cheer went up and all heads turned back to the wrestling match.

Kitty hardly noticed when the bell rang and the master of ceremonies held Sal's hand up in the air and handed her the leather purse.

Sal straightened her turban, which had slipped over one eye, waved the purse and blew kisses.

The crowd roared approval and then booed as Big Bessie limped away.

Nat was shouting and waving his arms in the air. He pulled Kitty to his side and kissed her. 'Ten guineas! I knew she could do it.'

'Nat, did you see that man?' She turned to look at King Midas again but he and his bullyboys had gone.

'What man?' asked Nat.

'The big one in the greatcoat.'

Nat shrugged.

'I've seen him before! He's dangerous.'

Nat looked at her, all amusement wiped from his face. '*You've* seen him before? All the more reason then not to ask questions.'

'But, Nat ...'

'No, Kitty! Never speak of him. He has spies everywhere and he's dangerous.' He touched a finger to her mouth. 'Don't look at me like that!'

Despite his forced smile, Kitty could see Nat was agitated. What else did he know about King Midas?

'Come on,' he said, 'we're going to celebrate Sal's win.'

Kitty glanced back to where King Midas had been standing and then went after Nat.

'Kitty!'

She yawned and stretched. She'd been dreaming, imagining she was walking along streets paved with gold, peering into brightly lit shops filled with silken shawls, embroidered parasols, painted fans and lace gloves.

Someone shook her shoulder. A girl's face was peering at her, illuminated by candlelight. It was freckled, with mousy hair and rabbity teeth. Dorcas.

'It's gone five, Slugabed. Didn't you hear the bells? Hurry now! I'll start the fires but don't be long.' The door slammed behind her.

Kitty held her head and groaned. Jesus God, she'd never had such a headache. Her mouth felt full of sand and she could do with a nip of gin to wash away the nasty taste. Shivering, she dragged on her short stays over her shift. Her stockings hung over the end of the bed and she grimaced as she pulled them on. There'd been a downpour after they'd left the Goat last night and she'd trodden in a puddle. She'd washed the mud off them in the scullery when she'd crept in. Although she'd rubbed them on her towel, they were still clammily cold and wet.

She swallowed, her stomach feeling queasy. She felt like a bucket of pigswill but what a night she'd had! Fumbling under her pillow, she pulled out the handkerchief Nat had given her. The clocks were striking two when he'd kissed her goodnight. Smiling, she remembered how he'd called her his best girl. Then, yawning, she made her way downstairs to work.

Chapter 9

Venetia sat at the dining table with a newspaper spread out beneath several damaged vases, lamp bases and china figurines. She particularly liked the pale green vase with its frieze of Grecian figures dancing around the base; carefully she painted the broken edges with glue.

'You'll never be able to sell that,' said a voice behind her.

'I'm perfectly well aware of that,' she said, her hackles immediately raised, 'but I'm hopeful I'll be able to effect a good enough repair to make it possible to display the piece on the high shelf in the shop.'

Major Chamberlaine came to sit down beside her. 'What's the point?'

He didn't sound derisory or critical, only curious, and Venetia's antagonism subsided. 'These items will help make the showroom look fully stocked. They're all samples that can be ordered. I've found out where to buy them and I hope to tempt customers to buy similar pieces.'

'I see.'

Carefully, she positioned the broken piece of china into the vase until the glued edges were almost invisible. 'Would you hand me that strip of pink silk?'

He watched her closely as she bound the vase. Wordlessly, he placed his finger on the knot while Venetia tied it. What long and elegant fingers he had, not at all how she'd imagined a soldier's hands might be. 'That should suffice to hold it in place while the glue dries,' she said.

'I came to see if you'd like me to accompany you on your visits to the various suppliers but if you're too busy ...'

'I can finish this later. If we don't coax the suppliers into lending us display samples it'll be impossible to open the shop.'

Major Chamberlaine sighed. 'Then we must use all our powers of persuasion.'

Venetia drew a breath of relief. That was the first time she'd heard him say 'we'. Perhaps he would co-operate after all.

An hour later a hackney carriage drew up in front of the premises of Louis Verbeke, a Belgian importer of carpets. Major Chamberlaine handed Venetia down and asked the driver to wait.

Mr Verbeke, full of obsequious smiles, greeted them in his showroom where Venetia explained who they were. His diminutive figure was neatly dressed and his dark hair glistened with scented pomade.

'I will be delighted to show you my range of carpets of the very best quality,' he said.

Carpets of all sizes covered the walls and the floor, their thick pile absorbing sound with a curiously muffling effect. There was a pervasive scent of dust and wool mixed with the sickly perfume of Mr Verbeke's pomade.

'I believe my father bought several carpets from you?' said Venetia, running her hand over a rug woven with a central medallion design in shades of celadon green and coral.

'Mr Lovell never went anywhere else.' Mr Verbeke smiled, his yellowing teeth slightly crossed at the front. 'I supply the finest Belgian flat-weave rugs, French Savonnerie carpets, Persian prayer mats, and intricately patterned Axminster carpets made from the softest wool, dyed in colours of your choice.'

'Initially, what we are looking for,' said Venetia, 'are some pattern books and a few sample carpets.'

'But of course!' said Mr Verbeke, waving his hand. 'Select what you wish.'

Venetia glanced at Major Chamberlaine and then looked Mr Verbeke in the eye. 'We're prepared to pay a small deposit to borrow these items for our showroom.'

'A small deposit?' Mr Verbeke's ingratiating smile disappeared. 'I do not understand.'

'We will encourage our clients to purchase your goods,' said Major Chamberlaine.

'You must pay in full for any carpets you take from this showroom.'

'But, Mr Verbeke,' said Venetia, knowing already that it was hopeless by the indignation in his expression, 'our clients may not wish to buy the exact carpets that we display. Suppose they want a different colour or design ...'

'Then they may visit me directly to make arrangements.'

'We can only send our clients to you if we have samples to show them,' said Major Chamberlaine. 'And we would require an introduction fee.'

'You expect me to allow you to take away my expensive carpets and leave only a small deposit? Do you take me for a fool?' Outraged, Mr Verbeke drew himself up to his full height of five foot two inches. 'Miss Lovell, Major Chamberlaine, you are wasting my time.'

'Mr Verbeke ...'

He held up a hand. 'Leave now. Our meeting is terminated.' He opened the door to the street. 'Good day.'

Mortified, Venetia stepped outside.

'I suppose,' she said, with feigned composure, 'that means we shall have to find another carpet supplier.'

Major Chamberlaine pursed his lips. 'Insufferable little man!' he muttered. 'Where now?'

'Furniture suppliers in Shoemaker's Lane.'

He gave the direction to the driver and they climbed back into the hackney.

A short while later he knocked on the front door of Messrs. Marsden and Harris with his silver-headed cane.

A young clerk came to greet them.

'May we speak with either Mr Marsden or Mr Harris?' asked Jack.

Venetia seated herself to wait on a hall chair, her hands clasped together nervously, while Jack stared out of the window. Although this was only one of her father's suppliers, it was one of the most important and, as their first meeting had gone badly, she feared if they met with another rebuff Jack Chamberlaine might withdraw his support for her scheme.

Footsteps echoed along the passage and a middle-aged man in shirtsleeves and wearing a canvas apron appeared. 'How may I help you?'

Venetia stood up. 'I believe you knew my father, Theodore Lovell?'

Marsden looked sharply at her. 'I was saddened to hear of his untimely passing.'

A moment later they were sitting on velvet-upholstered chairs before a magnificent inlaid desk in Mr Marsden's office. The walls were panelled with book-matched mahogany and a French carpet was soft under their feet.

'How may I be of service?' asked Mr Marsden.

'I hope that we may be of service to you,' said Venetia. 'My father had planned for me to join his business.'

92

Marsden frowned. 'He mentioned a daughter who designs paper hangings.'

'Together with Major Chamberlaine, I intend to continue the business.'

'I'm pleased to hear it.' Marsden ran a hand through his thinning hair. 'It's sad when the next generation isn't able to continue a tradition. My partner, Mr Harris, died of a broken heart when his son was killed at Salamanca.'

'War changes many things,' said Major Chamberlaine.

'You're a military man?'

'Until the Battle of Vitoria,' he said, gripping the head of his cane so tightly that his knuckles were white. 'Some might say I was lucky to survive.'

'Certainly luckier than young Frederick Harris.' Marsden turned back to Venetia. 'Have you come to order furniture?'

'Not yet,' said Venetia.

'I heard the shop was destroyed by thieves?'

'They caused significant damage,' said Major Chamberlaine. 'However, it's currently being refurbished.'

'It's a good time for a business such as yours,' said Marsden. 'There's a deal of house building going on and ladies are insisting on all the latest decorations for their new homes.'

'I agree,' said Venetia. Now she'd come to the point of asking the favour she was nervous again. 'I wish to ask if you'd be prepared to lend us some furniture samples.'

Marsden pursed his lips. 'It's customary to sell, not lend, samples to businesses such as yours.'

'I trust that we might reach an arrangement,' said Venetia. 'I'd like to promote your furniture to our clients. However, I'd need samples to satisfy them with regard to the quality of your workmanship.'

'Your father and I did a great deal of business together over the years.'

'We should like to continue that tradition. It would be a shame if we were obliged to use goods from another workshop.'

'What kind of samples had you in mind?'

'I have the idea of arranging set pieces,' said Venetia, warming to her theme. 'A lady's writing desk with a pretty chair, for example, placed before a length of beautiful curtain fabric. We'd dress the arrangement with decorative objects.'

'Is that necessary?'

Venetia noticed that Jack Chamberlaine was watching her with a half-smile. 'Many people have so little imagination,' she said, 'they cannot picture such items in their own home. These little vignettes will make it easier for them.' She held her breath while Mr Marsden tapped the desktop with his pen.

'An interesting idea,' he conceded. 'You hope to kindle your clients' imagination. But how are you going to draw these clients into your shop?'

Venetia stared at him. Surely people would visit the shop out of simple curiosity? 'We ...' She floundered. 'We'll have a good window display,' she said, aware of how unconvincing she sounded.

'And, of course,' said Major Chamberlaine smoothly, 'there'll be the Grand Opening of Lovell and Chamberlaine as soon as the premises are decorated. Invitations will be sent to Mr Lovell's clients, suggesting that they bring their friends. Refreshments will be served, including ices from Gunter's, and discounts given to those who place a commission with us on that day. Advertisements will be placed in the newspapers the week before.'

Venetia stared at him in astonishment.

Mr Marsden nodded. 'You've thought this through very carefully.'

'Indeed,' said Major Chamberlaine .

'Tell you what I'll do,' said Marsden. 'You shall have a selection of samples for three months. If you place a reasonable number of orders within that time and we're both satisfied, then I'll replace them with others. It's important to provide new items to keep catching the eye of your customers, don't you think?'

'Ladies can be very fickle in matters of fashion,' agreed Major Chamberlaine, glancing at Venetia.

'That would be splendid, Mr Marsden!' she said, ignoring the adversarial gleam in Jack Chamberlaine's eye.

'Then come and select the items you'd like to display.' Marsden led them down a passage and into the workshop beyond.

Venetia coughed at the powerful odour of fish glue.

Three men sat at benches under the windows. One worked a lathe turning chair legs and another sanded a small table. Sawdust motes swirled in the winter sunshine coming from a roof light. Half-finished tables, chairs, linen presses and writing desks were stacked against one wall.

'The furniture is made here,' said Marsden, 'and then taken to the finishing shop next door for French polishing. Come through to the storeroom,' he said, 'and you shall choose your pieces.'

There was a wide range of furniture available and Venetia considered each item carefully before selecting a rosewood drum table, a hall table with a gilt convex mirror to hang above, a satinwood games table with inlaid ebony chessboard, a variety of chairs, a calico-covered chaise-longue and a mahogany corner cupboard.

'It's been a pleasure doing business with you, Mr Marsden,' said Major Chamberlain.

Marsden smiled and held out his hand. 'I rather think we have still to do the business together but I look forward to that. Send me word when you're ready and I'll deliver the items.'

'Thank you, Mr Marsden,' said Venetia fervently.

'I liked your father,' he said, 'and I'm pleased to help.' His callused hand was firm and dry.

In the street again, Venetia shook sawdust off her skirt before they climbed into the waiting hackney. 'What a relief!' she said. 'After our earlier failure I wasn't at all sure we'd be able to persuade him.'

Jack Chamberlaine looked at her thoughtfully. 'You really care about the shop, don't you?'

She gripped her hands together in her lap. 'We *have* to make it succeed,' she said.

'I suppose you're right,' he agreed, slowly. 'And you're prepared to make that commitment?' His gaze bored into her, as if he were trying to see into the depths of her soul.

She looked straight back at him, trying not to be distracted by the intense blue of his eyes. 'If we don't,' she said, 'what will become of us all?'

After a long moment, he nodded. 'Miss Lovell, there's something else I wish to discuss.'

'Yes, Major Chamberlaine?' He looked uncomfortable and she mentally braced herself for a difficult conversation.

'I didn't want you and your family to come to Quill Court ...'

'You made that perfectly plain!'

'Will you listen to me?' He pulled awkwardly at his ear. 'I understand now that you had no wish to come to London either. However, like it or not, circumstances oblige us to mould ourselves into some kind of a family. To that end, I believe it's sensible to present a united front to the world.' Spots of high colour bloomed on his chiselled cheeks.

Good heavens, thought Venetia, he's embarrassed.

'I believe it's appropriate, despite our not being legally related, for you to address me as Jack.'

She raised her eyebrows but withheld her smile. Perhaps he was coming round after all. 'I agree,' she said. 'And I should be pleased if you will call me Venetia.'

Jack let out a slow breath. 'That's settled then. So now where?'

'Jepson Court,' said Venetia. 'Upholstery fabrics next. And then curtain materials and another carpet supplier. If there's time I'd like to call in on the upholstery workshop.'

Jack gave the instruction to the driver.

'So, the business is to be called Lovell and Chamberlaine, then?' asked Venetia as the carriage rolled away.

'I might have said Chamberlaine and Lovell.'

Venetia shook her head. 'Lovell must come first so that clients know it's a continuation of Father's business. But using your name too may give us some credence. Irritatingly, some clients may not wish to place their business with a mere female.'

Jack's lips twitched. 'There is that.'

'What made you think of such a marvellous idea as a Grand Opening party?' asked Venetia, unable to contain her curiosity any longer.

He smiled.

In fact, thought Venetia, his eyes positively twinkled and she caught a glimpse of the man Florence loved.

'It was your father's idea,' he said. 'He spoke to me of his plans in that regard at some length.'

'It might have been Father's idea but you saved the day,' said Venetia. 'And all we have to do now is to replicate that success with another dozen suppliers.'

Jack groaned and leaned back against the worn leather seat with his eyes closed.

☙

The following day Kitty went into the taproom of the Crosse Keys and saw Nat in conversation with a small boy wearing a tattered coat. The child handed something to Nat, who ruffled his hair and pushed his plate of half-finished pie towards him. The boy stuffed the pie into his mouth and darted away.

Creeping up behind Nat, Kitty placed her hands over his eyes.

'Guess who?' she said.

'Maria? Sadie? Or perhaps it's Lizzie?'

'Nat!'

He turned to face her, eyes full of laughter. 'It's my best girl, isn't it?'

Kitty sat down beside him, her cheeks pink with pleasure. He looked quite the gentleman again in a caped greatcoat and clean necktie.

'I knew you'd find a way to come.'

'I've only a few minutes,' she said. 'I'm on my way to Cheapside to help Miss Venetia.'

'Then I'll walk with you. I've finished my business here for the morning.'

'Nat, what is your line of business?' Kitty asked as they set off. 'You never said.'

'I'm a trader.'

'What kind of a trader?'

'This and that,' he said. 'Whatever takes my fancy that I can find a market for.'

'Do you have a shop then?'

'Blimey, you're full of questions!'

'Well, do you?' persisted Kitty. 'If I'm your best girl you shouldn't have secrets from me.'

Nat laughed. 'Everyone has secrets. But since it's you asking, I'll tell you. One day I'll have a shop but until then I've got me barrows. We'll pass a couple in Cheapside. I supply the goods and the old women who mind them take a percentage of what they sell.'

They turned into the tide of pedestrians strolling along Cheapside and Kitty's eyes were constantly drawn to the fashion-ably dressed ladies and the enticing displays in the shop windows. 'I've never seen so many lovely things,' she said, pausing to look at a mother-of-pearl fan painted with peacocks.

'What'd *you* do with a fan?' laughed Nat.

Kitty smiled. 'I'd have one of white swansdown and use it to flirt with my beau across a crowded ballroom.'

'Never seen a lady with a fan in the Goat and Compass.'

'Stop laughing at me!' she protested. 'It's not a crime to want pretty things.'

98

Nat caught her in his arms and kissed her nose. 'No, it's not. Now stay here for a minute.' He pushed his way through the throng and crossed over the road, weaving through the passing carriages.

Kitty watched him go then looked in the window of a milliner's shop and imagined herself trying on the red silk bonnet trimmed with ostrich feathers. Wearing a hat like that she'd look as fine as any lady. She'd mince along Cheapside, making the smallest bows to acquaintances, all hoity-toity. Sighing, she turned away. If Nat didn't get a move on Miss Venetia would have her guts for garters.

Nat was talking to an old woman leaning on a barrow. Handkerchiefs, ribbons and scraps of lace were tied to the awning and fluttered gaily in the breeze. Other items glinted in the light. Bottles, perhaps. Nat lifted up the sacking draped around the barrow, pulled out a box from underneath and began to sift through the contents.

A woman with a babe in arms stopped at the barrow. She pulled a piece of folded cloth out of the baby's shawl. Nat examined it before pulling a few coins from his pocket to hand to her. Then, as if he could feel Kitty's gaze on him, he glanced up. Quick as a flash the box was stowed and the old woman began to trundle the barrow away.

Nat crossed the road again, dodging between a yellow curricle bowling along and a dray travelling in the opposite direction.

'Did you buy something from that woman?' asked Kitty.

'Nice piece of lace. Belonged to her grandma.'

'I'm late and Miss Venetia'll be waiting for me. Annunziata made me polish the silver before I left.'

'I couldn't stand being at someone's beck and call all day.'

'Not much choice if you're a servant, is there?' said Kitty tartly.

'Don't be a servant then.'

'One day I'll find a rich man to marry me and then I'll lie about on silk cushions all day, eating grapes.'

Nat hooted with laughter. 'Have you been reading one of them ladies' romance stories?'

They stopped outside the shop and he kissed her cheek. 'Don't let Miss Venetia work you too hard, sweetheart.'

She waited until Nat disappeared into the crowd and then rapped on the window.

Miss Venetia hid behind the door as she let Kitty in. 'Quick,' she said, 'I don't want anyone to see me.'

Kitty had to stop herself from laughing. Miss Venetia had taken off her mourning dress and wore only an old shift with thick woollen stockings underneath. Her hair was tied up in a makeshift turban made from a piece of curtain material. 'Did you know you have paint on your face?' asked Kitty.

'I have paint on me everywhere,' said Miss Venetia. 'That's why I took off my dress, to save it from being spoiled.'

'Aren't you cold?'

'Quite the contrary,' she said, blowing a loose strand of hair off her cheek. 'I've been climbing up and down ladders all day and, after Raffie sloped off, I had to grind the paint pigments myself.'

Kitty glanced around the shop. It smelled of fresh paint. The high ceiling made the large space look bare but a fire crackled in the marble fireplace, dispelling the damp chill she'd noticed on her last visit.

'Will you wipe up any drips that might have soaked through the drop cloths on to the floor?' said Miss Venetia,

Kitty fetched a bucket and a rag from the little scullery at the back of the premises.

An hour later Venetia stretched out the knots in her shoulders. 'One last coat tomorrow should suffice.'

'You've made a good job of it,' said Kitty. Although she'd seen Miss Venetia redecorating at Spindrift Cottage the shop was much bigger.

'As I'm already paint-spattered, I'll wash the brushes,' said Miss Venetia. 'Will you start to clean the rooms upstairs? One will be a storeroom and I don't want to put any goods in there until the dust has gone.'

Kitty fetched a broom and dusters and went upstairs. She opened the first door and her footsteps echoed over the bare boards. It was a large, empty room with wood-panelled walls.

It was later, as she ran a duster over the panelling, that she found the secret door. She must have pressed a hidden catch because a section of panelling swung open. Peering inside, she caught her breath and then ran down the stairs. 'Miss Venetia! Miss Venetia!'

Miss Venetia, wearing her black dress again, came out of the office buttoning up her cuffs. 'What is it?'

'I've found something!'

A moment later Miss Venetia was carrying a portrait of a beautiful lady wearing an old-fashioned dress out of the secret store. She returned again to the closet and soon twenty paintings stood propped up against the walls. Eyes shining, she turned to Kitty. 'How clever of you! These are the missing items Major Chamberlaine mentioned to me. My father must have stored them here, ready to display in the shop. And there are packing cases, too.'

The tea chests were heavy and Kitty thought she'd break her back moving them. Miss Venetia pulled wisps of straw from inside and Kitty pursed her lips as they fell on the newly swept floor. Now she'd have to sweep up again. But then she forgot her irritation when Miss Venetia hefted a bronze statuette of a horse out of the chest. 'Oh, what a beautiful thing!' she breathed. The horse, about a foot tall, was rearing and shaking its mane. She touched it, almost surprised to find that it wasn't alive.

'Isn't it lovely?' she said. Miss Venetia lifted another statuette from the straw, a Roman maiden. Another six bronzes followed and an assortment of vases, marble urns and obelisks.

Kitty picked up one of the vases, in glorious blue porcelain, heavily decorated with gold.

'This is from the royal porcelain factory in Berlin,' said Miss Venetia. 'Look at the fine detail on the handles and the embossed decoration. I could design a colour scheme for a whole room around such a piece.'

'I suppose I'd better get on with the cleaning,' said Kitty.

Miss Venetia smiled. 'You've worked hard enough for today, I think. And without you, we wouldn't have found these treasures. Why don't you take the rest of the afternoon off and look at the shops? They're so tempting, aren't they?'

Delight made Kitty laugh aloud.

'Off you go then! Only be back in Quill Court by eight o'clock or Annunziata will scold me.'

'I will,' Kitty promised. Gathering up her broom, she skipped downstairs.

Chapter 10

Venetia, Florence, Mama and Raffie arrived at the shop with their arms full of cushions and baskets containing the vases and figurines Venetia had repaired.

Raffie climbed up and down the ladder, hanging the new-found paintings in the room to the rear of the showroom while Venetia supervised. She was particularly pleased with the portrait of a seventeenth-century beauty identified as Giulia di Pietro. Light from the long windows flooded the space, making it a perfect picture gallery. It gave her a great deal of satisfaction to unroll a beautiful blue and gold sample carpet and place it on the gallery floor. The new carpet supplier had been pleased to lend it to them, hoping to draw custom away from his old rival, Mr Verbeke.

Mama set to work pleating and draping lengths of curtain fabric over brass poles fixed to the walls, while Florence passed cushions to Venetia and pins and scissors to Mama.

Venetia stood back and studied her floor-to-ceiling arrangement of cushions with a critical eye. She was pleased with the shelves that Mr Marsden's joiners had made for them, forming a large rectangle on the wall and displaying twenty cushions, each in its own compartment. 'What do you think, Florence?'

'Perhaps the gold cushion would be more striking next to the blue one? And then the violet one could move along so that it's beside the pink silk.'

Venetia moved the cushions as suggested and then smiled. 'You have Father's eye for colour, Florence.'

The shop door burst open and Raffie shouted, 'The cart is here!'

Florence and Venetia hurried outside to find Mr Marsden and one of his men unloading the promised furniture samples. Before long they'd been carried in and carefully unwrapped.

'I added a few extra items,' said Mr Marsden. 'There's a sewing table, two armchairs, a small bookcase and a plant stand I thought you'd like.' He looked around at the shop. 'It's just as well, I reckon, since you've so much space to fill.'

'That's extremely kind of you,' said Venetia with a heartfelt smile. She'd been suffering an agony of anxiety that there would be too little to display.

Venetia and Raffie spent the next hour arranging the furniture into groups and selecting the most appropriate accessories for each display.

The doorknocker sounded and Florence ran to see who it was.

Venetia heard the murmur of voices and looked over her shoulder to see a man together with a woman holding a small parcel. They had a young girl in tow.

'Venetia, this is Mr and Mrs Benson and their daughter Jane,' said Florence. 'They own the baker's shop over the road and have brought us cakes.'

'How lovely!' said Venetia. 'Charles and Edwin Murchison from the bookshop next door mentioned that you bake exceedingly good custard tarts.'

'Our speciality,' said Mrs Benson, smiling. She was small and neat, while her husband was tall and lanky. 'We couldn't help seeing all the comings and goings and thought we should introduce ourselves.'

'Then you shall take tea with us.'

Raffie and Mr Benson gathered all the chairs around Mr Marsden's drum table.

Venetia glanced up with a smile as Jack arrived, carrying a small parcel. 'You're just in time to meet Mr and Mrs Benson who own the baker's shop opposite.'

'They've brought us cakes,' said Raffie.

'It was a terrible thing what happened to Mr Lovell,' said Mr Benson. 'He'd no airs and graces.' He shook his head. 'Wouldn't listen to advice, though.'

Mrs Benson placed her hand on his sleeve. 'William, not now,' she murmured.

'What advice was that?' asked Jack.

Mr Benson glanced at his wife. 'We talked about the unexpected overheads of owning a shop, that's all.'

Jack tore open the small parcel he'd brought with him, pulled out a rectangle of stiff card and handed it to Mrs Benson. 'Please accept this invitation to our Grand Opening next week.'

'Delighted, I'm sure.' Her face was wreathed in smiles.

'Excellent cakes,' said Raffie, licking crumbs from his lips.

'Perhaps we could order a quantity for the party?' said Venetia.

'We'd be happy to make something dainty,' said Mrs Benson. 'Miniature meringues and macaroons?'

Mr Benson nodded in agreement. 'Many fine ladies come to purchase our baked goods.'

'Perhaps, then,' said Mama, 'you might keep some of our invitations under the counter to offer to your best customers?' She lowered her voice. 'We want the right sort of person to come to the opening.'

'Of course we will,' said Mrs Benson.

After the Bensons had gone, Jack ate another of the ratafia

biscuits. 'I've spoken to Gunter's about supplying ices for the opening but we haven't really thought about who to invite. Since we're all new to town our circle of acquaintances is small.'

'I've invited Mrs Stanhope and her daughter Emily,' said Venetia. 'They live opposite us in Quill Court. We became acquainted when I was exercising the pugs.'

'It's all very well asking other shop owners,' said Mama, 'but we need customers with deep pockets.'

Venetia looked at her in surprise. That was a surprisingly perceptive comment for Mama to make. 'I've been so busy preparing the showroom that I haven't given that enough thought,' she conceded.

'Perhaps I could take the pugs out for a walk,' said Florence, 'and post invitations through the doors of the grandest houses I can find.'

'I'm not having you walking the streets alone, touting for business,' began Jack. He broke off, his face suddenly scarlet. 'What I mean ...'

'Of course not,' interrupted Mama. 'Nevertheless, it's an excellent idea. Raffie, will you accompany Florence and help her to distribute the invitations? You will, it goes without saying, not leave her side even for a second.'

Raffie gave her one of his angelic smiles. 'Yes, Mama. Perhaps Freddie's mother might come? His family live in a great big house in Hanover Square and his father's as rich as Croesus.'

'By all means,' said Venetia. A tapping noise made her turn around. A pale face peered in through the small gap between the curtains temporarily draped over the windows on to the street. 'Another visitor!' she said, going to investigate.

An elderly lady dressed in black waited on the doorstep. 'I do hope you will forgive the intrusion,' she said, 'but I often pass this way on my daily constitutional.' She fingered the heavy gold cross suspended around her neck. 'I became faint one day as I was passing and Mr Lovell bade me come inside and rest. Such a kind gentleman!'

'I'm his daughter,' said Venetia.

'I see the family resemblance. May I introduce myself? Mrs Grace Dove.' She proffered a small, gloved hand. 'It distressed me greatly to hear about the tragedy of poor Mr Lovell's passing. Rumour has it that you're continuing his business?' She peered past Venetia to look inside the shop.

'There's a Grand Opening next week,' said Venetia. Mrs Dove might be elderly, sixty perhaps, but she still had very blue eyes, attractively high cheekbones and a slim waist. She must have been exceptionally pretty in her youth. 'Perhaps you'd like an invitation?'

'How lovely! May I ...' She peered over Venetia's shoulder again.

'Would you like to see how the renovations are progressing?'

Mrs Dove's eyes twinkled. 'Dear Mr Dove always said I had an overdeveloped sense of curiosity.'

Venetia stood aside.

Mrs Dove made exclamations of delight as they walked through the showroom. She stopped in front of the display of cushions. 'Exquisite! The violet cushion is just what I should like for my boudoir. And this lady's writing desk is extremely elegant. Does the desk have a good, strong lock?'

'Indeed it does and a secret drawer.'

Mrs Dove smiled at Venetia. 'Then may I reserve these items?'

A sale even before the shop was open! She introduced Mrs Dove to Mama.

'If you don't mind our state of disarray, please take a cup of tea with me,' Mama said. 'We're newcomers and haven't met many neighbours yet.' She led the visitor away.

Venetia found Jack in the office working his way through a box of invoices. 'We have our first customer!'

'But we're not open yet.'

'A sale is a sale, isn't it?'

'Absolutely.' He brushed the dust off his sleeves and followed her to meet their unexpected visitor.

Venetia watched him as he bowed and made animated conversation with Mrs Dove, promising to oversee personally the conveyance of her purchases. There was no doubt that he was utterly charming and entertaining, when he chose to be. Perhaps this was the side of him that Florence missed so from the time before his war injury.

'Where would you like us to deliver your new acquisitions, Mrs Dove?' he asked.

'To Angel of Mercy House on the corner of Wood Street and Love Lane. Perhaps you've heard of it?'

'Not yet,' said Mama.

'I founded the charity and head the committee for raising funds to support women who've fallen from grace.' Mrs Dove sighed deeply. 'These wretched women and their babies often have nowhere to go.'

'A most worthy cause,' agreed Mama.

'We rehabilitate the women after their lying in and find them positions nearby so they can contribute to their babies' upkeep. And then, when the children are old enough, we train them for a trade.'

Venetia handed Mrs Dove an invitation card. 'Do come and see the shop when it opens.'

'I shall be delighted. Will you have many guests?'

'We'll deliver invitations to my father's past clients,' said Venetia, 'but we know few other people in London as yet.'

Mrs Dove rested a hand on Venetia's sleeve. 'My dear, you simply must open with a fanfare! Where the great and the good come, the rest will follow.'

'I'm sure they would,' said Venetia, miserably aware that she didn't know any such people and that Mrs Dove was regarding her with shrewd blue eyes, as if she realised it.

'Perhaps,' said their first customer, 'if you would not think it presumptuous of me, you would like me to pass on invitations to members of my committee? Lady Conningsby and Lady Goodhew would be most interested, I'm sure. And then Sir Peter might bring his wife and daughter, who is recently married and setting up home.'

'We'd take it very kindly,' said Mama, 'and please suggest that they bring any of their friends who may be interested.'

'Indeed I shall,' said Mrs Dove.

'Will you excuse me?' asked Venetia. 'I'm expecting a chandelier to arrive at any moment and I need to clear space for the men to put up their ladders.'

'Don't let me detain you,' said Mrs Dove. 'Now, Mrs Lovell, do tell me all about yourself ...'

Half an hour later Venetia was watching the workmen when Mrs Dove came to take her leave.

'I must tell you how much I have enjoyed my advance peep behind the scenes,' she said.

Venetia glanced around at the half-empty packing cases, discarded crumpled newspaper and furniture in disarray. She felt a tremor of panic in her stomach. 'I hope you'll find a great difference next week.'

'I'm sure I shall. I offer you all good wishes for the success of your new business.'

Mama ushered Mrs Dove to the door and then returned to stand beside Venetia as the men heaved on the rope and the great chandelier slowly rose from the floor, the prisms tinkling as they fell into place.

'Isn't it magnificent?' said Venetia.

'Quite the jewel in the crown.'

'Mama ...' Venetia hesitated, all her fears crowding in upon her again.

She put an arm around her daughter's waist. 'My dearest child,' she said, 'you have worked so hard to make the showroom beautiful and your father would have been very proud of you.' Tears sparkled on her eyelashes. 'I miss him so terribly, but we'll imagine him cheering us on and absolutely refuse to entertain the notion that this venture might not succeed. We've a lot to learn about running a business but we'll do it together.'

'I can't bear to think what might happen if we don't,' said Venetia, with a shiver.

'I have every confidence that Mrs Dove will send her well-connected friends to our opening,' said Mama. 'We must now exert all our charm to persuade them to part from their money.'

Venetia took a steadying breath and looked up at the still-swaying chandelier, glittering above them. At that moment a sunbeam shone through the window and tiny rainbows, as brilliantly coloured as a cloud of butterflies, danced around the showroom, flickering over the walls and floor.

'All will be well,' said Mama, firmly.

Venetia reached out to capture a rainbow on her palm. 'Yes, Mama,' she said meekly.

Nat unfolded himself from the shadows as Kitty closed the gate of the area steps quietly behind her. She ran to him and he caught her in his arms. His hair smelled of smoke and his lips were warm. Smiling, she pushed him away. 'Not here, Nat!' she whispered.

'Thought you were never coming.'

'At gone eleven Miss Venetia was still downstairs, sticking broken ornaments together.'

Before long they were threading their way through the deeply shadowed and noisome alleys of King's Castle towards the Goat and Compass.

Kitty was grateful for Nat's firm grip on her hand as he pulled her along. 'I'd be entirely lost if I came alone,' she said. A man pushed past them, muttering to himself, and she drew away.

Nat gave a low laugh. 'That, my beauty, is why me and my friends live here. We look after our own. There's only one way in or out of King's Castle. No one can find us without us knowing they're coming.'

Kitty clapped a hand over her nose at the sickly scent of putrefaction coming from the gutter. Perhaps Nat remembered to turn left at the dead rat and carry straight on past the pile of rotting cabbages?

'We'll call in at the Goat,' he said, 'and have a swift drink and then I've got something to show you.'

'What's that, then?'

'Wait and see!' She started in fright as a dog leaped out of the shadows, fangs bared and barking fit to wake the dead.

Cursing, Nat kicked the animal away.

Heart thudding, Kitty threw herself into Nat's arms. He kissed her, holding her tightly until she forgot the dog and returned his kisses with passion.

After a moment he held her at arm's length. 'Not here,' he said. 'You're too good for dalliance in a dirty alley.' He took her hand and they set off again.

Kitty's knees trembled. She hadn't wanted him to stop but she supposed she was pleased he respected her.

A few moments later she was enveloped in the smoky warmth of the Goat and Compass and holding a mug of gin in her hand. 'This gave me a terrible head last time.'

'Brought up on it meself,' said Nat, taking off his hat, 'and it never did me no harm. Ma Slattery used to give all the babies a rag soaked in gin to suck. Kept 'em quiet.'

Lennie and Ruth waved from a corner table. Black Sal and Billy sat beside them and shifted along the settle to make room.

As she sat down Kitty caught her foot in what looked like a bundle of rags under the table. 'There's a child asleep here!' The boy's clothes were so ragged she could see his naked skin. Curled up in a ball, he sucked his thumb and just for a moment Kitty felt a pang of homesickness for her little brothers. Nevertheless, she pulled her feet away with a grimace. He was bound to be lousy.

'Poor little sod,' said Sal. 'Benny's ma died last week and he's been following me around ever since I gave him a penny to buy a slice of pie. Found him asleep on my doorstep this morning.'

'Is he sick?' asked Nat, moving closer to Kitty so that she could feel the heat of his thigh pressing against her own.

'Nah,' said Sal. 'Starving, p'raps.'

'Tell you what,' said Nat, 'send him to me tomorrow and I'll see if he can make himself useful.'

Sal punched Nat on the arm. 'You're soft, you are.'

Nat laughed. 'And who was it who gave him a penny?' He called out to the landlord, 'Hey, Robert, will you let Benny sleep here tonight?'

'What, and be murdered in my bed? Not a chance!' He carried on wiping tankards with a grimy rag.

'You're not afeared of a scrap like that, are you?'

'Why don't *you* take 'im home then?'

'I've got plans,' said Nat, lifting Kitty's work-roughened hand to his mouth.

Kitty trembled as he kissed the inside of her wrist, his tongue flickering where the skin was softest. She couldn't help herself and reached out to touch his cheek. If they'd been alone she'd have wound her fingers through his dark hair and kissed him again.

'Plans, is it?' The landlord boomed with laughter. 'In that case, the little varmint can sleep in the coalhole tonight. I might even let him have the use of my pump to wash in the morning.'

'You're all heart, Robert!' Nat slipped his arm around Kitty's shoulders.

'She's too good for you, Nat,' said Billy, wiping his nose on his sleeve.

Kitty finished her drink without joining in the conversation. The gin made her sleepy and she was content to lean against Nat, half listening.

'Tired?' he whispered, his hand fondling a curl that lay against the back of her neck.

She nodded, smothering a yawn. 'Up before five.'

'Let's go. I've something for you at my place and then I'll take you back to Quill Court.'

Their goodnights were met by a chorus of ribald comments and they went out into the cold and dark. Shivering, Kitty clung to Nat's arm as they felt their way through the alleys. Her foot sank into the stinking drain and she made an exclamation of disgust at the mud clinging to her boot. The alley opened into a small court lined with ramshackle buildings.

Nat unlocked a door and pulled her inside.

A single candle in a wall sconce lit their way as they climbed the creaking staircase. On the landing Nat opened another door and Kitty followed him in.

She waited in the utter blackness, listening, as Nat crossed the room. It was as cold as the grave here and she hoped he couldn't hear her teeth chattering. Then came the sharp scrape of flint against steel until sparks showered downwards, as bright as tiny stars in a velvet night sky. Nat's face emerged from the dark as the candle he held to the glowing tinder caught alight.

Kitty looked about in the flickering light. There was only one chair in the small room and Nat rested his elbow on the seat as he tended the fire. She sat, shivering, on the edge of the four-poster bed and fingered its heavy curtains. The material was a rich red and made her feel a little warmer.

Nat stood up and brushed ashes off his hands. He opened a small cupboard and took out a package. 'For you,' he said, sitting down beside her.

She began to untie the string with eager fingers made clumsy by the cold.

Nat took a penknife from his pocket, sliced through the string and pulled aside the brown paper.

A waterfall of pale green silk embroidered with pink roses and tiny violets slithered out of the package and Kitty caught her breath. '*Ohhh*,' she said, on a long sigh.

Nat laughed. 'Like it?'

'It's the most beautiful thing I ever saw.' She gathered up the silk shawl and held it to her cheek.

'There's something else.' Nat reached underneath the shawl, took out a narrow cloth bag and shook it until a fan slid out. He waved it before his face.

'For me? It's really for me?' Tears smarted in Kitty's eyes. The soft swansdown that edged the white lace folded on mother-of-pearl sticks trembled in the draught. In her wildest imaginings she'd never thought to own such a treasure. The fan looked so delicate she was almost afraid to hold it.

Nat wiped her tears away with his thumb. 'I thought you'd like them.'

'I do! Oh, Nat, I do!' She stroked the soft feathers with her finger.

'Go on then, give us a flutter!' He smiled. 'You know, like you said, flirting with your beau across a crowded ballroom. I'm your beau, aren't I?'

She draped the shawl around her shoulders and eyed him provocatively over the top of the fan.

Gently, he took it from her and laid it on the side table. 'You're far too lovely to hide your face like that.'

'Nat, thank you,' she said, too moved to say all that was in her overflowing heart. She touched his cheek, overcome with love for him.

He cupped her face and kissed her.

She sat still, losing herself in the sensation of his kisses.

He took off her hat and buried his face in her hair.

Sliding her arms around his neck, she turned up her face to be kissed again. The shawl slipped unheeded from her shoulders.

And then Nat was kneeling on the floor and unlacing her muddy boots and pulling off her stockings. He kissed her toes and warmed them in his hands before removing his own boots and gathering her in his arms again.

They lay down on the bed as they kissed and his breath was hot on her cheek while he unbuttoned her dress and slid it down over her shoulders. The cold air brought her out in goose pimples.

'I want to look at you,' he whispered.

Half swooning, she arched her back while he covered her neck and breasts with kisses.

He released her long enough to drag off his shirt and breeches and then pull up the blankets over their shoulders. Under the covers, he untied the ribbons of her shift and slid it over her head.

Wrapped in his arms, she felt the heat of his body pressed against hers, heartbeat to heartbeat. When he gently parted her thighs, she opened up to him and welcomed him in.

The cry tore through the night, a sound so full of terror that Venetia reared up in bed, her heart hammering. Every muscle tensed, she listened, eyes wide open in the darkness. All was quiet in Quill Court except for distant street noise and the hooting of an owl.

After a moment her breathing steadied and she leaned back against the pillows, the blankets clutched to her chin. Perhaps she might not have heard the cry if she hadn't already been awake, fretting about the opening of the shop in the morning.

It was no good; she'd have to investigate. Slipping on her dressing gown, she relit her candle from the embers of the fire, snatched up the poker and tip-toed into the passage.

She tapped on her brother's door and went straight in. 'Raffie?' she whispered.

Nothing. Holding her candle aloft, she saw that the counterpane lay smooth and undisturbed across his bed. Where was he? He'd gone up to bed before her. Unease made her sprint downstairs. She peered into the drawing room, morning room and dining room. Each was empty and silent, shrouded in darkness.

It was then that she heard a whisper of a sound, a sob perhaps? A faint line of light showed under the door to Jack's study. What was Raffie doing in there? Creeping forwards, she turned the handle and inched the door open a crack.

Jack sat hunched over his desk with his head in his hands and a half-empty brandy glass before him.

'Jack?'

He started and lifted his head.

She took an involuntary step back. The candlelight cast deep shadows across his face. It pained her to see the desolation in his eyes. 'Jack, are you ...' she hesitated ' ... unwell?'

He drained the brandy glass and poured himself another with trembling hands.

'I heard something,' she persisted. 'And Raffie's missing.'

'He went out before I retired.'

'When was that?'

'About half-past eleven.'

'But ...'

'For God's sake, Venetia, go back to bed!'

Anger made her bristle but then she noticed how Jack's hands shook and even by candlelight she could see how pale he was beneath the black stubble of his beard.

He wiped one hand over his face. 'Sorry,' he muttered.

Leaving the study without another word, she went downstairs to the kitchen. She nearly dropped the milk she was fetching from the larder when she saw a white face at the window. And then it was gone again. Had she imagined it? She pressed her nose to the glass but all she could see was the empty area steps to the street.

A short while later she was whisking cinnamon and honey into the milk she'd warmed on the ashes of the fire when she heard the sound of a key in the back door.

'Raffie!' she said. 'Where've you been?'

He stopped dead when he saw her. His gaze was unfocused and he swayed slightly. 'I went to meet Freddie for a game of cards.'

117

'You might have been set upon by footpads or ...'

He closed his eyes and sighed. 'I wasn't. I'm going to bed.'

'Don't forget we need you for the Grand Opening tomorrow ...' But she spoke only to his back as he hastened down the passage. Venetia's lips tightened in anger. Really, she had no control over that boy any more.

Bubbles floated on the surface of the hot milk as she poured it into cups and carried them upstairs on a tray. She pushed open Jack's study door with her foot and placed the tray on his desk. 'Raffie's back,' she said. 'I've made spiced milk to help us sleep.'

'Milk?' He gazed at it with an expression of distaste. Then he sighed and lifted the cup to his lips.

Tentatively, she sat down on the other side of the desk. 'Was it you I heard cry out earlier on?'

'I apologise if I woke you. I have bad dreams.' Absent-mindedly, he slopped a large measure of brandy into his milk.

'Does your leg pain you?' A lock of black hair fell over his forehead and she had the sudden urge to brush it back into place, just as if he were Raffie.

He shrugged. 'So many died at Vitoria. I'm one of the lucky ones.'

She couldn't begin to imagine the horror he'd endured on the battlefield and his expression was so bleak she didn't dare to ask him about it.

They sipped their milk in silence and then she stood up. 'Will you sleep now?'

'I expect so.'

'Then good night, Jack.' Uncertainly, she turned, not sure if she should leave him.

'Venetia?'

'Yes?'

He glanced up at her, biting his lip. 'Thank you.'

'For the milk?'

A fleeting smile. 'For not pressing me to talk. I just can't ...'

118

She nodded and withdrew.

Back in bed again she ran over the conversation in her mind. It unsettled her to see him so wretched but, clearly, he didn't want to be mollycoddled. She couldn't settle to sleep, shuddering as she imagined the terrible sights and sounds he must have experienced.

It was an hour later that she heard his bedroom door close. Then, just as she was drifting into sleep, the floor above her creaked. One of the servants must be awake too.

Venetia looped a tasselled rope around a swathe of claret brocade suspended from a brass pole, arranging the pleats carefully to one side so that it looked like a curtain. She'd already gathered a drift of gossamer-fine muslin beneath the brocade so that the two materials framed a mirror on the wall. She stood back and studied the display through half-closed eyes.

'It looks exactly like a real window,' said Mama from behind her.

'I want to show our customers different ways of using curtain materials.'

Mama hurried away and Venetia gave the display a final tweak. She was exhausted. The past weeks had taken their toll, not only because of the unaccustomed physical work but because of her anxiety as to whether they could make a success of the business. Had she been foolish to sweep the whole family along with her in such a venture?

Sighing, she stood with her hands on her hips looking about her. The beautiful carpet that had been ruined by paint had been cut down the centre to remove the damaged part. The resulting runners, each four feet wide, had been turned around and the damaged parts tucked under the counters. She'd placed delicate gilt chairs there for customers to sit on while they chose from the swatches of fine fabrics and pattern books on the counters.

She'd completed the window displays earlier: glorious duck egg

119

blue silk draped as a backdrop for Mama and Florence's cushions in pale greens and aqua, decorated with contrasting rosettes and imitation pearls.

Mouldings had been applied to the walls near the back of the showroom, each panel displaying a different paper hanging. Eventually she'd design more patterns but for now Venetia's Rose was displayed alongside a variety of other designs she especially liked.

Florence was placing ruinously expensive cut flowers in vases and the air was fragrant with the delicate perfume of fresh greenery and narcissi. Kitty swept the floor and Dorcas rubbed the counters with lavender-scented beeswax. Annunziata was in the scullery making fruit punch.

Jack, leaning heavily on his cane today, came to stand beside Venetia, smiling approvingly. 'You have your father's knack of making everything look just right.'

'Praise indeed!' she said, her heart swelling at the compliment. Jack looked very handsome this morning in a tight-fitting black coat and pristine cravat.

He shrugged. 'You may think I'm harsh sometimes but I always aim to be fair.' There was little sign of his previous night's broken sleep, except for lines of pain etched around his eyes. 'You've worked very hard to make the showroom look splendid for the opening. I'm astonished by what you've achieved, and grateful to you too. I didn't believe it could be done.'

A warm glow of pleasure momentarily dispelled her exhaustion. 'Have you seen the rainbows in the chandelier? And doesn't the gallery look impressive?' She frowned. 'I do hope we've priced the paintings correctly.'

'Since we had the invoices for them I merely added the percentage your father usually applied.' Jack took out his silver pocket watch. 'Twenty minutes.'

'So soon!' Venetia took a deep breath, her stomach lurching. 'I must give the final instructions.'

'Don't look so worried, Venetia!' There was a warmth in Jack's eyes she'd rarely seen there. 'Everything is perfect and the ladies of the *haut ton* will soon be crowding at the door.' He clapped his hands and waited until all faces turned towards them. 'Gather round, if you please!'

Everyone formed a circle around Venetia and Jack.

'In twenty minutes we'll open the doors,' said Venetia. 'Kitty and Dorcas, go and put on your clean aprons now. Oh, and I want you to take special care of an elderly lady called Mrs Dove. She's the founder of Angel of Mercy House and several of her influential friends are invited.'

'How will we know her?' asked Kitty.

'She has a slender figure and dresses elegantly in black. She wears a gold cross around her neck.' Venetia turned to Annunziata. 'Did you collect the cakes from Benson's bakery?'

A smile spread across Annunziata's swarthy features. '*Ma naturalmente*! And the cakes,' she kissed her fingers, '*così bella*, are arranged like pretty jewels on silver trays.'

'Good. Florence and Mama, will you take up your stations behind the counters and be ready to show customers fabric or pattern books as required? Should anyone wish to discuss a design scheme, please bring them to me.' Venetia smiled, hoping that none of them noticed how her hands shook.

'What shall I do?' asked Raffie. His flaxen hair was neatly combed for once and in the unrelieved black of his best mourning coat he looked far too solemn for one so young.

'At two o'clock exactly you and Jack will pull up the window blinds and open the door. You'll welcome our guests with respect, whether they're neighbouring shopkeepers or, if they choose to attend, Mrs Dove's titled connections. Guide them to the furniture displays or the counters where Florence, Mama and I will serve them.'

'What if a customer wishes to buy something?' asked Florence.

'Write out the order in your books. Each counter has a cash drawer. Jack will regularly collect any cash and deposit it in the safe. If a customer wishes to open an account, ask Jack to arrange this.'

'But,' he said, 'as far as possible we wish to encourage customers to pay for their smaller purchases straight away. Many of them won't like that but we cannot replenish our stock until invoices are settled.'

'Please take up your stations in ten minutes,' said Venetia.

As the others drifted away she picked a loose thread off the chaise-longue and gave a last searching glance around the showroom. It looked wonderful. She felt a burst of pride and wished beyond anything that Father could have seen it. Sighing, she retreated to the office to tidy her hair. She pinched colour into her cheeks. At least her black mourning dress gave her enough gravitas to fool customers into believing she was experienced enough to hold a position of such responsibility. A growing queasiness brought her out in a cold sweat as she reflected upon what she'd taken on. It was utter madness.

'Venetia?' Mama's voice came from the showroom. 'It's nearly time!'

Jack and Raffie stood on either side of the door and Florence and Mama behind the counters. Nero and Caesar had crimson bows on their collars. Kitty and Dorcas waited as patiently as statues, holding silver trays of cakes. Kitty had dark shadows under her eyes, Venetia noticed. Perhaps it was she who'd been moving about so late last night?

'I wonder how many guests are waiting for us?' whispered Florence.

All at once Venetia wanted to run away. The churning in her stomach became more violent and she pressed trembling fingers to her mouth, wondering if she'd have to run to the privy.

Outside, one by one, the church clocks began to sound the hour. Two o'clock.

122

Jack nodded at Raffie and simultaneously they opened the shutters at the rear of the windows. Then Jack opened the door wide.

The usual relentless stream of people passed by, all intent upon their own business, but not a single guest waited for admittance.

Venetia's stomach plummeted. No one was coming. There were no customers and the whole idea was a dreadful failure. After a few seconds of spiralling panic, she suddenly became very calm. They'd have to sell the business to someone who knew what they were doing, one of Father's competitors perhaps, and invest the money. She'd seek a live-in position as a governess and send as much of her wages to her family as she could.

'Venetia?' Jack cupped her elbow. 'Are you faint?'

'Not at all,' she lied.

'Good, because we have our first customers.'

A surge of relief made her break out in a wide smile as Charles and Edwin Murchison came through the door, as small and neat as a pair of bookends. She was mortified that she couldn't remember which was which.

'I do hope we're not too early?' said one of them. 'Edwin assured me you would not think ill of us if we were the first to arrive.'

'Indeed I do not,' said Venetia with a welcoming smile. Edwin had a small mole on his left cheek and she mentally filed the information away for future reference.

The Bensons, in their Sunday best, were close on their heels, followed by two ladies Venetia had never seen before. They exclaimed in delight at the display of cushions and before long Mama was writing out the first purchase order as a trickle of guests began to arrive.

Kitty and Dorcas hurried hither and thither bringing glasses of punch, cups of tea and dainty cakes.

Raffie brought Freddie's mother, Mrs Crawford, and her sister to introduce them to Venetia.

'I require drawing-room curtains and have scoured the town for suitable material, entirely without success,' said Mrs Crawford, who wore a very long peacock feather in her hat.

'Allow me to show you our swatches and trimmings,' said Venetia. Mrs Crawford inclined her head so majestically that the feather did a dance all by itself and Venetia struggled to keep a straight face as she spread sample lengths of fabric over the counter.

Later, she saw Mrs Dove and a party of ladies advancing towards them. She beckoned to Florence. 'Please take your time examining the samples, Mrs Crawford,' she said. 'I'll leave you in the capable hands of my sister who will be pleased to advise. I shall return momentarily.'

Jack was already welcoming Mrs Dove and her party when Venetia joined them.

'What a feast for the eyes, Miss Lovell,' said Mrs Dove. 'A veritable treasure trove of delights! We have just finished our committee meeting and came straight here afterwards. I do hope we're not too late?'

'Not at all,' said Venetia. 'Perhaps you'd care to look at our furniture displays at your leisure and I'll be on hand if you have any queries. Of course, should you wish to discuss any requirements regarding colour schemes or the selection of fabrics or furniture, I shall be delighted to help.'

The next hour or so passed in a whirlwind of activity as more and more customers arrived. Many of the neighbouring shopkeepers came too and several placed small orders. Their neighbour in Quill Court, Mrs Stanhope, placed an order for Venetia's Rose paper hangings for her bedroom. The boy from Gunter's delivered the ices and Kitty and Dorcas served them in small glass dishes, to exclamations of appreciation.

Venetia booked three appointments in her diary for visits to customers' homes to advise on redecoration, one of whom was Lady Conningsby, who had a yearning for a crimson dining room.

'I shall try you out,' she'd said, regarding Venetia with hawk-like eyes, 'and if Lord Conningsby is satisfied then you may refurbish our house in Norfolk.'

'I'm sure you won't be disappointed, dear Lady Conningsby,' said Mrs Dove. 'I intend to engage Miss Lovell to redecorate my sitting room in Angel of Mercy House.'

'May I show you the paintings in our gallery, imported from Italy, Lady Conningsby?' said Jack. 'There may be something suitable for your dining room?'

'We have no need of new paintings since we have numerous ancestral portraits.'

'I have always thought,' said Jack, bestowing a winning smile upon her, 'that it's so *unsettling* to be watched by one's ancestors while one chews a tough piece of venison or wrestles with fish bones. How much more restful it would be to gaze at a scene of a sunset over a Venetian canal.'

Lady Conningsby smoothed the fur-trimmed collar of her pelisse and pursed her lips. 'I will agree that my husband's grandfather always appears to be watching me in a most disapproving way while we dine.' She held out her arm. 'You may escort me to view these paintings.'

Jack led her away, glancing back over his shoulder at Venetia.

'Major Chamberlaine has quite a way with the ladies, even the fierce ones, hasn't he?' said Mrs Dove, a twinkle in her eye.

'So it would appear,' said Venetia, finding it hard to reconcile the demeanour of the Jack she'd just seen, positively flirting with an imposing lady old enough to be his grandmother, with the angst-ridden man she'd plied with hot milk a few hours before.

'Your opening is going well.'

'Better than I dared to hope,' confessed Venetia. 'I must thank you for introducing your friends.'

'I was happy to do so,' said Mrs Dove. 'You've made a great deal of effort and your venture deserves to do well.' She patted Venetia's hand and nodded meaningfully at a lady examining one of the vases on the display shelf. 'Please don't let me keep you from a sale.'

Several hours later, Kitty watched with relief as Major Chamberlaine bolted the door behind the last guest. Her feet throbbed from standing about with a tray all afternoon and she was fit to drop.

She sniffed as she collected up all the cups and plates. Hanging around in the freezing coal cellar the night before had given her a chill. The last thing she'd expected when she'd returned to Quill Court was to find a light on in the kitchen. When she'd peeped in through the window she'd seen Miss Venetia coming out of the pantry and been forced to dive into the cellar. And then Raffie had returned, weaving from side to side, completely foxed. It'd been ages before she'd dared to creep indoors and she'd only had an hour's sleep before it was time to clean the grates.

Yawning widely, Kitty carried the tray of dirty crockery to the scullery. She scraped the plates and dropped a half-eaten macaroon on the floor for the pugs. Her deliciously illicit meetings with Nat were all very well but it was impossible to continue them without more sleep. She pictured his wiry body naked against hers as he whispered sweet words in her ear and had no regrets about giving herself to him. How lovely it would be to sleep in his arms all night instead of having to pick her way through the dark alleys of King's Castle back to her cold and lonely bed in Quill Court.

'Kitty, hurry up and wash the cups!' Annunziata's shrill call cut through her daydream like a knife.

'Coming!' She heaved the laden tray against her stomach and set off for the scullery.

Chapter 12

Jack was already demolishing his breakfast kipper when Venetia entered the dining room. 'I guessed you'd be the first down,' he said.

'Raffie came in very late again last night.' She poured herself a cup of coffee. 'I'm astonished he'd the energy to go out again after the opening.'

'Like many young men, your brother appears to have discovered the appeal of London night life,' said Jack, spreading butter on his toast. He hesitated. 'Venetia ...'

'Yes?'

'He looked directly at her. 'I was vastly unfair when you first came to Quill Court and I accused you of being a gold-digger. You've worked tirelessly to open Lovell and Chamberlaine and your father was right to believe you should come into the business. When you first suggested the idea,' he continued, 'I didn't believe it was possible.'

'That still remains to be seen,' said Venetia, 'but if it fails it won't be for want of trying.'

'I'll be honest,' Jack said, 'I've no ambition at all to sell curtains

127

to rich old ladies for the rest of my life but, for now, I promise to do whatever's necessary to support you.'

A warm glow blossomed inside her. 'That's a great relief to me,' she said. 'Interior decoration isn't all about frivolity, you know. Good design ensures that all is comfort and ease in the home. Luckily for us, many ladies have no idea how to achieve a pleasing effect.'

'I'm hardly the arbiter of fashionable taste, I leave that to you, but I can assist in ordering and despatching goods. And I'm keeping the books up to date. Since I've been studying the accounts, I realise that we *must* make the business succeed.'

'Are we in real difficulties, then?'

He rubbed his chin. 'I daren't order any more coal at present. The situation is worse than I thought. Your father was a shrewd business-man but there are several large and unexplained payments noted in the ledger, all just before he died.'

'Unexplained?'

'There's simply a crown scribbled against each one.'

'That's not like Father.' Venetia frowned, disquiet gnawing at her. 'He always said that good accounting was the foundation of a strong business.'

A smile flickered across Jack's lips. 'I remember. But bills are arriving daily now from suppliers who know he's passed on, and they want to be paid.'

'Didn't Father invoice his clients for the goods?'

Jack shrugged. 'I need to spend more time reconciling the ledgers to discover the exact situation.'

'I'd no idea things were so bad,' said Venetia, suddenly feeling as if a heavy weight pressed down upon her, flattening her exhilaration. 'I'll ask Mama to talk to Annunziata about economising.'

'Trimming the household bills won't be enough. If the shop doesn't thrive I suppose we could sell it, since your father bought the leasehold.'

128

'Absolutely not!' said Venetia. 'Don't you see, then we'd have no means at all of making a living?'

'I suppose you're right.'

'We'll simply have to seek more clients and work every hour we can.'

'Then I'll enter yesterday's sales into the ledger and, if your mother is happy to mind the shop, visit Mr Marsden to order replacements for items we've sold.'

'Mama and Florence will be downstairs directly.' Venetia sighed. 'But I'm not at all sure that Raffie's really grasped the fact that he's required to wait on customers every day, not just at yesterday's event.'

'Many boys his age have been earning a living and supporting their families for years.'

Venetia opened her mouth to defend her brother but decided it would be unfortunate to have a disagreement with Jack while bridges were being built between them. 'I'll go on to the shop now to prepare for my appointments.'

'I'll rally the troops here and we'll join you shortly.'

Later that morning, Mama and Florence were helping a customer to choose between a striped and a plain curtain silk. Raffie was expected at any moment. Apparently Jack had tipped him out of bed and told him to be fit for work in a quarter of an hour.

Venetia closed the shop door behind her. She'd bristled with indignation when she heard that Jack had taken it upon himself to discipline Raffie but perhaps it was a good thing.

Walking along Cheapside, she couldn't deny the exhilaration she felt to find herself amongst the teeming throngs sauntering down one of the best shopping streets in London. She still missed her wind-blown walks on the seashore but it was no good looking back.

It was as she passed Love Lane on her way to her appointment with a Mrs McGinty in Silver Street that she remembered Mrs

Dove had mentioned that Angel of Mercy House was on the corner of Love Lane and Wood Street. She saw it immediately, a forbidding redbrick building several storeys high. She mustn't forget that she'd promised to take tea with Mrs Dove very soon and to discuss a new colour scheme for her sitting room.

Two hours later Venetia left Silver Street with her head buzzing from discussions of Chinese bedrooms, Egyptian dining rooms, chandeliers fashioned from winged griffins, gilded acanthus leaves and laurel wreaths, and bedposts carved to resemble sphinxes. She'd taken pages of notes and sketches. Mrs McGinty had talked non-stop, changing her mind so frequently that it had been difficult to keep up. If they hadn't desperately needed the income Venetia might simply have walked away.

It was beginning to spit with rain when she reached the showroom and the sound of raised voices reached her as soon as she opened the door.

'I tell you, I saw it first!'

'No, you didn't!'

Two ladies grasped the bronze horse in an undignified tug of war while Mama and Florence looked on, aghast. The two pugs barked furiously.

Venetia hurried to take hold of the horse herself. 'Ladies, may I help? I'm sorry to tell you that this piece is already sold.'

'But it was on display!' The older of the two women, her mouth pinched with annoyance, let go of the horse's foreleg.

'I apologise sincerely,' said Venetia, catching sight of Jack limping out of the office towards them. 'This piece was sold a few minutes before I left for an appointment this morning and I didn't have time to remove it from the showroom.'

The other woman reluctantly released her hold on the horse's bronze mane. 'Will you order another?'

'I regret, this is a unique artefact.' She passed the horse to Mama, who secreted it under the counter. 'Have you seen this delightful statuette of Mercury, messenger to the gods?'

The older woman shrugged. 'I prefer the horse but let me see that dancing girl with the veil.'

Jack lifted the heavy statuette down from the shelf and Venetia placed Mercury on the counter, too, at a safe distance from the dancing girl. She watched as the customers eyed each other covertly while they scrutinised the two bronzes.

'These items are rare and unrepeatable,' said Jack, smiling charmingly at both customers. 'As you see, we have a limited number of pieces.'

Five minutes later both statuettes were sold.

'Had you really sold the horse?' asked Florence after the two ladies had left. Venetia shook her head.

'Well,' said Mama, 'that was a good piece of salesmanship. Two expensive items sold instead of only one and two satisfied customers.'

Venetia lifted the horse back on to the shelf. 'You know, I'm secretly pleased that he can stay with us a while longer. He's my favourite item in the whole showroom.'

'How was your meeting?' said Mama.

Venetia pursed her lips. 'Interesting.'

'In what way?' asked Jack.

'I must find a path between our client's taste and my own. It's important that the scheme for decorating Mrs McGinty's house pleases her but it must also demonstrate our goods and services in the best possible light. I fear a great deal of tact and a firm hand on my part will be required.'

Jack laughed. 'I suspect you'll make an admirable job of that.'

'Let's hope so,' said Venetia. 'Meanwhile, I'm going to make a pot of tea and retreat to the back office with the pugs and seek inspiration.'

Chapter 13

Naked but for the embroidered silk shawl around her shoulders, Kitty sat cross-legged on Nat's bed. The windows were shuttered and a fire flickered in the hearth.

'This is the first time I've been warm for days,' she said. 'Major Chamberlaine's so mean. There are to be no fires in the bedrooms at Quill Court and only a small one in the evening in the drawing room.'

'Why's that then?' Nat lay on his side with his head propped on his elbow, eating a plate of jellied eels.

Kitty smiled at him, the firelight casting shadows across his lean chest and sinewy arms. She couldn't get enough of looking at him. 'Because everyone's in the shop during the day, fires aren't needed, he says.' She picked up the last piece of eel off Nat's plate and ate it. 'He doesn't care if the servants are cold, of course.' She licked her fingers, careful not to drip grease on to her lovely shawl.

Nat yawned and pushed the plate away. 'I forgot to tell you, I saw your Miss Venetia's brother the other night.'

'Where was that then?'

'The Saracen's Head. He and another young buck were in the private parlour playing cards.' Nat reached out to caress Kitty's cheek. 'Bacon-brained fool. I know a couple of those card sharps around the table. They pick on greenhorns up from the country and get them half seas over before they pluck them.'

'Not much I can do about it, though, is there?'

'A quiet word maybe?'

'How can I? I'm meant to be cleaning the shop this afternoon, not lying in bed with my sweetheart, listening to gossip.' Kitty sighed. 'I'm going to have to go.'

Nat twitched the shawl off her shoulders and ran a finger down the curve of her breast. 'Not yet,' he coaxed.

Kitty shivered. She hadn't known before how a man's touch could make her burn with the fire of wanting him. Not any man, of course, only her Nat. She reached out for him and he gave a throaty laugh and pulled her on top of him.

'I've got you now, my beauty!'

She struggled in his tight embrace, shrieking in mock terror until he quietened her cries with kisses.

He loosened his hold and gave her that heavy-lidded look that meant he wanted her.

She bent her head to kiss him again, allowing her breasts to brush against his chest.

He wound his fingers through her hair so that she had to look at him. 'Kitty?' he whispered.

'Mmm?'

'I love you, you know.'

Kitty smiled, joy sparking like fireworks in her guts. 'I love you, too, Nat.'

'From the first time I saw you, splattered from head to toe with mud, I knew you had to be mine.'

'I was sure coming to London was the best thing I'd ever do, but now I've met you I know it was.'

He kissed her again, a warm and lingering kiss that made her wonder if she could delay her return another ten minutes.

A sudden, sharp rap at the door made her jump.

'Ignore it,' whispered Nat.

But another tattoo of knocks made it impossible.

Cursing, he sprang out of bed and scrambled into his breeches. 'Stay here!' He dragged the bed curtains closed around her.

She sat up, the sheet clutched to her breast, listening to Nat talking in an undertone to his visitor. Stealthily, she pulled on her clothes. Then she heard the click of the door latch and a moment later Nat drew back the curtains.

'Sorry, sweetheart. Business.' He pulled on his boots. 'I have to go out.' He picked up his coat. 'Can you find your way back by yourself?'

She stood up, alarm making her stomach turn over. 'Through King's Castle? It's nearly dark and I'll get lost in that maze. Nat, I can't!'

He bit his lip. 'Wait here and I'll send Benny to guide you. He won't be far away.' He kissed her. 'Lock the door and put the key on top of the doorframe.'

And then he was gone.

Well! One minute he was telling her he loved her and the next he'd gone off without a by-your-leave. She picked the shawl up from the floor and folded it carefully. She couldn't take it back to Quill Court because Dorcas, with her prying eyes, would want to know where it had come from. The feather fan was on the table and Kitty took some mincing steps across the floor, fluttering the fan in front of her face, imagining she was at Almack's.

She went to the chest where Nat stored her treasures and stubbed her toe on the edge of a floorboard. Bending over, she saw that it wasn't nailed down and prised it up to see what was stopping it fitting into place.

There were half a dozen sackcloth bags under the floor. Curious, she picked one up. Loosening the tie, she looked inside. Something glimmered in the firelight: a snuffbox wrapped in a handkerchief. One by one she drew out another five snuffboxes, eight gold watches, three silver spoons and a fistful of golden guineas. She stared at them. What was Nat doing with these things? Were they stock for one of his stalls? Surely, living in lodgings like these, he could never have come by them honestly?

A knock came at the door and she hastily crammed the items back into the sack and shoved it under the floorboard.

'It's Benny.'

'Just a minute!'

The boy waited outside, his nose red with cold in his pinched little face. 'Nat said to take you 'ome.'

'Lead me out of King's Castle and I'll find the rest of the way myself,' she said.

Benny set off as fast as his skinny little legs would go.

Kitty hurried after him, afraid she'd lose sight of him in the deep shadows and never find her way out of the endless warren of stinking passages. 'Benny!'

He must have heard the panic in her voice because he came to an abrupt halt and she skidded into him.

'Hold my hand.'

'I'm not afraid,' he said, his lip curling.

'But I am.' She grasped his icy fingers and they set off again.

Soon they emerged from a dark slit of a passage into a street Kitty recognised. 'You get off home now,' she said.

'Ain't got no 'ome.' He hurried back into the labyrinth of alleys and she walked in the opposite direction, troubled that his clothes were so threadbare against the cold. But then, there were street children everywhere she looked, huddled in doorways, begging on the street and asleep on the area steps when she crept in at night.

She fretted about the things she'd found in Nat's room. Had he stolen them? Deceiving the preventative officers with smuggling the odd bottle of brandy was one thing but there were so many snuffboxes and the like, surely they must be stolen? She was still worrying about it when she arrived at the shop.

The missus was chatting with Mrs Dove. Raffie and his friend Freddie were hunched over a table playing cards. She gasped as the cards suddenly flew from one of Freddie's hands into an arc high in the air and landed in a neatly stacked pack in his other hand. 'How did you do that?' she asked, full of wonder.

Freddie glanced up at her with a smug smile. 'Practice, my dear.' He handed the cards to Raffie.

Raffie's face was startlingly pale with a greenish cast and there were shadows under his eyes. He looked as sick as a dog. Must have been well in his cups last night.

He flexed the cards and sent them shooting up into the air to fall in an untidy shower over the table.

Freddie laughed.

The door to the office stood ajar and Miss Venetia sat on one side of the desk scribbling in her sketchbook, as usual, while Major Chamberlaine sat on the other, writing in his ledger.

Kitty went into the scullery and washed up the cups and plates. A custard tart sat on a plate on the table. It smelled of eggs and nutmeg.

Florence came in from the yard with the pugs and saw her looking at the tart. 'Would you like it, Kitty? Raffie couldn't eat his.'

'Thank you, Miss.' Kitty bit into the crisp pastry with its creamy filling and closed her eyes as she savoured it. She licked crumbs off her lips while the pugs looked up at her hopefully.

'I'll fetch an extra one for you next time,' said Florence in a conspiratorial whisper.

'That's very kind of you, Miss.' Kitty rinsed and dried the plate. 'Will you tell me when Mrs Dove goes so I can sweep the shop?'

'She came to arrange for Venetia to visit her tomorrow and then stayed to gossip. She won't mind if you're dusting.'

'I'll finish up here first.'

Kitty set to work sweeping the scullery, her thoughts roaming uneasily over her earlier discovery. Nat had said he loved her and she'd never been so happy. But now she'd found the snuffboxes, it was spoiled. He'd never told her about them and she didn't like to think of him as a thief.

Sighing, she went into the shop to begin the dusting.

The imposing panelled door had rendered pilasters to each side and Venetia noted that the black paint was fresh. The urn-shaped knocker gleamed in the pale sunshine.

A pretty girl in a blue dress opened the door. Her dark hair was neatly braided.

'I've an appointment with Mrs Dove,' said Venetia.

'Please come with me,' said the girl, keeping her eyes downcast. She led the way across the spacious hall and up the grand staircase.

The stairs were in the same pale stone as the hall floor and not a speck of dust was to be seen on the decorative wrought-iron balusters. Somewhere a baby wailed and a moment later another joined in.

They stopped on the wide second-floor landing but the stairs continued upwards for another two floors. A glass dome high above them illuminated the stairwell all the way down to the stone floor below.

There were a series of doors along the landing and Venetia paused at the sound of a woman crying behind one of them.

'My baby ... oh, give me my baby!' There was such desperation in the lament that Venetia caught her breath, but then the maid tugged urgently on her sleeve.

'Mrs Dove is waiting,' she whispered. Her grey eyes were so anxious that Venetia followed.

Mrs Dove sat in an armchair placed by the window. 'My dear Miss Lovell, please come in!'

'Mrs Dove, I heard a woman crying pitifully,' said Venetia. 'I wonder if she needs help?'

Mrs Dove sighed. 'That will be Belle. Her baby died this morning and there's no consoling her. It's sad to say, but it's probably a blessed relief. She'll be able to find work in a few weeks and her life will go on as before, without the impediment of a child to care for.'

'What an unhappy state of affairs.'

'It certainly is but we do everything we can here to help these poor girls,' said Mrs Dove.

'I'm sure you do.' Venetia had almost forgotten that Mrs Dove was a client since she'd become such fast friends with Mama. 'You've been very patient,' she said. 'In the weeks since the showroom opened I've received far more commissions than I expected.' She noticed that the lady's writing desk Mrs Dove had purchased stood at one end of the sitting room. A chair of unsuitably heavy proportions was placed in front of it and the mismatch made Venetia wince.

'Lady Conningsby is delighted with her refurbished dining room,' said Mrs Dove. 'She's telling all her friends about her discovery of a new and talented lady decorator.'

'I'm pleased to hear that.'

'I believe she's very taken with Major Chamberlaine?'

Venetia gave a rueful smile. 'At first it irked me that she hung on his every word while it was I who was busy working on the design, but I daresay she won't be the first to find it difficult to have confidence in a woman representing a business.'

'It's especially difficult for a woman as young and pretty as yourself,' said Mrs Dove. She leaned forward, her gold cross swinging against her chest. 'You must resign yourself to the fact that Major Chamberlaine makes an excellent figurehead for the business.'

'He does,' agreed Venetia. 'But it's galling.'

Mrs Dove patted her wrist. 'Never mind. I don't need Jack

Chamberlaine to flatter me into deciding what colour curtains to have in my sitting room. I understand from your mama that he's not your real brother?'

Venetia shook her head.

'He's charming.' Mrs Dove smiled at Venetia. 'Wouldn't you agree, Miss Lovell?'

Venetia was annoyed to feel herself blush. Jack was charming, when he chose to be. She hoped to see more of that side of his character. 'And what did you have in mind for your curtains?' Mrs Dove may look like an elderly lady but Venetia saw the light of lively intelligence in her eyes. It was good for Mama to have such a friend, even if her comments were a little too perspicacious at times.

'I'm not too old to want beautiful surroundings,' said Mrs Dove. 'As a young woman my circumstances were such that I wasn't able to indulge myself but now I can afford life's little luxuries. I saw a delightful trellised paper hanging in your showroom.'

'The duck egg blue with the cream trellis?'

'Exactly! And I fancy silk curtains.'

'Perhaps a slubbed silk in duck egg to match the wallpaper?'

'And a heavy weight, so it drapes well.'

What a pleasure it was to deal with a client who was easy to please. 'You bought two of our cushions in violet.'

'I did.'

'Then shall we trim the curtains to match?'

Mrs Dove clasped her hands to her breast. 'The very thing!'

'May I suggest a deeper violet upholstery to your sofa and perhaps a satinwood chair to complement the writing desk?'

'Delightful!'

'I shall bring samples to show you.'

'Please don't put yourself to the trouble. I'll see them in the showroom when I next visit,' said Mrs Dove. 'Oh, there's another thing,' she said. 'The committee room would benefit from fresh paint to the walls, heavy curtains to keep out the draughts and the chairs need to be reupholstered.'

Venetia tried not to smile too widely but it was impossible not to feel satisfaction that one commission had turned into two.

It was growing dark by the time she returned to the shop.

Jack was in the office and glanced up from the ledgers. 'I'm having trouble balancing the books today,' he said. 'Whatever I do, we seem to be ten shillings short. I suppose you didn't borrow any money out of the cashbox, Venetia?'

She shook her head.

'Then I'll just have to add it all up again.' He sighed heavily. 'How was your meeting?'

'Mrs Dove has asked us to decorate the committee room in Angel of Mercy House.'

'Another project!' He frowned. 'Will you have time?'

Venetia took a new folio from the drawer and carefully wrote *Angel of Mercy House* on the front. 'We can't afford to turn away any work, can we?'

'How was Mrs Dove's home for loose women?'

'Not at all what I expected,' said Venetia. 'Outside it's a dour redbrick mansion but inside it has a beautiful stone staircase winding up several floors, all lit by a glazed roof dome. Everything was spotlessly clean and there were paintings on the walls.'

'Did you see any inmates?'

It was remarkably quiet and well ordered. I heard babies crying and met one of the children. She looked well fed and her dress was freshly laundered. Somehow I expected it to be a dark and miserable workhouse.'

'Perhaps Mrs Dove keeps the fallen women and their babies in the cellar?'

'Surely she wouldn't …' Venetia broke off when she realised Jack was laughing at her. 'You're teasing me!'

He shrugged, his lips twitching. 'You looked so serious.'

'It *will* be serious if you keep interrupting me while I'm trying to write up my notes,' she said with mock severity. 'In any case, I must work late tonight.'

'Again?'

'I need to finish the drawings for Mrs Hilliard's drawing room.'

'Then Raffie shall accompany your mother and Florence home and I'll remain here until you've finished. I don't like you walking home in the dark on your own.'

Surprised, Venetia looked up from her notes. 'Then, thank you.' It was pleasing that Jack was concerned for her.

He nodded and turned his attention back to the invoices.

She picked up her pencil again. *Was* she too serious? Perhaps she did worry a great deal but then, there was a great deal to be worried about. But she couldn't help smiling at the memory of him teasing her.

An hour later the regular scratching of Jack's pen ceased and she glanced up from her schedule of works to find him watching her. For a second his penetrating gaze bored into her and she was quite unable to look away. Then he reached out to dip his pen in the ink-well and began to write in the ledger again.

Venetia stared at her schedule. There had been something strangely arresting in Jack's expression. It took her a moment to work out what it was. And then she smiled to herself and bent her head over her work.

Chapter 14

Two days later Nat was waiting for Kitty when she left the shop.

'I've come to walk you home,' he said, kissing her cheek.

She'd wondered if he'd turn up since she'd let him down the night before. She'd known once he'd got her in his bed she wouldn't be able to think straight and she wanted a truthful answer from him about the snuffboxes. 'I can't be long, mind,' she said. 'I have to finish the ironing.'

'They work you to the bone, that lot. Couldn't you get out last night?'

Kitty shook her head. 'I was so worn out I fell asleep waiting for Dorcas to finish her prayers. Next thing I knew it was time to get up again.'

'Poor little sprat!' Nat squeezed her hand. 'We'll get you a nip of blue lightning before you go back.'

He found them a quiet corner in the Cock and Bottle and Kitty plucked up the courage to ask the question that had been burning in her thoughts. 'Nat?'

'What is it, my lovely?'

Her heart began to race. He might get in a huff but she had to know he was honest with her. 'In your room I found ...' She swallowed, suddenly afraid to go on.

He put down his tankard very slowly and wiped the froth from his top lip. 'What did you find?'

'I found the sacks under the floor. Nat, where did you get those things?'

He turned up his palms. 'I'm a coster, a trader. I have to hide them because the world is full of thieves. People bring their little treasures to me and I buy them.'

'What kind of people?'

'People who've fallen on hard times. You saw that girl bring a bit of lace to my stall, didn't you?'

She nodded. 'Nat, are some of those things stolen?'

He shrugged. 'Usually.'

She didn't like his answer but at least he'd not lied.

'Kitty, I'd have no business if I asked questions. I've no mind to be sleeping on the streets again. Sometimes the thief-takers come to see me if there's a reward on a particular item. We both do nicely out of that and the cove gets his watch back.'

'But to make your living from theft ...'

Nat's voice was flat. 'Life is unfair. Look at all them rich people in their fancy carriages with footmen running behind. They never even notice the beggars starving in the gutter.'

That was true, all right. Those ladies wearing silk frocks that she'd seen looking in shop windows, deciding what else they'd buy, while Kitty only had two dresses to her name!

Nat gripped her wrist. 'Can you cross your heart and tell me that you've never, ever pinched anything?'

Kitty chewed her lip, remembering all the times she'd helped Tom and Pa to carry smuggled goods away from the beach. In a way they'd been stolen. And sometimes she'd slipped a jar of jam or a bit of leftover pie from Spindrift's pantry under her coat before she went home. Never felt guilty about it neither, not when the Lovells ate at every meal and her family went hungry. 'But, Nat, all those valuable snuffboxes and watches …'

'Rich people have so much they barely notice when they lose something. They don't get hurt and they'll buy a replacement without thought for the cost.'

That was true enough. All servants pinched things. Once Kitty had taken one of the missus's shifts and said it must have blown off the washing line. Anyway, Mrs Lovell had plenty more. It'd given Kitty a strange thrill to wear it under her work dress without the missus knowing.

'And then,' said Nat, 'there are poor little buggers like Benny. His ma was a draggletailed doxy who died of the pox. He never knew his pa. His ma probably didn't neither.' Nat's expression was bleak. 'I know what it is to fend for myself, never knowing where I'll lay my head at night or if I'll eat again.'

'I thought Ma Slattery took you in?'

Nat snorted with laughter. 'You don't think she kept me close for nothing, do you? There were a whole lot of us orphans and she taught us to filch handkerchiefs almost afore we could walk. And woe betide us if we didn't bring her something every day! I can still feel her birch switch across my bare backside.'

Kitty's stomach clenched with pity for the young Nat. At least her parents had tried their best for her.

'I've come a long way by living on my wits. I never hurt nobody and I'm making a better life for myself, however I can.'

She couldn't blame him for that. 'But what if you get caught?' The thought of it made her feel sick.

He rested his hands on her shoulders. 'I'm too canny. One day I'll have a shop as fine as your Miss Venetia's place. I'll sell watches and handkerchiefs and all the little geegaws people like.' He cupped her chin and made her look at him. 'You're the girl for me, Kitty, and I want you by my side in that shop. Your pretty smile will coax all the gents into buying trinkets for their dearies.' He smiled. 'And

144

when we're rich, I'll give you a hundred silk shawls and we'll have assistants to run the business while we lounge in bed eating jellied eels to our heart's content. What d'you say?'

The pounding in her chest made it hard for her to breathe and she couldn't look away from Nat's dark eyes. He loved her and he made her feel alive. One day he would be somebody of importance, she was sure of it.

'Kitty?'

His narrow face was anxious now. If no one was hurt, was it really so bad that the goods were stolen? He was right; life *was* unfair.

'Kitty? If you're to be my wife, I'll never keep secrets from you.'

Happiness bubbled up inside her and she smiled as she reached out to caress his cheek. 'So are you proposing?'

He gave a whoop of laughter and crushed her to his chest, smothering her face with kisses. 'Of course I am, you silly chit!'

A ribald cheer went up from a crowd of men drinking at the next table.

Nat stood up and swept off his hat. 'Gentlemen,' he lifted Kitty's hand to his lips, 'say how do to the future Mrs Griggs.'

The men cheered again and banged their tankards on the table.

Nat called to the barmaid and flung a handful of coins on the table. 'I'll buy ale for anyone who'll drink our health.' He pulled Kitty into the crook of his arm. 'I'll always look after you, sweetheart.'

She rested her head on his shoulder and sighed with happiness.

Venetia hurried back from her meeting with Mrs Warburton, a new client, with her head full of worry about how much work she had to do in so little time. As she crossed the road to the shop, the door burst open and two boys ran out. Each carried a cushion and, before Venetia had time to register it properly, Jack erupted out of the doorway, followed by Nero and Caesar.

'Stop, thief!' he shouted. Leaning on his stick, he hobbled after the two children but they separated, pushing their way through the legs of the crowd who'd stopped to gawp. One of the boys ran towards Venetia.

She grasped his ragged sleeve and he glanced up with desperation in his eyes as they engaged in a tug of war over the cushion. The pugs snarled and snapped at the boy's ankles.

There was a tearing sound and the silk rosette came away in the boy's grimy hand. Venetia tucked the cushion firmly under her arm and boxed the boy's ears. He yelled and lashed out with his foot before running off.

'Are you all right?' asked Jack.

Venetia called to the dogs and rubbed her shin. 'I'll have a bruise, I daresay.' She smiled in grim satisfaction. 'At least I saved one of the cushions. We can make a new rosette for it.'

'I apologise,' said Jack stiffly. 'I wasn't fast enough to catch them.'

'It wasn't your fault,' said Venetia. Oh, Lord! Did he think she was accusing him of failing to chase the little devils because of his limp?

'Raffie sloped off with Freddie Crawford,' said Jack, irritation plain on his face. 'If he'd been at his station those boys would never have got through the door.'

'Let's go back inside,' said Venetia, wrong-footed because Raffie had neglected his duties. She called to the pugs, who were eating something nasty in the gutter.

'Jack,' she said as she hurried towards the office, 'will you go and speak to the decorators?' She paused as they passed through the picture gallery and straightened the portrait of Giulia di Pietro. 'Mrs Warburton's drawing room must be painted this week.'

'This week?' He opened the office door and stood back to allow her to enter.

'We only have a fortnight. There's no time to make new curtains so Mama and I will have to improvise with plenty of cream muslin ...' She frowned while she thought. 'Perhaps Florence can help? I'll choose the furniture and Raffie can run round to see if Mr Marsden has the items in stock.'

'Venetia!'

'Yes?'

'Sit down.'

'There's no time! I must go to see Mrs McGinty.'

'There is time.' The tone of Jack's voice brooked no argument. 'Look at me! Now take a deep breath ...' He rested his hands on her shoulders. 'You cannot take on any more work until the current projects are finished.'

She couldn't help noticing again how firm and well-shaped his mouth was. All at once her knees were trembling and she wished she could lean against him until all their problems went away. The responsibilities she had shouldered were too great. 'We can't afford to refuse work.'

'Actually, we can.' He pushed the ledger towards her. 'We've made a small profit.' He smiled at her. 'And if you're on your sickbed, I'm hardly the best person to discuss with society ladies the benefits and disadvantages of Italian-strung window curtains or ...' he waved his hand in the air ' ... bugle-bead trimming. Or some such nonsense.'

Venetia gave a wavering smile. 'I'd no idea you even knew of the existence of bugle-bead braid. So, financially, we're out of the woods?'

'We'll need a steady supply of work but I'm surprised by how well Lovell and Chamberlaine is faring. There are still some irregularities in the books, including some missing money I can't account for, but I'm beginning to make sense of it all.'

Venetia leaned back and closed her eyes. 'I've been so worried, Jack.'

'Not without cause. I've also been pursuing your father's clients with requests to them to settle their bills, with some success.'

147

'I can't tell you how relieved I am not to have to keep the books and chase payments,' said Venetia.

Jack laughed. 'And I can't tell you how relieved I am that I don't have to choose curtain brocades for spoiled ladies' boudoirs. But, together, we can do this, don't you think?' He smiled at her, the corners of his eyes crinkling.

A slight tremor ran down her back, as if it were being stroked with a feather. A few months ago she'd never have believed that Jack would look at her with such warmth and had firmly pushed aside even the tiniest acknowledgement of how very attractive she found him. But those thoughts were becoming harder to deny.

He held out his hand. 'Friends?'

Slowly, she extended her fingers and he grasped them in a warm embrace. She looked at their clasped hands, her own small and white and his brown and strong, and something inside her shifted. Looking up, she met Jack's gaze and watched his smile fade.

'Venetia?' His voice was husky.

She moistened her lips, still looking at him. The other day she'd thought she detected a glimmer of interest in his eyes. It had been swiftly veiled, but now she was sure of it.

He lifted a finger towards her cheek but then the door opened and he hurriedly shuffled some papers on the desk.

Mama stood in the doorway. 'I've just taken an order for fifty yards of that expensive cream and burgundy striped brocade.'

'Splendid,' said Venetia.

Mama glanced at Jack's dark head bent studiously over the ledger and then back at Venetia. She smiled. 'In that case I shan't disturb either of you any longer.'

'You aren't disturbing us at all,' said Jack, standing up. 'I'm on my way to call on the decorators.'

'And I need to talk to you about muslin window drapes,' said Venetia, hoping that Mama hadn't seen the blush rising up her throat.

She followed her mother into the showroom and glimpsed Jack closing the shop door behind him.

All morning Venetia wondered what might have happened if Mama hadn't interrupted them, and if such a moment might come again.

Chapter 15

It was very late when Kitty and Nat arrived at the Goat and Compass. Billy and Sal, together with Lennie and Ruth, waited for them on a settle by the fire.

'So what's been happening?' asked Lennie.

'Not much,' said Nat, 'except that Kitty and me are getting spliced.'

Sal screamed in delight and hugged Kitty. 'My, Nat's a dark horse, ain't he? He never told us.'

'What, and have you squeak before I'd asked her?' said Nat.

Billy gave a hoot of laughter and slapped Nat's arm. 'Never thought to see you leg-shackled! You're punching above your weight with this one, that's for sure.'

'I've been biding my time for the right girl.' Nat hugged Kitty to his side. 'And now I've found her.'

Kitty smiled, her heart too full for her to speak.

'When did you decide she was the one for you?' asked Sal.

'First time I saw her,' said Nat. 'I'd gone to the Crosse Keys with my boys to meet the coaches and see if they could fetch me some wipers. Kitty was getting out of the basket. Even though she was splattered in mud I could see she was a diamond. Ma Cummings was there too, on the look out for game pullets, so I moved fast and nabbed her myself.'

'Ma Cummings?' said Kitty.

'Fat woman in purple with feathers in her hat. Very ample in the dairy department.'

Kitty screwed up her eyes while she remembered. 'I seem to remember a woman asking me if I needed somewhere to lodge. And then a boy stole Master Raffie's handkerchief.' She looked at Nat. 'And you chased him and got it back.'

Nat chuckled. 'Poor little bugger didn't know what'd hit him. One minute I'm telling him to lift the wipers and the next I'm making him give it back!'

'The missus thought you'd saved us,' said Kitty, 'and all the while you planned to fleece us!'

'But I didn't,' said Nat. 'Not once I'd seen you, my beauty.' He leaned over and planted a kiss on her mouth.

'You'll be wanting some extra blunt then,' said Lennie, 'and I've heard about a job at a leech's crib.'

'Oh, yes?' said Nat, his eyes gleaming.

'A little bird told me the leech's sister turned up her toes. He'll be off to bury her.'

Nat and Lennie turned away, whispering to each other.

Sal nudged Kitty's arm. 'Have you told your missus you're leaving?'

'Not yet,' she said. 'The banns have to be read.'

'Don't forget to ask for a wedding gift,' said Ruth. 'She's bound to give you a bit extra.'

Kitty yawned and sipped her gin.

Some time later Nat shook her awake and she lifted her head off his shoulder.

'Better get you home,' he said, a smile in his eyes.

They said goodnight and went out into the street. Kitty shivered. There was a frost and the ground was slippery.

'Another month,' said Nat, 'and we'll go home to bed together.'

'As long as you don't make me get up before the sun.' She breathed in the icy air to try and clear her head, muzzy with gin and exhaustion.

'Not a chance, sweetheart! I'll want you to stay in my bed as long as possible.'

'You're going to have to teach me how to find my way through this rat's nest of passages, though. I don't want to get lost every time I go to buy a loaf of bread.'

'There's a lot of things to teach you now we're to be riveted.'

'Shall I help you with your trading? I'm a quick learner.'

'The more you help me, the quicker we'll have that shop I talked about.'

At last they reached Quill Court and Nat kissed her lingeringly. 'Sleep tight, Kitty.' His eyes gleamed in the moonlight.

'What's that?'

'What?'

She cocked her head and listened again, hearing a faint sound, a moan perhaps. 'Someone's down there,' she whispered, peering over the area railings into the shadows. 'Nat, don't leave me!'

'A beggar, p'raps,' he murmured. 'I'll take a look.'

He crept down the steps while Kitty, shivering, waited at the top.

'Kitty?' his urgent whisper floated up to her.

She tip-toed down the steps and found him crouched over a body lying in a crumpled heap.

'I thought he was fuddled,' said Nat, 'but he's bleeding. He's either fallen down or someone's given him a basting.'

Panic fluttered in Kitty's chest. 'I've got to go in!'

Nat turned the figure over.

'Jesus God!' Kitty clapped a hand to her mouth. 'It's Master Raffie.'

Nat stood up and wiped his fingers on his handkerchief. The

moon was bright enough to show the bloodstains on the linen. 'We can't leave him here. He might bleed to death.'

'Nat, what'll I do? There'll be hell to pay if they know I've been out.'

'Let yourself in and put on your nightshift. Then you can wake Miss Venetia or the missus. Say you couldn't sleep and went to the kitchen for some milk. You thought you heard a noise, went to look and found him in the area.' He grasped her hands. 'Can you do that?'

'I have to. He'll die of cold otherwise.'

'That's my girl! I'll call by the shop tomorrow evening and catch you.' He dropped a kiss on her mouth and hurried up the steps.

Kitty looked at Raffie. Blood pooled darkly on the ground beside his head and she reached down to touch his cheek. He was already deathly cold.

Five minutes later she tapped on Miss Venetia's door. 'It's Kitty. Come quickly! It's Master Raffie ... He's hurt.'

❧

Venetia smoothed the heap of cream muslin voile over the counter. The showroom was free from customers and she'd taken the opportunity to enlist Mama's help in hemming Mrs Warburton's curtains. If she hadn't had so much work to complete and if dear Florence hadn't offered to sit with Raffie, she could never have left him.

'I don't know what the world is coming to,' said Mama, head bent over her sewing. 'To my knowledge we never had footpads in Kent.'

Venetia shivered, remembering how her stomach had turned over when she'd seen Raffie lying in a pool of blood. For one long, dreadful moment, she'd believed him dead.

'Still, boys will be boys,' continued Mama, 'and the temptation is too great for him here in London, after the quiet life we led at Spindrift Cottage.'

'I don't know how you can be so complacent about his injuries,

153

Mama.' Venetia pictured her brother's eyes, so swollen with purple bruises that they were mere slits. 'Why, he might have been murdered!'

'But he wasn't.' Mama nipped through the thread with her teeth. 'It'll be a lesson to him not to wander the streets at night.' She held out her needle. 'Will you thread this for me? I'm sure they make the eyes much smaller than they used to.'

'You need some spectacles, that's all,' murmured Venetia.

'I refuse to wear spectacles until you make me a grandmother and I'm finally obliged to sink into old age.'

'I'm unlikely to make you anything of the sort,' said Venetia, not quite liking the acerbic edge to her own voice, 'since Father's actions have rendered it impossible for any suitable man to wish to have me as his wife.'

'That's very unkind,' said Mama, 'and it sounds as if you blame me for it. Until you have known the power of True Love you cannot judge the actions of others.' She glanced up at Venetia from under her eyelashes. 'In any case, I wouldn't lose all hope for a husband just yet. I saw how you and Jack were looking at each other yesterday.'

Venetia blushed to the roots of her hair and glanced towards the office. Thank goodness Jack had gone to see Mr Marsden and couldn't have overheard them.

'And really,' continued Mama, regarding Venetia's glowing countenance, 'since there's no consanguinity, there is no reason why it shouldn't be a perfectly suitable arrangement.'

'Mama!' She was saved from protesting further when the shop bell jangled and Mrs Dove entered.

'I called by to see if my samples have arrived, Miss Lovell?' she said.

'Indeed they have.' Venetia put the muslin down, relieved to have an excuse to escape from an uncomfortable conversation. She took the samples from under the counter and spread out several snippets of duck egg blue curtain silk and cuttings of deep violet upholstery velvet and brocade.

Mrs Dove peered at them. 'This curtain silk is just what I had in mind.'

'The velvet would be my choice for your sofa,' said Venetia, 'but the brocade works well too, if you prefer it?'

'The velvet,' said Mrs Dove decisively. 'And I believe you ordered a sample desk chair for me?'

'It was delivered yesterday and I've placed it beside the panel of the trellised paper hanging that you liked. Shall we take the fabric samples and see how everything looks together?

Soon everything was settled between them and Mrs Dove sat down beside Mama.

'And what are you sewing here, Mrs Lovell?'

'A client requires over-curtains to be delivered in a hurry. She has a *soirée* planned and her husband's employer will be the honoured guest.'

'But do you not have curtain makers?'

'We've been so busy,' said Venetia, picking up her needle again, 'that they're fully booked for the next month.'

Mrs Dove gave her a sharply inquisitive look. 'So your business grows apace?'

'Jack tells me that we shall make a profit this month,' said Mama.

Venetia glanced at her and frowned. She would prefer that Mama didn't discuss such matters with others, even her friends.

Mrs Dove clapped her hands together. 'The very news I've been hoping for! I've always found plain sewing such a restful occupation. May I volunteer my services to hem the muslin? You would then be free, Miss Lovell, to continue your designing while your mama and I have a comfortable chat.'

'How very kind!'

'Many hands make light work!'

Half an hour later Jack returned.

'The specifications are finished for Mrs McGinty,' said Venetia. 'Would you prepare and deliver the orders, Jack?'

'After my errands I'll visit the shooting range and then return to accompany you home.'

Venetia regarded him covertly from under her eyelashes as he gathered up the paperwork but he made no comments of a romantic nature.

The remainder of the afternoon passed quickly as she toiled over colour schemes and carpet designs. She'd learned more from her father than she'd realised and was rapidly becoming more confident.

Mama left before dark, full of assurances that she'd sit with Raffie and, yes, she'd ask Annunziata to cook him a soft-boiled egg and soldiers, just the way he liked them, to tempt his appetite.

Venetia locked the shop door behind her and hung up the 'Closed' sign before riddling the scullery fire and boiling the kettle. Once her tea was made she returned to the office to light the candles and begin sketching curtain treatments for Lady Conningsby's second-best bedroom.

Chapter 16

It was past eight o'clock when Venetia heard the peremptory rap on the shop door. Jack must have forgotten his key. She snatched up a candle and hurried through the shadowy showroom. 'Coming!' she called.

As she turned the key in the lock the door burst open, its momentum thrusting her backwards. She gasped with pain and shock as hot wax seared her forearm and the candlestick clattered to the floor, extinguishing the light. Several men shoved their way in, slamming the door behind them.

It all happened so fast that she barely had time to comprehend it. Stale sweat stung her nostrils and rough hands propelled her towards the rear of the shop. She screamed and received a clout to her head.

'Shut up, if you know what's good for you!' said a hoarse voice in her ear. The man's rank, onion-laden breath was moist on her cheek as he clasped a hand over her mouth and nose. She couldn't breathe! Rising panic gave her strength and she bit into his palm. There was a muffled curse and a momentary release of pressure. She sucked in a lungful of air as the flat of his hand slammed across her cheek and sent her reeling.

'Come here!' The voice was cold and imperious.

Her assailant gripped her arms and pulled her up. Dazed, she shook her head. Candlelight glowed from the office, allowing her to make out the intruders in the shadowy picture gallery.

There were five of them. All were strongly built but one, taller than the rest and emanating a menacing air of authority in his caped greatcoat, stood directly before her.

'Fetch a light,' he commanded.

Venetia remained frozen in her captor's arms only half noticing that the big man spoke like a gentleman. The rapid, rackety beating of her heart rattled against her chest and fear churned in her stomach.

One of the men lumbered off to the office and returned holding a candle aloft.

Venetia recoiled as he thrust it at her face.

'A mere chit of a girl,' said the man in the greatcoat.

Venetia glanced up at him. A long nose, once broken and mended crooked. Cold eyes glittering in the candlelight. An elaborately tied cravat that would do justice to Beau Brummell.

'Let me go!' she said, her voice wavering.

Her captor wrenched an arm behind her back and she let out a gasp of pain. 'You don't, ever,' he hissed, 'speak to King Midas unless he gives you leave.'

'King Midas?'

The man in the greatcoat shook his head at the ruffian and she found herself released. 'The name is not of my own choosing, of course, but it serves well enough. You are Miss Lovell, I presume?'

Venetia forced herself to meet his cool inspection. 'I am.' She hoped he couldn't see how her legs trembled.

'I trust you are not as foolhardy as your father?'

'What do you know of my father?' But as she voiced the words she suddenly realised who these intruders were and ice formed in her veins. These were her father's attackers, the men who had

158

frightened him so much that his heart had simply given up under the strain, the men who had wrecked the shop and destroyed his dreams.

'Ah!' said King Midas. His thin lips curved in something like a smile. 'My reputation precedes me.'

'What do you want?' Shock made her lips so numb it was hard to form words.

'Two things in life are certain, Miss Lovell,' said King Midas. 'Death and taxes. Your father, foolish man, chose death when he could have continued to pay his tithe to me like others do. I've been generous enough to give you a few weeks to put the business back on its feet but now it's time to settle your dues.' He turned to one of the men surrounding them. 'Sammy, fetch the books.'

Venetia caught sight of Sammy's coarse features as he turned towards the light. He looked like a drinking man.

'What pretty pictures you have, Miss Lovell,' said King Midas studying the artwork on the walls of the gallery. 'Jem, bring the light.'

One of the men brought the candle.

'Hmm,' said King Midas, peering at a landscape. 'Venice, perhaps?' He moved to the next picture, the seventeenth-century portrait of Giulia di Pietro. 'Delightful! What a beauty!' He ran a finger slowly down her dark curls and on to the curve of the lady's painted breast.

Venetia had to bite her tongue to prevent herself from telling him to remove his filthy hands from the portrait.

He continued to comment on each of the paintings until Sammy returned, carrying the account ledgers. 'My man of business will study your books, Miss Lovell, to determine your income and then we shall return to collect our dues.'

'Your dues?'

'A tithe. It's not an unreasonable amount.' He turned to face her, his eyes narrowed. 'It would be a great pity if this elegant showroom should meet with further mishap ... a fire, perhaps. Your tithe will prevent anything unpleasant happening. We shall, of course, return every so often to inspect the books again.'

'How dare you!' Venetia could hardly speak for rage.

King Midas raised his eyebrows. 'Watch your manners, Miss, or I shall ask Jem to teach you a lesson you won't forget. And a friendly warning: I do not advise you to keep a second set of books in order to cheat us.' His gaze bored into her, as sharp as a gimlet. 'The last person to attempt that little ruse lost the fingers of his right hand. Now that wouldn't help your drawing, would it?'

Venetia glanced at him. Fear paralysed her even as hatred burned in her heart.

King Midas slipped a hand inside his coat and withdrew a knife. 'You will not talk of what has happened here tonight.' He angled the knife towards the light so that the blade gleamed. He reached out with his other hand and trailed his finger down Venetia's cheek. 'Pretty,' he said.

She flinched, unable to supress a gasp of terror.

King Midas raised the knife. Swiftly he turned and sliced the blade across the portrait of the dark-haired beauty. Slash, slash, slash.

Venetia whimpered.

'Not so pretty now! I think we understand each other, don't we?' he said with a cruel smile.

She stared at the portrait. Giulia's exquisite painted face was sliced open down one cheek and both eyes had been gouged.

Without another word King Midas turned and walked back through the shop, flanked by his men.

The front door slammed and then there was only the jangling of the shop bell.

Venetia's legs gave way and she leaned against the wall and slumped on to the floor. Waves of nausea rose in her throat and she closed her eyes, concentrating on willing them away.

And then the shop bell jangled again.

Her heart missed a beat and then rattled away so fast it nearly choked her.

He'd come back.

She scrambled to her knees and, crouched over, ran into the office. A candle still burned on her desk and she snatched up the paperknife and shrank behind the door. Peering through the gap in the doorframe, she held her breath.

The looming shadow of a man appeared on the gallery wall. Surely he must hear the rapid beating of her heart?

The dark shadow moved slowly and inexorably closer.

The paperknife shook in her clenched fist. She held it above her head, breathing so quickly and shallowly that a feather held before her nose would barely stir. Her only choice was to act swiftly and stab him immediately he came through the doorway. Coiled and ready to spring, she lifted the knife higher.

The door slammed back, a hand trapped her wrist and the knife was wrested from her grasp. She screamed again and again, lost in the grip of terror as her attacker shook her like a rag doll.

'Venetia!'

Eyes tight shut, she drew in breath to scream again.

'Venetia, it's me! Jack.'

She let out her breath in a shuddering sigh.

His face was tight with anxiety. 'Are you harmed?'

She shook her head.

He pulled her close and held her tightly. 'I was further down the street when I saw those men leaving. Although I couldn't see them clearly because of the fog, I knew at once that they couldn't be customers. I was afraid for you, Venetia. I thought they might have … hurt you.'

'I was so terrified, Jack!' She clung to him, not wanting to leave the safety of his arms as he kissed her hair and stroked her cheek. 'I thought you were *him* coming back.' She closed her eyes to shut out the terror of that memory. 'I was going to stab him. Jack, I might have killed you.' Her knees began to quiver again at the thought.

'Thank God you're safe!' He wiped away her tears. 'It was like the time I found your father ...' He swallowed. 'I feared it had happened all over again.'

'He said ... King Midas said ... that Father refused to pay him. He's taken the account books away and said we're to hand over a tithe on our profits. If we don't, they'll destroy the shop again.'

'You're trembling.' Jack patted her back and she looked up at him, holding on to his coat front. The moment stretched out and her fear turned to yearning.

He looked deep into her eyes. When she didn't drop her gaze but clung even tighter to him, he bent his head towards her.

His lips were gentle and she slid her arms around his neck and melted into his embrace. He wound his fingers through her hair, his breath quickening. She forgot what had just happened, drowning those fear-filled memories in his kiss. It was no longer fear but desire that made her knees weak.

Then he kissed her forehead and released her. He pulled out the desk chair and gently sat her down.

Her mind was spinning; so much had happened. Despite her earlier terror a peculiar kind of euphoria made her heart sing.

Jack's hands shook as he rummaged in the desk drawer, slopped brandy into a glass and thrust it towards her. 'Tell me everything,' he said.

Venetia tasted the brandy, the fumes pungent in her nose and stinging the back of her throat. 'I thought it was you when I heard the knock on the door.' She closed her eyes, remembering how she'd hurried to let him in, and began to relate the train of events. All the while the brandy burned like molten fire as it trickled into her stomach. Gradually, she stopped shaking. 'And then,' she said, 'he slashed the portrait of Giulia di Pietro.' She looked into her empty glass. 'It was a warning to me. He'll cut my face the same way if he doesn't get the money.'

Jack's hands clenched and unclenched on the desk. 'Hell's too good for him. It's the worst form of cowardice, to inflict pain and terror on those weaker than yourself.' He took Venetia's hand. 'But for now, let's get you safely home to Quill Court.'

Chapter 17

Fog curled down the area steps as Kitty let herself out of the back door.

Nat appeared at her side. He was carrying a large bag. 'It's well after midnight,' he whispered, kissing her cheek. 'What kept you?'

'I thought Miss Venetia and the missus would never go to bed. I hung about outside the drawing room because I heard them in there talking to Major Chamberlaine. You wouldn't believe ...'

'Tell me as we walk.' Nat took her hand and hurried her away from Quill Court.

'Miss Venetia was alone in the shop this evening when some men pushed their way in and knocked her about.' Kitty stumbled on a loose cobble. 'I can't keep up when you go so fast.

'Sorry, but we're late to meet Lennie. Is she all right?' He carried a lantern but the glimmer of light only made the fog look thicker.

'When I unlaced her stays, she was bruised. She didn't tell me anything but she seemed scared half to death. But I can't blame her, not after what I heard.'

'What was that?'

'Major Chamberlaine's going to report it to the constable in the morning. Nat, it was King Midas who broke in.'

He came to an abrupt stop.

'The man we saw at Sal's wrestling match.'

'I know who he is.' Nat caught hold of Kitty's shoulders. 'I told you before, you don't want to go messing with him. What do you know about him?'

'He came to the beach where I used to live in Kent. I told you my pa's a fisherman, didn't I? King Midas pays well when they smuggle guineas across to France for him.'

'I see.' Nat let out his breath in a slow whistle. 'So that explains it.'

'He had a man from our village killed.' She shivered at the memory.

'Only one?' Nat shook his head. 'For God's sake, keep clear of him, Kitty! He and his bullyboys run everything round here: the flash houses, brothels, fences, pawnshops and gambling dens. He takes ten per cent from them all. As a nipper I used to hide when he came round to collect his cut from Ma Slattery. He even took some of the prize money from Sal's purse when she won that fight.'

'He scares me.' Kitty closed her eyes for a second to blot out the vision of his powerful figure and those cold eyes.

'You're right to be scared, he's a bloodsucker. Come on.' Nat loped off again.

'If King Midas's patch is here, I don't understand why he got mixed up with smuggling in Kent?'

'It's the guinea road from London through Kent and Sussex to France,' said Nat. 'Napoleon wants to bankrupt Britain so we won't be able to afford to send enough soldiers to win the war. It's illegal to take gold out of the country in case the banks collapse. Boney encourages the smugglers to carry gold, usually guineas, to France. They trade the guineas for luxury goods. Midas pays off the smugglers and brings the goods to London where there's a market hungry for 'em. The wars have caused many shortages.'

'But where does King Midas get the gold from to send to France?' Kitty was out of breath as she trotted along beside Nat.

'He melts down jewellery and the like. It's safer that way. No one can recognise stolen pieces, 'cos there's no proof, see? And then every halfpenny he collects from the profit on a wiper lifted by some guttersnipe, every penny from a backstreet whore, every pound swindled out of the gentry at a gaming hell, every ten pounds he screws out of a business … all of this Midas funnels into the guinea route.'

'What about your bags of snuffboxes and gold watches?'

'I sell some from my carts. Others go to Uncle.'

'Your uncle?'

'The pawnbroker. I don't get full value but he shifts 'em for me. Sometimes Midas buys them from Uncle, who makes a bit, too. Then Midas melts down the gold and sends it to Boney.'

They hurried through the streets. The fog hung over them like a damp blanket, muffling the sound of approaching footsteps so that passers-by loomed up suddenly and then slid away into the swirling dark.

'Why are we in a hurry, Nat?'

'I told you, we're meeting Lennie. He's planned a job tonight. There's an empty house and we're going to pay it a visit.' He pulled her away from the main street and into an alleyway.

'A job? We're going to break in somewhere?'

'That's the size of it.'

'We're not going to hurt anybody?'

Nat shook his head. 'Don't hold with that. You need to learn how we make our living but I wouldn't be bringing you if there was anyone home.'

She let out a sigh of relief, but the thought of breaking in to a strange house gave her a feeling of excitement and terror mixed.

'The gent's a leech … a doctor. He and his missus are away to bury his sister. The maid accompanied them and he gave his housekeeper leave to visit her daughter until he returns.'

'What must I do?'

'Keep watch, most likely. Though there's little need in this fog. We can barely see six feet in front of us. We'll have to go single file through this alley. Watch where you put your feet.'

How could she possibly know where to put her feet when Nat's lantern gave out only the tiniest amount of light? It was slippery underfoot and Kitty wrinkled her nose in disgust. It smelled like a midden. She ran her fingers against the mossy walls on either side of the alley for guidance. Something brushed past her legs and she squealed.

Nat glanced back over his shoulder. 'Only a cat.'

A dark shape showed up in front of them, half blocking the passage. It rocked back and forth, grunting, and it wasn't until they pushed their way past that Kitty realised it was a whore and her cull. She was glad that Nat couldn't see how her cheeks burned.

'Nearly there,' he said. They turned into another alley and halfway along he cupped his hands around his mouth and hooted like an owl. He doused the lantern and they stood in silence in the vaporous dark.

There was an answering owl call and then Lennie appeared out of the mist.

'Thought you must have changed your mind,' he whispered. 'The kinchin's asleep.' He bent down and Kitty saw that Benny was curled up against a gate set in the wall. Lennie shook the boy's ankle until he woke up, yawning.

Nat laced his fingers together and gave Lennie a leg up.

Kitty peered anxiously into the fog, wondering which way to run if anyone came. Nerves made her want the privy but if she was going to marry Nat she was going to have to learn to help him.

A moment later the gate swung open.

Nat took her hand. 'I'm not leaving Kitty alone here,' he murmured to Lennie. 'It's too foggy for her to give a warning anyway.'

Kitty gave a sigh of relief and clung to his hand.

Lennie nodded in silent agreement and they went through the gateway and stumbled over a yard. Light glimmered through some of the shutters from the houses to either side.

Kitty's heart thudded and her mouth was dry. She wished she'd never come. What if someone saw them?

'Hold up your glym,' whispered Lennie. Nat opened the lantern and held it up while Lennie forced a small window.

'Up you go, Benny,' said Nat. He slid the boy's feet through the casement, gripping him by the waist. 'Remember what Ruth told you. The key's hanging in the larder and you've to unbolt the door. Stand on a chair to reach the top bolt.'

Benny nodded.

'Hold my hands and I'll let you down,' said Nat.

The boy slithered down past the windowsill and disappeared from view.

'What did Ruth tell Benny?' whispered Kitty.

'Where the larder and the back door key are.'

'How did she know?'

Nat grinned. 'Full of questions, aintcha? She made friends with the housekeeper in the market. One day she carried one of the baskets back and took tea in the kitchen with her. They shared a bottle of blue lightning and the housekeeper began to talk.'

There was the scrape of a bolt and then another. The lock clicked and the door opened.

Then they were inside.

'Leave the door open,' whispered Nat. 'Just in case.'

Kitty stood in the dark, the sound of her pulse thumping in her ears. What had Nat meant? Just in case the housekeeper hadn't gone after all? Or if the master came home unexpectedly? Jesus God, what had she got herself into?

Lenny lit candles from Nat's lamp. 'Nat and me'll spy out the land. Run like hell if we shout.'

Kitty's clothes were damp from the fog and she shivered as the two men disappeared down the passage, taking the light with them. The kitchen smelled of mould and mice and curdled milk. Her mouth was dry and her stomach churned. What if there was someone asleep upstairs? Benny opened the larder door and went inside and she heard him rootling about. She started in sudden fear as a floorboard creaked upstairs.

A moment later there was a flicker of light along the passage again.

'All clear,' murmured Nat. 'Where's Benny?'

Kitty nodded at the pantry and Nat snatched open the door.

Benny, cheeks bulging, sat on the floor with a pie dish on his knees.

Nat chuckled. 'Go to it, Benny boy! You're a few dinners short, I reckon.' He handed Kitty a candlestick. 'I'm going to the dining room with Lennie to sort through the silver. See what you can find in the way of the mistress's fallals upstairs. Leave it all neat, mind.'

Kitty gripped the candlestick and followed him into the hall. Nat mustn't see how afraid she was. She crept up the stairs, the skin of her back crawling, half expecting someone to jump out and snatch her ankle. Cautiously, she opened the first door. Inside it smelled stale, of a man's hair and unwashed clothes, but there was also the sweetish scent of lavender. She fingered the silky bed curtains and noticed a number of glass bottles with silver lids glinting on the dressing table. She sniffed the lavender water in one and dabbed a drop on her wrist. The bottles should sell for a tidy profit, she reckoned.

Pulling open the shallow drawer, she found a carved tortoise-shell comb amongst spilled powder and clumps of loose hair. After rummaging through hairpins and half-empty bottles of glycerine and rosewater, she caught the gleam of silver. A powder box. She turned it in her hand, admiring the chased silver and the turquoise enamelled lid inset with a garland of pink roses and ribbons. What a pretty thing!

All at once excitement and greed rose up in her. There was nothing to stop her taking whatever she could carry away! Hastily, she snatched up the powder box and comb and dropped them on the counterpane. A pair of embroidered women's slippers were tucked under the bed. Too large for Kitty but they'd have a value.

Outside, a dog began a frenzy of barking. Was someone coming? Hardly daring to breathe, she froze, listening until it stopped.

In a flurry now, she opened the chest of drawers and leafed through the neat piles of shimmies and petticoats with deft fingers, pulling out those with fancy lace or fine stitching. She didn't fancy the stays much; no doubt Madam had taken her best ones away with her.

Lifting the lid of a chest at the foot of the bed, she found folded dresses. One was of pale green silk with cream lace and she held it up against her chest and looked in the mirror, hardly recognising herself. Her cheeks were flushed and her mouth a little open as she stared at her reflection. The beautiful green suited her dark colouring and she looked like a lady of quality. She was definitely going to have that dress!

Turning back to the chest she found pelisses and capes, painted parasols and woollen shawls as fine as gossamer. And then, underneath, a jewellery box. Fingers trembling with excitement, she snatched up pearl earrings, a necklace of pale green stones that twinkled in the candlelight, a gold ring with a dark blue stone, and a coral necklace. Quickly, she tied the jewellery up in a fine lawn handkerchief and dropped it on the bed.

A door led to a dressing room where she scrabbled through a drawer and discovered two gold cravat pins, a pile of silk handkerchiefs and a pair of kid gloves. Her heart was thudding; she felt drunk with the power of taking whatever she wanted.

'Kitty?' Nat's whisper came from the landing.

'In here.' There wasn't time to gloat over her treasures. She dragged the slips off the pillows and bundled everything inside them, rolling up the silk dress and placing it on top. Quickly she straightened the counterpane and closed all the drawers.

'Find anything?'

She held up the pillowcases.

'Good girl! Let's go.'

In the hall, Lennie was hastily wrapping silver spoons in dish-cloths and stowing them in his bag. 'Quickly!' he said.

Nat snatched up his own bag and Kitty heard the chink of metal against metal. 'Silver dishes,' he murmured.

She wanted to whoop with glee but had to be happy with grinning from ear to ear. They were going to be rich!

Nat pressed a quick kiss on her lips and then they sprinted to the kitchen where Benny was stuffing a lump of cheese in his pocket. Nat blew out the candles and dimmed the lantern.

Lennie closed the door behind them and they slipped away into the foggy night.

Chapter 18

It was dark and Venetia was hiding. Her teeth chattered in terror and blood pounded in her ears. She made a tiny mew of distress as she saw the glimmer of light coming closer, growing brighter. Measured footsteps were approaching relentlessly. Pushing herself back into the corner, she made herself as small as she could, pressing a fist to her mouth.

The door flew open and he was there, surrounded by his faceless henchmen.

'You didn't think you could hide from me, did you?'

The cruel, amused tone of his voice made her skin crawl.

He snatched at her hair and yanked her painfully to her feet. 'I warned you what would happen. All the others have paid their tithe and you'll be no exception.'

Light glinted on the long-bladed knife he carried.

'No!' she whispered.

He smiled and her blood froze.

Slash. Slash. Slash.

She gasped as the blade sliced into her cheek.

He gripped her shoulders and shook her while she screamed and screamed.

'Miss Venetia!'

Her eyes opened.

A white-faced Kitty held her shoulders. 'You were having a bad dream, Miss.'

Venetia lifted a shaking hand to her cheek, expecting to find it slashed to the bone. She looked at her unmarked fingers in disbelief. No blood. 'It felt so real.'

'You're quite safe now,' said Kitty. 'Here, let me help you up.' She plumped the pillows and straightened the bedcover. 'I've brought your chocolate, Miss.'

Venetia glanced at the cup on the bedside. The chocolate was dark, rich, and comfortingly ordinary. 'Stay with me a while, will you, Kitty? I don't care to be alone until the nightmare has quite gone.'

'Of course I will.' The maid pulled a chair to the bedside.

Venetia sipped her chocolate. It wasn't surprising she'd had a bad dream after what had happened the night before. And then there had been Jack. She touched her lips with a forefinger, remembering his kiss. Perhaps their sudden passion had merely been a response to the terror of King Midas's visit? And yet ... She was shaken by the strength of her yearning for him to kiss her again.

She massaged her aching temples, full of dread at the thought of returning to the shop and unsure how to face Jack again.

'Does your head pain you?' murmured Kitty. She fetched Eau de Cologne and poured a few drops on a handkerchief before beginning to lay out clothes.

Venetia breathed in the bracing perfume. There'd been something else King Midas had said that she couldn't quite remember. It floated in the back of her mind, tantalisingly out of reach.

'I'll rise and dress now,' she said.

Some time later Kitty tied a ribbon around her mistress's hair. 'Do you still need me, Miss Venetia?' she asked. 'Only Annunziata ...'

'No, I'm quite recovered, thank you.'

Kitty went to put the scented handkerchief away in the drawer.

173

'Would you like to keep that, Kitty? You look tired, too, and it may revive you.'

A smile lit Kitty's face. 'Why, thank you, Miss.'

After the girl had gone, Venetia peeped around the corner of Raffie's door and saw that he still slept, his poor bruised face calm in repose.

Downstairs, she found Jack in his study engrossed in a newspaper.

'Good morning, Venetia,' he said. 'It appears Boney really will be removed from power.' His eyes gleamed with excitement. 'Troops are closing in on him and there are negotiations taking place now with the French government to force him to abdicate.'

'An end to the fighting after all these years can only be a relief,' she acknowledged. Was he actually going to ignore what had happened between them last night?

'I apologise,' said Jack, 'I was so caught up in the news from France I didn't ask how you are. Did you manage to sleep after your unpleasant experience?'

'I had bad dreams,' she confessed. She couldn't meet his searching gaze.

'It's not surprising. I'll visit the parish constable now to report what happened.' Jack sighed and admitted, 'I'm not confident any action will be taken in this case since he was singularly unhelpful after the attack on your father. Perhaps I'll visit the magistrate afterwards to discuss what might be done to overcome King Midas. Try and rest this morning, will you? And don't go to the shop.' His voice was gentle and she looked up, hope flaring. But he grasped his stick and left the room without a backward glance.

She called to the pugs and they came trotting out of the kitchen to sit with her in the morning room. Nero jumped on to her knee and Caesar curled up on her feet as she tried not to think of those cold eyes and the shining blade.

Then she heard Florence talking to Mama and a moment later the morning-room door opened.

'How are you today, my darling?' asked Mama.

'A little shaky,' admitted Venetia.

'What do you think made King Midas choose Lovell and Chamberlaine in particular?' asked Florence.

'That's it!' said Venetia. 'It wasn't only Lovell and Chamberlaine he targeted! He said something like "the others have paid their tithe".' Her jaw clenched. How *dare* that tyrant and his bullies force their way into her shop to intimidate her and demand money? *He* hadn't been the one who'd stayed up half the night working to complete a commission, or had to deal with the capricious demands of a rich client. How many other shopkeepers had been terrified into handing over their hard-earned income? 'It makes my blood boil,' she said.

'It's not fair,' Florence declared.

'No, it's not. And I'm going to find out if anyone else has been threatened.'

'What good will that do?' asked Mama.

Venetia sighed. 'Maybe, if there are enough of us, we could do say no.'

Despite her mother's protests she put on her hat and set off to Cheapside.

She called in at Benson's bakery first of all. There was a queue but it was no hardship to wait while breathing in the aroma of fresh-baked bread.

When it was her turn, Mr Benson smiled a greeting, bending his lanky form towards her. 'How can I help today, Miss Lovell? An apple tart perhaps? Or a slice of gingerbread or a Shrewsbury biscuit?'

'Three of your excellent custard tarts, if you please.' She watched while he wrapped her purchases. 'Mr Benson,' she said, 'I had a frightening experience in the shop last night.'

He paused in the act of folding the paper into a neat parcel.

'I wanted to ask you if you've ever received a visit from a man calling himself King Midas?'

The baker looked up at her, his face suddenly pale. 'What kind of a name is that?'

'It's the name of a man who frightens those weaker than himself into giving up a tenth of their profits to him.'

The man's meagre shoulders slumped. 'We're forbidden to speak of it,' he murmured. 'My daughter Jane is only ten years old. I'll do whatever is necessary to protect her.'

'He threatened to slice my cheek open with a knife,' said Venetia, shuddering at the memory.

'He'll do it, if you cross him,' said Mr Benson quietly. 'I beg you not to talk of this. He has spies everywhere.'

'But we can't just let him terrorise us and take our profits!'

'Miss Lovell, I urge you, for your own safety, keep your head down, pay him what he demands and try never to think of resisting. It's the only way to deal with it.' He handed her the package. 'Will that be all?'

Venetia sighed. 'I had hoped you'd help me …'

'My advice is the best help I can give.' He turned his back on her and began to wipe crumbs off the shelves.

There was nothing to do but leave. She crossed the road and pushed open the door of the Murchisons' bookshop.

Inside the usual hushed atmosphere prevailed. One customer and her companion were waiting for their purchases to be wrapped. Edwin came to greet Venetia.

'How delightful to see you, Miss Lovell!'

She held up her package. 'I wondered if I might invite myself to tea? I've brought custard tarts.'

Edwin's eyes gleamed. 'You remembered my weakness, Miss Lovell. Charles won't be a moment. Please, come through to the parlour.' He led her to the back of the shop, pulled aside a red velvet curtain and ushered her into a comfortable, if overcrowded, sitting room.

'How cosy!' said Venetia.

'It's as our dear departed mother left it but we like it just as it is. I'll ask Mary to make tea and we'll be with you in a moment.'

Venetia glanced around at the old-fashioned but well-made furniture, the walls painted in a rich garnet shade, embroidered cushions and scores of decorative knick-knacks. It perfectly reflected the Murchison brothers' fussy taste.

A moment later the curtain was pulled aside to admit Charles Murchison's portly little figure.

'My dear Miss Lovell,' he said. 'We hoped you might call upon us.'

Venetia waited until the tea had been poured and the custard tarts placed on bone china plates decorated with roses. 'Last night,' she said, 'after the shop was closed, men forced their way into the showroom and threatened me.'

'My dear Miss Lovell!' said Edwin, pressing a hand to his chest.

'The leader called himself King Midas.'

Charles replaced his cup in its saucer with shaking hands.

'The men were the same ones who frightened my father so badly that he died.' Venetia looked at Charles's suddenly pale face and knew the answer even before she asked the question. 'Has he threatened you?'

Edwin's hands twisted together in his lap and Charles's eyes were wide and fearful, but neither man spoke.

'I surmise that you have indeed had the dubious pleasure of making King Midas's acquaintance.'

'We cannot speak of it,' whispered Edwin.

'Then let me do the speaking. Has he asked you for a tithe of your profits and threatened to hurt you if it is not forthcoming?'

Charles gave Edwin an agonised glance.

Edwin, his small mouth twisting with emotion, gave a barely perceptible nod.

'Are there others who have been similarly menaced?'

Edwin nodded again, his chin quivering. 'He strangled our cat, Tabitha.'

'And then nailed her poor little body to the wall.' Tears glistened in Charles's eyes. 'He said he'd do that to us, too, if we didn't pay him.'

Venetia's stomach churned. She'd been lucky that it was only a portrait that had been destroyed. 'Can't someone stop him?'

Edwin shook his head. 'He has men everywhere, listening and watching. He takes our account books away and sends a collector for the money. He doesn't accept excuses and there are always repercussions if anyone tries to thwart him.'

'He may be having you watched in case you try to discuss last night's events with anyone else,' warned Charles.

The shop bell rang.

'There's a customer. We must ask you to leave now,' said Charles, hurriedly standing up. His custard tart lay untouched on his plate.

Venetia put down her cup. 'There has to be something we can do?'

'Do not even consider such a foolhardy idea, Miss Lovell.'

The Murchison brothers escorted her briskly through the shop and a moment later she was on the pavement.

She glanced around, the skin on her back suddenly crawling. Could the costermonger selling hot pies on the other side of the road be following her? Or was that man leaning against the wall, picking his teeth, watching to see where she went? Perhaps the couple looking in the window of the umbrella maker were staring at her reflection in the glass?

Someone touched her shoulder and she spun around, gasping.

'What are you doing here?' Jack scowled at her.

'I've been talking to the neighbours.'

He gripped her elbow, marched her to the shop and bundled her inside. 'I thought you had more sense than to wander about alone. King Midas is dangerous and you, of all people, should be very frightened of him.'

'Of course I'm frightened! But I discovered that the Bensons and the Murchison brothers have been intimidated by him, too.' Venetia blanched under the frosty glare this earned her but lifted her chin. 'It's so unfair ...'

'I'm not going to encourage you by arguing with you, Venetia. Do not poke a stick into a hornet's nest!' Jack walked towards the picture gallery while he visibly composed himself and then continued speaking in a gentler tone. 'We shall take care in future that none of us is ever alone here. And as soon as he's recovered from the footpad's attack, I suggest I take Raffie with me to the shooting range and teach him how to use a pistol. We must be able to protect ourselves.'

'And then what?' asked Venetia, following him. 'We fend off King Midas and make him so angry that he returns to the shop with his gang when we aren't here and destroys it all over again?'

Jack sighed. 'The truth is, I don't know what to do for the best.'

'We should discreetly find out about others who have been threatened.'

'To what end?'

'I don't know but ...'

'Listen to me, Venetia.' He turned to face her. 'It's worse than I thought. I've spoken to the parish constable and he knows all about King Midas. He says it's more than his life's worth to assist us. His wife and children will be harmed if he disobeys. King Midas has his finger in every crooked pie in this part of the city. He's powerful and entirely without pity and will bring to a violent end anyone who crosses him. The constable's advice is to pay up and keep quiet.'

'But that's monstrous!'

'He said that King Midas takes only what a business can afford. Like any parasite, he doesn't intend to kill his host.' Jack shrugged.

'But why don't people band together and refuse to pay him?'

Jack stopped in front of the ravaged portrait. 'This is why.'

Venetia saw again the violent slashes across Giulia di Pietro's beautiful face and shuddered.

Carefully, Jack lifted the portrait from its hook and Venetia followed him as he carried it into the office.

'We'll keep this as a reminder,' he said, his expression grim. 'King Midas's criminal network is too extensive for us to thwart it. If he hasn't broken your spirit, we'll continue our work here and hope the business flourishes. We'll pay his tithe promptly and try not to think about it for the rest of the time.'

'But ...'

'We can't fight him, Venetia!'

Her stomach lurched as she looked at Giulia's ravaged face and remembered that cruel voice saying, 'Not so pretty now!'

Jack turned the portrait towards the wall.

She clenched her fists. 'But we cannot let him get away with this!'

A few days later Venetia was dressed and ready to go downstairs when she noticed that her maid was hovering.

'What is it, Kitty?'

She hesitated. 'Please, Miss, might I have a word?'

Venetia wondered if Kitty was going to confess to some petty misdemeanour, a broken item of china perhaps.

'I thought I'd better tell you now.'

'Tell me what, Kitty?'

'That I'm leaving Quill Court.'

'Oh, Kitty!' Venetia looked at her in dismay. 'You're quite one of the family.'

Kitty's eyes sparkled and her cheeks flushed a delicate pink. 'I'm to be married, you see.'

'Married!' Venetia shook her head. 'I didn't know you had a suitor. How did you meet him? Not James, surely?'

'Oh, no, miss,' said Kitty, laughing at the very idea. 'It's Nat Griggs. Do you remember, he helped us when we arrived in London on the coach?'

'But we've been here only four months.'

Kitty lowered her eyelids, a secret smile on her face. 'Long enough to know he's the one for me.'

Venetia raised her eyebrows. Well! The sly little minx must have been meeting him at the kitchen door all this time. 'And nothing will persuade you to wait a little longer, to be quite sure you're making the right decision?'

Kitty shook her head. 'The last of the banns will be read on Sunday and we'll be wed the following week.'

'Then there's no more to be said other than to wish you well,' said Venetia.

'Thank you, Miss.' Kitty's smiling face glowed.

Venetia went downstairs to sit in the dining room until it was time for breakfast.

Sighing, she opened her sketchbook and began to draw illustrations of different curtain designs to use as a pattern book. It never ceased to surprise her how difficult many of her clients found it to picture the curtain styles she described to them. Curiously unable to concentrate, she botched the first sketch and had to tear out the page.

Kitty's news had unsettled her and it took her a while to admit to herself that she was jealous. Her maid had found a husband while Venetia herself had little prospect now of a good marriage.

Some half an hour later she conveyed the news to Mama and Florence as they joined her and Dorcas brought in the trays for breakfast.

'Well, I never,' said Mama. 'And she's not marrying the fisherman who used to call for her at Spindrift Cottage?'

'Apparently not.'

'Perhaps it's as well she's leaving,' said Mama, liberally spreading butter on her bread, 'since we'll be able to reduce our costs. I'm sure we can manage with the three remaining servants.'

'I shall miss Kitty,' said Florence. 'Dorcas always looks as if she's been sucking lemons.' She giggled, a hand over her mouth. 'But I suppose that's why no one wants to marry her.'

A door slammed and there was the sound of male laughter as booted feet clattered across the hall.

'Why are men always so noisy?' asked Florence as the dining-room door burst open.

'Good morning!' said Raffie, snatching up a roll.

Jack seated himself at the table and Mama rang the bell for fresh coffee.

'How did you do at the shooting range this morning?' asked Venetia.

'Famously,' said Raffie, his cheeks bulging with bread. 'Though my bruises still hurt when I lift my arms.'

'Sit down, dear. You're spreading crumbs everywhere,' admonished Mama.

'Raffie has surprised me,' said Jack. 'He's proved to be a fair shot. He'll become a useful marksman with some practice.'

Raffie's pale skin suffused with colour at the compliment. 'I'm not a complete novice. George and I used to take a gun out after rabbits on his father's farm.'

'I have my father's duelling pistols,' said Jack, 'and I intend to keep them in the shop.'

'Is that wise?' asked Mama.

'I sincerely hope we'll never need them.'

'I wonder when King Midas will return our account books?' Venetia shuddered at the thought. She was constantly looking over her shoulder, waiting. 'I still think we should talk to the owners of other neighbouring shops about resisting his demands.'

'If we all refuse to pay him, he might go away,' said Mama.

'Or step up his intimidation,' said Jack.

Raffie put down his fork. 'Don't go poking your nose into things you don't understand, Venetia. Jack's been telling me what the constable said about King Midas. And I'd already heard something about him.'

'You had?' Venetia put down her cup.

Raffie shrugged. 'I heard about a man who had his thumbs cut off by King Midas's men when he couldn't pay his gambling debts.'

'So he's involved in the running of gaming hells, too?' said Jack. 'I hope you aren't foolish enough to patronise such establishments, Raffie?'

'Where would I find money for gambling?' he said, shortly.

In the interests of harmony, Venetia decided to change the subject.

Chapter 19

Kitty rinsed the last of the breakfast plates and laid it upside down on the draining board. She stretched out her hands and splayed her fingers. They were still chapped despite the goose grease she'd been rubbing in every night but now that spring had arrived at least her chilblains had healed. And before the day was out she'd have a wedding ring on her finger. She jigged from foot to foot and happiness thrummed through her veins.

Dorcas's footsteps came along the passage.

'Miss Venetia wants to see you in the morning room,' said the maid, looking as if she'd swallowed a fish bone.

Kitty held back a laugh at the other girl's pinched expression. Green with jealousy! She gave Dorcas a pitying smile and escaped upstairs.

After knocking softly upon the door she went into the morning room, where the ladies of the house sat.

Miss Venetia looked up from her sketchbook and smiled. 'Well, Kitty, have you packed your box?'

'Yes, Miss.' It struck her again how alike Miss Venetia and Miss Florence were, with their heart-shaped faces and beautiful blue-green eyes. Only their contrasting hair colour gave away the fact that they had different mothers.

'But I hope you might still have room for this?'

Kitty took the package that Miss Venetia handed to her and unwrapped it. Inside was a china shepherdess with a frilled skirt and a curly-haired lamb at her feet. 'Oh, how lovely!' She ran a finger over the girl's straw hat and smiled at the fat little lamb.

'I thought you'd prefer something pretty rather than a saucepan,' said Miss Venetia.

'Oh, I do!'

'And this is from me,' said Florence.

Kitty unwrapped the tissue paper and several coils of cream silk ribbon fell out. Tears blurred Kitty's eyes as she gathered them up, feeling their slippery softness catch on the rough skin of her fingers. 'I haven't any so fine. I'll wear them to my wedding.'

'And I'd like you to have this,' said Mrs Lovell. 'I remember you admired it.'

Kitty took the missus's second-best shawl of lilac wool and held it to her cheek, blinking back tears. 'You've all been so kind.' It was thoughtful of them, even though she knew now that she could have any fancy trinket she wanted just by taking it from some rich woman who'd never notice it was gone.

'We all wish you every happiness in your new life,' said Mrs Lovell.

Miss Venetia took her hand. 'I shall miss you,' she said. 'We all will.'

All at once Kitty felt almost sad she was leaving but that didn't last long when she thought of Nat waiting for her at the altar. Then she could hardly wait to get out of the door.

Black Sal and Billy leaned against the railings at the top of the area steps.

'Ready?' asked Billy. He hoisted Kitty's box on to his shoulder.

Sal linked arms with her. 'We're going back to our place for you to change into your wedding dress,' she said, 'and by then it'll be time to go.'

Kitty glanced over her shoulder for a last look at the house in Quill Court and a sudden flutter of nerves made her stomach churn. Miss Venetia was right; she hadn't known Nat for very long.

Sal gripped Kitty's arm. 'You're not going to faint on me, are you?'

Kitty shook her head.

They arrived at Sal's and Billy's lodgings and he took himself off to the alehouse while Kitty changed.

'Nat brought your beautiful silk dress and shawl here yesterday,' said Sal. 'You're going to look as fine as fivepence. And look at what I fetched you from the market. Aren't they pretty?'

Kitty took the posy of primroses Sal held out to her.

Ten minutes later Kitty looked at her reflection in Sal's little mirror. It was a shame she couldn't study all of herself at once but she could see that her hazel eyes were shining, made to look more green that usual by the silk dress. Sal had threaded the cream ribbons and some of the primroses through Kitty's dark hair and she reached up to tuck a loose curl behind her ear. 'Will I do?' she asked, suddenly overcome with nerves again.

Sal gave a shout of laughter. 'Do? I should think so! Nat'll be fighting off his rivals in droves.'

Nat, looking very fine in a brown velvet coat and starched neck-cloth, waited outside the church with Ruth and Lennie.

'Don't you look dimber?' said Ruth, as she kissed Kitty.

'Well, let's be looking at you!' said Lennie. He took her hand and twirled her around to show off her finery. 'Bang up to the mark, ain't she, Billy?'

Nat took Kitty's hand and kissed her cheek, his eyes shining. 'You look beautiful, sweetheart.'

'And I've never seen you look so handsome.'

Nat laughed. 'Then we'd better get through them church doors before our heads swell too big to fit.'

Kitty paused in the doorway, her heart knocking so hard it was a wonder the others didn't hear it. The inside of the church was shadowy and damp-smelling, the same as the little church in her home village. She wished that Ma and Pa and the little ones were there but it was impossible for them to make such a journey just to see her married. That was another life and soon she and Nat would make their own family.

She clung to his arm as they walked with echoing footsteps towards the altar where the vicar waited for them. All at once a great calm descended upon Kitty. Her fears melted away like morning mist and she knew with deep certainty that there would be no other man for her than Nathaniel Griggs.

The ceremony began. Nat made his oath and looked at Kitty with such love in his eyes that she was nearly undone but she managed to make her own promises in a clear and steady voice.

The vicar pronounced them man and wife.

Nat felt for Kitty's hand as he kissed her lips gently and the final knot was tied. They would be together until death parted them.

At the church door, the vicar shook their hands and blessed them.

'Well, Mrs Griggs,' said Nat as they walked away, 'I've worked up quite an appetite.' He winked at her when Billy guffawed. 'But perhaps we'll make do for now with a whacking great slice of beef pie and mash?' He leaned closer and whispered in her ear, 'All afternoon I'll be thinking about when we're alone together tonight.'

Kitty blushed. 'So will I,' she whispered.

Nat had reserved a private supper room for them in the Queen's Head and Kitty drank red wine and ate her dinner amidst a flurry of good wishes.

'All right, Mrs Griggs?' murmured Nat.

'Never happier,' said Kitty, glancing at the gold ring glinting on her finger, her heart almost too full for her to speak

Billy and Lennie began to sing a boisterous drinking song but Nat held up his hand for quiet. 'A toast!' he said. 'A toast to my lovely wife, who has today made me the luckiest cove in the world!'

Kitty blushed as they all raised their glasses and Nat kissed her, his mouth tasting of wine.

'I've a surprise for you,' he announced.

He took Kitty's hand and led them all through the inn to the courtyard beyond where they found a cart wreathed with flowers and greenery, hitched up to a dappled grey cob with red ribbons in his mane. A driver sat holding the reins.

'Your carriage awaits, Milady,' said Nat, sweeping off his hat and bowing low. He lifted Kitty into the cart. The seats were draped with soft wool blankets. Sitting down beside her, he tucked a blanket over her knees as tenderly as a mother with a new babe.

'You've gone to a lot of trouble, Nat,' she said, as the others clambered in with a deal of good-natured joshing.

'I was determined this journey'd be more comfortable than the one that brought you to London.' He laughed and squeezed her hand. 'Fair froze to death you were, but never a complaint from your lips.'

The driver flicked the reins and drove them north out of the city. It was a balmy April day as the cob trotted along and the wedding party sang and drank ale as they went, having a fine old time.

Kitty's heart swelled with happiness as a crowd of small boys ran after them and people waved and cheered as they passed. A gentleman on a horse threw a handful of coins into her lap and kissed his fingers to her.

They took the City Road and passed Bunhill Fields and the vinegar manufactory, where the fumes made their eyes water, but very soon they left the houses behind and came to open fields.

'Where are we going?' asked Kitty. She leaned her head against Nat's shoulder, watching puffy white clouds scudding across the blue sky.

'I'm taking us to Sadler's Wells to see a play.'

'A play?' She sat bolt upright. 'I've never been to a theatre before! How did you know it's the very thing I've always wanted to do?'

He laughed. 'Because you've mentioned it several times.'

She gave him a dazzling smile. 'I've *never* been so happy.'

'I'm glad.' He kissed her, slowly and thoroughly, while Billy hooted and Lennie catcalled.

'Nat?' she murmured when he released her. 'We won't be home *too* late tonight?'

He laughed. 'Not a chance, sweetheart! Now that I've made an honest woman of you, I want you to myself as soon as possible.'

They arrived at Sadler's Wells and there were already a great number of people milling around amongst the horses and carriages massed outside.

The theatre was crowded and they had to squeeze past people's knees to reach their seats. Kitty had never seen such a large crowd, all chattering and laughing. The noise was deafening and the air heavy with curling tobacco smoke, candle grease and the sharp scent of orange peel. It was hot and she plucked at the sleeves of her dress, wishing she'd brought her fan.

Nat had secured good seats near the front of the gallery. Gents in the tiered boxes to either side were standing up to ogle the young ladies opposite and there was a sea of people spread out before them in the pit. Suddenly there came a cry of 'A fight! A fight!' and Kitty heard screams and shouts as the wrong-doers were dragged apart and pelted with pieces of bread.

'Perhaps I should sort them out?' said Sal with a chuckle. 'Wouldn't know what's hit 'em.'

Ruth ducked as a piece of orange peel sailed overhead.

Billy and Lennie pushed their way along the row carrying stacked glasses of porter and handfuls of little cheesecakes.

'Tell you what,' said Nat a few minutes later, 'watching these people is almost as good as a play. But mind you look out for your pocket handkerchiefs!'

Billy guffawed. 'No one's going to snitch any wiper of mine. They didn't call me Fingers for nuffink when I were a bantling.'

Gradually the candles in the wall sconces were snuffed out. The audience drummed their feet on the floor. Slowly, the scarlet curtains on the stage were drawn apart.

Kitty gripped Nat's hand. She'd never seen anything so wondrous. The stage was brightly lit with a backdrop painted to look like a row of houses. It seemed so real she couldn't believe the houses weren't made of stone. There were even small trees in the courtyard in front. Lights gleamed in the open windows and up above a pretty girl in a pink dress leaned out over a balcony.

The audience quietened, although this didn't stop someone from lobbing an orange at the performer. She lifted up her arms and then began to sing:

> *'There were three travellers, travellers three,*
> *Hey down, ho down, lack a down derry.*
> *And would go travel the north country*
> *Without ever a penny of money.'*

A cheer went up as the girl mounted a hobbyhorse and pretended to ride it over rough roads.

Kitty glanced at Nat whose eyes were fixed on the singer but he turned to her with a smile.

> *'At length, by good fortune they came to an inn*
> *and they were as merry as e'er they had been.*
> *A jolly young widow did smiling appear . . .'*

A host of catcalls and whistles came from the pit as the singer curtseyed in welcome.

'She gave them a banquet of delicate cheer.
They drank to their hostess a merry full bowl.'

The girl mimed offering a glass of wine to the audience.

'She pledged them in love, like a generous soul.'

The singer pulled the pins from her hair and her long blonde tresses fell down to her shoulders, to the delight of the men in the house. Waving her arms, she encouraged everyone to join in the chorus:

'Hey down, ho down, lack a down derry.'

The audience roared out the refrain and Kitty had to put her hands over her ears.

'The hostess, her maid and cousin, all three,
they kissed and made merry, as merry could be.'

Coyly, the singer clasped her hands to her bosom and then slowly began to unbutton the neckline of her dress while several of the men called out ribald comments.

'The handsomest man of the three, up he got,
He laid her on her back and he paid her the shot.'

The audience rose in their seats and stamped their feet in a frenzy of enjoyment.

'Then, taking their leave, they went merrily out.
Hey down, ho down, lack a down derry.'

After the third noisy repetition of the chorus the singer curtseyed while people threw their hats in the air and whistled.

Next a clown with a painted face came tumbling out of the wings, turning cartwheels and spinning plates on poles and making everyone laugh at his antics.

'That's Grimaldi,' said Nat. 'He'll be in the play, too.'

There were several other acts, two men singing comic songs, a strongman who supported nine people on his shoulders in a pyramid, and a talking dog in a red jacket who jumped through a hoop of fire.

During the interval Kitty, Sal and Ruth stretched their legs and fanned their overheated faces while they waited for the men to bring them another glass of porter.

'We're having such a fine time, I'm going to miss you all,' said Sal.

'Miss us?' echoed Ruth.

Sal nodded. 'Billy and me are travelling up north next week. He's got a friend near Manchester who says the alehouses are crying out for quality acts. Big Bessie and her man are coming too.'

'I thought you hated Bessie,' said Kitty.

Sal laughed. 'All part of the act, isn't it?'

Nat, Billy and Lennie returned just in time as the play, *Kaloc, The Pirate Slave*, began.

Kitty enjoyed watched the actors strutting across the stage, laughing at their jokes and again when one of the actors forgot his lines and was hissed off the stage.

'It's only a play, sweetheart,' said Nat, passing her his handkerchief when, later on, she cried at Kaloc's misfortunes.

At last the play ended and the wall lights were lit again. When the red curtains finally closed there was a stampede for the doors.

Kitty was swept along by the tide of people. She couldn't see Nat anywhere and panicked for a moment. Then she saw Sal a few feet away and behind her was Nat, waving. A moment later he caught hold of Kitty's arm as they were thrust outside by the crowd and into the moonlit night.

The night air was chilly and Nat slipped his arm around her.

She'd remember this day as long as she lived. Yawning, she leaned her head on his shoulder. The swaying of the cart made her sleepy.

She woke when the cart pulled up and the others descended in a chorus of good wishes. Nat and Kitty waved goodbye and the cart set off again. Very soon it stopped.

Kitty shivered in the cool night air as Nat opened the door of his lodgings. They tip-toed up the creaking staircase.

Nat lifted her into his arms. 'I'm going to carry you over the threshold, Mrs Griggs,' he whispered.

A fire burned merrily in the grate and the candles were lit, casting a warm glow over the red curtains surrounding the bed. A carafe of wine and two glasses waited for them on the table and now there were two chairs in the room.

'It looks so welcoming,' breathed Kitty as Nat laid her carefully on the mattress. Clean sheets, too, she noticed, breathing in the faint scent of lavender. Bless him, he must have sent them to a laundry!

'I paid Benny to come in and light the fire and the candles this evening,' said Nat.

Kitty wound her arms around his neck. 'Today has been perfect.'

'And it isn't finished yet,' he whispered.

Afterwards, she lay in Nat's arms, sated with love but too wide awake to sleep. Kitty wasn't much of a one for church but she sent up a silent prayer of thanks that God had sent her a good man who was kind to her and who loved her. And what was more, she didn't have to leave the drowsy warmth of his bed to creep through the dark, stinking alleys and return to a cold attic in Quill Court.

Smiling into the dark, she listened to the soothing music of her husband's sleeping breaths. And, at last, she slept.

Chapter 20

By the time Venetia reached Angel of Mercy House, Mr Marsden's waggon had come to a stop outside, behind a smart yellow carriage.

'Am I late?' she asked.

Mr Marsden shook his head and began to unload the reupholstered chairs for the committee room on to the pavement.

A gentleman and an expensively dressed lady came out of the house. The lady cradled a baby in her arms. It began to cry the thin, high wail of a newborn as she climbed into the yellow carriage.

Venetia watched as they drove away, wondering if Mrs Dove had found adoptive parents for the baby.

'That's the last one,' said Mr Marsden, placing the twelfth chair beside the others.

Venetia ran a hand over the claret velvet-covered seats. 'They look splendid.'

She knocked on the door of Angel of Mercy House and one of the young inmates admitted them to the hall before going to inform Mrs Dove of their arrival.

There was the tap, tap of quick footsteps and Venetia looked up the central stairwell to the impressive glass dome at the top.

Mrs Dove leaned over the banisters. 'Good morning, Miss Lovell! As prompt as ever, I see.'

Mr Marsden carried the chairs into the committee room and then discreetly left. The walls had been repainted and the new curtains hung the previous week. Mrs Dove was delighted with the finished result.

'I shall write a testimonial to Lovell and Chamberlaine,' she said, 'and call on your mother this afternoon to deliver it.'

'If only all my clients were as easy to please as you,' said Venetia, bathing in the warmth of her praise.

'Miss Lovell,' said Mrs Dove. 'There is something else I wished to mention.'

'Yes?' said Venetia.

'Forgive me, I have no wish to interfere but as your mama's friend, I've been concerned for you.' Mrs Dove bit her lip. 'Your mother mentioned to me, in confidence of course, that you'd been visited by a dreadful man calling himself King Midas. I understand he threatened you in the most vile way?'

'I do wish Mama wouldn't rattle on so,' said Venetia, determined to speak to her about being more discreet.

'She said this King Midas person demanded a regular payment from you?'

'I shan't pay him a penny,' said Venetia.

'After his threats, aren't you worried about what might happen if you do not?'

'I'm not the only one who has been frightened. I've been speaking to the other shopkeepers.'

'I see,' said Mrs Dove. 'What do you all intend to do?'

'I'm not sure yet.'

'If you'd like to discuss it at any time, I'd be happy to listen.'

It was a kind sentiment but what did an elderly lady know of such matters?

Mrs Dove smiled. 'I can see you don't wish to talk about it

further,' she said, 'so let me change the subject. Have you seen a newspaper today? Napoleon has abdicated at last. Our soldiers will be coming home.'

'What excellent news!' said Venetia, relieved she didn't have to discuss King Midas. 'Wives and mothers will be so happy to have their loved ones returned to them.'

'But,' said Mrs Dove, 'what will we do with the men who come home all seeking work at once?'

Venetia considered the implications of this as she walked back towards Cheapside but there was something else of more immediate concern to her. She hadn't dared to mention to Jack that she'd continued, one by one, to visit the neighbouring shopkeepers to discover if they, too, were in thrall to King Midas. Almost all, after some probing questions, had finally admitted it was so and she believed that those who didn't admit it were simply too frightened to speak.

Lost in thought, she walked a little too close to the road to avoid a small group of ladies who had stopped to greet each other. A dark green carriage bowled by, missing her by inches. Catching her breath, she glanced up and froze, teetering on the kerb. For a moment, she'd thought that it was King Midas's profile that she'd seen in the carriage. But couldn't have been him; his great town coach was black. Her nerves were on edge, never knowing when he might return and that made her imagine he and his bullyboys were spying on her.

She shook her head, chiding herself for her being fanciful, and continued her journey.

Raffie opened the shop door to her. His bruises had faded and over the last couple of weeks he appeared to have turned over a new leaf. He hadn't gone out in the evenings at all and had been on time for work every day. Perhaps he was growing up at last.

'Raffie, this came for you.' She withdrew a letter from her reticule. 'I found it slipped under the front door as I left home this morning.' She paused a moment. Home. How strange! But it was true that she had begun to consider Quill Court her home at last.

Raffie glanced at the note and stuffed it in his pocket.

'Aren't you going to open it?'

'Later.' His expression was morose again as he turned away to rearrange the display of urns, vases and bronzes.

She watched him for a moment, wondering who might have sent him the letter that he didn't want to open in front of her.

Jack was writing out a sheaf of orders and invoices in the office and glanced up when she entered. He sighed. 'I'm having to keep a note of all transactions as I can't enter them in the account books.' He looked directly at her. 'I still can't balance the cash transactions, either. I don't suppose you or your mother borrowed any money from the cashbox?'

Venetia shook her head. 'I'd write a note and put it in the box, if I had.'

'I see.'

She sighed. 'It's dreadfully unsettling not knowing when King Midas might turn up with the ledgers.'

'But you won't have to deal with him on your own this time. Did Mrs Dove's chairs arrive?'

Venetia nodded.

'Then I'll send her our invoice.'

'She's coming to visit Mama this afternoon so you can give it to her then,' said Venetia.

Opening her folio for Mrs de Vere's Berkley Square drawing room, she glanced at Jack from under lowered lashes. It disappointed her that he'd been polite but unforthcoming over the past fortnight, just as if they'd never shared that kiss. She wondered if she'd done something to annoy him.

Sighing, she pulled a furniture pattern book towards her and flicked through the pages until she came to sofas but her mind still ran on the hold King Midas had over them all. Could the shopkeepers form their own defence force? She must plan how such a scheme might work.

'Venetia?'

She jumped. The blue scrutiny of Jack's gaze made her flush.

'You're daydreaming! Having trouble deciding on the upholstery for a sofa? You've been staring at that page in the pattern book for ten minutes.'

'Daydreaming is a necessary part of the design process,' said Venetia, maintaining her dignity. And that was certainly true, whether you were selecting the items of furniture that made up an elegant drawing room or planning ways to turn a disparate group of shopkeepers into a united militia.

'In that case,' said Jack, 'carry on!'

A while later Mama put her head around the office door. 'Mrs Dove is here,' she said. 'Will you join us for tea?'

'I'll leave you ladies to have your gossip without a mere male putting a damper on the proceedings,' said Jack. 'You can give her this invoice, though.'

'Gossip?' retorted Mama, taking the envelope. 'We're talking about Napoleon's abdication. Besides, it never does any harm to be friendly to one as well connected as Mrs Dove.'

'Let me tidy these papers away first,' said Venetia.

A few moments later, as she walked through the picture gallery, Raffie hurried towards her.

'I'm going to deliver those parcels to the townhouse in Greville Street,' he said.

They were walking together through the gallery towards the showroom when Raffie caught her by the sleeve. 'Venetia, can you give me some money? You said you'd pay me a salary.'

'The profits aren't significant enough to pay any of us a salary yet.'

'I must have some money!' His grip on her arm increased and his face was taut and pale.

'What do you need it for?'

'It's ...' His gaze slid away from her. 'It's for Freddie.'

'I don't understand.'

'He's got himself into debt. It's not the first time and his parents won't stump up the blunt any more. There are some men threatening to come after him if he doesn't pay up.'

'We've enough difficulty paying our own bills, especially if we are going to have to pay a tithe to King Midas. Freddie will have to confess to his parents. They're rich enough.'

Raffie made a sound of disgust and hurried away.

Venetia pressed her lips together in annoyance. He must choose his friends more carefully in future.

Mrs Dove sat with Mama and Florence. The pugs waited hopefully at their feet for cake crumbs.

'Still hard at work, Miss Lovell?' enquired Mrs Dove. Nero placed a paw on her lap and sniffed inquisitively at her reticule.

'I shall enjoy a short break,' said Venetia. She watched Raffie out of the corner of her eye as he collected an armful of packages from under the counter and then banged the door rather too hard behind him.

Mrs Dove lowered her voice. 'Miss Lovell, may I use your necessary house? I hadn't meant to be out for long but your mama had so much news.'

'Of course! Let me show you the way.'

Mrs Dove followed her through the showroom.

'Your mama is very anxious about King Midas,' she said. 'Do you know yet when he'll return for his payment?'

Venetia shook her head. 'No, and it's nerve-wracking.' She unlocked the back door and showed Mrs Dove the privy in the yard.

The injustice of being put in such a fret of anxiety by a jumped up bully made her tap her foot. No matter what Jack thought, she'd call a meeting of the other shopkeepers and present it to him as a *fait accompli*.

After Mrs Dove had returned to Angel of Mercy House, Venetia went back to the office to finish the design scheme for Mrs de Vere. She glanced across the desk at Jack, wondering if the time was right to tell him about her meetings with the other shopkeepers. He was scowling as he tried to balance the accounts and she decided to wait for a more propitious moment.

Two hours later, Florence tapped on the door.

'Jack? Venetia? I'm worried about Nero. He was sick earlier and kept falling over. Now he won't get up.'

They hurried after her into the showroom.

Nero had crawled under the writing desk. Caesar stood beside him, whining.

Venetia gathered the little dog into her arms but his breathing was quick and harsh and he barely stirred, even when she called his name. She kissed his velvety ears and rocked him in her arms.

Florence began to weep. 'He wouldn't even eat a morsel of custard tart,' she sobbed. 'Then he was ill and his whole body began to twitch.'

Jack took Nero from Venetia and stroked his nose. 'Caesar seems well, so what's the matter with this poor little chap?'

All at once Nero arched his back and began to convulse, his mouth foaming.

Florence cried out and then the pug went limp.

Jack bent his head to the dog's nose but the harsh breathing had stopped. He shook his head. 'I'm so sorry. He's gone.'

Venetia stared at Nero in disbelief. He couldn't be dead! Not the precious puppy Father had given her. It had been a frosty winter's day two years ago when he'd returned from one of his trips. He slid down from Dante's back and opened his coat and she'd been enchanted to see the puppy nestled in his waistcoat against his chest. She'd fallen in love with the pug at once.

Florence burst into noisy sobs and Venetia, with tears running down her own face, held out her arms to her sister.

*

The following morning, after they'd buried Nero in the garden at Quill Court, Venetia and Jack arrived to open up the shop. As she walked through the gallery towards the office a cold draft stirred her hair and she knew at once that something was wrong. She held her breath to listen but at that moment the church clocks began to sound the hour in their usual noisy cacophony. Hurrying into the scullery, she discovered the cause of her disquiet.

'Jack!' she called. The back door stood wide open to the walled yard.

'What is it?' he said, appearing at her side. He ran his fingers over the splintered wood. 'It's been forced.' Grim-faced, he cast a glance around the yard.

'Nothing looked to be disturbed in the showroom,' said Venetia.

'I'll arrange for some bars and extra bolts to be fitted,' he said as they went into the office.

Venetia caught her breath. The portrait of Giulia di Petro had been propped up on the desk and turned around so her ruined face was the first thing they saw. And this time her other cheek had been slashed, too.

Jack smothered a curse and picked up the envelope tucked into the frame.

Venetia felt as if she'd swallowed a great ball of rough twine and it was lodged in her throat. The portrait rested on top of the ledgers. 'Look!' she said. 'The account books.' A shiver ran down the nape of her neck.

Jack scanned the contents of the letter and sat down, the blood draining from his face.

'What is it?' asked Venetia.

He handed her the note.

It was an invoice written in a clear, confident hand and signed with an extravagant flourish by King Midas. But it was the words written at the bottom of the page that made her gasp.

Pay your dues tomorrow evening or your other lapdog will be poisoned.

Sickened, Venetia whispered, 'So King Midas killed poor Nero! How could he?'

'He has no heart,' said Jack. 'He's damnable!'

Venetia wiped away a tear. 'I'm frightened, Jack. What else might he do? And now I'm not sure which is worse: knowing that he's broken into the shop or anticipating his next visit.'

Jack kicked the leg of the desk. 'Damn his eyes!' He snatched up the ravaged portrait, shoved it in the store cupboard and slammed the door.

'I have to go out,' said Venetia. There was no time to lose. She would make an attempt to rally the other shopkeepers to rise up against King Midas before further damage was done.

Chapter 21

Kitty and Nat sauntered arm in arm through Petticoat Lane's rag fair. Rows of clothing pinned to a rope fluttered in the breeze, breeches, chemises and muslin dresses all tangled together. Second-hand clothes were mounded on the stalls or piled on the ground beside boots freshly blacked to disguise flapping soles.

'All right, sweetheart?' asked Nat as they pushed their way through the mass of bargain-hunters.

Kitty nodded, loving the noise and bustle. Life throbbed through Petticoat Lane like a beating heart. Her ears rang with the stallholders' hoarse shouts and from the hammer blows resounding from a nearby building site. She caught a drift of pipe smoke and then the aroma of onion gravy as they passed a woman with a basket of pies on her shoulder. A rat streaked along the gutter and an emaciated cat set off purposefully after it.

'Let me know if anything takes your fancy,' said Nat, as they worked their way through the throng.

'I've never seen so many clothes together,' said Kitty. Most of them looked shabby and their fusty stench overpowered even the oozing drain. She'd rather go with her husband the next time he went housebreaking and choose something from a lady's wardrobe.

'I have to call on one of my barrows before we go to the Saracen's Head,' said Nat.

A gang of tattered children raced past, yelling and nearly knocking Kitty flying as they twisted and turned in a game of tag. A barking dog lolloped behind.

Nat came to a stop before a barrow manned by an old woman in a battered hat.

She gave him a gap-toothed grin. 'Brought me any new stock, dearie?'

'Not today, Betty. How's business?'

Shrugging, she reached into the pouch she wore tied across her chest and pulled out a handful of coins. 'Could be better,' she said.

Kitty smiled behind her hand. She'd have thought Betty might have chosen something smarter from the stall instead of her ragbag of shabby clothes.

Suddenly Nat whirled around and clouted a small boy on the side of his head. 'Little varmint! Don't you try dipping *my* pocket or you'll get more than you bargained for.' The child howled and ran away.

'He can't have been more than four!' said Kitty. 'He should be at home with his ma.'

'She's probably asleep after working the streets all night,' said Nat.

Two girls came to rummage through the contents of the stall. One held up a pair of greasy leather stays and her friend shrieked with laughter.

Quick as a flash, Betty rapped her on the knuckles. 'Don't fiddle with my goods unless you're buying.'

'Hark at her!' said the girl, poking out her tongue. 'Cat-faced old harridan.'

'Young people today!' said Betty, shaking her head as the two girls flounced away.

Nat took Kitty's arm again. The rag fair gave way to more general merchandise: vegetables, pots and pans, straw bonnets and baked goods. Then they came to a stall with a dozen wooden birdcages hanging from the roof.

'Oh, look!' said Kitty, drawing Nat closer. Each cage housed a canary or a little greenfinch, except for the largest where a bright green parrot swayed from side to side on his perch. 'Aren't they pretty?'

Nat sighed but his eyes twinkled. 'Which one do you want? Please say it's not the parrot.'

Kitty eyed the bird's fierce beak and cold eyes and shuddered. 'The canaries are singing so sweetly.'

The stallholder put down his tankard of ale and moved in to close the sale. 'Finest singing birds you'll find,' he said.

Five minutes later Nat carried a birdcage in one hand. 'You'd better take it when we reach the Saracen's Head,' he said. 'Can't have Lennie and Billy thinking I've turned into a Miss Molly.'

Kitty kissed his cheek. 'No one would ever think that.' She glanced up at him from under her eyelashes. 'Especially not me.'

When they arrived at the Saracen's Head, Sal and Billy had already finished their first drink. Ruth and Lennie arrived a moment later. The two women cooed over the canary.

'How's married life under the cat's foot, Nat?' asked Billy.

He glanced at Kitty, his dark eyes alight with mischief. 'We rub along well enough and I don't need to beat her more'n six or seven times a day.' He leaned closer to kiss her on the lips while the others whistled and drummed their feet on the floor.

'I'll get another round in,' said Lennie. 'We'll drink a toast to Billy and Sal.'

'What time are you leaving?' asked Kitty. She was sad that these new friends were off to another life.

'We'll be on the afternoon mail coach,' said Billy.

'Must you go?' asked Ruth.

Sal nodded. 'I'm sick of that bastard King Midas ...'

'Quiet, Sal!' said Billy, glancing over his shoulder.

'I'm tired of him pinching half my winnings,' she murmured. 'We're going far enough away that he can't grow fat on my success any more.'

'Nasty piece of work,' said Nat, lowering his voice, too.

'But he hasn't yet found a way to weasel money out of honest housebreakers like us,' whispered Lennie with a grin. 'He'd have to catch us first!' He leaned closer to Nat. 'Talking of that, there's a bit of business I'm chasing.' He tapped the side of his nose with one finger. 'It's a big one and there might be something in it for us.'

'I'm in,' said Nat, glancing at Kitty. 'Got a wife with expensive tastes to support.'

Nat and Lennie went into a huddle, talking in an undertone.

'Whatcha calling your canary?' asked Sal

'Clara,' said Kitty.

'Let's hear her sing, then.'

They took it in turns to encourage the canary, falling about with laughter as they warbled at her and sang snatches of ballads while she watched them with bright eyes, her head on one side, stubbornly refusing to open her beak.

'You're cork-brained, the lot of you,' said Billy, downing the rest of his ale.

Soon it was time for Sal and Billy to gather up their baggage and they all went into the courtyard to wait for the coach.

Later, as it trundled away, Kitty and Ruth waved their handkerchiefs until it disappeared from sight.

Nat was uncharacteristically quiet as he and Kitty walked home.

'All right?' asked Kitty as he unlocked the door to their room.

He shrugged. 'Billy and I grew up together at Ma Slattery's flash house. He's the closest I have left to family and now he's gone. Not the first neither. Three dead, two transported and four gone away.'

'And my family are miles away in Kent,' said Kitty. 'But now we have each other.'

Nat hung up the canary cage by the window and then turned to take her in his arms. 'I'm the luckiest man in the world,' he said, kissing her gently.

He gazed into her eyes as he laid her on the bed and stroked the hair off her face with such tenderness that it brought her to tears.

'I'll always love you, Nat,' she whispered.

'We'll make our own family, won't we, sweetheart?' he said. 'And we'll keep our littl'uns close and give them the comfort I never had.'

Kitty nodded and buried her face in his shoulder as he unbuttoned her dress.

Later, Nat called out her name at the height of his passion and she clung to him, vowing to herself always to let him know how much he was loved. As he curved himself around her, a shaft of sunlight burst through the window.

Clara turned to the sun, flapped her wings and began to sing.

Venetia rearranged her pencils yet again and aligned her papers and catalogues precisely with the edge of the desk. Brushing a tiny piece of fluff off her skirt, she glanced up at Jack from under her eyelashes. The sudden yearning she could feel made her catch her breath sometimes when she looked at him. Had he completely forgotten that he'd kissed her? There was no sign of the passion he'd shown then. But for now it wasn't possible to delay any longer; she must tell him what she'd done.

'Was there something?' he murmured, without looking up from his writing.

She swallowed. 'Some of the neighbours will be calling round to see us in a moment.'

Jack's pen ceased scratching. He looked at her through narrowed eyes. 'A social call?'

'Not exactly.'

He raised one dark eyebrow.

'I've spoken to business owners around here and some of them are coming to discuss how we might stop King Midas's demands,' she blurted out, nervousness making her angry.

'I thought the other shopkeepers were too frightened to talk?'

'They're also furious. The injustice they suffer rankles with them.'

'You know my opinion,' said Jack in a dangerously calm tone. 'It's not wise to meddle.'

'I'm surprised that you of all people, Jack, a *soldier*, are prepared to turn your back on wrongdoing.' As soon as she'd spoken the words she knew she'd gone too far. She hadn't meant …

His face blanched and a muscle clenched in his jaw. 'I apologise if I disappoint you, Venetia. Contrary to the way you continue to judge me, it isn't cowardice that makes me draw back. We cannot conquer this powerful gang leader. The most successful generals will tell you it's important to know when to make a strategic retreat.'

'We aren't fighting a war, Jack!' She didn't want to argue with him. It made knots in her stomach.

'It will be war, if you persist in this course of action. And there'll be serious consequences.'

Venetia pushed back her chair and rose to her feet. 'We *must* defeat this enemy.'

Jack slammed his hand down on the desk, making her jump. 'And die in the process?'

'No, of course not …'

'King Midas has a network of criminal associates that stretches all over the city and beyond. He takes a percentage from several houses of ill repute, whose draggle-tailed doxies steal from their customers. He encourages the vilest flash houses where children are raised to pick pockets and indulge in petty thievery for his profit.'

'Then all the more reason to stop him!' Venetia drew a breath to steady herself. 'I suggest we wait until the others arrive and discuss this all together.'

Jack sighed heavily. 'I pray that good sense will prevail.' He bent his head over the paperwork again.

Venetia couldn't settle. Despite her insistence that she must rally the other shopkeepers against King Midas she had severe misgivings. He was an even more powerful foe than she'd imagined.

Half an hour later Raffie pulled down the shop blinds and, one by one, the neighbouring shopkeepers arrived. Soon the showroom was crowded with forty or fifty people.

Venetia clapped her hands for attention, her heart thudding in nervous anticipation. Was she making a terrible mistake in stirring up trouble? The chatter continued and she glanced at Jack who was leaning against the wall with his arms folded. Damn him! He wasn't going to help her.

Mama caught her eye and smiled reassuringly.

Venetia clapped her hands again and shouted for quiet. Gradually the conversation ceased.

'Thank you all for coming here today,' she said, her voice trembling a little. 'I'll come straight to the point. We've all suffered at the hands of King Midas in one way or another and he continues to leech away our profits under the threat of violence.'

'What have you in mind?' asked Mr Benson.

'We must all refuse to pay this monster another penny.'

A murmur ran through the crowd and Venetia saw Edwin and Charles Murchison shaking their heads in unison.

'He'll kill us, or worse, if we don't,' said Mrs Benson. 'I'm frightened for my daughter.'

'He frightens me, too,' said Venetia, 'but if we don't take a stand, it'll never stop.'

'Your father made a stand and look what happened to him,' said Mrs Benson.

'He had a weak heart,' said Venetia, 'and he was alone.' The thought of it made her falter but as she pictured his face she imagined him smiling at her in encouragement. 'We must find ways to help and protect each other.'

'How can we? We never know when King Midas will attack next.'

'We need to form ourselves into a peacekeeping militia.'

'And then what?' called out Mr Bernstein.

'We can support any shopkeeper he intimidates. There's safety in numbers. If we refuse to pay and he sees us presenting a united front, then he'll leave us alone and go somewhere he'll find less opposition.' Out of the corner of her eye she saw Jack straighten up.

He took a couple of steps forward and waited until everyone was looking at him. 'King Midas is involved in every dishonest dealing in this part of the city and he's made himself so rich he fears no one. What will happen after your shop closes for the evening?' he asked. 'Some of you live on the premises. Are you going to remain awake all night waiting for him?' He turned to fix Edwin and Charles Murchison with a penetrating stare. 'For you can be sure he'll make his visit when you least expect it.'

Somewhere a woman began to sob and all at once Venetia was overcome with anger.

'This must stop! We're all living in absolute terror of that man. We take the financial risks and stand for hours every day behind our counters, with our backs and feet aching, smiling at difficult customers. And then, after closing time, the books still need to be balanced and the shelves restocked.' She thumped her fist on the counter, making several shopkeepers jump. 'How *dare* King Midas make us so terrified that we meekly hand over our hard-earned money? It's completely wrong, it's unjust and we have to stop him.'

'How can we stop him?' called out Mr Elliot.

'I tell you,' said Venetia, her fists clenched in fury, 'if we *don't* stop him, he'll go on and on and on stealing from us. His greed will grow and grow and never be sated if we don't oppose him now. Don't you see that it's absolutely essential for our long-term survival to take a stand against him?'

There was silence and then people began to whisper amongst themselves.

Venetia waited, her stomach churning. 'I don't mean to add to your worries,' she insisted. 'I just want us to discuss how we might protect ourselves from our common enemy. Perhaps, for example, we could share the cost of a watchman for a night patrol?'

'There'd have to be at least two,' said Mr Hayes from the glover's, 'so one could run for assistance. And they'd need to be armed.'

A woman in a blue coat waved to catch Venetia's attention. 'Perhaps the watchmen could carry whistles.'

'That's a good idea,' said Venetia. Were these the first signs of growing support?

The wife of the glove-maker waved a hand for attention. 'Now Napoleon has abdicated our son will be coming home, along with many other soldiers. Perhaps he and some of his friends could help us?'

'I'm an old soldier and still have my musket,' said Mr Wheeler of the grate and stove shop.

'King Midas is a vicious man,' said Jack, 'and you're right to be afraid of what he or his minions might do if you oppose him.'

'All the more reason to put an end to his tyranny,' Venetia spoke up. 'If we don't act, nothing will change!'

Voices were raised as the shopkeepers argued amongst themselves until Venetia called for quiet again.

'I suggest we vote to see how many of us wish to unite to protect ourselves,' she said, 'and how many prefer to let matters continue as they stand.'

A murmur of assent rose from the gathering.

'In that case, raise your hand if you want to leave things as they are.'

Charles and Edwin Murchison were the first to vote, quickly followed by Jack.

Venetia wasn't sure if she was relieved or sorry as, one by one, more and more hands went up. At least half of the assembly seemed to be voting to do nothing. She counted the show of hands. 'Nineteen,' she called out.

Jack nodded in agreement.

'And now please lift your hand if you want to take part in ending this tyranny.'

The hands were raised more hesitantly this time but then Mama raised hers confidently, smiling at her neighbours. Raffie thrust his arm in the air, quickly followed by Florence and Mr Bernstein the furrier. Gradually others voted, too.

Venetia raised her own hand and then began to count. 'Twenty-two!' she called out.

'Objection!' Jack scowled at her. 'My sister is too young to have a vote.'

Venetia hesitated and then nodded. 'But there's still a majority.'

He turned his palms up and shrugged. 'In that case, I must bow to that majority, whatever I may think of the wisdom of the decision. Now we need to discuss our next steps.'

He'd taken defeat better than Venetia had expected.

'Those of you who wish to leave are welcome to do so,' said Jack, addressing the gathering.

Four people stood up to go: Mrs Benson, the Murchisons and Mr Johnson from the stationer's. Mrs Benson waited for her husband but he sat with his hands clenched in his lap, staring at his boots. After a moment she sniffed and followed the others to the door.

'Tomorrow evening,' said Jack, 'Lovell and Chamberlaine expect a visit from King Midas to collect our first payment. Does anyone else anticipate a call from him tomorrow night?'

'I do,' said Mr Bernstein.

'Yes,' said Mr Elliot the draper.

'I tell you now,' said Jack, 'if we commit ourselves to this course of action there can be no going back. Ever. There are bound to be repercussions and we must stand united and vigilant. Do you all understand?'

He waited, looking around the shop to see if anyone wavered. Several people shuffled their feet but no one walked away.

'We must discuss our strategy for the confrontation between the Shopkeepers' Militia and King Midas tomorrow night,' he said. 'How many of you have weapons?'

Several men crowded around Jack and suddenly Venetia felt quite light-headed. Weapons? She'd set a train of events in motion that would place them all in terrible danger. There would be fighting and men might kill or be killed. Feeling apprehensive she went to sit beside Mama and Florence.

Some time later Jack left the group of men arguing over tactics and came to speak to them. 'So your impassioned plea for action has borne fruit, Venetia, and our course is set,' he said. 'I sincerely hope we don't regret it.' He sighed. 'I'm going out now. I have urgent business to attend to so don't wait up for me.'

Venetia watched him leave, a heavy weight in her heart. Had she driven a further wedge between them?

Mama squeezed her hand. 'Your father would have been so proud of you,' she whispered.

Tears sprang to Venetia's eyes. Or would Father have considered her unutterably reckless? Whatever he might have thought, it was too late for her to go back now.

Chapter 22

Kitty finished unpicking the embroidered name from the last hand-kerchief and put down her scissors.

'You've made a neat job of that,' said Nat.

'If the doctor's name hadn't been Higginbotham I'd have been quicker,' she said with a smile. 'Next time pick a house-hold where they're called Lee.' She plucked the iron from the fire, which sizzled when she spat on it. She smoothed the hand-kerchiefs, folding them neatly so that any darns were on the inside.

Nat closed the shutters and then grunted as he heaved up the floorboard. He withdrew two of the sacks. 'Here, you open one,' he said as he untied the drawstring.

Kitty worked her thumbnail under the coarse string and released the knot. She took out several gold snuffboxes, a couple of watches, four silver teaspoons, a gold seal and several pieces of jewellery. Amongst them were the pearl earrings, the necklace of green stones, two cravat pins and the sapphire ring that she'd taken from the bedroom in the doctor's house. She slipped the ring on to her finger and held out her hand. Now that it wasn't always red and cracked from scrubbing it could almost pass for a lady's hand. Smiling, she lifted the necklace to her throat and felt the cool, heavy stones on her neck. They sent a shiver of excitement down her back.

'Don't go getting no ideas,' said Nat. 'We need to sell this lot.'

'I know that, don't get in a kerfuffle!' said Kitty.

'Don't take too much at once.' Nat fingered the jewellery, picking up each piece one at a time, and taking it near to the candle for a closer look. 'Go to two different pawnshops. Spin them the yarn that you've only recently arrived in London and need to sell these family pieces to tide you over until you've found work.'

Kitty nodded. That didn't sound too hard. Why, it was almost the truth!

'You can wear the ring for today. Never does any harm to look well off as they're less likely to think you've pinched the pieces. And it's not so valuable that anyone'll be on the look out for it. Take the necklace and the cravat pins to the pawnshop and the pearl earrings and the silver spoons to Mary Spiggott.'

'What about the handkerchiefs?'

'They're going to my barrows. I'll do the rounds now while you visit Uncle. I'll shift more of the silver plate over the next few days. I always let it go a few pieces at a time. Draws less notice that way.'

Kitty collected up the items to sell and placed them into the pockets tied around her waist under her skirt. Pockets were old-fashioned and spoiled the line of her dress but she wasn't going to risk having the jewellery pinched on the way to the pawnbroker's. King's Castle was full of villains.

Nat tucked the handkerchiefs into his coat. 'All set?'

On the bottom step the red-headed Irishman from the downstairs left sprawled snoring, reeking of ale. Kitty grimaced but Nat took no notice at all. Candlelight had made his lodgings look romantic but since she'd seen them by day she'd been shocked to discover how squalid everything was. Rags were stuffed in broken windows and the flaking paint had faded to a dingy brown. The stairs were filthy with years of encrusted dirt and the leaking roof made the walls black with mould. Once the goods were sold she was going to insist they move somewhere better.

The landlord, Mr O'Leary, peered out of his door as they passed. He gave Kitty the shrims, always creeping about on the stairs and watching her as she came and went. His eyes were perpetually bloodshot and he stank of gin and piss.

Nat kept a tight hold on her arm as they wended their way through the maze of alleys until they reached the Goat and Compass. 'Cobbett's Court is down this alley and you need to turn into Salt Lane. Halfway down on the left is a house selling red herrings. Go in the side door and ask for Mary Spiggott.'

Kitty frowned. 'If I'm supposed to have just arrived from Kent, how would I know about her?'

'Tell her you met Ruth in the Goat and she said to visit her. And you'll find Moses Levy's pawnshop in Tanner's Yard a bit further down the alley. There are golden balls hanging up outside. He's a hard bargainer. Will you be all right?'

'I've never done this before.' Suppose she couldn't sell the goods?

'Don't worry, sweetheart, you'll manage. And when you've finished come back to the Goat and wait for me. I'm meeting Lennie there to find out more about this job he's got wind of.'

Kitty watched him walk away, his hat set at a jaunty angle, and smiled to herself. There were women who'd give their eyeteeth to marry a man as handsome as her Nat, never mind as kind.

Grubby washing was festooned from the rotting timber galleries that clung to the crumbling brickwork on the upper storeys of Cobbett's Court. Barefoot children crouched in the gutter, busy damming the flow of putrid water with clumps of mud.

She glanced up as she heard a casement creak open and leaped backwards as a woman emptied a bucket of stinking slops out of the window.

'Watch out!' Kitty yelled. Up above, the casement slammed shut but not before she heard the woman cackle. Filthy slattern! Shaking her skirts, Kitty picked her way through the foul puddle. There was poverty at home in Kent but none of the women she knew there would have dreamed of living in such nasty conditions.

She crossed the court and entered the narrow passage between two ramshackle houses, unsure if this was Salt Lane. A moment later she caught the pervasive whiff of smoked fish and guessed she was in the right place after all. Red herrings, tied in pairs by their tails, were hung up inside the open door.

A fat woman in a stained apron peered out at her. 'Nice bit of fish for your dinner, dearie?'

Kitty shook her head. 'I'm looking for Mary Spiggott.'

'Round the side.'

The staircase was steep and rickety but there was a door half-open at the top. 'Mrs Spiggott?' Kitty called.

The door creaked. 'Who wants her?' A woman with a pock-marked face and her hair in grey-streaked rat's tails peered out at her from behind the door.

'I'm told you buy things. I've some spoons.'

'Who told you?' Mary's voice was sharp.

'Ruth. I met her in the Goat and Compass.'

The door opened wider, releasing the fetid smell of unwashed bed linen

'Whatcha got?'

Kitty delved in her pocket, took out the four silver teaspoons and the pearl earrings, all wrapped in a silk handkerchief, and put them on the table.

Mary's sunken eyes gleamed as she looked at them. 'Very nice. Pawn or sell?'

'Sell,' said Kitty.

Mary picked up one of the earrings and scraped the pearl against a blackened tooth. 'Real, then.' She looked at Kitty through narrowed eyes. 'I'm not going to have the constable knocking on my door?'

Kitty opened her eyes very wide. 'Certainly not!' she said. 'My grandma was a lady's maid and her mistress gave them to her. And the spoons have been in my family for years.'

Mary went to her chest of drawers and Kitty heard the chink of coins. She forced herself not to grin.

Mary placed the coins, one by one, on the table.

'But that's not enough! The spoons alone are worth more than that.'

Shrugging, Mary waited.

Two could play at that game! Kitty gathered up the spoons, polishing the fingerprints off on the handkerchief. 'That's a handsome pattern on the handle. No scratches neither and there's a set. Still, if you don't want them, I'll take 'em elsewhere.'

'Won't make no difference.'

'I'm not desperate,' said Kitty. She began to wrap the spoons in the handkerchief.

Mary placed another coin on the table.

Kitty looked at it and raised her eyebrows, picked up an earring and held it to her ear, turning to show Mary. 'Pretty, ain't it? Maybe I'll keep them after all.'

Mary sighed. 'My, but you're a hard-hearted girl.' She slammed another fistful of coins on the table.

Pursing her lips, Kitty counted them. That was more like it! 'I'm still not sure.'

One more coin joined the rest.

'You've got yourself a bargain,' said Kitty, gathering up the money.

Mary snatched up the spoons and earrings.

'Do you mind?' said Kitty. She whisked away the silk handkerchief wrapped around the spoons. 'That's extra.'

'Get along home with you,' said Mary, a sour expression on her pockmarked face.

Kitty was halfway out of the door when Mary called after her.

'Come and see me when you want to sell that ring.'

Kitty clattered down the stairs.

In Tanner's Yard three golden balls, sadly tarnished, hung above a low doorway where the name *Moses Levy* was painted on a signboard. She peered in through the window but the glass was too grimy for her to see anything.

Inside it took a moment for her eyes to penetrate the gloomy interior. A lamp burned on the counter, shedding a feeble glow. Shelves of folded blankets and clothing and cabinets of silver and trinkets lined the walls. All at once the hairs on the back of her neck prickled. She was being watched.

'Hello?' she said.

There was a faint sound and she saw an elderly man sitting in the shadows, a blanket tucked over his knees. White hair fell to his shoulders from under a black skullcap. He levered himself to his feet and regarded her with sharply inquisitive dark eyes. 'You have something for Moses?'

She withdrew the items from her pocket.

He picked up the cravat pins and then the necklace with a claw-like hand, nails yellow and thickened with age. Holding the necklace towards the lamp, he studied the stones. 'Where did you get this?'

'It was my grandmother's,' lied Kitty. Nan had never owned any jewellery except for her wedding band.

'It is precious to you?' asked Moses.

'I don't want to sell it but since I've come to London it's taken longer than I thought to find work.'

Moses glanced at her wedding ring. 'Does your husband not provide for you?'

219

'Oh. He ...' Kitty swallowed. She hadn't expected to be questioned. 'He died,' she said. 'A storm at sea. He was a fisherman.'

Moses felt inside his grimy coat and dropped a fistful of coins on the counter.

Kitty stared at them. 'They're worth far more than that.'

'I'll write you a ticket. You must pay me back in a month or I'll sell them. The stones aren't of the best quality and the gold of the cravat pin is not pure.'

'But ...'

He hunched his shoulders.

'Can't you give me more?'

He shrugged, turning his palms up. 'Do you want to see a poor old man starve? Take it or leave it.' He drew an inkwell towards him and began to write the date and the description of the items on a scrap of paper.

One by one, she picked up the coins. Miserable old nipfarthing! He laid down the quill and Kitty snatched the ticket and thrust it in her pocket, along with the measly handful of coins.

It was as she turned to leave that she saw it. She peered into a glass-fronted cabinet. 'Where'd you get that?' she asked, pointing.

'Not for sale ... not yet,' said the old man.

'Let me see.'

Slowly, Moses Levy pulled a key chain out of his pocket. He rested it on the counter and thumbed through the thirty or so small keys until he found the right one.

Kitty bit her tongue with impatience as he unhurriedly fitted the key in the cabinet lock.

At last he lifted the item out of the cupboard and, taking the weight in both hands, placed it on the counter.

Kitty touched the cold metal. The bronze horse still shook his mane and pawed the ground, frozen at a particular moment in time, just as she remembered him. Could Miss Venetia have brought it in? But she'd loved the little statuette and had even jokingly said she hoped it never sold so that she could keep it. 'Where'd you get this?' asked Kitty.

Moses looked at her, his eyes wary. 'My business is confidential. Would you like it if I blabbed to all and sundry about our little transaction?'

'It's stolen,' said Kitty.

He looked at her, eyebrows raised. 'That's an unfounded accusation. And you still say that the necklace and cravat pins came from your grandmother?'

'Of course.' But she couldn't meet his eyes.

'Go now.' He picked up the horse and turned his back on her while he locked it away again. Then, muttering under his breath, he hobbled through a door behind the counter, closing it firmly behind him.

Kitty gnawed at her fingernail. There was nothing for her to do except leave.

Kitty's gaze searched the taproom of the Goat and Compass. Two lads, already bleary-eyed, called to her to sit with them. She pushed past without answering, slapping their hands away as they snatched at her skirt. Ignorant oafs! Then she saw Ruth, waving.

'Nat and Lennie ain't here yet, then?' Kitty asked as she sat down.

Ruth shook her head, pushing a glass of port towards her. 'I got one in for you.'

The landlord's dog, a young lurcher, came to sniff her hand.

'Thanks.' Kitty sipped her drink and patted the dog, who curled up by her feet. She glanced around but no one sat too close. 'Nat told me Lennie's heard about another job?' she whispered.

Ruth pulled a face and then drained her glass.

'What's the matter?'

'Oh, I don't know.' Ruth's freckled face was worried. 'Lennie always been ...'

'Go on!'

221

'He's a simple soul. That's why I love him. But he believes everything he's told, even by me.' She grinned. 'He says I look on the black side but someone's got to.'

'How d'you mean?'

'It's this job, see. Ask Nat what he thinks of Samuel Horne. He's older than Nat and Lennie. Another of Ma Slattery's boys but I don't like him.'

Kitty didn't see what Ruth was on about. 'What's he got to do with anything?'

'It's Samuel who told Nat about this job. Can't put my finger on it but …' She broke off as they saw Nat and Lennie coming into the taproom, followed by a skinny man with ginger hair and a cocksure swagger.

'That's Samuel,' said Ruth, nudging Kitty in the ribs.

'How's my best girl?' asked Nat, sitting down beside Kitty. He bent to pat the dog. 'Did you sell the goods?'

'I did. But I saw something in the pawnshop …'

He laughed. 'You can't go spending the money straight off!'

'I'm not,' she protested.

'Are we going to talk about this job or not?' said Lennie. 'Only Samuel wants to know today.'

The other man nodded, rasping his fingers over the gingery bristles on his chin. 'Else I'll let someone else have it. Need to move fast.' He stared at Kitty and then at Ruth for a moment and jerked his thumb over his shoulder. 'Out. This is men's talk.'

Indignant, Kitty glanced at Nat.

He squeezed her hand under the table. 'Better go, sweetheart. Wait for me outside, eh?'

Lennie kept his eyes fixed on his tankard of ale.

Ruth, red in the face, stood up too. 'Come on, Kitty. Let's find better company.'

'Watch your mouth, baggage!' said Samuel. He kicked the dog away and plumped down on the settle.

As they left the taproom Kitty glanced back at the three men, leaning over the table with their heads together. Samuel seemed to be doing the talking.

'That's a nasty piece of work if ever I saw one,' she said.

Chapter 23

Venetia hurried through the darkening streets. She'd promised Jack to return before dark and hadn't meant to be so long at Mrs de Vere's house in Berkeley Square. The wretched woman had been unable to make up her mind between the figured silk and the Indian chintz and then rattled on for an hour about the style of curtain and choice of trim.

Venetia had listened to the hall clock ticking the minutes away while she was involved in a trivial conversation about *passementerie* tassels and galloon braid. Growing increasingly anxious, she'd eventually suggested that Mrs de Vere should borrow the samples and then Venetia made a hasty retreat.

The lamps were being lit above the shop doors when she reached Cheapside. Carriages were driving along at a spanking pace and pie sellers briskly touted their wares. All good wives had gone home. The remaining women parading the pavements were of a different class entirely, either hanging on to the arm of chance-met gentlemen or importuning them from the shadows.

Venetia glanced at each shop as she walked past, noticing that several had sign cards propped up in the window display that read:

Protected by the Shopkeepers' Militia. Her breathing quickened and she began to run. It really was going to happen then; they were uniting to see off King Midas.

Mr Bernstein was lighting the lamps in the window of the furrier's and waved at her. She opened the door and went inside his shop.

'Are you prepared?' she asked. The odour of mothballs rose up from the fur hats, muffs and tippets arranged on the counter but it was impossible for her to resist running her fingers over the silky softness of the sealskin coats and luxurious blankets trimmed with silver fox.

Mr Bernstein reached under the counter and showed her a wooden crow-scarer. 'My son Jacob is keeping watch outside. If he hears this, he'll bring help.'

Venetia put her hands over her ears to keep out the deafening racket as he whirled it around his head. 'My brother's on watch, too,' she said.

'One of my cousins from Spitalfields has been paying King Midas for years and he's here to support us.' Mr Bernstein's jowls wobbled as he shook his head sorrowfully. 'That man's tentacles reach far and wide. I've sent my wife to her sister's house for the evening.'

'I'm going to wait with Major Chamberlaine.'

'You should be at home with your mother,' said Mr Bernstein, concern on his face.

Venetia gave a half smile. 'Since I instigated the militia I can hardly draw back now, can I?'

'Many ladies would,' said Mr Bernstein, folding his hands across his stomach. 'Take care, Miss Lovell. We all know this piece of dreck likes to pick on those weaker than himself.'

Soon after, as Venetia passed the draper's, Mr Elliot was peering anxiously out of the door.

'Are you ready?' she asked.

'My apprentice and three of my brothers are outside,' he said.

'And my clerk waits with me. We have a butcher's knife and a stout stick, but I don't mind telling you I'm a peaceful man and hold no hope of being able to protect myself with a knife.'

'I trust it won't come to that,' said Venetia. Mr Elliot, undersized and skinny, didn't look like a man who'd do well in a fight. 'The others will be watching and will run to your aid if necessary. Who knows? If we make a stand at the first shop that King Midas visits, he may not call on the others.'

'But then he might come back another time.' Close to tears, Mr Elliot ran a hand over his thinning hair. 'I have my wife to support. Heaven knows what would happen to her if I ...'

'Is your whistle to hand?' Earlier that morning, after he'd been to the rifle range with Jack, Venetia had sent Raffie out to buy all the whistles he could find and distribute them to the shopkeepers.

Mr Elliot pulled a whistle out of his waistcoat pocket and she smiled at him encouragingly. He wiped beads of perspiration from his forehead. 'I hope we haven't made a terrible mistake.'

'We cannot live with this kind of fear, Mr Elliot,' said Venetia. 'King Midas's greed will continue to grow. If we unite to fight him we'll make him realise that his hold over us has weakened. It's the only way.'

'I don't look any further ahead than praying we're still alive in the morning.'

'I must go,' she said.

A high-perch phaeton, going much too fast, raced by and, as she stepped back from the following cloud of dust, a hand snatched at Venetia's sleeve. Whirling around in fright, she found her brother behind her. 'You scared me!' she said, pressing a hand to her heart.

'Sorry.' Raffie's face was pinched with apprehension. He looked far too young to be risking such danger.

'You haven't seen King Midas yet?'

He shook his head. 'We're posted outside every fourth shop. As soon as he appears we'll follow him. There are a considerable number of friends and relatives with us. If we can, we'll send a runner on ahead to warn the shopkeepers.'

'I'm going to wait with Jack.'

'Don't worry, Venetia.' Raffie's face was pale in the half-dark. 'I won't let that Midas brute hurt you again.' He sloped off without a backward glance.

Now that she was looking, Venetia saw other shopkeepers: kicking their heels as they stared into the illuminated shop windows or lurking in groups of two or three at the end of alleys. Another four slouched beside a stall selling hot potatoes. Several carried heavy canes and she wondered if they also had knives or pistols.

The 'Closed' sign was already facing the street as she pushed open the door to Lovell and Chamberlaine.

'There you are at last!' said Jack, drawing her swiftly inside.

'I called in on Mr Bernstein and Mr Elliot to see if they were prepared ...' She broke off as she saw that Jack held a pistol in his hand.

'I've given the other one to Raffie,' he said. 'We've put in considerable practice at the shooting range and I'm confident that he's capable of using it.'

Venetia swallowed. 'It frightens me to think of what might happen if you have to use them.'

'It's too late for that.' He took hold of her shoulders and turned her to face him. 'Venetia, I admire you for fighting for what you believe in but in my opinion you were wrong to propel a group of very ordinary shopkeepers into thinking they can defeat King Midas. Blood will be shed.'

'I can't bear the injustice of his actions.' She noticed the gleam in Jack's eyes and frowned. 'In spite of your opposition, the prospect of action excites you, doesn't it?'

Carefully, he placed the gun inside his coat. 'I do not care for gratuitous violence. However, you have set our course and it's pointless to look back. It won't be easy to overcome the enemy, probably impossible, but now there's no choice but to give it our best shot.' He smiled. 'Literally, if needs be.'

Fearful of what she'd started, Venetia peered out at the street.

'We'll sit here, where we can see what's happening,' said Jack, pulling two chairs nearer the window. He'd already lit candles and they cast a warm pool of light.

Dread made Venetia queasy. When would King Midas come? Could he be persuaded that none of the shopkeepers would pay him any longer? She closed her eyes, remembering the man's cruel smile.

Jack took a hip flask from his pocket. 'Dutch courage,' he said, offering it to her.

'I don't feel brave at all,' said Venetia, taking a sip.

'You are brave,' he said quietly. 'It's courageous to stand in the face of danger to uphold your principles.'

All at once she wanted to cry. And she wanted Jack to put his arms around her and tell her that everything would be all right and that he'd keep her safe. She closed her eyes for a minute and when she opened them again he was still looking at her. The candle glow highlighted his face with gold and it was all she could do not to reach out to him.

'Venetia?' His voice was low.

'Yes?' she whispered. How she longed for him to kiss her again! To tell her that he cared for her.

Slowly, he moved his hand across the table.

She held her breath.

The tips of his fingers brushed hers and it was as if a wave of shimmering heat seared through her very bones. Drawing in her breath, she felt a sweet, sharp stab of desire in her belly.

He leaned towards her until his face was inches away.

Melting, she closed her eyes and waited for his kiss.

And then came a piercing blast from a whistle.

Jack reared to his feet and went to the door.

Venetia blinked, shocked out of her trance.

Another whistle blew and then another. A man shouted.

She ran to stand by Jack at the door and peered outside. On the other side of the road a great black coach drawn by four black horses had stopped in front of Elliot's the draper's. As she watched, men appeared from doorways all down the street and ran towards it.

'Is it King Midas?' she asked, her heart beating faster.

'I'm going to see,' said Jack, opening the door.

'Poor Mr Elliot was so frightened.' Although they'd all been expecting King Midas, it sent tremors through Venetia now that he'd actually arrived.

'Stay here, out of harm's way.'

She shook her head decisively. 'I'm coming too.' She couldn't bear to be alone, not knowing what was happening.

Jack took one look at her determined expression and shrugged. 'Stay close, then.' He tucked the pistol into the front of his jacket. 'And lock the door. We don't want to find that thieves have helped themselves.'

A crowd of men had gathered around the coach, shuffling uneasily from foot to foot. Most carried heavy sticks. A few held swords or muskets and there was a sprinkling of pitchforks. The door of the black coach remained firmly closed. The coachman up on his high perch stared woodenly ahead.

Venetia glimpsed Mr Elliot's frightened face pressed against the glass in the shop door.

Jack pushed his way through the throng and she stayed close to his side as the men stepped back to allow him through.

'What now?' asked Mr Hayes from the glove shop.

'We must talk with King Midas.' Jack rapped on the carriage door with his cane.

Venetia noticed that a gold crown was painted on the door. The insufferable conceit of the man!

Faces in the crowd were tense. Venetia's mouth was dry and

her stomach churned. Why, oh, why, had she started this? No good would come of it and someone might be hurt.

And then the coach door opened. Two burly bodyguards descended and stood as immovable as mountains at the foot of the steps, arms folded.

King Midas ducked his head as he climbed out of the carriage and stood at the top of the steps, looking down his crooked nose at them.

Venetia had forgotten how tall and broad he was in his caped greatcoat. She noticed it had a scarlet lining. The man carried such a palpable air of power and menace that she shivered.

'My, my!' he said. 'A welcoming committee.' His voice was smooth and amused.

'On the contrary,' said Jack firmly. 'You and your henchmen are unwelcome here. You will leave Cheapside and not return.'

King Midas twisted his lips into a sneer. 'Not until I collect my dues.'

Venetia's apprehension turned to boiling anger. 'We owe you nothing!' How *dare* he frighten people out of their wits and steal their money?

Jack placed a restraining hand on her arm.

Slowly, King Midas turned to look down at her with a reptilian stare. 'Miss Lovell, is it not? I do hope you aren't going to be a troublemaker like your father.'

'We won't allow you to steal from us.' Her hands were balled into fists to stop them from shaking and her nails bit into her palms. 'There'll be no more payments. Not one.'

King Midas sighed. 'Then there's going to be a great deal of unpleasantness.' He scanned the crowd. 'Are you going to risk your businesses and your lives by allowing this sprig of a girl to stir up trouble? I'm a reasonable man. Make your payments on time and your businesses, and those you love, will be safe.'

Kitty caught sight of Raffie's face in the crowd as he stared at King Midas's bodyguards.

'We'll no longer be intimidated by your threats,' said Jack.

King Midas raised one eyebrow. He searched the crowd until his gaze rested on Mr Wheeler. 'You advertise your patented stoves and grates as bang up to the mark with unrivalled safety features. How ironic if your shop should burn down!'

Mr Wheeler raised his stick and shook it. 'We're not letting you terrorise us any more. Just you try it and see what happens!'

'Idle threats, Wheeler,' said King Midas. 'I shall strike when you least expect it. I never tolerate insolence and you will pay thrice-fold for it. Who can say if your family will be burned alive while they sleep?'

Mr Wheeler's face turned as white as whey.

King Midas scanned the faces turned towards him and focused his attention on the baker. 'You there.' He pointed. 'What a pity if you put your pretty daughter in harm's way, Benson. She's ten years old, I believe. You cannot watch her all the time. My associates will pay a good price for a virgin. And with the judicious use of pig's blood, she can remain apparently pure for at least thirty men. After that, of course, she'll have fallen victim to the pox and be of no further use.'

'You lily-livered bastard!' Mr Benson raised his stick and lunged towards King Midas, scarlet-faced with fury. 'I'll kill you if you come within a stone's throw of my daughter.'

King Midas threw his head back and laughed.

The bodyguards stopped Mr Benson in his tracks. One of them caught his wrist and twisted it until he yelped and dropped his stick. The two men set about him with their fists and, when he moaned and collapsed to the ground, began to kick him mercilessly.

'Don't just watch!' screamed Venetia. 'They'll kill him!'

Jack grabbed her arm and pulled her back. 'Go to the shop! Now!' He took the pistol out of his jacket, raised it in the air.

Jolted out of inertia as the shot ricocheted around the street, the crowd surged forward. Venetia was sent spinning by men pushing

231

past her, shouting and yelling as they bore down on the coach. From his high perch at the front, the coachman laid about the mob with his whip.

Jack thrust Venetia to one side and hurled himself into the action.

She huddled in the doorway of the draper's shop, unable to believe how fast the violence had escalated. Then she saw Mr Benson curled up on the ground while the others trampled him underfoot in their determination to reach King Midas. She thrust her way through the horde and, crouching down, grabbed hold of the baker's collar.

Mr Benson's hands were over his ears. His eyes opened when he felt Venetia tugging at his clothing. Shocked, he stared at her, blood dripping from his nose and mouth.

'Come on!' she shouted, then yelped as a heavy boot came down on her fingers. Hauling on Mr Benson's arm, she rolled him on to his knees. Groaning, he forced himself into a crouch and she put her arms around his waist and dragged him up. Panting with effort, she pushed and kicked a passage for them through the mob. They emerged from the melee, buffeted and bruised, and she half carried him into the doorway of the draper's shop.

Mr Elliot let them in. 'It's a calamity! King Midas will kill us all.'

'Fetch this man some brandy,' said Venetia. 'And warm water and clean cloths to bind his wounds.' She set Mr Benson down on a chair and loosened his necktie.

'Thank you,' mumbled Mr Benson. One bloodshot eye was rapidly swelling and his mouth and cheek were cut.

The shop door burst open and Mrs Benson ran in. 'Where is he?' Sobbing, she hurried to her husband and threw her arms around him.

He cried out in pain

'I thought they'd killed you.' She smothered him in kisses, stroking his hair. 'And why aren't you out there, helping them?' she demanded of Mr Elliot.

232

Venetia left her to minister to her husband and returned outside. A stone whistled past her ear and the coachman clapped a hand to his head. He looked at the blood on his fingers and roared, redoubling his efforts with the whip, lashing out at the men scrambling on to the coach.

The two bodyguards fought like madmen, their superior strength and physique enabling them to swat their adversaries away as if they were flies.

King Midas remained on the coach steps, surveying the commotion with a scornful smile.

Venetia stared anxiously into the heaving mass of men. Where was Jack? His bad knee would make him vulnerable. She glimpsed Raffie's blond head and then he'd gone again. Please God, don't let either of them be hurt!

A knot of ragged children were throwing stones, shrieking with glee. A dog sank its teeth into Mr Bernstein's ankle and refused to let go.

One of the bodyguards snatched a pitchfork from a shopkeeper and, laughing, broke it across his knee.

The owner of the perfume shop had levered up a paving slab. He lifted it high and brought it down with a thud on the head of the laughing man, who dropped like a lead weight.

A roar of approval went up from the crowd and they set about the remaining bodyguard with pitchforks, sticks and fists.

King Midas's scornful smile slipped. He took a pistol from inside his coat and took aim. A sharp crack rang out and a man screamed and fell to the ground.

A woman shrieked.

One of the horses whinnied and took fright, rearing up and pawing the air while the coachman tried to regain control.

King Midas disappeared inside the coach.

The other bodyguard dragged his henchman off the pavement and threw him into the coach.

The coachman cracked his whip and the wheels began to roll. The next moment the street echoed to the thunder of horses' hooves as King Midas and his men made a rapid escape in a swirl of dust.

Chapter 24

Kitty, wearing her green silk dress and a new hat, ambled along Cheapside. She practised a gliding walk, taking small steps and kicking her skirts out in front of her.

She tarried before any window display that caught her eye, looking at frilled silk parasols, lace gloves and trimmed bonnets. It made her smile to think that now there was no one to scold her and tell her to get back to work.

Peering into Wheeler's grate and stove shop, she studied the gleaming black stoves. One of them, made of steel with brass trimmings, was just what she'd like, when they had a better place to live. Then she'd be able to show Nat that she could cook a tasty beef and oyster pudding instead of having to bring something home from the pie shop.

She stopped before the draper's because the blinds were pulled down. Funny that, in the middle of the day. On the edge of the pavement, waiting until a carriage swished past before she crossed the street, a loose paving slab rocked under her foot and she nearly turned her ankle.

Once safely over the road, she made for Lovell and Chamberlaine.

Master Raffie opened the door for her. 'Good morning, Madam,' he said.

Kitty laughed. 'Mrs Griggs it is now. Don't you recognise me?'

'Kitty?' Master Raffie's eyes danced with sudden amusement. 'You're looking all the go, if you don't mind my saying so?'

'Delighted, I'm sure! How's tricks?'

The amusement faded from Master Raffie's face. 'There was a riot yesterday and Mr Elliot from the draper's shop was shot and badly injured.'

'Here, in Cheapside?' She glanced outside at the pavement crowded with shoppers. 'What happened?'

'Well, there's a man called King Midas and he's been demanding money from the shopkeepers. If we don't pay him, he'll send his men to break up the premises, or worse. We've told him we're not paying him any more and he didn't like it. When Mr Elliot came out of his shop King Midas shot him, to make an example of him, I suppose.'

Kitty winced. 'I've heard about King Midas. He's a dangerous cove and no mistake.'

'Major Chamberlaine went with some of the men to report him to the constable,' said Master Raffie. 'You'd think they'd hang this King Midas character, wouldn't you? But no one seems to know where he lives. In any case, the constable is frightened witless and he's not going to look very hard.'

'Disgusting that he gets away with it,' said Kitty. She glanced around the shop and saw Mrs Lovell and Florence measuring out a bolt of cloth together at the counter. 'May I have a word with Miss Venetia?'

'She's in the office.' Raffie set off with Kitty following. The office door was ajar. 'Mrs Griggs to see you, Venetia,' he said.

She looked up and Kitty couldn't help but notice the dark shadows under her eyes. Nevertheless, she smiled.

'Kitty! How lovely to see you looking so well. Married life must be suiting you.'

236

'Oh, it is, Miss Venetia! I'm sorry for the disturbance but there's something I should tell you.'

'Oh?'

'There's a shop in Whitechapel, a pawnshop ...'

'I'm not sure I understand.'

'You said there isn't another one like it but I've seen one in the pawnshop ... the bronze horse, Miss. It must be yours.'

'But our bronze horse is here.' Miss Venetia frowned and rose to her feet. 'I'm sure it must be. Shall we go and see?'

They walked into the showroom but could not see the statuette.

'Have you moved the bronze horse, Mama?' asked Miss Venetia.

Mrs Lovell shook her head.

'I dusted it only the other day,' said Miss Florence.

'Kitty has seen a horse just like it in a pawnshop.'

'But there is only one!' said Mrs Lovell. 'Could a customer have stolen it?'

'Surely we'd have noticed?' said Miss Florence.

'Kitty, will you give me the direction to this pawnshop?' asked Miss Venetia.

'Don't go on your own, Miss. It's not a nice place for a lady.' She described how to find it.

'I'll ask Major Chamberlaine to accompany me.'

'I'll be off then,' said Kitty.

Miss Florence walked with her to the door. 'Are you happy?' she asked.

Kitty was struck again by the girl's lovely eyes. The dead spit of Miss Venetia, she was. 'Happier than you can imagine,' she said.

'I'm glad.' Miss Florence smiled. 'Come and see us again.'

'I will,' said Kitty, touched. Miss Florence was a sweet girl with no airs and graces. She closed the shop door behind her and set off home.

The last of the light was fading when Kitty stretched and threw back the sheet.

The canary in the cage by the window tucked her head down on her breast.

Kitty turned and smiled at Nat, still dozing beside her. She had to keep pinching herself to be sure she wasn't dreaming. Only a few months ago she'd never have believed she'd be married to a man she loved with all her heart, lazing around in bed after making love in the afternoon.

Nat's dark eyes were open now and she touched his thin, clever face, running her fingers over the stubble on his chin.

He kissed her palm. 'We're going places, you and me.' He glanced at the mould stains on the wall. 'Don't think I haven't noticed you turning up your nose at our lodgings. Hadn't really noticed it meself but you're used to better. And you shall have better, my queen.'

Kitty bit her lip. 'I don't mean to be ungrateful.'

'I know that, sweetheart.'

'Only ... imagine if we had a little kitchen where I could cook your dinner.'

'And you shall have it.' He trailed his fingernails down her bare shoulder in a way that made her shiver with wanting him again. 'This job of Samuel's tonight,' he said, 'it's a big one. I couldn't decide whether to go for it at first but if we pull it off we'll be in new lodgings within a week.'

'Really?' Kitty sat up in bed with her arms around her knees, imagining a couple of rooms with fresh paint and a sunlit window.

'Samuel knows of a coiner, see.'

'A what?'

'A queer bit-maker.' Nat laughed and ruffled Kitty's hair as she frowned in puzzlement. 'By day he's a watchmaker but at night he makes coins: sixpences, half crowns, guineas and Portugese *moidores*. He's a widower and there's no live-in servant neither so, when he's out, the crib's empty. Samuel's persuaded one of the girls from Mother Murray's nunnery to sweet talk the watchmaker. So the cove's falling over himself trying to get under her skirt and she's promised to show him her muff if he'll take her to the theatre first. The house'll be empty this evening.'

'Crafty!'

Nat nodded. 'Samuel always were wily. Bit tricksy sometimes but quick.'

'Ruth told me he was at Ma Slattery's too.'

'Felt the rough side of his hand a few times when I were a nipper but there weren't no real harm in it.'

Whatever Nat said, she didn't like Samuel. Not one bit. Gave her the creeps. Nat'd have to watch his back to get his fair share from the job. 'I want to come with you tonight,' Kitty said.

'Samuel wouldn't like that.'

'Please, Nat! I can help to move the goods away more quickly.'

He sucked his teeth thoughtfully for a moment. 'Tell you what, tag along ... but if Samuel's not happy you'll have to leave.'

She nodded.

'And you'd better put on some of my togs. You can move faster in breeches.'

Kitty laughed. 'What a lark!'

'Get up then, you lazy baggage.'

She stood up and stretched.

Nat smacked her across her naked backside and, when she squealed, threw back the sheet and chased her round the room before carrying her back to bed.

Kitty, Nat, Ruth and Lennie left the Goat and Compass fortified by a nip of gin and made their way by moonlight through the alleys and backstreets of Whitechapel.

Samuel was waiting for them in the shadows on the corner of Plough Street, leaning on a handcart. 'Who's this?' he asked, lifting up his lantern and staring at Kitty.

'She's going to help shift the swag,' said Nat.

'And Ruth's going to keep watch,' said Lennie.

Kitty didn't like the way Samuel looked at her legs revealed by Nat's breeches.

Samuel shrugged. 'They aren't getting a share.'

'Fair enough,' said Nat.

They followed him as he pushed the handcart through an archway into Lead Yard, which was edged by ramshackle houses, and then into an alley behind.

'You!' He caught hold of Ruth's arm and nodded his head at a doorway. 'Wait here. If anyone comes down the passage, hoot like an owl.'

She took up her station without a word.

'Will you be all right?' whispered Kitty.

Ruth nodded. 'Don't fancy going inside the house anyway.'

Samuel forced the lock on a back gate and pushed the handcart into the yard.

The house was in darkness. For a few minutes they waited, listening. Then Lennie levered open the kitchen casement and shutter and scrambled inside.

Samuel parked the handcart by the back door, dragged back the canvas cover and gathered up a pile of sacks.

Kitty jiggled up and down. Nerves made her want the privy. She was flooded with that strange excitement she'd felt last time they'd gone housebreaking, a mixture of terror and elation. She was scared but what was that against the hope of such rich pickings? She almost laughed aloud at the thought of what they'd do with all those golden guineas.

Inside, Lennie scraped back the bolts and then they were in.

Uncovering their lanterns, they looked around. The kitchen, none too clean in Kitty's opinion, led to a parlour. The dining table was littered with fancy clocks, watches, brass pendulums, tiny gear wheels and painted clock faces.

'Cellar's under the kitchen,' said Samuel. 'You,' he nodded at Kitty, 'go upstairs and check there's no one here.'

The hairs on Kitty's neck stood up. 'I thought there weren't any live-in servants?'

'Don't argue!'

Silently, Nat handed her his lantern.

Kitty crept up the staircase, wondering if her trembling knees would reach the top. What did Samuel expect her to do if someone was there? She had no weapon to defend herself. At the top of the stairs she stopped, listening, but all she could hear was the blood pulsing in her ears.

It was a mean little house and neither of the two bedrooms had anything of interest in them. If the watchmaker hoped to bed his wench in that fusty-smelling room she wouldn't have to be too particular.

Downstairs again, Kitty found the kitchen table pushed to one side and the trapdoor lifted. Peering into the hole, she heard the men's muted voices. She let herself down the creaking ladder and held up the lamp. There was a workbench against one wall with a shelf above lined with half-used candles. On the bench were files, presses, basins and piles of sixpences and shillings but no guineas.

The brick walls were lined with shelves, all crowded with tea chests, broken chairs, old boots, cooking pots, wine bottles and the remains of a smoked ham. The cloying stench of damp and mould nearly choked her.

'Where are the guineas?' muttered Lennie as he and Nat rootled through the junk.

'They must be here!' Samuel began to sweep everything off the shelves.

Kitty jumped back as a bottle shattered on the stone floor and wine splashed over her shoes. She peered under the workbench. 'Here!'

Grunting with the effort, Samuel elbowed her aside and dragged out a metal chest.

Nat and Lennie hurried to help, heaving the chest into the

241

middle of the floor. Nat grabbed a file from the workbench and wrenched open the hasp.

Samuel raised the lid.

Kitty held up the lantern and gasped.

Lennie let out a low whistle.

'We'll be fixed up for life if we can pass off this little lot,' said Nat.

Samuel laughed and buried his hands in the mass of golden coins, lifting them up high and letting them trickle through his fingers. He kissed a handful of them and threw them in the air. They spun around, catching the lamplight until they fell to the ground.

Kitty picked one up and held it wonderingly in the palm of her hand. She'd only ever seen a guinea once or twice in her life but this one looked just like the real thing.

'The chest is too heavy to get up the stairs,' said Nat.

They hurried to scoop handfuls of coins into the sacks Samuel had brought and, when the chest was empty, began to haul them up the ladder.

'Douse your lights,' said Samuel as he opened the back door.

They formed a chain, passing the sacks swiftly from hand to hand, while Samuel stacked them on the cart.

A bubble of laughter began to build in Kitty's chest. In a moment they'd be away and a share of the guineas would be theirs. They'd find new lodgings, eat off silver dishes and she'd have a new dress every week. How could she have wasted her life scrubbing other people's floors when housebreaking was so easy? Of course, she'd needed Nat to show her how it was done. She shivered, half from the cold night air and half with a sudden pressing need. She couldn't wait any longer.

Nat passed the last sack to her from the kitchen doorway.

'Nat, I really need to go,' she whispered.

'Now?' He scratched his head. 'Do you have to?'

She nodded vigorously.

'Go to the bog-house in the yard. Be quick, mind! And open the back gate again so we can push the cart through.'

She hurried to open the gate and then lifted the latch on the lean-to, unbuttoning her breeches as she went inside. The place stank but she sighed with the sweet relief of release as she sat on the wooden board over the pit. It was as she was buttoning up again that she heard the shouts. Her stomach did a somersault and she snatched open the privy door.

Samuel raced past with the handcart and pushed through the gate.

Rage rose up inside her. The bastard was going to cheat them! But then a scream came from inside the house and she felt an icy finger of terror on the back of her neck. Her heart rattled nineteen to the dozen as she ran back to the kitchen. She stopped dead in the doorway.

A hulking great man was viciously laying about Lennie with an iron bar. Lennie screamed again, blood pouring from his head as he was knocked sideways with each blow. Another man was tussling with Nat, who squirmed and kicked in the bigger man's grasp. The men must have got in by the front door.

Kitty panicked, her breath coming in short gasps as she ran about frantically searching for a weapon.

Then Nat saw her. 'Run!' he shouted.

She couldn't leave him!

'Now! For God's sake, do as you're told! And don't come looking for me.' He grunted as another clout caught the side of his head.

Lennie fell to the floor. He wasn't screaming any more.

She turned and ran. There must be something she could use as a weapon! But the yard was empty. Sobbing, she darted through the back gate. Voices. She squinted into the moonlight. Three men were arguing with Samuel a little way along the alley. The handcart was beside them. It was then that she recognised the outline of the tallest man and it felt as if an icy hand clutched her throat. King Midas!

The men began to move towards her and she dodged back into the yard. Holding her breath, she heard the wheels of the handcart coming closer. She couldn't run back to the house and she couldn't go into the alley. The privy! Slipping inside, she pulled the door to behind her.

The handcart came to a stop outside and she heard the click of the back gate's latch. Circles of moonlight filtered through the ventilation holes in the door as she stood trembling behind it.

'You didn't think you could cheat me, did you, Samuel?' The man's voice was cold and hard.

'N-n-no ...' he stammered. 'I was bringing the guineas to you. I heard about Griggs's plan for the robbery and went along with it so I could find out more.'

There was the sound of a blow and Samuel whimpered.

'Don't lie to me!'

Holding her breath, Kitty pressed her nose to the door and peered out through the ventilation holes. King Midas was no more than six feet away. Jesus God! What if he could hear her heart thumping away fit to burst?

One of the men had Samuel's arms twisted up behind his back.

'You've nothing but water and pips in your head, Samuel,' said King Midas. 'Mother Murray came to tell me of the plan you and her doxy cooked up together. I called on the watchmaker and he was happy to co-operate with me, once I'd explained the consequences if he didn't.'

'Never meant no harm!' Samuel's voice was a nasal whine.

'As one of the guards on my guinea route to France,' said King Midas, 'you have betrayed my trust.'

'I'm sorry!' snivelled Samuel.

'There is no forgiveness.' The big man stepped back and nodded at one of his bullyboys.

Kitty saw the glint of moonlight on a blade but then the man stood in her line of sight.

Samuel wailed and began to make a strange gurgling sound. After a few moments the bully moved away. She couldn't see Samuel.

Footsteps came from the house and the other two men appeared, dragging Nat with them.

Kitty pressed her fist against her mouth to stop herself crying out. Nat sagged in his captor's grip. There was blood on his face but he was alive.

'The other one's snuffed it,' said the guard, 'and there was one who ran away.'

'He'll be too far off to catch now,' said King Midas.

The guard gave Nat a shake. 'Do you want me to finish this one?'

A shriek began to rise in Kitty's throat and her nails bit into the palms of her hands.

'Tie him up inside,' said King Midas. 'Make sure the trap to the cellar's hidden. The watchmaker will go to the police station in Lambeth Street now to report the break in. He can tell them that this man murdered his partner in crime. I want him punished as a warning to others not to meddle in my affairs. You shall stay to guard him and then make a fast exit when you hear the police arriving. I will not be connected with this affair.'

'What about Samuel?'

'Put the body on the handcart and sell it to the resurrection men.' King Midas chuckled. 'Might as well turn the evening to a profit, don't you think? Oh, and there's a dead girl in the alley for them, too. Samuel's lookout, I believe.'

Kitty's legs began to shake uncontrollably. Nat was to be taken up by the constable and Ruth, Lennie and Samuel were dead. A great roaring sound began to echo in her ears. Her knees gave way and she sank down on to the wooden seat and then, mercifully, everything went silent and black.

Chapter 25

'It's impossible to imagine that people live here,' Venetia said, wrinkling her nose at the reeking gutter. A dog paused in the act of eating a fish head and bared its teeth at them before returning to his prize.

'It's a different world from Cheapside,' Jack agreed. 'There!' He pointed his cane at a passageway beside a smoked fish shop.

The passage smelt like a cesspit and Venetia wished she'd worn stouter shoes. The rank slime underfoot seeped through the thin leather and her toes were unpleasantly moist. Stepping over a puddle, her foot plunged into a heap of stinking ordure. She'd have fallen if Jack hadn't caught her around her waist. His cane clattered to the ground as she clung to his shoulders while she found a foothold.

He teetered for a moment while he regained his own balance. 'Steady now?' he asked.

His face was only inches away from hers. A pulse began to flutter in her throat.

He must have read the desire in her eyes but he released her and she hid her mortification by picking up his cane.

He took it from her, linked her arm with his and they set off again.

The pawnbroker's, identified by the tawdry golden balls hanging above the crooked shop, had windows thick with grime.

The shop bell jingled their arrival in the murky interior. Feeble lamplight revealed a white-haired man unfolding his gaunt frame from a chair.

Venetia ran her gaze over the crowded shelves and glass-fronted cabinets but didn't see what she was looking for.

The man spread gnarled fingers on the counter. 'Do you have something for Moses Levy?'

'We do not,' said Jack. 'However, I believe you have in your possession a bronze statuette of a horse?'

Levy's sharp gaze moved slowly from Jack to Venetia.

'My maid came to tell me she had seen it here.'

'The fisherman's widow?'

Venetia frowned. What kind of story had Kitty told him? 'The statuette was stolen from us.'

'I don't accept stolen goods,' snapped Levy.

'I'm sure you don't. At least, not knowingly,' said Jack, 'but it would be awkward, would it not, if I were obliged to bring a constable to search your premises? Show us the bronze horse and we'll know if it's what we seek.'

Levy pursed his lips. 'Can you prove it belongs to you?'

Jack reached into his pocket and retrieved a bill of sale. 'You'll see several numbered items listed, all purchased from Italy. Our bronze has the numbers 4753 marked on the base.'

Slowly, Levy foraged under the counter while Venetia held her breath. Then he lifted up the horse.

'That's it!' said Venetia, reaching out.

Levy took a step back. He traced the number underneath with a yellowed fingernail. 'I paid for it in good faith.'

'Who brought it in to you?' asked Jack.

'A young pigeon fresh up to town and ripe for the plucking.' Levy shook his head, apparently considering the stupidity of the young. 'Cards and dice were his downfall, he said.'

'Can you give me a description?'

Levy gave a cynical laugh. 'What do they all look like? But he had yellow hair.'

Venetia caught her breath. Dear God! Surely it couldn't have been Raffie?

'I see.' Jack reached into his pocket and place a few coins on the counter. 'We'll take our property now but this is for your inconvenience.'

'It's not enough,' said Levy.

'I think you'll find that it is,' said Jack. 'Unless you'd like me to fetch the constable?'

Muttering under his breath, Levy lifted up the coins, tested them with his teeth and waved his visitors away.

Jack tucked the horse firmly under his arm.

Venetia couldn't bear to look at him as they crossed Tanner's Yard. Raffie had come to her for money and she'd turned him away. Had he pawned the horse to save Freddie from his creditors?

'We need to have a private word with your brother,' said Jack, his voice curt.

'I can't believe ... I don't want to believe that Raffie has done something so dreadful,' said Venetia, her eyes smarting.

'Perhaps this is the time to tell you that several small sums of money have disappeared from the cashbox recently.'

'Stolen? But why didn't you tell me before, Jack?'

'I did ask you about it. I thought ...' He walked on without looking at her.

'You suspected it was Raffie?'

He hesitated. 'I didn't know who it was. I only knew it wasn't me or Florence.'

Venetia stopped. 'And you thought it had to be one of my family?'

Jack's face was expressionless. 'Now, I believe it might have been your brother.'

Distress made Venetia almost lose her footing. 'But before that you thought it could have been me? Is that why you've ...' Tears sprang to her eyes. It was a bitter pill to swallow that he'd thought, even for a second, she might have been capable of theft. But if it had been Raffie who stole the horse, he might also have taken the money. All the efforts she had made to bring them together as a family had been undone. She could have wept.

They returned to Cheapside in silence.

A chattering crowd had gathered outside the furrier's shop and Mr Bernstein stood in the doorway, wringing his hands. Mrs Bernstein had collapsed, sobbing, into the arms of one of the female onlookers.

Jack glanced at Venetia and they pushed their way through the crowd.

'What happened?' asked Venetia.

'Oy vey! My shop has been defiled.' Distraught, Mr Bernstein dashed tears from his eyes.

Venetia went inside and stopped so suddenly that Jack walked into her. She pressed a hand over her nose.

In the centre of the floor was a tumbled pile of sable tippets, gloves, fox-trimmed blankets, velvet and beaver hats, sable-lined capes and sealskin coats. The air reeked with the metallic stench of blood and a scarlet lake seeped out of the furs, staining the luxurious carpet. Dripping animal intestines were draped from the chandelier, arranged in stinking coils on the velvet chairs and in heaps on the counter. But there was worse. Atop the mound of blood-soaked furs was a whole slaughtered pig wearing a beaver hat at a jaunty angle.

Aghast, Venetia looked at Jack. 'A pig! King Midas knows this is absolutely the worse thing that could happen to Mr Bernstein's stock.'

249

'May the Fiend take him and all his men!' said Jack through gritted teeth.

'We can't leave the Bernsteins to deal with this alone.' Burning with anger, she marched outside to talk to the onlookers.

Ten minutes later Venetia, together with Mr and Mrs Bernstein, arrived at her showroom.

Raffie opened the door and Venetia's heart was heavy at the thought of the forthcoming and, no doubt, difficult discussion. But there was no time for that now.

Mama and Mrs Dove were taking tea together while Florence assisted a customer in choosing some picot edging suitable for spotted muslin curtains. Caesar was curled up like a black velvet cushion on Mrs Dove's knee.

'Mama, Mr and Mrs Bernstein have had a terrible shock,' said Venetia. 'I'm going to make hot sweet tea.'

'Whatever has happened?' said Mama, rising to take Mrs Bernstein's hand. 'You look quite undone.'

Venetia took the empty teapot and left Mama administering sympathy.

In the scullery, waiting for the kettle to boil, misery engulfed her again. Jack had believed her to be a thief. The bitter hurt of it sliced through her, leaving her sick and shaking.

The kettle was singing when Mrs Dove's elegant form appeared in the scullery doorway. 'Allow me to help you.'

'I'm only waiting for the kettle.'

Mrs Dove shook her head. 'I heard about all the pig entrails in Mr Bernstein's shop.'

'It was a particularly dreadful thing to happen to people of the Jewish faith,' said Venetia, measuring out tea leaves.

'I fear it may not be the last outrage if the shopkeepers persist in their misguided notion of routing King Midas. He appears to have far too great a hold to be dislodged by a few men shaking sticks at him.' Mrs Dove rested a hand on Venetia's arm. 'My dear, you look so strained and I fear for you all if you continue on this course.'

'Part of me wishes we'd never started it,' said Venetia. There was a cold, tight feeling in her chest that told her she was to blame for others' suffering. She kept picturing Mr Elliot's terrified face before he'd been shot. He was still gravely ill and it was uncertain if he'd recover.

Mrs Dove's blue eyes were kind. 'Why don't you make the payments before anything else terrible happens?'

'It's too late.' Venetia lifted the kettle off the fire.

Mrs Dove sighed. 'I can see you don't want an old lady's advice.'

'Shall we take the tea into the showroom, Mrs Dove?' said Venetia.

Mrs Bernstein still wept and shook but she sipped her tea and allowed Mama and Mrs Dove to soothe her.

Then Raffie opened the door to admit Charles and Edwin Murchison.

'We've come to a decision ...' said Edwin.

'... after a great deal of discussion,' continued Charles. 'Since Mr Elliot was injured we can no longer hide behind the curtains while the rest of you fight our common foe.'

Charles pressed a manicured hand to his velvet coat front. 'We shall take up arms and join the shopkeepers' militia.'

'You're most welcome,' said Venetia. Their change of heart wouldn't make a great deal of difference in defeating King Midas but their support warmed her heart.

Edwin turned to Mr Bernstein. 'Major Chamberlaine is even now occupied in setting up a working party to scrub away all evidence of that outrage.'

'And we have undertaken to see what might be rescued,' said Charles, 'and to receive your instructions on what to do with the ruined stock.'

'We sincerely wish to make this burden a little lighter for you,' said Edwin.

Mr Bernstein's face worked but he was too overcome by emotion to speak.

'We'd be honoured,' said Charles, 'if you'd stay with us until all is restored to order. Mother's old room is very comfortable and if Jacob will not mind the box room for a few days ...'

Mrs Bernstein burst into tears again. 'Such kindness!' she sobbed.

The Bernsteins left with the Murchisons and Mrs Dove followed a moment later.

Venetia washed the teacups while she gathered the strength to speak to Raffie about the bronze horse and the money. It would be far better to have an argumentative discussion without Jack being present.

She went into the showroom to look for her brother just as a man, shabbily dressed but of upright bearing, came into the shop. He didn't appear to be the kind of person who'd be interested in new curtains.

'May I help you?' Venetia asked, glancing over her shoulder and wondering where Raffie was.

The man didn't face her directly but half turned away as if he might run off given the slightest provocation. 'Is Major Chamberlaine here?' He glanced doubtfully over her shoulder at the showroom.

'Not at present.' As he turned his head she saw that one side of his face was terribly scarred. A ragged red line curved from his left eye down to his chin and had been badly stitched together so that it puckered his cheek. It was all Venetia could do not to gasp at the sight. She understood now why the poor soul didn't care to look directly at her.

He took off his hat. 'Richard Norreys,' he said. 'Major Chamberlaine wrote to me, you see,' he said, averting his face again.

'Would you care to wait?'

She left Mr Norreys perched on the delicate French hall chair and, since she could see that Raffie was deep in conversation with Florence, went to help Mama tidy a box of trimmings. She'd wait to speak to Raffie until after the visitor had gone.

'Who's that?' asked Mama, nodding at the man.

'He's waiting for Jack.' She watched curiously as Mr Norreys examined the carving on the hall chair and ran his hand over the velvet upholstery. He wandered over to the lady's writing desk and peered closely at the satinwood inlay. He appeared to be genuinely interested.

The door opened and Jack, carrying the bronze horse under his arm, caught sight of his visitor. 'Sergeant Norreys!' he declared with every sign of delight. 'You're looking well, man. Come in, come in.' He placed the bronze horse on the counter.

Raffie saw it and blanched.

Venetia knew then that what she'd feared was true.

Jack made brief introductions and then retired to the office with his visitor, shutting the door behind them.

'I wonder what that's about,' said Mama, winding up some galloon braid.

'A military acquaintance, I assume,' said Venetia, watching her brother return the bronze horse to the shelf. 'I'm just going to have a word with Raffie,' she said.

When he saw Venetia bearing down on him, he turned and hurried out of the shop door.

'Raffie!' She stood in the doorway and watched him weaving his way swiftly through the crowds.

'Whatever has upset you so?' asked Mama.

'That boy will have a piece of my mind when he returns,' said Venetia, almost in tears. She described how she and Jack had recovered the bronze horse. 'And he thought that one of us might have taken money from the cashbox. After all we've done to work together to open the shop, it's so hurtful.'

'I'm insulted that Jack thought we might have done such a thing,' said Mama, indignation written across her face, 'but Raffie needs to be taught a lesson. He's really let down the family honour.'

Jack's going to be awfully angry with him,' Venetia said,

unhappily, 'and I cannot blame him. I'm angry with him myself. I doubt Jack will be happy until he's punished Raffie.'

Mama gave her a sharp look. 'You've always been a mother hen to your brother but don't let him come between you and Jack. It's been so much more comfortable for us all since we've become united. Or, at least, I thought we had.'

Venetia turned away so that Mama wouldn't see her unhappiness and began to tidy the rolls of curtain fabric. Had the blossoming friendship with Jack been no more than a thin veneer?

It was an hour later that Jack and Sergeant Norreys emerged from the office, both wreathed in smiles. Jack came straight over to them.

'Sergeant Norreys has agreed to stay in the rooms above the shop until the present difficulties are over,' he said. 'He'll be armed and any intruder will receive short shrift from him.'

'Well, that would certainly bring us peace of mind,' said Mama.

'After what happened to the poor Bernsteins,' said Florence, 'who knows when King Midas might call?'

'Is it not too much trouble for you?' asked Venetia.

'Not at all, Miss Lovell,' said Sergeant Norreys. 'I'm but lately returned from the Peninsula, now that Bonaparte has been subdued, and staying temporarily with my sister.'

'But the rooms upstairs aren't decorated, Jack,' protested Venetia.

Sergeant Norreys laughed, his face still turned away from them. 'Believe me, Miss Lovell, if you'd seen where I've been sleeping on campaign during the past few years, you'd know that your room, decorated or not, will be a palace to me.'

'Nevertheless,' she said, 'I'll arrange for a bed and some other pieces of furniture to make you comfortable.'

He made a small bow. 'Obliged to you, Miss Lovell.'

The shop bell tinkled and Raffie sidled in. He slipped past them and disappeared into the back of the shop.

Venetia watched him, a hollow feeling in the pit of her stomach.

'You'll fetch your kit and return tonight?' Jack said to Sergeant Norreys.

'Before you close,' he said. 'I'll guard your premises right away.'

'Let me see you to the door,' said Jack.

When he returned, Venetia said, 'I suppose you know Norreys well? If he's going to have access to the showroom, we must be sure he's honest.'

Jack put his hand to his heart. 'Venetia, I trust him with my life. In fact, he saved my life. I owe him my utmost gratitude.'

'Why is that?' What did she have to do to inspire Jack to trust her as much as he trusted Sergeant Norreys?

'When I was wounded at Vitoria he carried me off the battlefield and sought medical help for me. It was utter carnage there and men were dying all around us.' Jack closed his eyes. 'I still dream of it. Without Sergeant Norreys I'd have died where I fell, as so many did. At the very least I'd have lost my leg.'

Venetia shuddered.

'Soldiers are returning home in their thousands now,' said Jack. 'But what are they coming back to? Some are so damaged they'll never be the same again, either in their bodies or their minds. Will they find work? Have a family life? How long will it take the public to forget what all those men have done for us and turn away from them?'

Venetia didn't know what to say in the face of Jack's passionate outburst. 'At least we can make Sergeant Norreys welcome,' she said at last, all the while wondering when Jack was going to talk to Raffie.

'There's a truckle bed in the box room in Quill Court,' he said. 'I'll ask Raffie to take a note to Annunziata. She can pack up some linen and send it back with him.' He sighed. 'But first, I want to ask that brother of yours for an explanation of his behaviour. Will you bring him to me in the office, please?'

Venetia's heart was heavy as she went to find Raffie. She didn't want to think him a thief but, if he denied it, a cloud still hung over the Lovell family.

Raffie was leaning against the open door to the yard, hands in his pockets, staring morosely at a couple of starlings squabbling over some titbit.

'Jack wants to see you,' she said.

He looked at her, his eyes wary, and then at the yard, as if hoping there was a way out. There wasn't.

'Now, Raffie, if you please!'

Dragging his feet, he followed her indoors.

'You may leave us, Venetia,' said Jack.

'I prefer to stay,' she said firmly as she sat down.

'As you wish.' Jack fixed his steely gaze on Raffie but didn't ask him to sit. 'You will have seen that we've returned the bronze horse to its rightful place. I require a full explanation of how it came to be in a pawnshop.'

Raffie glanced desperately at Venetia.

'The truth, Raffie,' she said.

His face was so pale it was almost green.

'I wish to give you the opportunity to present your side of the story,' said Jack.

Raffie shifted from one foot to the other, staring at the floor.

'Get on with it!'

'It started soon after we arrived in London,' he said slowly.

'Go on,' said Venetia encouragingly, ignoring Jack's frown.

'I met Freddie Crawford in an alehouse,' said Raffie. 'I didn't know anyone here. I couldn't bear to be in the house in Quill Court, knowing that Father had lived there with his other family. He'd lied to us and nothing in the world was safe or true any more.' The boy ran a hand through his hair, leaving it standing up in tufts. 'And a shop selling curtains may interest you, Venetia, but greeting customers and being a glorified delivery boy certainly isn't how I want to spend the rest of my life!'

'You know that we cannot send you to university, Raffie.' Venetia spoke gently to him. 'We've all had to accommodate ourselves to our change in circumstances.'

'Less self-pity, please, and tell us about the bronze horse,' said Jack.

Raffie cast him a look of loathing. 'Freddie took me to places to have some fun. At cards and dice mostly. All the *ton* enjoy games of chance.'

'But, Raffie, we're from the merchant classes,' said Venetia. 'We don't have the wealth necessary to gamble.'

'Do you think I don't know that now?' He buried his face in his hands. 'Freddie had more money than I, which wouldn't be hard,' he said bitterly. 'He lent me enough to get started and we went to a gaming club. At first I had a run of luck.' A smile flickered across his lips. 'But then both Freddie and I began to lose badly at dice.'

Jack sighed. 'And then the owner of the club called in the debts?'

'How did you know?' Raffie stared at him.

'Oldest trick in the book.'

'Freddie asked his father to pay his debts since even his allowance wasn't enough. He cut up rough about it and Freddie's been sent to stay with some old aunt in the country. But those men are still after me to pay. I begged for more time. They beat me up.'

Venetia gasped. 'Was that when Kitty found you in the area? It wasn't footpads?'

Raffie shook his head. 'I was desperate and that's why I took the bronze horse.'

'You pawned it to pay the debts?'

'It wasn't anything like enough. And I'm sorry but I took money from the cashbox, too.' Tears started into Raffie's eyes.

Jack glanced at Venetia. 'I guessed that but I'm pleased you've been man enough to own up, Raffie.'

'But now I'm *really* frightened,' he said. 'I still owe a lot of money and the men who beat me up ...' He swallowed. 'I couldn't believe it when I recognised them outside Elliot's shop the other day. The men are King Midas's bullies. He must own the gambling club.'

Venetia caught her breath, fear turning her insides to water. Was there no escape from that terrible man?

'If I don't pay them by the end of the month ...' Raffie's lips quivered. 'They asked how I'd like living with only one hand.'

Jack closed his eyes and pinched the bridge of his nose.

'I'm sorry,' said Raffie, his head bowed, 'but I'm *begging* you to lend me the money to pay them off.'

'Jack,' said Venetia, 'we must find it!'

'I see,' he said, his blue eyes becoming icy. 'You want the shop-keepers to risk everything by refusing to pay King Midas but *you* are prepared to pay him to let Raffie off the hook?'

'But it's different! He's young and can't defend himself.'

'And what about the threats to the baker's defenceless ten-year-old daughter? You encouraged everyone to stand together and ride out the storm. You can't go back on that now, Venetia, simply because it's Raffie who's in jeopardy.'

'But ...' She knew he was right. But this was Raffie, her dearest little brother, no matter what he'd done.

'Enough!' Jack picked up his pen and scribbled a brief letter. 'Raffie, take this to Annunziata. You will wait until she has filled the handcart with the items I've requested and then return straight here.'

Raffie took the note and left the office without another word.

Venetia blurted out, 'You'd find the money if it were Florence who needed help.'

Jack dropped his pen on the desk, splattering it with ink. He left the office without looking at her.

Venetia's her heart was beating uncomfortably fast. Angry and tearful, she wrestled with his comments. *Was* she being unfair?

Chapter 26

Kitty floated in a shadowy half-sleep full of echoing shouts and King Midas's pounding footsteps. She was running and running with tears dripping off her chin, running for her life while she tried not to remember that terrible gurgling sound Samuel had made as the blood pumped out of the wide slash across his neck.

A knock on the door started her fully awake with her heart banging. Her feet were uncomfortably twisted up in the blankets and she realised she'd fallen asleep still wearing her boots. It was then that she remembered everything. Sitting bolt upright, she moaned. Nat had been caught and was festering in gaol somewhere. Samuel, Ruth and Lennie were dead, all killed by King Midas's men. A keening wail rose from deep inside her and she twisted the sheet in her hands. Nat! Dear God, what was going to happen to Nat?

The door handle began to turn and she stared at it, frozen with dread. Had King Midas's men seen her running away last night and come after her? There was a hard thump on the door. The key bounced out of the lock and, as she watched, a piece of wire appeared and hooked it under the door. A moment later the lock turned and the door began to open slowly. Shrinking back against the pillow, she waited for King Midas to enter the room.

A small figure stood framed in the doorway. Benny.

'Got anything to eat?' he asked.

Kitty let out a wavering sigh. 'There's bread in the cupboard. Make yourself at home, why don't you?' She could hear the note of hysteria in her voice.

'Where's Nat, then?' asked Benny a few moments later, his cheeks bulging.

She buried her face in her hands, tears seeping through her fingers. 'We were on a job that went wrong. Some men killed Samuel, Lennie and Ruth. And Nat ...'

Benny stopped chewing. 'What 'bout Nat?'

'They fetched the constable and took him to Lambeth Street police station.' She shivered, remembering how she'd followed the constable and the watchmaker as they'd dragged Nat away, half insensible. She'd lurked in the shadows outside but after the watchmaker had left the police station no one else had gone in or out. Eventually, when the sun rose, she'd crept home with no more tears left to shed and collapsed on the bed.

'He'll have been moved this morning. Want me to find out which gaol they've sent him to?' Benny wiped his nose on his cuff. 'It'll cost you, though.'

'Just find him!'

The door slammed behind the boy.

Kitty's mind was full of fog. There was no one she could turn to. All her friends were dead now, except Black Sal and Billy, who'd gone away. There'd be a trial. What if Nat was transported? Jesus God, she couldn't bear to think of it! She paced the floor, trying to clear her head. Perhaps she'd give herself up and then she'd be transported, too. At least they'd be together.

She caught sight of the china shepherdess on the mantelshelf. If she sold it she could use the money to grease the palm of Nat's gaolers and maybe they'd let him go. Her spirits lifted a little. She changed out of Nat's breeches, wrapped up the shepherdess in a pillowslip and set off.

No one spoke as they sat round the breakfast table. Venetia ached with misery as she sipped coffee as black as sin in an effort to brace herself to face the new day. It could hardly be worse than yesterday. The Bernsteins were deeply distressed and had declared they'd never be able to return to their desecrated shop. Mr Elliot was still gravely ill with the gunshot wound to his chest. Jack had thought she might be a thief. And then there was the terrible threat to Raffie hanging over them. He looked as if he hadn't slept either.

Jack drained his coffee cup and consulted his pocket watch. 'Time to open the shop.'

'Mama has taken a headache powder and returned to bed for an hour,' said Florence.

'Raffie, you will stay and escort your mother to the shop later,' said Jack. 'We can't take any risks while everything is so unsettled.'

Venetia glanced at Jack, whose expression had remained forbidding ever since they'd argued over Raffie's debts. Then he'd gone out again for several hours without telling anyone where he was going. Their closeness of a few weeks ago appeared to have entirely evaporated. Nevertheless, she'd ask him, at an appropriate moment, to reconsider his decision not to pay off Raffie's debts. A shudder ran down her spine at the thought of what might happen otherwise. Later, as they turned into Cheapside, Florence lifted her chin and sniffed. 'Smoke,' she said.

Smog from the city's coal fires always hung in the air but this was stronger than usual. Venetia looked at Jack. 'You don't think . . .'

'Hurry!'

Jack doubled his pace but Venetia could see his jaw gritted in discomfort as he limped along.

Smoke, black and acrid, began to swirl around them and flakes of charred paper floated to the ground.

A crowd had gathered further along Cheapside. Coughing, they pushed their way through the throng until they saw that Johnson's the stationer's was now no more than a burned out shell. Black smoke still belched out of the windows.

Jack raised a hand and shouted: 'Mr Hayes!'

Venetia recognised the owner of the glove shop coming towards them, his face smeared with soot.

'King Midas?' asked Jack.

'It was him, all right,' said Mr Hayes, his expression grim. 'I was on the night patrol with three of the other men. At two o'clock this morning we heard a coach rattling down the road, driven hell for leather, with men hanging off the back of it whooping and shouting. We thought it was young bloods but it was King Midas's coach. It slowed down just enough outside the stationer's for the men to throw bricks and flaming torches through the windows.'

'Was anyone hurt?' asked Venetia.

'We got Mr Johnson and his wife out but the water engine came too late to save his poor old mother upstairs. God rest her soul.'

Florence pressed a hand to her mouth.

'She wouldn't have suffered, Miss,' Mr Hayes said gently. 'She was asleep and the smoke ...'

Florence reached for Jack's hand.

Mr Hayes wiped a hand over his face. 'Where will King Midas strike next?'

Venetia saw Florence's anxious expression and said, 'We'd better hurry on to open up the shop, Mr Hayes.'

He nodded. 'Your man Norreys came to help us last night when he heard the commotion. Useful sort of a chap.' He lifted a hand and turned away.

Sergeant Norreys opened the door for them as they arrived.

'I heard you were called out last night,' said Jack.

Norreys shrugged. 'A raiding party. You weren't overstating the situation. King Midas is a nasty piece of work, isn't he?'

'We must put him out of action, Sergeant Norreys.'

'Sooner the better, sir!' The good side of Norreys's face twisted into a smile. 'But now you're here to hold the fort, I'm going to catch up on my sleep.'

❦

Benny was crouched on the doorstep, waiting for Kitty.

'Did you find out where Nat is?' she asked.

He wiped his nose on his sleeve. 'What's it worth?'

Kitty fumbled in her basket and handed him a coin.

He bit the edge and nodded. 'Newgate,' he said. 'He'll be up before the beak soon. I reckon they'll hang 'im.'

Kitty clutched the door handle. 'What d'you mean?' she whispered. Her bones had turned to ice. 'I thought they'd transport him.'

'Not for murder.' Benny looked at her pityingly.

'But he didn't murder anyone! He'd never ...' She pulled at the neckline of her dress, struggling for breath.

'They fink he did.' The boy shrugged. 'I'll be off then.'

'No! Benny, wait ...' But he had gone. Light-headed with shock, Kitty sank down on the stairs and wept.

❦

Venetia was sitting at the counter drawing in her sketchbook when the shop door suddenly flew open, banging back against the wall with a crash.

Venetia's head jerked up. Was it King Midas and his men returning?

But it was Mrs Elliot who stood in the doorway, her hair hanging loose about her tear-stained face.

'What is it?' asked Mama, alarmed.

Full of dread, Venetia knew at once what had happened.

263

Mrs Elliot looked wildly about her. 'You!' she shouted, and ran towards Venetia, hands outstretched.

Her palms thudded against Venetia's chest with such force that she staggered backwards against the wall, winded.

'It's your fault!' screamed Mrs Elliot. Hissing and spitting with grief and fury she pounded Venetia's head and shoulders in a violent frenzy.

Shielding her face with her arms, Venetia received blow after stinging blow.

Mama tried to pull Mrs Elliot away and received a punch on the jaw.

'You came here, stirring up trouble,' yelled Mrs Elliot, kicking Venetia's shins. 'You promised everything and delivered nothing.' She spat in Venetia's face. 'I hate you!'

The blows suddenly ceased. Venetia tentatively lowered her arms to see that Raffie had grasped the struggling woman.

Jack was hobbling towards them from the office.

'She killed him!' Mrs Elliot shrieked. 'My husband died this morning and it's *her* fault.' She burst into a storm of noisy weeping, beating her fists on Raffie's chest.

Jack hurried to his aid.

Venetia's chin trembled with distress.

'Come with me.' Florence tugged at her sleeve and she allowed herself to be led away.

In the scullery Florence bathed Venetia's bruised face while Mrs Elliot's shrieks echoed through the showroom.

Tears cascaded down Venetia's cheeks as she wept in an agony of self-recrimination while Florence patted her back.

At last Mrs Elliot's cries subsided and then ceased.

A moment later Jack came into the scullery. 'Raffie and your mother have taken Mrs Elliot home,' he said.

'She's right,' wept Venetia. 'It is my fault. And there's Mr Johnson's mother, too.'

Jack took her in his arms and stroked her hair, soothing her as if she were a child. 'Of course it wasn't your fault! It was King Midas who shot Mr Elliot, not you.'

'But Jack …'

'Shhh! The poor woman is distraught and doesn't know what she's saying.' He took a handkerchief out of his pocket and carefully dried Venetia's eyes.

'I should have listened to you,' she sobbed. 'We can never win against King Midas.'

'Perhaps not,' said Jack, 'but you're right about how unjust it is that he terrorises a whole community. You've been braver than anyone else in standing up to him and we'll all do our utmost to defeat him. The time has come to call in reinforcements.'

She felt his lips brush against her hair and buried her face in his shoulder. If only she could stay safe in his arms and make all the misery go away!

'You've had a shock. 'I'm going to put you in a hackney carriage and Florence will take you home and put you to bed.'

Home! Suddenly all she wanted was to be at home in Quill Court, safely tucked up in bed in her room decorated with Venetia's Rose paper.

There was nothing she could do to help poor Widow Elliot.

Kitty rose before dawn and walked with leaden steps through the darkness until she came to St Paul's Cathedral. She crept inside and knelt down in a pew. The memory of Nat's trial was still like a gimlet in her head and she didn't know how to bear the pain. The watchmaker had said terrible things about Nat but he stood upright and stared straight ahead, answering all the questions and accusations in a clear voice.

Jostled on all sides in the public gallery, Kitty had wept into her handkerchief all the while. After Nat had been condemned, he caught her eye for one long moment and mouthed, "I love you" before they led him away. Her knees wouldn't hold her then and she'd sunk to the floor, blinded by tears.

Bowing her head in the shadows now, Kitty struggled to pray. She'd never been one for church but she didn't know what else to do.

After the trial she'd tried to bribe Nat's warder to let her visit him but he'd laughed at her.

'You can't just walk into the condemned cell! Next you'll be trying to persuade me to smuggle in a file for him.'

'Would you? I have money.'

'Have you now?' The warder rasped the bristles on his chin. 'More'n my job's worth. But you could buy him a little comfort. He'll be terrible hungry and gasping for a drop of ale.'

After a deal of wrangling he'd taken all her money from the sale of the china shepherdess and promised to pass on a message to Nat and get him a decent dinner. Kitty had a nasty feeling the man would pocket all the money and Nat wouldn't see any of it. She'd laboriously written him a note but how could she convey in a few words the agony of her feelings and the deep love she felt for him?

Light began to filter through the cathedral windows. Kitty sent up one last prayer. *If you're there, Lord, please save my Nat or at least make his passing quick.*

It was almost light outside and horse-drawn delivery waggons were trundling along the echoing streets.

A milkmaid with a wooden yoke across her shoulders called out, 'Milk below!' and the scent of baking bread wafted from a bakery. Despite her misery, Kitty's mouth watered. She hadn't eaten a morsel since Benny brought her the terrible news.

Turning off Ludgate Street into Old Bailey, she passed the Session House and then the forbidding stone bulk of Newgate Prison loomed over her. Workmen were tightening the bolts on the high scaffold erected outside the Debtors' Door. The sight of it made her feel sick.

People were already gathering. Booths had been erected for the sale of refreshments and costermongers with baskets of hot pies, apples and sausages cried their wares.

A man thrust a paper at her. 'Only a penny, Miss, read all about the condemned.' Dazed, she handed him a coin and took the broadsheet. A juggler moved among the crowd and she heard a violin and a penny whistle start to play a lively jig. It was like a hideous carnival.

An hour passed, during which time Kitty stood before a wooden barrier set up to keep the crowd back from the scaffold and read the broadsheet. She couldn't look at the dreadful drawing of a previous hanging but ran a trembling finger along the lines of text until she came to the part about Nat:

> Nathaniel Griggs. Convicted of house breaking and murder most foul. From a child he formed an intercourse with abandoned companions and commenced that profligate career which brings him to his untimely end. His life was spent in the perpetration of every species of vice. His mind became so familiarised with guilt that he scarcely seemed sensible of his depravity and thus, in the natural progress of iniquity, was carried away with his wickedness.

It wasn't true! Kitty wept at the injustice of describing him so. As a child Nat had only ever done what he needed to do to survive. He was the kindest man and would never murder a soul!

The gathering crowd jostled against her back and she was pressed hard against the barrier. She barely felt the discomfort but kept her eyes raised to the Debtors' Door, where Nat would appear. A curious numbness overcame her as she waited, unable to think, only to whisper his name again and again. The noise of the chattering throng echoed dully in her ears and jagged shards of light hurt her eyes as she stared up at the scaffold.

A red-headed girl standing beside her, eating an onion tart, nudged her in the ribs. 'Been to a hanging before?'

Kitty shook her head.

The girl licked the grease off her lips. 'There's usually some good dying speeches. Can't abide the snivellers, though.'

Kitty, unable to speak, returned her gaze to the Debtors' Door.

Someone in the crowd began to sing about a highwayman:

> *'I never robbed any poor man yet,*
> *Nor any tradesman did I beset,*
> *I robbed both lords and the ladies bright,*
> *And brought their jewels to my heart's delight.'*

Vendors thrust their way through the heaving mass and Kitty, suddenly light-headed, bought herself a cup of ale. It was thin and sour but she couldn't risk fainting and missing Nat.

The crowd joined in the singing, linking arms and swaying from side to side:

> *'And when I'm dead and in my grave,*
> *A flashy funeral pray let me have,*
> *With six bold highwaymen to carry me.'*

The bell in St Sepulchre's began to sound and the nightmarish clamour clanged through Kitty's aching head. She pressed her hands over her ears until it ceased.

'Eight o'clock,' said the girl beside her, jigging up and down.

The nervous excitement of the crowd increased and the noise swelled.

And then the Debtors' Door opened. The crowd roared and whistled.

'What'd I tell you?' The red-headed girl nudged her again.

Kitty broke out into a sweat as several figures emerged, her heart beating so fast she thought it'd jump out of her chest. There was a chaplain, the hangman, two guards, and then five men and a woman in chains, all wearing white caps. She gripped the barrier, barely noticing the splinters in her palms as she looked for Nat. And there he was! She made a mew of distress.

The girl standing beside her frowned. 'Do you know one of them?'

A great sob burst out of Kitty's chest. 'That's my husband up there. He never murdered no one, no matter what they say.'

'Blimey!' The girl looked at her with renewed interest. 'If you're his wife they'll let you have a few minutes to say goodbye.'

'Will they?' Kitty clutched her fists to her chest. If she could only hold him one last time, kiss him and tell him she'd love him 'til her own dying day …

The crow of a chaplain said a few prayers, his black vestments flapping in the gusty breeze. Then one by one the convicted stepped forward to address the crowd. The woman was sobbing so hard no one could understand what she was saying. One of the men swaggered forward and boasted of his exploits on the highways and the crowd booed him. He responded with an obscene gesture at the hangman and the fickle crowd roared approval, throwing their hats in the air.

When it was Nat's turn, Kitty strained to hear him over the noise. 'I repent all my sins,' he said, 'but as God is my witness, I never committed murder. Those who falsely accused me must make their own peace with the Lord.'

Tears streamed down Kitty's face. He was so brave. The last man gave his dying speech but Kitty couldn't bear to take her eyes off Nat, not even for a moment.

'Go on then!' said the red-headed girl. 'The others are going up now.'

There was a ladder leading to the scaffold, guarded at the bottom by two men, but a few members of the crowd were beginning to mount it to say their goodbyes to the condemned. The bell in the tower of St Sepulchre's began to toll, a sound so mournful that the crowd quietened.

Nat was staring out across the sea of faces and Kitty jumped up and down, waving her arms to catch his attention. 'Nat!' she shouted.

He turned and saw her as she waved then shook his head.

'I'm coming!' she called, beginning to climb over the barrier.

Nat cupped his mouth with his hands and shouted, 'Go! Now!' He pointed into the crowd.

She stood still and tried to see what he was looking at. It took her a moment and then she gasped.

'Run!' Nat's desperate cry was half snatched away by the wind.

King Midas's black-caped figure stood a head taller than the rest of the crowd and his men were clearing a path for him as he pushed his way towards her.

'Run!' shouted Nat. 'Don't go home!'

Uncertain, she glanced at him again. King Midas knew there'd been another person at the coiner's house. Did he know it was her? Could he know that she'd witnessed him murdering Samuel?

The hangman was leading the condemned, one by one, to their places on the gallows. A noose was hanging down in front of Nat.

The crowd was hushed now, holding their breath.

Kitty looked behind her. King Midas was only fifteen feet away.

The hangman pulled Nat's white cap down over his eyes and dropped the noose over his head.

King Midas was ten feet away, close enough for her to see the steely intent in his eyes. His men were on either side of him. She looked again at Nat's hooded face, turned and frantically pushed her way through the press of people.

Behind her, the crowd groaned.

Glancing over her shoulder she glimpsed the six condemned jerking up and down in their nooses. She let out a wail of anguish, the pain of Nat's death piercing so deeply into her breast that she thought she'd fall. But she mustn't think about him now.

King Midas shouted after her.

A man in the crowd began to sing again:

> *'Six pretty maidens to bear my Pall,*
> *Give them white garlands and ribbons all.*
> *And when I'm dead they will speak the truth,*
> *He was a wild and a wicked youth.'*

Kitty emerged from the crowd and ran, her feet skittering across the cobbles. Head down, she skidded around a corner and into Fleet Lane. Her legs pumped as she ducked into an alley and then another. She glanced behind her as she crossed Bacon Lane. There was no sign of King Midas or his men. She sprinted up Castle Street and into Fleet Market.

She hid behind a poulterer's stall and rested her hands on her knees while she heaved for breath. At last she recovered enough to peer out from behind the stall. She waited fifteen minutes but no one had followed her.

Agony throbbed within her. King Midas had taken away her last opportunity to hold Nat in her arms, however briefly, and to kiss his dear face for the final time.

A deep and terrible hatred welled up in her heart. Wiping the tears from her face, she vowed that she'd never rest until she'd made King Midas suffer for what he'd done.

Venetia stood on a stool in the shop window, hanging up a waterfall of pale blue silk.

'How does that look?' Running her fingers down the under curtain, she formed the muslin into soft folds.

Florence stood on the pavement outside, looking in. Hands on her hips, she studied the display through narrowed eyes. 'That's better now.' She glanced along the street and it was then that Venetia saw a carriage drawn by high-stepping black horses approaching at a rollicking pace.

The coachman lashed his whip and the horses broke into a canter. Someone shouted and pedestrians scattered out of the way. A man leaned out of the carriage's window waving his arm above his head.

It happened so fast that Venetia barely had time to blink.

The black coach raced past. A missile flew past Florence's head, causing her to cry out in fright.

The windowpane shattered with a crash and something heavy thumped into Venetia's chest. Shocked, she lost her balance and fell backwards off the stool. Her head thudded against the floor and everything went dark.

The next thing she knew, Mama was waving smelling salts under her nose.

Venetia winced as she touched the back of her head and found a painful swelling, oozing blood. Her face stung as if she'd been attacked by a swarm of bees.

A pair of strong arms lifted her into a semi-sitting position. Jack, his face ashen, wiped her cheek with his handkerchief.

'Is she all right?' asked an elderly lady customer.

'A little shaken,' he said. 'I apologise, Madam, but I must ask you to return when we are not in such a state of disarray.'

The lady nodded, her feet crunching broken glass underfoot. 'A disgraceful state of affairs, to be terrorised while out shopping! I only wanted three yards of braid.'

By the time the customer had gone and the sign had been turned around on the door, Jack had deposited Venetia carefully in a chair and Florence had brought her hot, sweet tea. Raffie stood beside them, his hand on his sister's shoulder.

Mama stroked a curl off Venetia's face. 'What a shock! You are in the wars this week! There are some little cuts on your cheek, my darling but they're so small they won't leave any permanent mark.'

Shaking, Venetia fingered her smarting face.

'Did you see who it was?' Jack leaned towards her and carefully picked a splinter of glass off her shoulder.

'A black coach.' Venetia's teeth chattered against the edge of her cup and Jack reached out to steady her hand. 'It wasn't *him*, though. One of his minions, I expect.'

'A message from King Midas,' said Raffie, holding it out to Jack. 'It was wrapped around the brick that smashed the window.'

Jack read the note aloud:

Pay your dues or there will be a surcharge of fifty per cent to cover the cost of my inconvenience. And tell young Mr Rafaele that my patience is at an end. He knows the penalty if he

doesn't settle his gambling debts. He has until the end of the
week.

Venetia felt terror, shock and rage combine in her chest until it was
all she could do not to scream and rail against him.

There was a knocking on the front window and Sergeant Norreys
looked in through the broken glass.

'Missed an enemy attack, did I?' he asked, after Raffie let him in.
The sergeant carried a paper parcel. 'You'll be wanting that window
boarded up and I see we have a wounded civilian. Shall I fetch the
sawbones?'

'I don't believe Miss Lovell needs a physician,' said Jack, 'only
her mother's tender care. We'll close the shop for the rest of the
day.'

'I'll arrange for a new pane of glass,' said Norreys. He held up his
parcel. 'I'll eat my pie first while it's hot, if you don't mind. Set me
up for the long night watch.'

'I don't mind saying,' said Mama, watching Sergeant Norreys's
retreating back, 'that I'm relieved to have another man about in the
current circumstances. He appears to be eminently practical.'

'Indeed he is,' said Jack with a faint smile. He turned to Raffie.
'Please will you escort your mother and sisters home? I have some
urgent business to attend to and cannot return until later.'

'I can't go home, Jack,' said Venetia. 'I'm expecting a delivery of
chairs.'

'Sergeant Norreys will take them in.'

Jack went into the street to find a hackney carriage to convey
them to Quill Court. While he was gone Charles and Edwin
Murchison tapped on the door.

'We heard the commotion,' said Charles.

'My dear Miss Lovell, you are injured!' Edwin twisted his hands
together in distress. 'We saw the black coach thundering off along

274

the road and knew it could only mean King Midas was up to no good again.'

'No lasting harm,' said Venetia as a hackney carriage drew up outside. She became dizzy when she stood up and was glad of Jack's supporting arm. Her head ached abominably.

'Raffie, take care of your mother and sisters,' said Jack once they were settled in the carriage, 'and I'll return home when I can.'

The carriage jerked forwards and Venetia leaned her head back and closed her eyes. She wished Jack had come with them and wondered what was so important that he'd abandoned her when she felt so vulnerable.

Once at home in Quill Court, she went to bed and slept all afternoon. When she awoke the early-evening sun cast lozenges of light through the windowpanes on to the walls. Raising a hand, she gently touched the lump on her head.

'Does it still pain you?'

She turned her head on the pillow. 'I didn't know you were there!'

Florence was sitting beside the bed with a book on her knee. 'Mama thought you shouldn't be alone. Can I fetch you anything?'

Venetia shook her head and then wished she hadn't. 'I'll come downstairs now.'

'Then I shall go down and ask Annunziata to make tea.'

Brushing her hair, Venetia peered into the looking glass at the small cuts she had sustained. She was lucky the damage wasn't any worse, bearing in mind King Midas's earlier threats to slash her face.

Jack called out to her as she passed his study.

'How are you feeling now?' He pulled up a chair for her.

'Better.'

'I don't believe King Midas meant to harm you this time. It was merely unfortunate you were standing in the window when the brick came through.'

'But he means to harm Raffie if we don't pay his debts.'

'Those debts amount to nearly five hundred pounds. And although he might have been foolish, I do believe he was cheated out of that sum.'

'Five hundred pounds!' gasped Venetia.

'We cannot pay it.'

Tears sprang to her eyes. 'But if we don't his hand will be cut off. It makes me sick to think of risking such a terrible thing. We *must* pay!'

'I'm not insensible to your distress, Venetia, but we cannot.' Jack's tone was adamant. 'I've no wish to put Raffie in any extra danger. I suggest that he stays safely at Quill Court for the time being. I'd like Florence to keep away from the shop, too.'

Venetia nodded.

'It will remain closed and you will stay here, too, until you've recovered.'

'But I have an appointment with Lady Draycott in Cavendish Square tomorrow afternoon. Cavendish Square! Jack, this could be a very lucrative project.'

'We'll see how you feel tomorrow.'

'I shall make quite sure I am recovered,' she said.

'You are a very determined young lady.' He gave her a brief smile. 'There's something else,' he said, picking up a sheet of paper off his desk. 'I thought you should read this. It was wrapped around Sergeant Norreys's beef and oyster pie. I hope it's not too greasy, I had to wipe off the gravy.'

Venetia took the paper and grimaced to see an illustration of a hanging. 'What in this lurid broadsheet could be of interest to me?' She scanned the text and a name jumped out at her. 'Nathaniel Griggs!'

Nathaniel Griggs. Convicted of house breaking and murder most foul ... which brings him to his untimely end.

'I can't believe it,' she said. 'They've hanged Kitty's husband. What a terrible thing!'

'It's a salutary lesson to us always to take care who comes into our home.'

'I've known Kitty for years,' protested Venetia. 'She's not a thief or a murderer.'

'King Midas's evil web is so widespread, Griggs might have been one of his gang.'

'Poor Kitty! Then she's been terribly deceived.' Venetia remembered the girl's face shining with joy when she'd announced she was to be married.

'But who knows whether he might not have led her along the path to wickedness?'

'I don't want to believe that.'

'In any case, she'll find being a hempen widow will condemn her to a life of shame.'

'Not if we ask her if she'd like to come back to Quill Court.'

'Absolutely not!' said Jack. 'She might open the door in the night and let King Midas in to murder us in our beds.'

❧

Kitty peered around the corner of the alley. Washing was festooned from the upstairs windows and there was the usual heap of ash and rubbish by the front door of their lodgings but no sign of anything untoward.

Darting across the dank court, she slipped through the front door. She took the stairs two at a time. Stopping dead in her tracks, she saw the door to their room was already open. She held her breath and peeped through the narrow opening. Apart from Clara, singing in her cage by the window, all was quiet so she sidled in and closed the door behind her.

The room was empty. Everything had gone, except for the chest and the bed, which had been stripped. Disbelieving, she ran to the chest and lifted the lid. Her clothes, the green silk dress, her feather fan and the lovely silk shawl, had all gone.

Suddenly ice cold, she ran to the loose floorboard, falling to her knees to lever it up. The space beneath was empty. She reached under the other boards, running her fingers through dust and cobwebs. Nothing.

She sat back on her heels, her hands over her eyes, and sobbed. Everything had gone. She was penniless.

The door creaked open. The landlord shuffled in, reeking of stale drink. 'Thought you'd gone.'

Kitty stood up. 'Who said that?'

'Griggs's friends said he'd been hanged for murder, so they did.'

'He didn't murder anyone!'

He shrugged. 'Got any rent money?'

'It's paid up to the end of the week.'

'He never paid me last week.'

'That's not true! And where are all our things?'

'Griggs's friends took 'em to pay for the burial. Needed to get the room cleared before I let it again, didn't I?' He narrowed his bloodshot eyes at her. 'P'raps you'd be after wanting to rent it yourself?'

'Since you let those men steal everything I own, I haven't any money for rent, have I?' she snapped.

O'Leary let his gaze wander up and down her body, lingering on her breasts. 'We might come to an accommodation,' he said, 'depending on how accommodating you'll be.'

'What do you mean?' asked Kitty, but she had a nasty feeling she knew.

'It's a lonely life since my Bridie died, God rest her soul.' O'Leary licked his lips. 'If you'll be nice to me ...' He stretched out a hand and pinched Kitty's breast.

'Get your hands off!'

'Beggars can't be choosers, Missy.' His eyes gleamed. 'I used to look through the keyhole and watch you with Griggs.'

'How dare you!' Outrage and fear made her shout.

He spread his hands wide. 'Where else are you going to go? Be nice to me and you can stay here.' He rubbed at his crotch and smiled, showing the blackened stumps of his teeth. 'Close your eyes and you'll never know it isn't Griggs.' He grabbed her and, before she could escape, kissed her, forcing his tongue into her mouth.

She struggled, retching at the sour taste of him, while his hands kneaded her buttocks. Throwing back her head, she yelled, 'Don't touch me, you filthy bastard!'

He pulled up her skirt, his hot, moist hands delving between her thighs. 'Come on, my pretty little colleen,' he cajoled. 'I saw you with Griggs and know how you love it.'

Revulsion and fury exploded within her. She lifted her knee and drove it into his crotch with all the force she could muster.

O'Leary let out his breath with a sound like a deflating pig's bladder and doubled over, groaning.

Kitty ran to the door, skidded to a stop and raced back to the window to snatch Clara's cage from its hook. Then she was off again, clattering down the stairs and out through the court, leaping over the oozing filth and sprinting down the alley as if the hounds of hell were at her heels.

Rage fuelled her as she ran, imagining that nasty little bog-trotter watching her with Nat during their most private moments. It made her feel dirty and spoiled her memories of those precious times.

She stopped running at last and walked along with Clara's cage banging against her knee. Sniffing and panting for breath, she looked around and realised that her feet had led her to Gracechurch Street, only a step away from Quill Court. The sky was already darkening.

Two minutes later she was standing on the pavement looking into the drawing room of the house in Quill Court. A lamp had been lit and Miss Venetia, Mrs Lovell and Florence sat bathed in its golden glow. A sob escaped from her lips. The ladies of the house had no idea how lucky they were to be in the safety of their own home. Kitty didn't know where she'd sleep that night. Dare she beg Miss Venetia for her old job back?

She went down the area steps and tapped on the kitchen door.

Dorcas's sandy eyebrows shot up on seeing her. 'What are you doing here?'

'I'd like to speak to Miss Venetia.'

Dorcas laughed. 'Major Chamberlaine told Annunziata not to let you in, you being the wife of a murderer an' all.'

'How did they know about Nat?' she whispered.

'Major Chamberlaine read it in a broadsheet.'

Swallowing her pride, Kitty said. 'I've nowhere to go tonight and nothing to eat. Can you let me have a bit of bread?'

'I'm not risking my place for you,' said Dorcas with a sniff.

Kitty stared at the ground, trying to control her temper while her fingers itched to slap that bran-faced bitch across the face. You'd have thought she might have learned some kindness from her continual praying.

Clara began to sing and Kitty lifted up the cage and stroked her wing through the bars. There was no way she could care for the bird now. Perhaps she should let her fly free? But Clara wouldn't know how to defend herself if the wild birds picked on her. Kitty made up her mind. 'Will you give my canary to Miss Florence? Tell her that she's called Clara.' Thrusting the cage into Dorcas's arms, Kitty turned and ran up the area steps before the other girl could see her tears.

Kitty slumped against the settle, a glass of blue lightning in her hand. The Goat and Compass was bursting at the seams. The men at the next table were laughing as they boasted about the number of pocket watches and silk handkerchiefs they'd dipped that afternoon. The crowd watching the triumphal procession of King Louis of France riding from Hyde Park to Grillon's Hotel had been too caught up in the spectacle to notice pickpockets moving stealthily amongst them.

'May I sit here?' said a voice. Kitty looked up to see a plump but smartly dressed lady smiling at her. 'I don't care to sit beside the men while I'm on my own.'

Kitty shrugged. It was all the same to her. Nothing mattered except where she was going to lay her head that night and what was going to become of her.

'Mrs Cummings,' said the lady. 'And you are?'

'Kitty Griggs.'

'Well, Kitty Griggs, I'm going to have a nice port and lemon. Can I get you another tipple?'

'That's very kind of you.' Tears started to Kitty's eyes again. She'd been all evening going into alehouses asking for work and no one had been kind to her. She'd just spent the last of her money on another gin and she'd no idea what to do next.

Mrs Cummings waved her fingers at the landlord and a moment later their drinks were set before them.

'You have a lovely country girl complexion,' said Mrs Cummings, 'so I'm guessing you haven't been in London long, Kitty. I may call you Kitty, mayn't I?'

Kitty nodded. 'Four months ago.' Only four months! Misery rose up like a black fog again and she took a deep gulp of her drink. The fiery spirit helped to stop her thinking.

'And have you found employment?' asked Mrs Cummings. 'I ask because I'm desperately seeking a good maid.' She sighed. 'My last girl upped and left without a by your leave. No notice at all!'

Kitty sat up straight, her heart suddenly beginning to beat faster. 'I was working as a maid,' she said, 'but I left my last house to get married.'

'Oh, I see,' said Mrs Cummings, glancing at Kitty's wedding ring. 'So you won't be wanting employment then.' She drained her port and stood up.

'But I do!' Kitty rose unsteadily to her feet. 'My husband died.'

'Died?'

281

Kitty thought quickly. She couldn't say Nat had been hanged, and if she said he'd had a fever Mrs Cummings might think she'd sicken too. 'He was older than me,' she said, 'and he had an apoplexy.'

Mrs Cummings's face broke into a wide smile. 'Too lively for him, were you? You might suit very well. Why don't you come home with me? If you like, you can start straight away. What do you say, Kitty?'

She sent up a brief prayer of thanks. 'Thank you, Mrs Cummings,' she said. There was a God after all.

Chapter 28

Kitty was drooping with exhaustion by the time they reached Winchester Street. It was too dark to see much except that it appeared to be a good-sized house.

A maid let them in, giving Kitty a searching look.

'This is Kitty, who has come to join us, Annie,' said Mrs Cummings. 'Fetch her supper on a tray, will you?'

The sound of singing and a piano playing a jolly tune came from behind a closed door in the hall.

'It sounds as if the girls are enjoying themselves,' said Mrs Cummings with a smile. 'You look half dead, Kitty, so I'm going to take you upstairs straight away.' She picked up a candlestick from the hall table.

Kitty followed her up the staircase. Gin-fuddled, she tripped on one of the steps.

Mrs Cummings opened the door to a room on the second floor and set the candlestick down.

Kitty's eyes widened. It was a larger room than she'd ever slept in before. The ceiling sloped on one side and the window was small, but the walls were not the whitewash she was used to but painted pink and with stencilled daisies. She took in the small wardrobe, a table and chair, and a washstand with a flowered china bowl. 'This is for me?' She could hardly believe it.

'Pretty, isn't it?' said Mrs Cummings. She smoothed the pink frilled counterpane on the double bed heaped with cushions. 'Have you a box to be fetched?'

Kitty shook her head. 'It was stolen,' she said.

'You poor lamb! I'll see what we can find for you.'

Kitty blinked back tears, unable to believe how her luck had changed.

Annie brought a tray of soup and bread and set it on the table. 'Is there anything else, Mrs Cummings?'

'Bring warm water, a clean nightgown and a comb, will you?'

Kitty sat at the table and ate her supper while Mrs Cummings watched with an approving smile. The vegetable soup was warming, even if she didn't quite like the slightly bitter taste of the herbs.

'Better now?' asked Mrs Cummings.

Kitty supressed a yawn and nodded, fighting to keep her eyes open.

Annie returned with a jug of water and poured it into the washbowl before closing the door behind her.

'Let's get you into bed,' said Mrs Cummings. 'Nice clean sheets so you must wash first.'

'I'm too sleepy,' protested Kitty.

'It won't take but a minute.'

Kitty sat on the edge of the bed with her head drooping. Her mouth was dry and her head swam. She barely noticed when Mrs Cummings helped her out of her clothes and washed her from top to toe with a clean flannel.

'Good, you look perfectly healthy,' she said, drying Kitty's back with a soft towel.

She felt Mrs Cummings combing her hair, parting it carefully and

284

inspecting her scalp. 'I'm not lousy,' she protested. Her lips were numb and she slurred her words.

'Best to make sure, dear,' said Mrs Cummings.

A nightgown smelling of lavender was slipped over Kitty's head and then she was curled up under crisp sheets with a soft pillow beneath her head. It felt as if she were floating on a sea of thistledown.

Mrs Cummings blew out the candle. 'Goodnight, Kitty.'

She tried to mumble her thanks but sleep was irresistible.

The door closed and, as she drifted away, Kitty heard the click of the lock.

It was light when Kitty awoke. Her head was muzzy and she lay staring at the ceiling, trying to remember where she was. Vaguely uneasy, she pushed herself into a sitting position. There were daisies stencilled on the walls.

Outside, the church clocks began to sound the hour. Ten o'clock. She must have overslept! She should be at work. Swinging her legs over the side of the bed, she felt a rag rug beneath her toes but her head was full of boulders and her mouth dry as dust. She relieved herself in the rose-patterned chamber pot and splashed her face with water.

Her clothes weren't on the chair. The borrowed nightgown was pretty but it was such fine muslin it barely hid her nakedness. There was a faint smell of mothballs in the empty wardrobe. Despite her nightgown being so thin, she'd have to find Mrs Cummings.

She raked her tangled curls with her fingers and went to the door. It wouldn't open. She rattled the handle and called out, 'Mrs Cummings!'

She waited, listening, and then rapped on the door. 'Mrs Cummings!' A sudden stab of fear made her bang on the door with her fist.

'Stop that!' called a girl's voice outside in the corridor. 'I'll fetch her.'

285

Kitty sat on the edge of the bed, biting her fingernails.

A short while later the key turned in the lock and Mrs Cummings came in. She carried an armful of clothes and, in her other hand, an inkwell and pen. 'So you're awake?'

Kitty nodded. 'You locked the door.'

Mrs Cummings smiled. 'Since I took you into my home, despite never seeing you before last night, surely you cannot blame me for taking such a precaution? My last girl fled with the silver teaspoons.'

Kitty bit her lip. Mrs Cummings had been kind and it was true there was no reason for her to trust someone she'd just met. 'Shouldn't I start work?'

'All in good time.' Mrs Cummings laid the clothes upon the bed. 'Try these on, dear.' She went to look out of the window.

Kitty pulled off her nightgown and scrambled into a chemise edged with lace. Over this she tried a pair of embroidered short stays. They laced at the front and were designed to lift her breasts up high. Fancy having embroidered stays when no one would see them! Despite her embarrassment at dressing in front of a stranger, she couldn't help but feel a spark of pleasure at such delightful fripperies. The lawn petticoat had a deep frilled hem and the stockings were undarned. As she reached behind her to button up the spotted muslin dress, Kitty glanced up to see Mrs Cummings watching her in the mirror on the dressing table. She blushed at the memory of allowing the woman to wash her naked body the night before.

Mrs Cummings came to do up the top button and tie the blue sash in a neat bow. 'Come and see!'

Kitty went with her to the dressing table and stared at her own reflection. She looked pretty with the blush still staining her cheeks. The new clothes showed off her slender figure. She'd have to put on a sensible apron to keep the white muslin clean.

'I'll ask one of the girls to dress your hair,' said Mrs Cummings, lifting up Kitty's dark curls. 'Blue ribbons, I think, and caught up to show off your neck. How old are you?'

Kitty blinked. 'Eighteen.'

Mrs Cummings pursed her lips. 'Hmm. You'll pass for less. Your complexion is clear and the white muslin makes you look innocent.' She took a piece of paper out of her pocket and placed it on the table next to the inkwell. 'I must ask you to sign this.' She dipped the pen in the ink and held it out to Kitty.

'What is it?'

'It's to say you've borrowed these clothes and that I'll take the cost of them out of your wages until they're paid for.'

Kitty couldn't argue with that. Without Mrs Cummings she'd be out on the streets. She signed her name, slowly and carefully, taking care not to splatter ink on her new dress.

Mrs Cummings blew on the ink, folded the paper and slipped it in her pocket. 'There's nothing to do for the moment,' she said, 'though some visitors will come during the afternoon.'

'You'd like me to clean the parlour?'

'Kitty, you're too pretty to spoil your hands with dirty jobs. I have other duties in mind that will make better use of your talents and, perhaps, lead you on to tremendous opportunities.'

'I don't understand.'

'Let's not beat about the bush,' said Mrs Cummings. 'I have four girls here and this house takes gentlemen callers. You will be required to entertain the gentlemen in your room and do whatever is asked of you.'

'But ...' Kitty gripped the edge of the table. Her blood ran cold.

'I do hope you aren't going to be awkward, Kitty. It's a nice clean house and I personally select the gentlemen. No beatings allowed and regular doctor's visits.'

'But I'm not a whore!'

'That's not a word we like to use,' chided Mrs Cummings. 'Please don't make me think you ungrateful. Cast your mind back to last night when I found you at your wit's end. You had no money, nowhere to go and no references. I can guarantee that in those circumstances you'd have been obliged to sell yourself in some dark alley before the week was out. You may count yourself fortunate that I found you first.'

'I won't go with strange men!' Kitty's heart thudded and blood pounded in her ears.

'I assure you they won't be strange once you've been properly introduced and I have in mind someone special for you. A virgin up from the country is always popular.' Mrs Cummings smiled. 'There's the slight obstacle of your husband, of course, but we won't mention him. You'll pass for sixteen and I'll give you a bladder of blood to mark the sheets.'

'Give me back my clothes!'

'Why don't you rest awhile? I'll come to see you later.'

Kitty ran to the door and snatched it open.

A man, solidly built, stood outside. He caught hold of her wrist in a grip of iron.

'Don't be stupid, Kitty,' said Mrs Cummings. 'You really wouldn't like it if I asked Bruno to subdue you. His methods are really quite ...' she paused ' ... violent.'

Bruno pushed her back through the doorway and she heard the click of the lock behind her. She hammered on the door. 'Let me out!'

'Be quiet!' Mrs Cummings sounded irritated. 'Or I'll let Bruno in to keep you company.'

Kitty retreated to the corner of the room and began to weep.

Four days later Mrs Cummings unlocked the door. Annie stood behind her holding a supper tray.

Kitty, curled up on the bed, pushed herself painfully into a sitting position. She was thirsty and her stomach growled. Twice a day Mrs Cummings had come to see her and offered her food and water, if she'd do as she was told. Twice a day Kitty had sent her away.

'So, Kitty, are you going to be sensible now?'

The smell of the soup, chicken she thought, made Kitty's mouth water.

'There's no need for all this, dear.' Mrs Cummings sat on the side of the bed. 'Eat your soup and then I'll bring a nice gentleman to see you. I have just the one in mind. He's well set up and generous. Who knows where that might lead? A discreet little townhouse of your own, perhaps?'

'I'm not that kind of girl,' said Kitty, hearing the sulkiness in her voice.

Mrs Cummings sighed. 'Then you're free to go,' she said, standing up.

'Free?'

'I wash my hands of you. There are plenty of girls out there who'd give their eyeteeth for this opportunity. Still, you know best. I'm sure you'll find a man to give you a penny for a knee trembler in some dark alley. But you might like to think about what happens after that.'

'I'll find work,' said Kitty.

'Not without a reference, you won't.'

'I'll go home to Kent!'

'You do that. Back to whatever it was that made you leave in the first place. I'll fetch your old clothes and I want you out of here in five minutes, you ungrateful hussy.'

Mrs Cummings slammed the door behind her.

Slowly, Kitty reached up to undo the ribbons on her nightgown. She hadn't a penny to her name for the coach home so she'd have to walk. But after several days without food she was too weak for that. And where would the next meal come from? Mrs Cummings was right, what was she going back to? Marriage with Tom if he still wanted her, living all cramped together with his family and being poor for the rest of her life.

Closing her eyes, she summoned up Nat's cheeky smile, remembering the way his dark eyes had shone with love for her, imagining the warm smell of him as he nuzzled her neck. But he'd gone and she'd never love like that again.

Mrs Cummings returned. She held up Kitty's patched work-dress. 'Here,' she said. 'Or if you want to change your mind you can take this one.' In her other hand she held the lovely white muslin dress.

Kitty's mind raced. She looked at her old brown dress. Since she'd never love any man other than Nat, did it really matter what she chose to do?

'Well, Kitty?' Mrs Cummings was tapping her foot.

If she put on the white muslin she'd never have to scrub floors again. All she had to do was stop thinking while she was with one of Mrs Cummings's gentlemen.

'Well?'

Kitty held out her hand. 'I'll take that one.'

Mrs Cummings smiled and handed her the white dress. 'I knew you'd see sense, Kitty dear. Now, how about some supper?'

Henry's fleshy face turned scarlet and drops of sweat beaded his brow as he panted his way to a satisfactory conclusion. One last huff and he collapsed on top of her. Kitty turned her head away from his hot breath. She thought she'd made all the right noises to convince him she was intact. Mrs Cummings had coached her carefully and promised her a little extra if she managed it successfully. It hadn't been as awful as she'd expected, so long as she thought about something else until he was done.

A wave of euphoria washed over her. She'd come through. And now she had somewhere to stay and there'd be food on the table.

Henry let out a snore and she jerked her legs to wake him up before she suffocated.

He sighed and withdrew from her.

Kitty crossed her arms over her breasts and turned away.

He inspected the smear of pig's blood on the lower sheet and smiled. He stood up and dressed hurriedly without looking at her. The door closed behind him.

Ungrateful wretch! If he'd believed it was her first time he might have said a kind word to her or left her a penny or two. Kitty got out of bed and washed herself thoroughly in the strangely shaped china basin that Mrs Cummings had brought her. It fitted comfortably between her thighs and the vinegar in the water washed away any lingering musky smell. She dressed again, except for her stockings, which she'd not had the chance to take off before Henry had grabbed her.

There was a knock at the door and Mrs Cummings came in. 'All right, dear? No nastiness?'

Kitty shook her head.

'He certainly seemed very satisfied. Now make your bed neatly ready for the next client.'

'The next ...' But of course, she thought, her spirits plummeting again.

'There's no other gentleman here yet so why don't you come down and meet the rest of the girls? We're all one happy family here.'

Chapter 29

Florence laughed as the canary pecked at the proffered slice of apple.

'She's a pretty little thing.' Venetia's smile faded as she thought about Kitty. The poor girl might have made a bad choice of husband but there was no malice in her. It would be hard for her since only the most menial kinds of work in less than respectable households, or worse, would be available to her without a reference. If only she'd known Kitty was there when she'd called at the kitchen door, Venetia would have written her a recommendation.

Caesar barked and looked up intently at the birdcage on the table.

'He's jealous!' said Florence.

Venetia bent to pat the pug. She was fond of Caesar but he didn't compensate for the loss of Nero.

The morning-room door opened and Jack came in, his expression good-humoured. 'Are you ready, Venetia?'

She nodded. He was freshly shaved and carried with him a tantalising aroma of lime and bergamot. Last night he'd come in very late and she couldn't help wondering where he'd been.

'I miss being in the showroom,' said Florence. 'There's always something interesting happening there.'

'Including bricks being thrown through the window,' said Jack, dryly. 'Now remember, you're not to go outside, except into the garden.'

'Raffie's going to teach me another card game.' She gave Jack an impudent grin. 'But we'll keep the stakes to matchsticks only.'

'Make sure you do, Miss!' Amusement gleamed in his eyes.

Mama came in. 'Have I kept you waiting?' she said. 'I must say, now we have to shift for ourselves, I realise how much I took Kitty for granted. She always laid out my clothes and advised me on what to wear.'

It was warm as they walked to Cheapside. Ladies strolled with their friends, taking advantage of the sunshine to show off their delicate muslin dresses and pretty bonnets.

Venetia yearned to cast aside black and wear something colourful; a primrose dress in lawn with ivory lace, or lilac perhaps. Then Jack might look at her in that singular way of his again, the way that made her heart thud and her knees go weak, and tell her that he'd never really believed she'd stolen money from the cashbox.

'You're unusually quiet, Venetia,' he said.

She flushed. He'd think her very shallow if he knew what she'd been imagining. 'I'm planning what samples to take with me to show Lady Draycott today.'

'I shall accompany you to Cavendish Square.'

'That would set my mind at rest,' said Mama. 'I don't like to think of Venetia being exposed to any risks in the current circumstances.'

When they arrived at Lovell and Chamberlaine they discovered Mr Marsden was there, talking to Sergeant Norreys.

'Good morning, Marsden,' said Jack.

Mr Marsden tipped his hat. 'I came to bring the walnut sewing table Miss Lovell ordered.'

'Is that for Mrs Dove?' asked Mama. 'I expected it last week.'

'I apologise for its late arrival, Ma'am,' said Mr Marsden, 'but, as I was telling Sergeant Norreys here, we're short of skilled workers at present. Since Fred Harris was killed at Salamanca and his father died of a broken heart, it's hard to oversee everything myself without a business partner.' He rubbed a hand over his homely face. 'Can't seem to find the right quality of apprentice, neither.'

As Mr Marsden walked off down the street Venetia heard the sound of a whistle being blown urgently outside. Her stomach did a somersault. King Midas! She looked at Jack and saw that he was already alerted.

'Lock the door,' he said, 'and go upstairs with your mother.' He snatched up his pistol from its hiding place behind the counter and went outside.

Sergeant Norreys followed close on his heels, already reaching for the pistol inside his jacket.

Venetia locked the door behind them.

'We must do as Jack says,' said Mama. Her eyes were frightened.

Venetia took her hand and they ran upstairs.

Sergeant Norreys had made a comfortable billet for himself in one of the front rooms and Venetia led her mother into the other one.

'We can see the street from here,' said Venetia, throwing up the sash window.

'Come in at once!' said Mama. 'The men have pistols and we've no idea what might happen.'

Venetia ignored her and leaned out to scan the street. Whistles blasted and men ran out of the shops armed with rifles, pitchforks and sticks. Further down the street she saw King Midas's black coach forcing its way through the gathering crowd of shopkeepers. The coachman's whip licked at the men attempting to climb on to the carriage. Three of King Midas's men, all dressed in their customary black, hung off the back of the coach, beating off the shopkeepers' grasping hands with cudgels.

A couple of women in the crowd threw eggs and potatoes at the coach, screaming abuse.

'He's here!' said Venetia.

Mama let out a moan of terror.

'And he's stopped outside.' Venetia's heart hammered.

Five men leaped out of the coach and tried to force their way through the crowd to Lovell and Chamberlaine's door. Scuffles broke out as the mob prevented them from gaining access.

'He must have come to collect Raffie's gambling debts,' said Venetia.

'We must pay him at once!' Mama wrung her hands. 'I don't care if it bankrupts us. I cannot go on for another day wondering when that man will appear and hack off Raffie's hand. His life will be ruined!' Her voice rose with impending hysteria.

Venetia took a deep breath to quell her own rising fear. 'Raffie's safe at home in Quill Court and we haven't five hundred pounds to give King Midas.'

'Five hundred pounds!' shrieked Mama. 'Five hundred? Then we'll never be rid of him. He'll go on terrorising us, one by one, until we're all dead. Why did you insist we fight him? Jack was right, we'll never beat him.' She could barely breathe as hysteria threatened to overwhelm her.

'Stop it!' Venetia shook her mother's shoulders. 'We can't change what's happened. We have to show King Midas that there are too many of us for him to overcome. We'll be so much trouble to him that he'll leave us alone.'

The sound of a pistol shot outside reverberated along the street.

Mama screamed and Venetia ran back to the window. The street seethed with yelling, fighting men. She looked frantically for Jack. Please God he wasn't hurt!

King Midas stood on the top step of the coach, holding a smoking pistol. 'Stop!' he commanded.

Someone in the crowd shouted and an egg smashed against the coach door.

Then another shot rang out.

King Midas clasped a hand to his shoulder and then looked disbelievingly at the blood oozing out from between his fingers. A stone soared past his head and his guards fought their way back to the coach.

Five men clambered inside, pulling King Midas in with them, and the other three leaped on to the back, lashing out with their boots as the shopkeepers attempted to pull them off their perch.

The coachman cracked his whip and the black horses tossed their manes. The coach, spattered and smeared with rotten eggs, rolled forwards.

The jeering mob ran alongside it, thumping the coachwork with their fists until it gathered speed and set off down the street at a furious pace.

Venetia ran downstairs and unlocked the door with her mother following behind.

Jack and Sergeant Norreys stood outside with a group of men, laughing and clapping each other on the back.

Venetia clasped a hand to her chest while her heartbeat steadied. Jack was safe!

'Good work, Sergeant,' said Jack. 'Nothing like a shot across the bows to put the fear of God into the enemy.'

'My aim was at fault though,' said Sergeant Norreys, rubbing at his nose. 'I only meant to let a bullet whistle past his ear and give him a fright.'

'Thank goodness you didn't kill him!' said Venetia.

'King Midas certainly isn't worth swinging for,' said Jack.

'Still, it seems to have done the trick. He and his men have galloped off with their tails between their legs,' said Mr Wheeler.

'That's the last we'll see of *them*!' said Mr Benson, rubbing his hands together with satisfaction.

Mr Hayes, who had blood dripping from a cheek wound, took himself home.

Venetia watched the men congratulating each other. They all seemed very pleased with themselves following the skirmish but, although the battle was won, she doubted the war was over yet.

Kitty sat in Mrs Cummings's parlour, buffing her nails and listening to the other girls chatting.

'Settling in, Kitty?' asked Ruby. Dark-haired and lively, she'd been at the brothel the longest. Full of stories, she was still popular with the gentlemen, even though she was nearly thirty.

'We didn't know if you'd be staying,' said Diamond.

'Neither did I,' said Kitty. Diamond's swarthy skin and wide, white smile reminded her of Black Sal.

'Some of the girls Ma Cummings brings home leave after a few days. They get uppity about working here, but you're lucky Mother found you else you'd be on the streets now.' Ruby shuddered theatrically and rolled her eyes. 'And that's really frightening. Street whores never make old bones.'

'You never know who'll pick you up,' said Hazel. 'It's safer here, though you want to watch out for men like that John Haig.'

Ruby cackled with laughter. 'He don't try it on with me no more because I tipped the chamber pot over his head last time. *And* I told him I'd follow him home and tell his wife he'd been indulging in unnatural practices with a donkey.'

Kitty clapped a hand to her mouth. 'You didn't?'

'Lots of them like to talk dirty and smack you about a bit,' said Hazel, yawning. She began to shuffle a pack of cards.

Diamond chuckled, her black face beaming. 'Me, I just close my ears, and my eyes too if he's ugly, and let him get on with it. It's all over quicker that way.'

'And remember, if a gentleman gets up to nasty tricks,' said Hazel, 'scream for Bruno and he'll come and give the tosser a good thump. He's always hanging around listening for trouble. He carries a master key and can let himself into any of the rooms.'

Belle, pale and delicate-looking, stared at her feet and said nothing as usual.

'How long has Mrs Cummings had this house?' asked Kitty.

'Lor' love you!' said Ruby. 'She doesn't own it, for all her airs and graces.'

'She doesn't?'

'Nah! She was a working girl herself, once. There's a man as calls himself King Midas who comes once a month to collect the rent and a share of the profits from her …'

'King Midas?' Kitty looked at Ruby in horror.

'Heard of him, have you? Not surprising. He runs everything around here, including the knocking shops.'

'I know he's not a man to cross,' said Kitty bitterly, picturing her Nat jerking on the end of a rope. Then a cold sweat prickled under her arms. 'I won't have to see him, will I?'

Diamond gave a throaty chuckle. 'He wouldn't even notice the likes of us.'

'He's a nasty piece of work, all right,' said Ruby. She looked thoughtful. 'But he may not be as clever as he seems. I've been with Ma Cummings a few years now but in my last place I overheard him talking to the madam. She asked him whether he'd like to invest in another brothel, one she wanted to open in Westminster. The house needed a lot spending on it but was in a good position for the House of Lords. He said something then about having "to ask my superior".'

'I see,' said Kitty, frowning. So was there still a man above King Midas who gave him his orders? She shivered, imagining him to be even more merciless.

'Who's for a game of Speculation?' asked Hazel, laying out the cards.

A while later the doorknocker sounded and Kitty's heart sank.

'Here we go, girls,' said Ruby. 'Smiles in place and ready for the off!'

The girls put down their cards as Mrs Cummings opened the parlour door and ushered in a gentleman. Portly and with thinning hair, his coat buttons barely restrained his stomach.

'Say good evening to Harold, girls.' Mrs Cummings showed her teeth.

Kitty knew by then that her smile never reached her eyes.

The girls did their best to look interested, especially Ruby who was saving up to retire and rent a place of her own.

Harold looked at them one by one with his hot, piggy eyes.

Kitty held her breath. She didn't like the look of him but beggars couldn't be choosers. She had to have at least four clients a night or she'd be out on her ear.

He pointed. 'That one,' he said.

Mrs Cummings smiled again. 'A good choice. Belle dear, take Harold upstairs.'

Belle rose to her feet and led him away.

Mrs Cummings returned to her private parlour.

'Why does Belle always look so sad?' asked Kitty.

'She lost her baby a few months ago,' said Hazel. 'It died soon after it was born but she's got a bee in her bonnet that it didn't die but was stolen from her.'

'It takes some women like that, the death of a baby,' said Diamond.

'Still,' said Ruby, 'at least she's only gone quiet. Bedlam is just over the way and you can hear the inmates howling sometimes when there's a full moon.'

Hazel shivered. 'Fair gives you the creeps, that does.'

The doorknocker went again and Mrs Cummings ushered a young man into the parlour. 'This is Digby, girls,' she said. 'He comes to us following a recommendation so I'm relying on you to make sure he isn't disappointed.'

Kitty smiled at the nervous young man. He had fair hair and reminded her a little of Master Raffie.

Mrs Cummings saw Kitty smiling at him as he dithered. 'May I suggest Kitty?' she said. 'Fresh up from the country and quite unspoiled.'

Digby nodded.

Kitty forced a smile and stood up.

Chapter 30

There were no customers at present and Venetia hummed to herself as she sat in the showroom, sketching designs for paper hangings. The meeting in Cavendish Square had gone well, culminating in a lucrative contract to redecorate Lady Draycott's townhouse. She was young and had taken to Venetia immediately. She'd also taken to Jack, and Venetia had tried not to be jealous as she listened to their light-hearted banter.

The shop bell jangled violently, making Venetia drop her pencil. Her first thought was that it must be King Midas.

Sergeant Norreys must have feared the same because he raced towards the door, pistol in hand.

Venetia was relieved when she saw that it was only Raffie, bent over with his hands on his knees, catching his breath.

'Whatever's the matter?' asked Mama.

Jack hurried from the office to see what was happening.

Sergeant Norreys put his pistol away and waited for Raffie to speak.

At last he lifted his head and Venetia gasped. One eye was blood-shot and his face was mottled with purple bruises. Blood dripped off his chin.

301

She ran to him. 'What happened?'

'I'm sorry,' he said, his chin quivering. 'I fought them but they were too strong for me.'

'King Midas?'

He nodded, his eyes glistening with tears. 'They've taken Florence.'

'Dear God! Not Florence!' Fear knifed into Venetia's stomach.

Mama let out a shriek and the colour drained away from Jack's face. He swallowed and clasped his hands together, cracking his knuckles. 'Tell me exactly what happened,' he said quietly.

Raffie drew a shuddering breath. 'I never let her out of my sight, except when she went into the privy. I stayed at a discreet distance. They must have been watching. The gate at the end of the garden burst open. There were four of them and King Midas.'

'Please, no!' Tears slid down Mama's face.

'I thought they'd come to cut off my hand.' Raffie closed his eyes for a second. 'They snatched open the privy door and dragged Florence out. She screamed and screamed.' His voice broke. 'I couldn't find anything to use to beat them off, except for an old besom. I ran at them, shouting and flailing the broom.' His shoulders sagged. 'I knew it was hopeless, of course.'

'You were very brave, Raffie,' said Venetia.

'They punched me to the ground. Two of them kicked me and I heard my ribs crack. I was sure I was going to die. And then I heard Florence stop screaming.' He closed his eyes while he composed himself. 'I thought she was dead.'

Mama moaned and began to sway and Sergeant Norreys caught her.

'I struggled to my feet,' said Raffie, 'and staggered after them. King Midas's coach was outside the back gate. I saw them bundle her inside. She had a sack over her head and her hands were tied behind her back.'

Jack gripped Raffie's bruised wrist. 'Did they say anything? Anything at all that might give a clue as to where they've taken her?'

He winced and unclasped Jack's fingers. 'Nothing,' he said. 'I heard them laughing, though. One of them said something about "fresh meat". I didn't know what to do. I was going to go to the constable but he hasn't been much help up to now. So I came straight here to you.' Tears glittered on his lashes. 'I'm sorry, Jack.'

He nodded. 'Yet again those bastards have used their superior strength.' He spoke as if his mouth hurt. 'So they know where we live.' He banged his fist on the counter. 'How could I have been so foolish as to think that you were both safe in Quill Court?'

'Nowhere is safe any more!' Mama burst into great gulping sobs.

'What are we going do?' asked Venetia as she patted her mother's shoulder and wiped away her tears. 'We don't even begin to know where to start looking.'

'We must put ourselves in our enemy's shoes,' said Sergeant Norreys briskly. 'Miss Florence is valuable to them and they're unlikely to harm her at this point.'

'Do you really think so?' Mama plucked at his sleeve.

'I do, Mrs Lovell,' he said. 'They'll have taken her as a hostage and I daresay we'll receive their demands soon enough. Now, shall we go to the kitchen and make a good strong brew with plenty of sugar?'

He led Mama away but Venetia couldn't help intercepting the glance he cast at Jack over his shoulder. It didn't give her any real hope for Florence's safety.

Jack limped backwards and forwards with his hands clasped behind his back. 'I'll go to the parish constable and offer a reward for information regarding Florence's whereabouts but I can't emblazon her name all over the place or her reputation will be ruined. And then all we can do is wait and see if we receive a ransom note.'

'And then what?' asked Venetia. 'If we haven't five hundred pounds to pay off Raffie's so-called gambling debts then we don't have enough to pay a ransom for Florence.'

'I must find it.' Jack's face was ashen and sweat beaded his brow. 'Somehow.'

Venetia suppressed a stab of anger that he hadn't been prepared to protect Raffie but it was different now that his precious Florence was at risk. But then her anger died away, overcome by her fears for the young half-sister she had grown to love. It hurt to imagine her, alone and frightened, in the hands of cruel captors.

'All we can do now,' said Venetia, 'is wait and pray.'

The house was still quiet when Kitty woke. She lay in bed since there was nothing yet to get up for. Drifting in and out of sleep, she thought about Nat and pretended he was curled up behind her, remembering how she'd fitted so neatly into the curve of his body. She wept as she pictured his smile, now fading a little from her memory.

She dozed until she heard heavy footsteps and the click of her door being unlocked. She held her breath until she heard Bruno's footsteps move away. Nasty piece of work, that one. The door always remained locked overnight but now Mrs Cummings trusted her enough to unlock it in the day. In any case, she'd never get through the front door as Bruno kept watch there and the down-stairs windows were nailed shut to prevent the gents from escaping without paying.

Sighing, Kitty dressed. She ached all over. It'd been a busy night and there'd been more callers than she cared to remember. At last, in the early hours, she'd fallen into her bed alone, the sheets all sticky and crumpled.

Thank the good Lord that she hadn't been a virgin when she arrived. All those men, one after the other, would leave you shocked for the rest of your life if you had been. The only way she could do it was, like Diamond said, to close her eyes and think about some-thing else.

She carefully washed out the little sponge Mrs Cummings had given her and hung it from the window catch to dry. Wrapped in a gauze bag with a piece of ribbon sewn to one end, it twirled gently in the breeze. Kitty had to soak it in a mixture of olive oil and quinine and then insert it deep into her private parts every evening.

'You can fish it out by the ribbon,' Mrs Cummings explained. 'Don't forget to use it because you're no use to me here with a brat in your belly. I'd just got the last two girls trained when they fell pregnant.'

The thought of that horrified Kitty and she took care to use the sponge and to wash herself thoroughly after each client. She couldn't help but think that if her mother had been given such a device there wouldn't have been so many mouths to feed and they wouldn't have been so poor.

The girls mostly slept until the middle of the afternoon so Kitty sat by the window to pass the time. The sun was shining and she could see over the roof of Bedlam Hospital to Moor Fields behind.

A big coach swayed down the street, drawn by four black horses. Curious, she watched as it drew to a halt outside and leaned out of the window to take a better look. It was early in the day for a gentleman to visit; none of the girls would be dressed.

The door of the coach opened and a man in a black greatcoat and hat got out. Kitty caught her breath in shock. King Midas! Supposing *he* came to her room? The thought made her quake.

Two other men followed him out of the coach, pulling a girl between them. All Kitty could see was that she was slender and had a fall of black hair. The doorknocker banged. A moment later there were clumping footsteps on the stairs and then outside her room.

She retreated to the corner and held her breath, while her heart banged like a blacksmith's hammer. She heard the door opening to the empty room next door. A moment later it slammed and she heard Ma Cummings speaking in a low voice.

'You can be sure I'll keep her fast,' she said.

'It'll be the worse for you if you don't,' said King Midas.

Kitty came out in a cold sweat. She'd never forget the horror of overhearing him as he planned Nat's murder. Pressing her ear to the door, she listened while the heavy footsteps retreated downstairs. She hurried back to the window and sighed in relief as the black coach drove away.

The house was quiet again.

Kitty stealthily turned her door handle and tip-toed out on to the landing. She peered over the banisters and glimpsed Bruno sitting on the hall chair with his arms folded. She tried to open the door to the adjacent room but it was locked. All was silent. Perhaps the girl was drugged? Mother Cummings had said she needed more girls.

Downstairs the dinner gong sounded and Kitty stopped pondering and went down.

The following morning Kitty sat up in bed and yawned. It had been another busy night. In fact there had been so many gentlemen that the girls had protested.

'I'm not turning away good business,' Ma Cummings had said. 'It's only for a little while, until I find a couple of new girls. I'll visit the Crosse Keys a few times this week and meet the coaches coming up from the country. That's usually time well spent.'

Kitty suddenly remembered where she'd seen Ma Cummings before. It was when she got off the coach from Kent and a fat lady in purple had come to speak to her before Nat shooed her away. He'd joked about it later. The old witch must have been trying to procure her even then.

The whole thing sickened Kitty. How could any girl choose to work in a brothel? The hasty couplings with no soft words were nothing like the delicious times she'd spent making love with Nat. One or two of the men had been rough, some were ugly and most had bad breath.

'Don't let the punters kiss you,' Ruby had advised when she complained of this. 'Just remember to look as if you like it. No punter'll waste his money stuffing a sack of straw.'

Kitty guessed she was performing well enough since two of the gentlemen had left a few coins on the table. She'd hidden them in a handkerchief on top of the wardrobe lest Ma Cummings pinch them. If she could save enough, in time she'd be able to leave. She refused to think how long that might take.

It was then that she heard weeping. Sliding out of bed, she pressed her ear to the wall. Definitely weeping. She remembered how utterly alone she'd felt when she'd been locked in. They were probably starving this poor creature, too. Tentatively, she rapped with her knuckles on the wall. The weeping stopped.

Tap, tap, tap.

Running to the window, Kitty slid up the sash and leaned out.

A moment later she heard the window in the next room scrape up and then a girl peered out.

Kitty gasped. 'You!' She stared at Florence's tear-stained face and tangled hair.

'Kitty? Oh, Kitty! Help me!' she sobbed. 'They beat Raffie and dragged me into a coach and brought me here.'

'Shhhh!' she said. 'They'll hear you!'

Florence clapped a hand over her mouth and glanced fearfully over her shoulder. 'Did they steal you, too?'

'Something like that,' said Kitty. How could King Midas have brought Florence, hardly more than a child, to a place like this?

'I want to go home!'

Kitty leaned dangerously out of the window and reached out, trying not to look at the ground two floors below. Try as she might, she couldn't touch Florence's outstretched fingers.

'Have they hurt you, Florence?'

'I'm bruised. I fought them when they caught me.'

'That's all?'

Florence nodded. 'I'm hungry and I want to go home.' Tears began to slide down her cheeks again.

Kitty breathed a sigh of relief. The girl was still unsullied but for how much longer? 'I haven't the key.' A burning anger rose up in her at the cruelty of those who would use an innocent young girl without mercy.

'What are we going to do?'

The desolation in Florence's expression made Kitty want to weep. 'I'll try to fetch help. It might not be today and you must stay quiet as a mouse and not make a fuss.'

Florence nodded.

'I'll talk to you later.'

Inside her room she paced up and down. She couldn't unlock the door to Florence's prison so she'd have to fetch help from outside. But even if she could escape, would the constable take any notice of her? As soon as he knew that she was a whore he'd laugh at her. No, the only thing to do was to face up to the shame and speak to Miss Venetia. She'd tell Major Chamberlaine and he'd get Florence out.

If Ma Cummings found out that Kitty was a traitor, she'd be out on her ear . It made her sick to the stomach to think of walking the streets, alone, at night, and taking men against a wall in a back alley. They wouldn't be gentlemen neither, and she'd probably catch a foul disease. It didn't bear thinking about. But Florence's woebegone face had awoken pity in her and Kitty refused to ignore it.

Venetia sat by the drawing-room window looking out into Quill Court while her mother, overcome by terror, lay deep in a sedated sleep upstairs. Jack had reported Florence's kidnapping and then they'd sat up all night waiting, dreading, hoping, for news.

'King Midas is deliberately tormenting us,' Jack had said, at three o'clock that morning. 'I'm sure he'll let us know what he wants in exchange for Florence's safety but he's prolonging the agony until we're so desperate we'll give him anything he asks for.'

Venetia watched him rub his bloodshot eyes. He looked exhausted and worn down with sorrow and she ached to hold him in her arms and make his pain go away. What if King Midas killed

Florence as a warning to the other shopkeepers of what would happen to their loved ones if they didn't give up the battle?

Jack fell into a restless sleep in the armchair beside her. She watched him, longing to stroke away the black curl that fell across his brow.

He opened his eyes again after a while. 'Florence will be ruined if we don't get her back soon,' he said bleakly. 'We can't conceal her disappearance for ever.'

If we get her back, thought Venetia, close to tears.

'Coffee,' he said, at dawn.

She'd sent for a pot of scalding hot coffee as black as King Midas's heart and they sat quietly together while they drank it, neither of them finding the words to express their anguish.

Jack had drained his second cup and then rested his hand briefly on her shoulder before going out to speak to the constable again.

Gritty-eyed with exhaustion, Venetia continued to wait. Whenever anyone walked into Quill Court her muscles tensed. She watched Mrs Stanhope and her daughter Emily scatter breadcrumbs on the ground while the sparrows fluttered around their feet. A girl ran across the court with a hoop, a nursemaid running after her. Two brown dogs had a snarling match over a bone.

Annunziata brought her hot chocolate. '*Quella povera ragazza!*' She mopped her eyes on her apron and returned to the kitchen.

Half an hour later a ragged boy crossed Quill Court clutching a piece of paper in his hand.

Venetia sat up straight and watched him, holding her breath.

He looked about as if unsure where he was going.

She didn't wait a moment longer but hurried outside.

'Have you brought a note,' she asked, 'for number five?' Her stomach turned over when she saw that there was an imprint of a crown pressed into the red wax seal on the note he clutched.

The boy squinted up at her suspiciously. 'The gen'leman said I'd get a penny.'

'Did he now?' said Venetia, grimly.

He snatched the coin from her and gave her an impudent grin before running off.

She unfolded the paper with trembling fingers and scanned the elegant black script.

For the attention of Miss V. Lovell
and Mr J. Chamberlaine

I will tolerate no further resistance. Should you and the shopkeepers continue your opposition, one member from each family, including your own, will be executed every week, continuing until all the overdue fees have been collected.

Your sister is in my keeping and her maidenhead will be auctioned to the highest bidder. If you wish to prevent the auction you have one opportunity only to purchase her safety. Miss Lovell will go, alone, to Leadenhall Market at ten o'clock on Thursday morning and leave a bag containing one thousand pounds beneath the poultry stall.

Venetia sank down on the bench under the oak tree and stared at the missive. Thursday morning. Three days to find a thousand pounds. It was impossible. Florence would be ravished and killed. Then, one by one, each shopkeeper's family would be decimated. And it was all her fault. Fatigue and distress gripped her like a steel band around her chest until she could hardly breathe. Jack had pleaded with her not to set in motion a runaway waggon but she'd carried on regardless. Her foolishness was going to kill them all.

Chapter 31

Kitty tip-toed downstairs, avoiding the step that creaked. If she could find a way out through the kitchen, she might be able to fetch help for Florence.

But it was no good.

Bruno stirred on his chair in the hall and looked up at her suspiciously from under his heavy brows. 'Where d'you think you're going?'

'I was going to the kitchen for a drink.'

'You've got water in your room.'

'I ...' Kitty bit her lip. 'I spilled it.'

'More fool you.' He stood up and prodded her with his forefinger. 'Get back upstairs.'

Defeated, she went up again. She stopped outside the room next to her own and tapped on the door. 'It's me, Kitty,' she whispered. She heard the bedsprings creak and footsteps patter over the floor.

'Kitty, let me out. Help me, please!'

'I'm trying to find a way.'

A stair creaked behind her and as Kitty turned fearfully to see who was coming, she was struck a blow to the head that sent her reeling. She screamed and banged her face on the banister rail as she fell to the ground. Dazed, she tried to sit up. A booted foot landed on her back, throwing her forwards. Then she was lifted up and her head thumped against the wall.

'Stop it!' Mrs Cummings's shriek cut through the agony in Kitty's head. 'What are you doing, Bruno? Haven't I told you again and again not to damage the goods? We're short enough of girls already without you putting them out of action.'

'She was talking to the new girl.'

Ma Cummings's face swam into Kitty's view. 'Is that right?'

'I heard her crying,' said Kitty. 'I thought if I soothed her she'd be less trouble.'

'Hmm.' Ma Cummings tipped up Kitty's chin and looked at her with suspicious eyes.

Kitty held her gaze while waves of pain throbbed in her head.

'I'll give you the benefit of the doubt this time,' said Ma Cummings. 'Bruno, fetch a basin of water and a cloth. And be quick about it! Look at this girl's lip! And there's blood on her white dress. It'll cost us at least a night's earnings. You've got to keep that bloody temper of yours under control! I'm going to dock your wages to teach you a lesson.'

Bruno stared at Kitty and she shivered at the burning hatred in his eyes.

'And you, Miss,' continued Ma Cummings, 'can share the loss with him, to remind you not to interfere in things that aren't your business.'

A short while later Kitty's face had been bathed and she'd been issued with a blue dress made of a shiny, cheap-looking material. Ma Cummings left her in her room with a cold compress on her mouth to reduce the swelling on her lip.

But something had to be done about Florence. Creeping down to the first-floor landing again, Kitty peered over the banisters to the hall. Bruno was still on the chair before the door.

There was a window on the landing overlooking the back yard.

Cautiously, Kitty pushed up the sash and leaned out. She looked down and saw what must be the washhouse next to the privy. It was a fair drop down and looking at it made her head spin. But as long as she didn't break an ankle it might be possible. She climbed up and crouched on the windowsill.

Two minutes later she'd turned on her stomach, her body see-sawing over the sill while she summoned the courage to push herself over the edge. Sweat prickled under her arms and her fingers were clawed as they gripped the windowframe.

Downstairs a door opened and footsteps began to mount the stairs.

She let go and landed with a thud on the slate roof where she teetered for a moment until she had her balance. Making her way, crablike, across the roof, she climbed down to the brick wall surrounding the small garden and jumped to the ground. She slid back the bolts on the garden gate and hurried into the alley.

Kitty was out of breath by the time she reached Quill Court. She was wondering if she dared to go to the front door when she saw Miss Venetia sitting on the bench under the oak tree.

She looked up as Kitty's shadow fell across the piece of paper she'd been reading. 'Kitty!' Her eyes were red-rimmed from weeping and her hands trembled. 'What happened to your face?'

Kitty sank down beside her. 'I've found Miss Florence,' she said.

Miss Venetia let out a sob.

'She's alive, not harmed ...'

'Thank God!'

'King Midas brought her. She's locked in a ...' Kitty could hardly bear to say it. 'She's in a bawdy house.'

'A bawdy house?' whispered Miss Venetia. 'The note said King Midas is going to auction her ...' She looked away, her face shocked. 'Where is this?'

'The house with the red door, Winchester Street, near Bedlam Hospital.'

'But how did you find her, Kitty?'

The girl licked her throbbing lip, remembering Bruno's violence, but she had to tell the truth now, however shaming. 'Because I live there. I've fallen on very hard times, Miss.' She couldn't bring herself to say what she'd become. 'Nat's dead.' Miss Venetia looked at her with such compassion then that Kitty couldn't stem the flood of tears that sprang to her eyes.

'I read it in the paper, Kitty. I'm so very sorry.'

She rubbed her eyes with the heel of her hand, unable to speak.

'I wish you'd come to ask me for help,' Miss Venetia said softly.

'I did,' sobbed Kitty. 'But Dorcas turned me away. She said Major Chamberlaine gave orders.' She took a deep breath. 'Anyway, it's too late now. But you must tell him to fetch Miss Florence quickly. If you don't, she'll be ravished.'

Venetia pressed a hand to her mouth. 'Couldn't you have helped her escape with you?'

'I haven't the key to her door and she's at the top of the house. It's too high for her to climb out of the window. I'm risking my life by coming here as it is. If Mrs Cummings finds I've escaped, she'll set Bruno on me again. I must hurry back now.'

'But you can't possibly go back!'

Kitty buried her face in her hands. 'If I don't, I'll be tramping the streets at night with nowhere to lay my head and praying some drunk will give me a penny to have his way with me. I have nothing! Even the clothes I wear are borrowed. At least there I have regular meals and a roof over my head.'

Venetia squeezed her hand but couldn't hide the shock in her eyes.

'I couldn't let Miss Florence be harmed but don't, please don't, let Mrs Cummings know I told you how to find her!' Kitty touched her swollen lip. 'Bruno'd kill me.'

'But how shall we get Florence out?'

Kitty stood up. 'I don't know, but if you'll walk with me I'll show you where the house is. Then you and Major Chamberlaine can make plans.'

They left Quill Court and hurried along Gracechurch Street while Kitty described the layout of the house.

'Bruno holds the keys and guards the front door,' she explained. 'He roams about the house while we're working, listening outside the bedroom doors. He throws the gentlemen out if they're drunk or beat the girls too hard.'

'Couldn't you steal the key out of his pocket, Kitty?'

'No, I couldn't.'

'I only thought that you …'

'No!' said Kitty. The thought of trying to filch a key from Bruno and what he might do to her then was terrifying. 'Even if I could get Florence out of that room, we'd still have to get past Bruno and he's looking for an excuse to beat me up again. Mrs Cummings isn't likely to let down her guard, neither. I heard King Midas threatening her.'

Miss Venetia was quiet while she thought. 'Major Chamberlaine will have to come to the house and pretend to be a client.'

'If she thought I'd done anything to help Miss Florence escape, anything at all, she'd tell King Midas. There'd be nowhere for me to run after that.'

'That man has control over the entire London underworld,' said Miss Venetia bitterly.

'Not just London, neither. Did you know he was behind the smuggling from the beach near Spindrift Cottage? He runs the guinea route to France.'

Miss Venetia stopped and turned to face Kitty. 'His network reaches as far as Kent?'

Kitty nodded. 'He takes a rake-off from most of the brothels and businesses round here, too. Though one of the girls told me that she'd heard he takes his orders from someone else.'

As they passed the Crosse Keys, Kitty added, 'Do you remember when we first arrived here?'

'I do,' said Miss Venetia.

'Mrs Cummings spoke to me as I got off the coach,' said Kitty, 'but Nat sent her away. She fools young girls up from the country by promising them work and taking them to her house. She seems to be kind but she drugs them and makes them sign a paper to say they owe her for the new clothes she gives them. And then she tells them the kind of work they're going to have to do.'

'She deceives them?'

Kitty nodded, remembering how she'd thought Ma Cummings was her saviour. It was only Miss Venetia's presence that stopped her from spitting on the ground in disgust.

They had turned into Threadneedle Street before Miss Venetia spoke again.

'I've a plan. Tell me if you think it'll work.'

Venetia sighed in relief as she peered through the window of the Crosse Keys. It had taken her a moment to spy a woman dressed in purple sitting at a table in the corner, sipping a port and lemon, just as Kitty had said she'd be.

She retreated to the other side of Gracechurch Street and pretended to peer into the window of a silversmith's shop while studying her reflection in the glass. She meant no disrespect to Father but it was a pleasant change not to be wearing mourning. A straw bonnet, decorated with ribbons that matched her blue muslin dress, made her look young and pretty again.

Was she completely mad to attempt such a plan? Of course she was, but she'd never forgive herself if she didn't make every effort to save Florence. Even if her reputation were destroyed, at least they'd have each other, two unmarriageable sisters, one ruined by a sojourn in a brothel and the other the product of a bigamous marriage.

The mail coach appeared and rattled along the street. Venetia's pulse began to race. She gripped her travelling bag and hurried close behind the coach as it turned into the courtyard of the Crosse Keys.

The coach door opened and she pushed her way past the descending passengers and sat down inside. There was a deal of noise and confusion as the ostlers changed the horses and the luggage was brought down from the roof. Several boys ran about importuning the passengers to let them carry their bags.

Once she was the only remaining person inside the coach, Venetia stood on the top step surveying the commotion in the courtyard. It only took a moment to see the woman dressed in purple advancing towards her. Suddenly dry-mouthed, she descended and walked slowly towards the inn, looking about her as if uncertain of her whereabouts. Wandering into the taproom she found a free table, ordered a pot of coffee and sat down to wait.

It didn't take long. Within a few minutes the woman in purple was standing beside her.

'May I sit here?' she asked.

Venetia smiled, wondering if the other woman would notice how her hands shook. 'Please do. I've just arrived on the coach.' She did her best to sound like a girl up from the country.

'I'm Mrs Cummings,' said the woman. 'Pleased to make your acquaintance. And you are?'

'Lizzie Dowling.'

'Well, Lizzie Dowling, I'm going to have a nice port and lemon. Can I get you a tipple?'

'That's very kind. I'll have the same.'

Mrs Cummings waved her fingers at the landlord and a moment later their drinks were set before them.

'So you've just arrived, Lizzie,' said Mrs Cummings. 'I may call you Lizzie, mayn't I?'

Venetia nodded, sipping the sweet yet vinegary drink. It wasn't at all like the port Father used to buy.

317

'And do you have employment to go to?' asked Mrs Cummings.

'Not yet,' said Venetia. 'I'll knock on the back doors of some of the big houses.'

'Now that is fortunate!' Mrs Cummings smiled. 'Would you believe it but I'm desperately seeking a good maid.' She sighed. 'My last girl upped and left without a by your leave. It's not even as if the work's too hard.'

'You have a vacant position?' asked Venetia.

'I do and you might suit very well, a bright, pretty girl like you. Why don't you come home with me and, if you like, you can start straight away. What do you say, Lizzie?'

'Yes, please, Mrs Cummings!'

Venetia followed her from the taproom, heart beating with a mixture of exhilaration and terror. She was going to gain entrance to the house where Florence was being held but would she ever be able to leave it again?

Chapter 32

Venetia, all rouged and tricked up in a flounced and frilled red dress with a great deal more of her bosom on display than usual, sat with Mrs Cummings in the parlour. It had given her a strange illicit thrill to behave in this impudent way that was so at odds with her usual demeanour. Kitty had warned her about the soup that was likely to be drugged and so, when she'd arrived at the house, she'd winked at Bruno and professed herself willing to entertain gentlemen straight away.

'I knew you were a sensible girl, Lizzie dear,' said Mrs Cummings.

Venetia shrugged. 'Well, between you and me, I've already found seeing to a gentleman's needs beats scrubbing floors.' She crossed her fingers behind her back, praying that Jack had found her note. If he hadn't, or if he didn't follow her instructions to the letter, she'd soon be in very deep water indeed. She breathed slowly and deeply, hoping that Mrs Cummings couldn't see how scared she was behind her bold manner.

There were footsteps on the stairs and a moment later the door opened. Several girls entered in a flurry of muslin and cheap perfume.

'Come and say hello, girls,' said Mrs Cummings. 'Mother's brought you a new sister. Lizzie, here are Belle, Diamond, Ruby, Kitty and Hazel.'

Venetia smiled, relieved that it appeared Kitty had managed to get back into the house unscathed. 'Happy to make your acquaintance,' she said.

'Pleased, I'm sure,' said the dark-haired girl called Ruby, while the others nodded in a friendly way, except for Kitty who didn't meet her gaze. Venetia noticed that Kitty wore thick face paint in an unsuccessful attempt to disguise the split in her lip.

'It's early for callers so I'll leave you to chat,' said Mrs Cummings. 'But, Kitty dear, try and smile, will you? You look as miserable as sin.'

After she'd gone Ruby sat down on the sofa next to Venetia. 'So, where did Ma Cummings find you?'

'I'd just arrived on the coach from the West Country.'

'You'll not be the first she's picked up that way,' said Hazel.

'First time I've been in a smart house like this, though,' said Venetia. 'This'll be easier than working my fingers to the bone in a kitchen.'

'Mostly,' said Diamond. 'Just remember, you can yell for Bruno if you need help.'

'Am I likely to?'

'Only if some young buck is half seas over and gets rough.'

Venetia nodded. She'd expected these girls, whose way of life had damned them, to be hard and lewd and yet they seemed so ordinary, even showing concern for her. She glanced at Kitty again but she sat, back rigid, with her head turned away.

The girls chatted desultorily amongst themselves and Hazel began to shuffle a pack of cards.

Venetia was too apprehensive to concentrate as the game of Speculation got under way and dropped her cards twice.

'Nervous?' asked Ruby.

'A little,' said Venetia with a fleeting smile. In fact, she was so anxious that it was hard not to run straight out of the front door. But then, Bruno was sitting in the hall, as solid as a rock.

'It's not so bad,' said Belle quietly. 'You do get used to it.'

Before Venetia could answer, the door knocker sounded.

Belle sighed. 'Early start tonight, then.'

'Stand by your beds, girls!' said Ruby.

Venetia's heart began to knock fit to burst. What if her plan failed? She gripped the edges of her chair, battling down a rising wave of nausea.

The door opened.

'Here are my lovely girls,' trilled Mrs Cummings as she ushered two men into the parlour. 'Here are John and Dick come to visit us for the first time. See that you make them welcome.'

John, the taller of the two, had a scowl on his handsome face, while Dick kept his half-turned away.

Ruby stood up and sashayed across to John. 'My, you're a fine-looking fellow. See anything you like?' She rested her hands on her hips and gave him a provocative smile.

He took a step back and scanned the faces turned towards him. 'The blonde.'

Venetia felt a flood of burning heat rise up her throat.

Ruby pouted and returned to her chair.

'An excellent choice!' said Mrs Cummings. 'Lizzie is fresh from the country today.'

Slowly, Venetia stood up, feeling weak as a newborn lamb. What had possessed her to come to this wicked place?

Dick glanced at the girls and nodded at Kitty.

All four of them trooped into the hall and Venetia's back crawled as Bruno watched them while they silently mounted the stairs. On the first floor she opened her bedroom door. Pausing in the doorway, she watched Kitty lead Dick up to the second floor. Wishing she were anywhere else in the world, she followed 'John' into the bedroom.

321

He was sitting on the bed removing his boots but the moment she shut the door, he pulled her roughly into his arms. The stubble on his face rasped her skin as his mouth came down on hers and he kissed her so hard that her senses swam. Her knees buckled.

Then he drew back and tipped up her chin, pinching it painfully between his finger and thumb so she was forced to meet his intense blue gaze.

Still reeling with shame and desire, she squirmed in his grip but he only held her tighter. She began to tremble.

His eyes burned with fury. 'In the name of all that's holy, what the bloody hell do you think you're playing at?' he hissed. 'What if it hadn't been me who came to take you upstairs, Venetia?'

'You're hurting me, Jack!'

'Do you have no conception of the danger you've put yourself into?'

She stared at him boldly. 'Have you a better plan for releasing Florence?'

He let go of her and stepped back. 'Clearly not but yours had better be fool-proof or we're all going to die.'

'I had to snatch the opportunity,' she whispered. 'I had so little time and none at all to discuss it with you.'

'Is Florence still safe?'

'I believe so but we must act quickly. Do you understand what we need to do?'

Jack nodded. 'I read your letter.' A brief smile flashed across his face. 'I'll give credit where it's due. Given that you had so little time and it's unfamiliar terrain, you've planned this like a military campaign.'

'Kitty gave me the information we needed.'

'Time to go into battle then.' He turned the door handle stealthily.

Venetia slipped off her shoes and placed them beside Jack's boots just inside the door before following him.

He looked over the banisters and nodded to her when he saw that Bruno was still at his post on the hall chair.

They tip-toed upstairs.

Kitty was waiting, peering out from behind her door with Sergeant Norreys beside her.

'Where's Florence?' whispered Jack.

Kitty went to the wall beside the bed, tapped three times and then opened the window.

After a moment Venetia heard the sash of the window in the next room sliding up.

'Florence,' murmured Kitty, 'they're here.'

Jack pushed Kitty aside and leaned out of the window. 'It's all right, sweetheart,' he said, softly. 'Don't cry! But you must be absolutely silent and do exactly as we say. We're going to try and get the key so be ready to come with us if we unlock the door. Understand?'

'Kitty,' said Venetia. 'It's time.'

Deathly pale, Kitty took off her dress and lay on the bed with her shift pulled up above her knees, unable to look at them.

Sergeant Norreys, slightly pink about the ears, took several lengths of thin rope and proceeded to tie her ankles and wrists firmly to the four corner posts.

'Ready?' asked Jack. He took a wooden cudgel from inside his coat.

Kitty nodded.

Jack and Venetia pressed themselves flat against the wall behind the door.

'Remember, Kitty,' said Venetia, 'you need to cry out loud enough to bring Bruno but not so loudly that all the others come running.'

'I'm frightened,' she whimpered, looking at Jack. 'If they find out I've pulled the wool over their eyes, they'll kill me. You're going to have to hit me hard enough to leave a mark.'

323

Jack recoiled. 'I can't hit a woman!'

Sergeant Norreys stepped forward. 'She's right, Major.' He turned to Kitty. 'I'm so sorry,' he said, then whacked her across cheek with the back of his hand.

Kitty screamed. 'Again,' she sobbed.

Venetia turned to face the wall with her hands over her ears.

Kitty screamed again. And again.

Heavy footsteps hurried up the stairs. Bruno burst into the room and ran towards Sergeant Norreys, holding up a crowbar.

Jack stepped forward and brought his cudgel down on the back of Bruno's head with a satisfying thud.

The man's knees buckled and he sank to the floor.

Sergeant Norreys hastily tied the man's wrists together behind his back, yanking viciously at the rope.

Jack gagged the prostrate man with his handkerchief and then searched his pockets until he found a ring with several keys attached.

Venetia snatched it from him and hurried to the adjacent room. One by one she tried the keys in the lock until she found the right one and the door sprang open.

Florence fell into her arms.

Venetia felt her hot tears soaking into her shoulder and held her tightly, whispering, 'You mustn't make a sound.' She pulled Florence on to the landing and Jack came to enfold his sister in his arms.

Venetia went back to Kitty, embarrassed to see her spread-eagled and half naked, on the bed. 'We can't leave you here like this!'

'You have to,' she said. Her cheek bore the scarlet imprint of a hand and the split on her lip had opened up again.

Venetia was troubled, knowing that, however helpful Kitty had been in rescuing Florence, Jack wouldn't want her in the house.

Tears glinted in Kitty's hazel eyes. 'Just go!' She turned her face to the wall.

Downstairs the doorknocker sounded.

Venetia caught Jack's sleeve. 'Hurry, before the next couple come upstairs!'

On the floor, Bruno groaned.

'Give me the keys, Miss Lovell,' murmured Sergeant Norreys.

Venetia gave Kitty one last glance and handed him the keys. He locked the door, hiding Kitty from view.

Jack took Florence's hand and they crept downstairs to the first-floor landing.

Venetia collected her shoes and Jack's boots while he slid up the window sash. It was a long drop down to the roof below and her pulse began to skip. What if she slipped and fell?

Jack laid a hand on her arm and whispered in her ear, 'Sergeant Norreys and I will go down first and catch you.'

She nodded, hoping he couldn't see how terrified she was.

Sergeant Norreys climbed out. Jack, grimacing in pain as he forced his bad knee over the sill, took a little longer. He held up his hands for his boots.

'You now, Florence,' whispered Venetia, slipping on her shoes.

Florence scrambled on to the windowsill then balked. 'I can't!'

'Yes, you can,' said Venetia firmly. 'Turn on to your front and slide down.' A moment later she grasped Florence's wrists, nudged her over the sill and lowered her down to Jack's waiting arms.

It was Venetia's turn. She swallowed her fear and climbed on to the sill, twisting herself on to her stomach. It was then that she saw Belle coming up the stairs.

Belle stopped dead and clapped a hand to her mouth as she saw Venetia half in and half out of the window. A man's footsteps were coming up the stairs behind her.

Venetia pressed a finger to her mouth and gave Belle an imploring look.

She nodded and turned to face the man as he reached the top

step. She lifted his hand and placed it on her breast. He wasn't look-ing at anyone climbing out of the window as he pulled up Belle's skirt and ran his hand up the inside of her thigh.

Dry-mouthed, Venetia closed her eyes and slid over the sill.

Jack caught her before she landed and held her tight against his chest for a heartbeat.

Florence and Sergeant Norreys were already sliding down from the roof to the garden wall below.

A moment later they let themselves out through the gate into the back alley.

Jack hurriedly put on his boots. 'I've a hackney waiting,' he said.

They ran to the end of the alley, scrambled into the carriage and were away.

Venetia, her teeth chattering with the aftershock, said, 'I can't believe we've escaped!'

'Thanks to you,' said Jack. He slipped his arm around Florence, who had her face buried in his shoulder.

Venetia closed her eyes while she composed herself. It terrified her to think how easily her plan could have gone horribly wrong.

They drew up outside the house in Quill Court and Florence disentangled herself from Jack's arms. 'Home!' she said. 'I expect Mama's been worried.'

Jack laughed. 'That's the understatement of the century. You run in while I pay the driver.'

Sergeant Norreys handed Venetia down from the carriage. 'You've been extraordinarily brave, Miss Lovell,' he said. 'Not many ladies could've held their nerve to a successful outcome.'

'It was Kitty who was brave.' Guilt at leaving her in that place churned in Venetia's stomach. She plucked at the tawdry material of her red dress. 'I'd better hurry inside before the neighbours see me.' She forced a wavering smile. 'We'd never live it down.'

Mama was in the drawing room, laughing and crying at the same time while hugging Florence. She looked up and saw Venetia. 'My darling girl! Come to me at once. I've been frantic with worry for you both.'

Venetia ran to her and Mama pulled her close and kissed her face again and again. 'I nearly had an apoplexy when I heard, Venetia. I'd have utterly forbidden it if I'd known.'

'That's why I didn't tell you,' she said. 'I knew I mustn't think twice or we'd lose the opportunity.'

'I was so frightened I'd lose you both.' Mama dabbed her eyes dry.

Caesar put his paws on Florence's knee and yapped until she made a fuss of him.

'Thank heavens!' said a woman's voice.

Venetia turned to see Mrs Dove.

'I came to visit your mother,' she said, 'and heard about the terrible catastrophe that had befallen you all.'

'I don't know how I should have come through these past hours without you, Grace,' said Mama.

'But now all is resolved.'

'My cup runneth over,' said Mama, kissing Venetia and Florence again.

'And Florence is quite unharmed?' asked Mrs Dove.

Florence nodded her head vigorously and smiled up at Jack.

'It's a relief, isn't it, Major Chamberlaine?' said Mrs Dove. 'A girl's reputation is so easily spoiled.'

'And for that reason,' said Jack, 'I'm sure you'll understand if we ask for your absolute discretion in this matter?'

'Not a word,' she said, touching a finger to her lips.

'Florence,' he said, 'I'm going to send you to stay with your god-mother.'

She wrinkled her nose. 'Aunt Mullins is so strict! And there's no one to see in Highgate, except all the old tabbies who call to take tea.'

'But you'll be safe,' said Mama.

'Where's Raffie?' asked Florence.

'Resting,' said Mama. 'King Midas's thugs broke his ribs.'

'He tried so hard to save me.'

The door closed behind her and Mrs Dove rose to her feet. 'What a world we live in! I shall take my leave of you, Fanny, and allow you to spend time with your reunited family.'

'Thank you for your kindness today, Grace,' said Mama.

'That's what friends are for,' said Mrs Dove, kissing Mama's cheek.

Jack escorted her to the front door and then returned to the drawing room.

'There are bound to be repercussions once King Midas finds we've released Florence,' he said.

'Take her to her godmother's house immediately, Jack,' said Mama. 'It would be too terrible if he snatched her again.' Her mouth quivered and tears overflowed. 'It's dreadful living like this, as if we're waiting for an earthquake. I can't sleep for worrying. Can't we pack up and move somewhere he'll never find us?'

'We have everything invested here,' said Jack, 'and having stirred up the shopkeepers into an army, we cannot abandon them, can we?'

Jack was right and Venetia felt entirely to blame. She put one arm around her mother. 'Why don't you go and rest?'

'Perhaps I will.' She dabbed at her tears with her handkerchief.

'I'll come upstairs with you and wash the paint off my face and change my clothes before that sour-faced Dorcas sees me.'

As they climbed the stairs, arm in arm, Venetia caught a glimpse of Jack through the drawing-room doorway. He sat slumped in a chair, his bad leg straight out in front of him, his head in his hands.

Chapter 33

Venetia heard a commotion down the area steps and peered out of the morning-room window.

'I'm not leaving until you let me speak to Miss Lovell!'

Dorcas had her hands on her hips. 'I've already told you, Kitty's gone and you can't speak to Miss Lovell.'

'Are you looking for me?' Venetia called.

The man's face and fair hair was familiar but she couldn't think where she'd seen him before. He didn't look dangerous, only agitated.

He snatched the hat from his head. 'Miss Lovell, Tom Scott, begging your pardon.'

'Tom Scott?' She frowned, trying to recall where she'd seen him before. 'Oh!' she said. 'You're the fisherman who used to call for Kitty at Spindrift Cottage on her afternoon off.'

'I did, Miss.'

Dorcas was looking at her with her mouth pursed up as if she'd been drinking vinegar. 'Please go and open the front door for Mr Scott, Dorcas,' Venetia said.

The maid stepped back as if she'd been slapped.

A short while later Tom Scott stood in the drawing room, awkwardly twisting his hat round in his hands.

'You're looking for Kitty?' said Venetia.

'I've come all the way to London on business and hoped to see her. Your maid tells me she's gone.'

'That's correct.'

'Will you tell me where?'

Hesitating, Venetia studied his earnest and hopeful expression.

'I mean Kitty no harm,' he said. 'The truth is, I expect to collect some money owing to me very soon and then I'll be able to provide for her.'

'I see.' How could she say Kitty was working in a brothel? 'But I'm not sure she'd want me to tell you her direction.'

'I'll camp on your doorstep until you do.' Tom's face worked in distress. 'I'm sorry if you think me rude and ignorant but I must find her!'

Venetia sighed. 'You're a very determined young man.'

'You know something,' said Tom. 'Please, Miss Lovell, whatever it is, tell me.'

The poor man was so anxious. Would telling him the truth cure him of this painful love? 'It's unhappy news,' she said.

'Tell me!'

'Kitty left us to be married.'

'Married!' he groaned.

'But her husband was hanged. Kitty said a certain King Midas ...'

Tom clutched his hat to his chest. 'King Midas! He's the reason we're in London. What does Kitty have to do with him?'

'He murdered a man and Kitty told me he placed the blame on her husband. King Midas is a vicious tyrant,' said Venetia. 'But why does he bring you to London?'

Tom glanced away. 'You know I brought silk and brandy from France for your father,' he said. 'But King Midas used us to smuggle guineas to Napoleon. Now Boney's been defeated the trade has stopped. King Midas still owes us for several trips. We risked our lives for him and he kept saying he'd pay us next time, but he never has.'

'That doesn't surprise me,' said Venetia. 'He'd betray his mother for sixpence.'

'Without us he'd never have made such a vast profit. Twenty-three of us have come to London to seek him out and force him to pay.'

'We've suffered at his hands, too,' said Venetia.

'You?'

'He was responsible for my father's death. He kidnapped my ... a girl from my family and attacked my brother. And then there are the shopkeepers.' Venetia explained what had transpired since they had arrived in London.

'We're going to root him out,' said Tom, a determined expression on his face. 'But now I must find Kitty.'

Venetia drew a deep breath. 'You may not want to find her, once I've told you what I know. After her husband was hanged, King Midas's men stole everything from their lodging house. Kitty was destitute. But there's worse. She was tricked with an offer of employment into going to a house where she's been forced to ...'

'Forced to what?' Tom's voice was anguished. 'For the love of God, don't say what I think you mean!'

'She's in a brothel,' said Venetia quietly.

Ashen-faced, he reared to his feet and slammed his fist against the wall, letting out a howl of anguish. 'I'll kill the bastard!'

'Then you'll surely hang.'

'Tell me where she is!'

Perhaps Tom might overlook what had happened and marry Kitty anyway? Venetia made up her mind. 'She's in the house with the red door in Winchester Street, near to Bedlam Hospital.'

'Thank you, Miss,' said Tom. 'I'll not forget you helped me. I'm staying at the Ship's Bell in Hugging Lane, near to Queen Hithe stairs, if there's anything I can do for you.'

331

'Perhaps you'd let me know if you discover where King Midas lives?'

Tom nodded.

Venetia went with him to the front door and watched him hurry away down the street.

It was growing dark by the time Jack returned from Highgate.

'You left Florence safely with her godmother?' Venetia asked.

He nodded.

'I shall miss her very much and Mama is bereft.' He looked tired, she thought.

Jack closed the door and limped into the room. 'I've seen how much you've all grown to love my sister and I'm ashamed of the way I spoke to you when you first came to Quill Court. And, more than that, I apologise for even suspecting that it might be you who took money from the cashbox.'

Venetia couldn't prevent the tears from starting to her eyes. 'It hurt me very deeply.'

He bit his lip. 'I know and I'm so sorry.'

'We were never the gold-diggers you thought us.'

'You've proved that a thousandfold.' He took her hand and lifted it to his lips. 'The personal risk you took to save Florence was extraordinary. I can never thank you enough.'

A shiver ran up her arm at his touch and her heart sang at his apology.

'How's Raffie?'

'Recovering from his injuries,' she said, 'but he still blames himself for Florence's abduction.'

'He's young,' said Jack, 'and lacks a father's discipline. Although his foolishness drove him to behave dishonourably, he acted with great bravery in attempting to beat off Florence's attackers. Perhaps, with your permission, I might take on a father's role and attempt to give him guidance?'

'Jack, that's the very thing he needs!' A great weight lifted off Venetia's shoulders.

'Then that's agreed,' he said with a smile.

'I had a visitor this afternoon,' Venetia said, and told him all about Tom Scott. 'So there are twenty-three smugglers baying for King Midas's blood, or at least out to claim what he promised to pay them. Tom's staying at the Ship's Bell and he'll let us know if they find out where King Midas lives.'

'I doubt they'll get their money.'

'It's so frightening never knowing when he'll strike again. We're all living on a knife edge.'

'I'm taking steps to resolve the problem,' said Jack, 'but it's too early to say if I'll be successful. I wish I could give you comfort by saying that it'll soon all be over but there's no certainty.' He sat down on the sofa beside her and rubbed his eyes.

'I do so hope Tom will take Kitty away from Mrs Cummings.' said Venetia. 'I feel dreadfully guilty at leaving her in that place after she was so brave.'

'It was her own choice to stay,' said Jack.

'Choice?' said Venetia. 'She has no *choice*. What else could she have done? No one will give her a position without a reference. Would you let her work here again?'

He shook his head. 'Not with Florence in the house.'

'She would have been ruined if it hadn't been for Kitty.' Annoyance made Venetia speak sharply. 'I must do something for her. If Tom doesn't help her and you won't, then I shall at least give her a reference.'

'You'll ruin your own reputation if you do.'

'She must be allowed to erase the memory of the last few weeks from her life! Would you have refused to allow Florence to come home to us if she'd been ravished?'

'How can you possibly compare an innocent and gently brought up young girl with a maidservant who has fallen into the depths of sin?'

'But it wasn't Kitty's fault!'

'Venetia,' he said gently, 'there's nothing we can do for Kitty now and there's much we need to do to rid us all of King Midas.' He stood up. 'I must go out again,' he said. 'Don't wait up for me.' He touched her shoulder and then he was gone

Venetia sighed. She would have to hope that Tom Scott's love for Kitty would prove strong enough to save her.

Kitty pulled the sheet up over her shoulders. She had a chill and a sore throat. Her head ached and she alternately shivered and burned with fever. Tears of self-pity seeped from her eyes, as she conjured up Nat's smiling face. She'd never be happy again. The agony of missing him and of what she'd become made her heart feel as if it had turned to a lump of stone.

There was a tap on the door. 'I've brought you a drop of soup,' said Belle, sitting down on the edge of the bed.

Kitty sat up slowly, her head swimming. 'You're very kind.' At least someone cared about her.

'Even if you feel rotten, the bruises on your face are fading and your lip is healing,' said Belle.

'But what if it leaves a scar and Ma Cummings throws me out?' Dread lay uneasily in Kitty's belly. 'I'll not be able to work if the punters don't fancy me. And she was really angry at me after Lizzie and those men ran off, even though it wasn't my fault.'

'There was ever such a ruckus between King Midas and Ma Cummings,' said Belle. 'He came round in a rage; that horrible quiet rage that means something awful will happen. We listened outside her private parlour. She said Lizzie bamboozled her into coming here and she let the men in and they stole the other girl away. Kitty, what really happened?'

'Did Ma Cummings send you to ask me?'

'She did not! I saw Lizzie climb out of the window but I didn't call Ma Cummings. I'd *never* help her. She's in league with all the others.'

'What others?'

'King Midas, a whole ring of brothel keepers, pickpockets, thieves, flash houses, pawnbrokers. This city is as rotten as a cheese full of maggots.'

'Then why do you stay here, Belle?'

'Why do you?' Tears glittered on Belle's eyelashes. 'What's left for girls like us? I had a good position once as a housemaid but the master's son took a fancy and one night he forced himself on me. Next thing I had a babe in my belly and the mistress turned me off. The bitch accused me of seducing her son!'

'How could she deny her own grandchild?'

'Kitty, you're still such an innocent.' Belle sighed. 'Try and sleep. I'd better go or Ma Cummings will be after me.'

Kitty dozed all afternoon and felt a little better when Ma Cummings came to get her up and dressed for the evening's trade.

The other girls chatted amongst themselves in the parlour, squealing with laughter at Ruby's tale of her last client's peculiar fascination with her feet. 'He had to suck my toes before he could do it,' she giggled.

Kitty, rubbing her temples, didn't even look up when Ma Cummings brought a gentleman into the parlour. He loomed over them while he made his choice.

'Kitty!' Ma Cummings's voice was sharp, even though she still smiled with all her teeth showing. 'Kitty dear,' she said in more melodious tones, 'this is Tom.'

Mechanically, Kitty stood up and held out her hand. As the man pressed his callused palm, warm and dry, against hers, she glanced up. His face was weathered by years of sun and wind and his scrubby fair hair tousled. Her mouth fell open but he shook his head slightly and squeezed her hand so hard she winced.

'Hello, Kitty,' he said.

Bruno, sitting in the hall and trimming his nails with a knife, watched them go upstairs.

Kitty led him into her room and closed the door behind them with shaking hands. She could see their reflections in the dressing-table mirror, like a painting.

'How did you know I was here?' she whispered.

'Miss Lovell told me.'

Kitty turned her head away so that he wouldn't see her shame. 'She shouldn't have done that.'

'I made her.'

'Come to gloat, have you?'

He tried to take her hand again but she snatched it away. 'She told me about your husband,' he said.

His sea-grey eyes were full of concern. A great bubble of grief forced its way up from deep in Kitty's chest. Her mouth opened in an ugly square and she heard herself wail in anguish while tears rolled down her face. 'I loved him so and King Midas sent him to the gallows.'

'Oh, Kitty love!' Tom drew her to his broad chest.

She clung to him like a limpet, breathing in the familiar tang of sea salt on his clothes, and sobbed until there were no tears left.

'I'm going to take you home,' he said.

All at once she wanted more than anything to leave the stinking, hateful city behind and go back to Kent where the air was fresh and the beach washed clean by the sea every day. She sniffed and sobbed. 'I can't return now, not after …'

'What happened wasn't your fault, Kitty. No one has to know. Listen to me!' He tilted up her chin and wiped her tears away, just as he had when they were children and she'd fallen and cut her knee. 'I've come to London with the rest of the fishermen. We're going to find that bastard King Midas and collect the money he owes us. And then I'm going to take you home.'

She shook her head. 'You can't. I'm soiled goods now.'

'Not to me, you're not.'

'Tom …'

'Come on, we're leaving right now.'

'Ma Cummings won't let me. I owe her money for my clothes and she'll put me in the debtors' jail if I can't pay. And Bruno will beat me again if I try to leave.' She pressed her fingers to her temples. Her headache was worse.

Tom put his hand inside his coat and withdrew a pistol. 'I'll do whatever I have to.'

Kitty stared at the pistol. 'Where did you get that?'

'We've come prepared to do battle with King Midas.'

Outside the door a floorboard creaked.

Kitty pressed a finger to his lips, her heart thudding.

There was a knock on the door. 'Time's up!'

'It's Bruno,' whispered Kitty. Jesus God, what if he'd heard?

'One minute!' Tom called out. He kissed Kitty's cheek and whispered in her ear, 'Stay close.'

Once Bruno's footsteps had faded away, Tom opened the door and they crept downstairs.

Kitty's heart sank as Bruno watched them from his chair by the door. He must have sensed something wrong because he stood up. 'Get back in the parlour, Kitty,' he said.

Tom pointed the pistol at him. 'She's coming with me. Let us out.'

Bruno hesitated and then opened the door.

Tom stepped through the doorway, pulling Kitty by the hand.

She saw the street and freedom ahead but, as her foot crossed the threshold, the door slammed against her wrist. A shaft of excruciating pain made her scream.

Tom yelled and shouldered the door open. There was a flash and a deafening bang and Bruno yelped, clasped a meaty hand to his arm and slid down the wall to the floor.

Nursing her wrist against her chest in a haze of pain, Kitty saw Belle run into the hall as Ma Cummings burst out of her private parlour.

Belle stuck out her foot and Ma Cummings went sprawling on top of Bruno.

Tom, white-faced with the smoking pistol at his side, was staring at the puddle of Bruno's blood spreading across the hall floor.

'Run!' shrieked Belle. She leaped over the two tangled bodies on the floor, snatched Kitty's arm and dragged her outside. She grabbed Tom's hand and sprinted off down the street, pulling them along.

They ran until they were sure no one was following them, finally coming to a stop in a churchyard off Bishopsgate.

'Bloody hell!' said Belle, sinking down to sit on a tomb. 'What've I done? I can't never go back there no more.'

'Come with us,' said Tom. 'I'd never have got Kitty out without you.'

Kitty watched in amazement as Belle smiled. She'd never seen the girl smile before.

'First time you've shot anyone?' asked Belle.

Tom nodded. 'There was so much blood.'

'Bruno'll be all right. More's the pity.' Belle lifted Kitty's hand and inspected her wrist. 'You're going to have a cracking bruise but I don't think it's broken. So what do we do now?'

'We'll go back to the Ship's Bell,' said Tom, 'and you'd better meet the others.' He spoke to Belle but he was smiling at Kitty.

It had all happened so fast. Kitty smiled tremulously back at him. Tom wasn't the love of her life, like Nat had been, but just maybe they might rub along together. Somewhere, deep in her heart, there was the smallest glimmer of hope.

Chapter 34

Venetia stared out of the shop window, lost in contemplation.

'You're looking very solemn,' said Mama, coming to stand beside her.

'I've been thinking about what I can do for Kitty,' said Venetia.

'But surely there is nothing you *can* do?' said Mama, doubt written across her face.

'Jack's of the same opinion,' said Venetia, 'despite Kitty risking her safety to help Florence.'

'But, Venetia dear,' Mama rested her hand on Venetia's wrist, 'you must know we cannot have Kitty back here? It would be entirely unsuitable. We're already in a delicate situation with regard to your father having had two households. If it should become common knowledge that we've taken in a girl from a house of ill repute we might as well close the shop immediately since we'd have no more customers.'

'It's too late today,' Venetia said, 'but I'll visit Mrs Dove and ask if she can find a situation for Kitty. She finds places for the fallen women from Angel of Mercy House.'

'I'm sure Grace will help if she can,' said Mama.

The shop bell jangled and a street boy handed Venetia a note. 'It's for Jack,' she said.

She went to find him in the office. 'This came for you.'

He looked up at her, his expression wary 'Not another missive from King Midas?'

Shaking her head, she said, 'It's different writing.'

He opened the note and scanned it, then scraped back his chair, rising abruptly to his feet. 'Florence has a high fever and is asking for me. I must go to her straight away.'

A wave of relief that it wasn't King Midas up to no good again washed over Venetia. 'Shall Mama or I come, in case she needs nursing?'

'Thank you but you're needed here. I'll send for you if necessary.'

'It'll be dark when you reach Highgate. You'll have to stay the night.'

'Sergeant Norreys will guard the shop. Lock up carefully when you go home to Quill Court tonight, won't you?'

She nodded. 'Take care, Jack! And send my love to Florence.'

'I will.' He reached out and touched her cheek. 'Venetia ...'

'Yes?'

He sighed. 'We'll talk when I return. But stay vigilant, won't you?'

A few moments later he'd gone.

It was after closing time and Raffie had gone upstairs to lie on Sergeant Norreys's truckle bed to rest his aching ribs while Venetia and Mama tidied the showroom.

'I hope Florence recovers soon,' said Mama, a worried frown on her forehead.

Venetia glanced up at the shop window as a carriage, going too fast, lurched past. And then a woman screamed. The familiar feeling of dread enveloped her.

Mama paused in the act of dusting a bureau and was listening, too. 'There's a disturbance. Do you think it's ...'

The shop door burst open and Mama screamed for Sergeant Norreys as half a dozen men surged into the showroom.

Venetia gasped as one of them wrenched down the curtain display in the window and smashed the windowpanes. Another overturned a table, sending an arrangement of delicate china skittering in shards across the floor. Remembering the pistol Jack had hidden under the counter, she ducked down and scrabbled about amongst the shelves. Panic fluttered in her stomach. Where was it?

The thugs, yelling with excitement, began to sweep all the vases, urns and obelisks off the shelves and to tear down the draped lengths of silk. A man with ginger hair slit a cushion and threw it in the air, laughing at the snowstorm of feathers. Another joined in the fun, slashing the remaining cushions to tatters.

Sergeant Norreys, who'd been in the kitchen, ran into the showroom with a pistol in each hand. 'Stand!' he shouted.

One of the thugs ran at him, a knife gleaming in his hand.

Sergeant Norreys took aim.

Mama screamed, hands over her ears, as a shot rang through the air.

The man bellowed and dropped the knife, his sleeve blossoming scarlet.

'Who's next?' shouted Sergeant Norreys, snatching up the knife.

One of the men pulled out a pistol but Norreys was too quick for him. The man yelped and clasped his knee.

Venetia shouted, 'Stop!' as the ginger-haired man reached inside his coat.

He turned to look at her and saw the pistol in her hand, aimed at his chest. He laughed, his eyes gleaming with excitement. 'Put it down, girl!'

She lifted her chin and tried to keep the pistol steady. 'Leave these premises now or I'll shoot,' she said. Out of the corner of her eye she saw Sergeant Norreys reloading his weapon as fast as he could. Whatever happened, she must not waver or faint.

341

Footsteps hurried down the stairs and then Raffie was there, a pistol in his hand, too. 'If my sister doesn't kill you, I will,' he said.

The ginger-haired man stopped laughing.

'Now get out!' said Venetia.

Sergeant Norreys came to stand beside them, his pistol primed. 'Better do as the lady says. She never makes idle threats.'

Venetia breathed shallowly while her pulse beat a tattoo, concentrating hard on not fainting.

'We've finished here anyway,' said one of the men, backing out of the door. One by one the others followed him, supporting the wounded.

Ginger Hair stopped in the doorway and narrowed his eyes. 'We'll be back. And next time it won't just be a few bits of broken china.'

The door slammed behind him, leaving the bell jangling.

'You can put it down now, Miss Lovell,' said Sergeant Norreys.

Frozen with fright, she couldn't move.

One by one, he levered her fingers off the pistol. 'Have you ever used one of these before?' he asked mildly.

Mutely, she shook her head.

'I thought not.'

Raffie caught her just as her knees buckled.

'It was lucky you were here, Master Raffie,' said Sergeant Norreys.

Raffie gave a lop-sided grin. 'Except that my pistol isn't loaded. I heard the shots and there wasn't time ...'

'You stupid boy!' said Venetia, hugging him tightly. 'You might have been killed!'

'I could say the same about you!'

Mama, trembling like an aspen leaf, came to kiss and fuss her children while Sergeant Norreys went outside to see what was happening.

'Is it never going to end?' whispered Mama.

Venetia looked at the trail of destruction. How many times could

342

they go on picking themselves up and repairing the damage caused by King Midas? She bent to pick up a broken fragment of green china. A tear ran down her cheek as she saw that it was part of the vase with the lovely frieze of Greek dancers, the one she'd so painstakingly mended after the attack that killed her father.

Angry shouts came from the street and a stream of people ran past.

Sergeant Norreys returned. 'It's chaos outside,' he said. 'Several of the shops are on fire. King Midas has brought in reinforcements and our militia is trying to fight them off. You must lock yourselves in while Master Raffie and I go and put out the fires.'

'I'm coming, too,' Venetia said.

'Miss Lovell ...'

'I'm not wasting time arguing.'

'Venetia!' Mama clutched at her arm.

'I started this whole thing and cannot skulk away in hiding while people need help.' She kissed her mother's cheek. 'Why don't you tidy up some of the mess?'

Mama nodded, her eyes wide and frightened. 'But what if King Midas's men come back?'

'Lock yourself in the office and hide in the cupboard. Take this pistol with you.' Venetia spoke briskly but she was trembling inside. 'We'll not be too long,' she said, and followed Raffie and Sergeant Norreys outside. For all her brave words she wished beyond anything that Jack was at her side.

Three shopkeepers raced past them towards a pall of smoke coming from further along the street. 'The haberdasher's shop is alight!' shouted one of them.

It was growing dark and Venetia's heart turned over as she saw the glow of the burning building. 'The apothecary and the tailor's shop are on fire, too.'

They joined the crowd milling about outside the haberdasher's shop. Drawers of trimmings and buttons, chairs, a table and several boxes were heaped haphazardly on the pavement as the owner and his apprentice ran in and out of the shop trying to save their possessions. Mrs Gilbert, the haberdasher's wife, keening with distress, wielded a broomstick to guard the goods from thieving street children.

Raffie hurried to help her.

Sergeant Norreys pointed out the Phoenix fire mark on the side of the building. 'They've called for the water engine but the fire's taking hold.'

A chain of men passed leather buckets from hand to hand, filled from the public fountain, attempting to douse the flames.

'Can't we help?' said Venetia.

'It's too far gone for us to make a difference.'

A noisy fight had broken out and half a dozen men grappled in the gutter. One youth was having his head beaten against the ground by a ruffian in a shabby coat.

Venetia recognised the boy. 'It's Jacob Bernstein!'

Sergeant Norreys grasped the offender by the collar and smacked his head against a wall.

Glass shattered in a nearby window and Venetia ducked as a bottle sailed past her head. The whirling smoke made her cough. She hardly recognised her surroundings. The elegantly dressed shoppers had fled and the street had become a dangerous battle-ground.

They hurried to the tailor's shop to discover that the fire was confined to the front of the building. Venetia pushed herself into the line of men throwing water on to the flames and Sergeant Norreys took off his coat and went to beat out the blaze licking up the window-frames.

The leather buckets were heavy and water slopped down Venetia's skirt and filled her shoes. She gritted her teeth and passed the buckets on as quickly as possible. The heavy weight of guilt churned in her stomach. All of this was her fault.

The water engine clattered into the street, the horses tossing

344

their heads and snorting as they came to a stop outside the haberdasher's. The watermen unrolled their hoses and began to pump a jet of water on to the burning building. Hissing steam billowed all around until the lead trough in the engine was empty. The chain gang directed their efforts to refilling it.

At last the fires were smouldering, leaving the air full of acrid black smoke.

The sound of galloping horses made them look up and Venetia gasped as she recognised the big black coach. That devil King Midas had come to gloat.

The coach slowed down. Men stopped fighting and cursing, and stood silently watching as it rolled slowly past.

Venetia saw King Midas's face as he stared out of the coach's window and held her breath, wondering if he was going to stop.

She shuddered as his hooded gaze, cold and lizard-like, rested on her for a long moment. It made her feel violated, as if he were seeing her naked, defiling her with a slimy touch.

The corners of his thin mouth lifted in an amused smile and he nodded his head just a fraction in acknowledgement of her.

A terrible hatred expanded inside her chest and Sergeant Norreys grasped her wrist as if he sensed the red haze of rage that rose to cloud her vision. If she'd still had the pistol she'd have shot King Midas dead and laughed, not caring about the consequences.

With a flick of the coachman's whip, the coach drove away.

Once it had gone it was as if King Midas had sucked the energy out of the street with him. The troublemakers slunk away and the shopkeepers began to tend to their wounded and start clearing up the trail of destruction.

Raffie returned some hours later, yawning but with his eyes shining. His face and coat were smeared with soot and he pressed a hand against his aching ribs.

Mama ran to hug him. 'I was worried, Raffie. You were gone for such a long time.'

'I helped with the clearing up,' he said. 'The shopkeepers are worried there'll be no trade if it looks too dangerous to shop here.'

'At least it happened after closing time,' said Venetia.

'You look done in, Raffie,' said Mama. 'Come and sit beside me.' It was past two in the morning. Sergeant Norreys had prised up floorboards from an empty room upstairs and fixed them over the broken windows. 'That'll do it until we can fetch a glazier,' he said, hammering home the last nail.

Venetia had cleared away the damaged china, righted the furniture and swept up the feathers that had alighted on every possible surface including the chandelier. Suddenly exhausted, she yawned and looked at Mama and Raffie fast asleep on the sofa together.

'We've got away lightly, compared to some of the others,' said Sergeant Norreys.

'I know,' said Venetia, full of remorse. 'The haberdasher's shop was completely burned out and Mr Gilbert and his wife plan to leave Cheapside and stay with relatives in the country. Jack warned me not to interfere and I wish now, beyond anything, that I'd listened to him.'

There was a sharp rap on the shop door and Venetia looked up in fear.

Sergeant Norreys took out his pistol. 'Stay here, Miss Lovell.' He went to the door and stood behind it, his weapon raised. 'Who's there?' he demanded.

'Let me in, man!'

Sergeant Norreys unbolted the door.

Jack pushed his way in. 'Are they safe, Norreys?'

'Mrs Lovell is sleeping like a baby,' he said. 'Worn out, poor lady.'

Jack saw Venetia. 'Thank God!' he said.

'Is Florence better?' she asked.

'She wasn't ill,' he said shortly. 'The note was a decoy. Aunt

346

Mullins knew nothing about it but clearly someone had found out where we sent Florence. I've asked Aunt Mullins to take her to stay with friends. Then I galloped back to Quill Court and discovered you weren't there. When I arrived in Cheapside I was terribly afraid that something might have happened to you.'

'We were very lucky in comparison to others,' said Venetia. 'King Midas's bullies forced their way in and began to tear the shop apart.'

'But you should have seen Miss Lovell holding one of the thugs at gunpoint, Major,' said Sergeant Norreys with his twisted smile. 'Put the fear of God into him and they all left, sharpish. Master Raffie came out with his pistol cocked, too, even if he hadn't loaded it.'

'What?' Jack's face was a picture of shock.

'It was pure bluff on our part,' said Venetia, 'whereas Sergeant Norreys drew blood from two of the men. Though I'm pleased to say it didn't stain the carpet.'

'How can you joke about it?' said Jack. 'You might have been killed!'

'I joke about it because I was so frightened I thought my heart might stop,' she said. She sat down on a nearby chair, suddenly close to tears. 'I can't stop thinking about the haberdasher's wife. She's lost her home and business and she'll have to go and live on her sister's charity.' Venetia looked down at her shoes so that he wouldn't see the tear running down her cheek. 'And it's all my fault.'

'Time to go home,' said Jack briskly. 'There's been quite enough excitement for one day.'

Chapter 35

Venetia tidied away her pattern books and went into the show-room. It was empty except for Mama, sitting at the counter. Caesar was asleep on her knee and she stared listlessly out of the newly repaired shop windows.

'Are you all right, Mama?'

'I was thinking about Spindrift Cottage. A blowy walk along the beach always made everything better.'

'Wouldn't that be lovely?' said Venetia, imagining the soothing rhythm of the restless sea.

'It's so quiet today.' Mama glanced anxiously at the street. 'The troubles are keeping the customers away. If it goes on like this we'll have no business left.'

'And that won't do King Midas much good, will it?' said Venetia tartly. 'Where are Raffie and Jack? I've hardly seen them all day.'

'They shut themselves away in the study before breakfast this morning and then went out together while you were in the office,' said Mama.

'Perhaps they've gone to the shooting range. I expect Jack has been bamming Raffie for not having loaded his pistol last night.'

Mama closed her eyes. 'It doesn't bear thinking about!'

'But thank goodness Raffie was there.' Venetia swallowed down the memory of her terror that she might have to kill someone to save her family. 'His arrival tipped the balance and made those thugs leave.'

'I need something to distract me from worrying about King Midas,' said Mama. 'I was hoping Grace might call by. She was asking about her walnut sewing table the other day.'

'Oh! I completely forgot about it,' said Venetia. 'It arrived just before Florence was kidnapped and went right out of my mind with all the upset.'

'Do you want Raffie to deliver it for you?'

'It's very light, little more than a sewing box on legs, so I shall manage. In any case, I want to ask her if there's anything she can do to help Kitty.'

'You mustn't walk there alone,' said Mama. 'Sergeant Norreys will find you a hackney and then come and keep me company until Jack and Raffie return.'

Half an hour later the carriage stopped outside Angel of Mercy House and Venetia descended with the little sewing table in her arms. The doorknocker echoed inside and one of the inmates, a curly-haired girl of about eleven, let her in.

Venetia sat down to wait in the hall, watching the child trot up the curved staircase to the second floor. Two floors above that, the great glass dome framed blue sky. Dust motes twirled in a shaft of sunlight filtering down to the hall floor below. After a few minutes in the peaceful warmth, exhaustion caught up with her and her head began to nod.

A door opened on the other side of the hall and a woman dressed severely in black came out, carrying a birch switch.

'Come along, girls and boys!' she said. 'No dawdling.'

A stream of silent children, perhaps a dozen of them, traipsed after her up the stairs.

Venetia sat up straight again and watched them file past in their uniform of blue dresses or shirts and brown breeches, their boots scuffing the stone stairs. One or two glanced her way but they didn't return her smiles. They were a curiously good-looking group of children.

Then two young women, each near to her time, crossed the hall from the back of the house carrying piles of clean linen. They wore grey dresses with cotton aprons stretched over their swollen stomachs. Embarrassed, Venetia looked away. Whatever would have happened to these unfortunate girls if Mrs Dove hadn't so kindly taken them in?

'Miss Lovell?'

Venetia started. She'd been lost in thought and hadn't noticed the girl coming downstairs again.

'Mrs Dove says to go up.'

She picked up the walnut sewing table and climbed the stairs beside the girl. 'Have you been here long?' she asked. The girl looked up and Venetia saw that she had the loveliest hazel eyes fringed with black lashes.

'Always.' Dimples appeared when she smiled. 'But I'm going to work for a gentleman. He's going to give me a new dress and honey cakes to eat.'

Venetia paused halfway up the next step. 'A gentleman? Did he tell you what your duties would be?'

'Yes, miss. He's ever so kind. He sat me on his knee, stroked my hair and said I was very pretty. I only have to be good and do exactly as he says.'

Venetia stared at the girl. Surely no gentleman should say such things to a young scullery or housemaid?

'Miss?' The girl's expression was anxious. 'Mrs Dove's waiting for you.'

'Yes, of course.' Inwardly perturbed, Venetia followed her into the private sitting room.

'My dear Miss Lovell!' Mrs Dove came towards her. Sunlight from the window glinted on the heavy gold cross she always wore. 'How delightful to see you! And you've brought my sewing table. I would have sent one of the boys to carry it, if I'd known.'

'It's not heavy,' said Venetia.

'Sally, bring tea for two, please.'

The girl bobbed a curtsey and left.

'What an attractive child,' said Venetia. 'She was telling me that she's soon to start work for a gentleman.'

Mrs Dove smiled. 'How that girl can rattle on! But, yes, she'll be leaving Angel of Mercy House. It's always such a happy day when a child we've nurtured and trained for years is placed in a suitable position.'

Venetia lifted the lid of the sewing table to show Mrs Dove the satin lining, the embroidery scissors, a needle case and other sewing necessities.

'It's beautifully made,' said Mrs Dove. 'But do tell me, has poor Florence recovered from her frightening experience?'

'I believe so,' said Venetia. 'But King Midas must have discovered where she was hiding. Jack received a note purporting to have come from her godmother, telling him that Florence was dangerously ill. But it turned out to be a ploy to draw him away.'

'Whatever do you mean?'

'While Jack was absent, King Midas's thugs came calling on the shops.'

'How frightening!' said Mrs Dove. 'I'd heard about another disturbance in Cheapside.'

'Mama's nerves are in shreds,' Venetia said. 'There was fighting in the street. Three shops were burned and windows broken. Men forced their way into our showroom at gunpoint and overset the furniture. Nevertheless, we were luckier than many.'

'It's become a war, hasn't it, between King Midas and the shopkeepers?' Mrs Dove's blue eyes were full of concern. 'I did wonder

at the time if you might not have been a little impetuous in insti-
gating such a rebellion.'

Misery and fatigue swept over Venetia. 'I did what I thought was
right. I hate injustice but I was naive to imagine we could overcome
such an enemy.'

The door opened and Sally carried in a tray.

Mrs Dove poured the tea and offered Venetia a piece of short-
bread. 'Unfortunately the braid on my new curtains has become
unstitched,' she said.

'I apologise for any faulty workmanship,' said Venetia, concerned.
'May I see?' She ran her fingers down the edge of the curtain and
found the section of braid that had come loose. She held the curtain
up to the light at the window. 'This certainly shouldn't have happened and I'll ...' She stopped talking, her attention arrested by
what she saw outside.

Down below, beyond the end of the garden, was a paved courtyard and mews. A dark green coach had rolled to a stop into the
courtyard and she caught her breath as King Midas and two bodyguards stepped down. A groom ran out of the stable and started to
uncouple the horses. Another stable hand opened wide the carriage
house doors and inside Venetia saw a great black town coach with a
gold crown painted on the side.

'Miss Lovell?' said Mrs Dove.

Frozen to the spot, Venetia watched King Midas take a key from
his pocket and unlock the garden gate leading to a townhouse
on the opposite side of the mews. She blinked and he was gone.
Turning her gaze away from the window, she examined the curtain
again with trembling hands. What was King Midas doing *here* of
all places? Clearly, his horses were stabled in the mews and he'd
entered the rear garden of the townhouse with every appearance of
familiarity. Exactly as if it were his home, in fact.

'Miss Lovell? What is it?' Mrs Dove went to look out of the
window.

Venetia stared at the trim figure of her mother's friend who turned to regard her with cool blue eyes. Sudden unease made Venetia cautious as she tried to order her thoughts. Had Mrs Dove recognised the black coach? Why had she never mentioned King Midas resided in a property so close to her own? Surely, she couldn't *not* be aware of that but in all the time they'd known her she'd never mentioned it.

'Miss Lovell?'

'I'll speak to the curtain maker,' Venetia said, just as if her world hadn't tilted on its axis. 'I'll ask them to come and make the repair.'

'Perhaps on Thursday?'

'I'll send you a note to confirm it,' she said. King Midas, *here*, his horses stabled behind Mrs Dove's home? It was impossible to comprehend.

'I'll pour you another cup of tea,' said Mrs Dove.

Venetia sank down on the sofa. Something began to nag at her memory, something important, but she couldn't put a finger on it.

'Dear Miss Lovell, are you quite well?'

Venetia smiled weakly. 'A headache. I slept badly after last night's excitement.'

'I'm not surprised.' Mrs Dove's tone was sympathetic. 'Why, you look as white as paper. I shall fetch a headache powder for you.'

'No, really ...'

Mrs Dove patted her shoulder. 'I shan't be a moment.' The door closed behind her.

Venetia massaged her temples. She did have a headache, brought on by lack of sleep and trying to understand the alarming thoughts whirling round and round in her head. Drawing in a deep breath, she went back to the window. The carriage house doors were closed now, hiding the black town coach from view. Burly men were on guard either side of the gate to the townhouse garden. Just supposing everything she'd believed about Mrs Dove was turned upside down? Could she have been allied with King Midas all this time? What possible reason could she have?

Even the thought of a connection between them was so disturbing that Venetia knew she couldn't rest until the mystery was solved. If she could find proof … Hurrying to the glass-fronted bookcase, she scanned the spines of the books not quite sure what she was looking for. She opened the glazed door and hooked out one of three ledgers and flipped it open. Scanning the pages, it was apparent that this was a record of children apprenticed to seamstresses, milliners, blacksmiths and grocers. The second was the household accounts and the third was a register of births and deaths.

She pushed the register back into place and glanced at the other volumes on the shelves. Closing the bookcase door, she looked around the room. Of course, the writing desk!

It was locked. Without hesitation, she ran to the new sewing table and took out a small pair of scissors with storks-head handles. She forced them into the lock on the writing desk and a moment later it unlocked with a satisfying click.

Standing still, she listened in case Mrs Dove was returning but all she could hear was her own galloping heartbeat pulsing in her ears. She opened the desk and rifled through the neatly arranged contents. A number of bills folded into one of the compartments. A penknife and an inkwell, a pair of glasses, a pile of visiting cards and some writing paper. Relief that she was wrong after all made her let out her breath.

But then she remembered Mr Marsden telling her about the desk's secret. She fumbled underneath it until she found a small lever. A panel inside the desk sprang forwards. A hidden drawer. Her heart somersaulted when she saw the notebook. Snatching it up, she saw a folded note poking out from between the pages. Hastily, she smoothed it flat and saw that it was dated a month before.

My dear Mrs Dove,
I am pleased to inform you that we go on well enough at
Winchester Street. The girls complain I work them too hard but, as

you are aware, we have had losses due to illness, pregnancy and
absconding. I am taking steps to procure fresh blood and have taken
in a new 'virgin', one Kitty Griggs. She is proving stubborn but
hunger will bring her round. The girl is eighteen years old but she
looks younger. Clients seeking virgins are registered with me and we
will obtain a good price for her maidenhead.

Belle Hawson, since her troubled arrival, has now settled,
assisted by judicious doses of laudanum to keep her quiet and good.
She still cries for the child at night but is able to perform her duties.

The account books are ready for your inspection at your earliest
convenience and I believe you will be pleased with the takings for
this quarter.

> *Your ob't servant*
> *Letty Cummings (Mrs)*

Venetia stared at the note. So Mrs Dove was not the charitable lady
she appeared to be but a wicked woman supported by immoral
earnings! Shaken, Venetia opened the notebook with trembling
fingers and cast her eye over the neatly inscribed entries. It took
only a moment to discover that it was a record of children sold, some
newborn, others as old as twelve. There were no entries to indicate
that any were to be apprenticed.

Hardly able to credit such wickedness, she thrust the notebook and
letter inside her bodice, pushing them down securely into her stays.

A sound made her head jerk up. She closed the desk with a flick
of her wrist and ran back to the sofa.

'My dear Miss Lovell,' said Mrs Dove, as she opened the door,
'you do look pale!'

'My headache is grown worse,' said Venetia, which was the truth.

'How tiresome! Take this straight away, my dear.' She placed a
small glass of water and a box of Rodwell's Headache Powders on
the table beside her.

Venetia examined the box. It was new and unopened. She broke the wafer and extracted one of the folded papers inside. There couldn't be any harm in it and her head did ache abominably. She slid the contents of the packet into the glass of water and swirled it around until the white powder dissolved.

'I've sent one of the children to find a hackney,' said Mrs Dove in a sympathetic tone. 'You must go home to bed.'

Venetia drank the bitter medicine. The sooner she left with the purloined notebook, the better. She must find Jack at once and tell him what she'd discovered.

'I always find it helps a headache if I close my eyes.' Mrs Dove's voice was gentle. 'You sit there quietly and I'll tell you when the carriage arrives.'

Leaning back against the sofa, Venetia closed her eyes while her thoughts raced. Mrs Dove had often visited the shop. Had she encouraged Mama to talk indiscreetly and relayed the information to King Midas? It was as she took a deep, calming breath that Venetia realised what it was that had been worrying at her, pricking like a splinter in her finger. Florence! It was now so clear to her that her eyes snapped open.

Mrs Dove was sitting with her hands folded in her lap, looking at her.

Out of the corner of her eye, Venetia saw that she'd left the stork-headed scissors on top of the desk and that a corner of writing paper poked out from the flap she'd so hastily closed.

Mrs Dove's gaze followed Venetia's to the desk. Then, slowly, she turned to look at Venetia again. All traces of concern had fled and her eyes were as icy clear as a mountain stream. 'You know, don't you?' she said softly. 'What a shame!'

'What do you mean?' Venetia sat up straight.

'Don't insult me by dissembling, Miss Lovell.' Mrs Dove's voice was unaccustomedly hard.

Venetia rubbed her forehead. Her thoughts were jumbled, as if her head were full of feathers. She must leave at once.

'What gave the game away?' asked Mrs Dove. 'You can tell me.' She smiled, her high cheekbones and heart-shaped face still attractive, despite her age.

Venetia pushed herself unsteadily to her feet.

'Was it Nero?' persisted Mrs Dove.

'Nero?' Venetia's tongue felt thick and her mouth was numb.

'The silly little creature wouldn't leave me alone that day in your shop. Sniff, sniff, sniff! He could smell the piece of poisoned liver right through the velvet of my reticule. Still, in the end, his greed cost him his life. I guessed he'd scent it out from where I hid it behind the privy.'

Shock and outrage ricocheted through Venetia's body and her knees began to give way. She sat down again.

'Ah, so it wasn't Nero, then.' Mrs Dove frowned. 'I knew how you all doted on him and I really thought that would be sufficient to make you give up that preposterous nonsense of the shopkeepers' militia.'

'You, you …' Venetia couldn't find the words for the rage and the sorrow that burned in her heart. 'You harridan!' she said at last.

Mrs Dove laughed, her eyes twinkling. 'Is that the best you can do? Now do put me out of my misery, what was it that gave me away?'

Venetia wasn't going to risk telling her about the notebook. She struggled unsteadily to her feet again. 'Apart from my family,' she said, 'you were the only other person who knew that Florence had gone to stay with her Aunt Mullins in Highgate.' Her voice echoed back to her from far away.

'Careless!' said Mrs Dove, nodding her head. 'Still, it did the trick and lured Jack Chamberlaine away. Do sit down again, Miss Lovell. I'm afraid you might fall down if you don't. Such a determined girl you are, bordering on pig-headed. But, do you know, I've become rather fond of you. We're alike in many ways.'

The floor seemed to be slipping sideways. Venetia sank down on to the sofa. So tired … No! She must leave now. Jack. Find Jack.

'We both run a business in a man's world,' said Mrs Dove. 'Both of us were forced into it through circumstances beyond our control while we were young. I wasn't as lucky as you because I didn't have any family worth their salt to fall back on. I do envy you having a mother's love, even if dear Fanny really isn't awfully clever.'

Anger and indignation made Venetia open her mouth to speak but no sound came out. Her eyelids were so very heavy.

'My father was a minister of the church,' continued Mrs Dove. 'He disowned me when Lord Danvers's heir seduced me. I was only seventeen. Mother was a poor thing and simply watched and wept when Father threw my belongings out of the window after me. It was raining too.' Mrs Dove sighed. 'Still, Johnny Danvers was besotted enough to set me up in a nice little house. He even supported me for a few years after the baby was born but then the inevitable happened. He was seduced by younger flesh.'

There was silence for a moment and, through half-closed eyes, Venetia glimpsed Mrs Dove walk to the window and stare outside.

'I had no protector and a child to keep. Johnny paid me off and I sold the jewels he'd given me. Some of them turned out to be paste, the cheapskate! Still, I had enough to start out with a couple of girls in a rented room. One of them was Letty Cummings. You've met her, I understand? She's stayed loyal to me to this day. In five years I ran three profitable brothels and there are many more now. Men are insatiable, aren't they?'

Distaste made Venetia wrinkle her nose but she was too sleepy to speak. Behind her, the door opened.

'And now the business has branched out and grown beyond anything I could have imagined,' continued Mrs Dove. 'It became like a drug to me, not only the riches I made but the power they gave me. It's not always easy, is it, for a woman to gain acceptance in a business setting? We spoke of this before. You have Jack Chamberlaine to front your business. I have my son.'

A shadow passed over Venetia. She shivered, her eyelids fluttered and she looked up, straining her eyes against the light. A commanding figure dressed in black towered over her, the same imposing figure that had given her such terrible nightmares.

King Midas put his arm around Mrs Dove and kissed her cheek. 'Dearest Mother! I see you've brought me a present.'

'A veritable prize, I should say.' Mrs Dove looked up, smiling fondly at her son.

'But a meddlesome girl nonetheless and it's time to bring a halt to her interfering. We'll let her family sweat for a while but perhaps now we have the means to make the shopkeepers lay down their arms,' said King Midas.

'If the battle continues much longer,' said Mrs Dove, 'the shops will all be destroyed and there'll be no profit for any of us. The wretched shopkeepers are cutting off their noses to spite their faces.'

'Talking of cutting off noses,' King Midas reached out to lift Venetia's chin, 'she's pretty, isn't she? At the moment, that is.'

The last thing Venetia saw before she drifted into oblivion was King Midas's cruel smile.

Chapter 36

Tom had given Kitty and Belle his room at the Ship's Bell and moved into the inn's hayloft over the stables. He'd left them a few coins for food and then gone out with the rest of the fishermen again to make enquiries about where King Midas might be found.

Kitty, still slightly feverish, lay on the lumpy bed. The stench from the river made her gag but it was too warm to close the window.

'Belle,' Kitty said, examining the purplish bruising on her wrist, 'what did happen to your baby?'

Belle turned to look at her and her face was so stricken that Kittty wished she hadn't asked.

'The mistress didn't know I was pregnant until I was six months gone,' she said. 'She gave me half an hour to leave.'

'Whatever did you do?'

'One of the other maids whispered that her sister'd got caught like that and she'd stayed at a workhouse where she'd been given a job in the laundry. After she had the baby she had to leave but they found her a place somewhere as a kitchen maid. Her baby stayed at the workhouse and she sent money every week for it to be looked after. I went there and asked if they'd take me in.'

'To the workhouse?'

Belle nodded. 'Then my baby was born and she was the sweetest little thing. I called her Violet.' She pressed a fist to her mouth and let out a sob. 'I fell into a deep sleep after the birth and in the morning they told me I'd overlaid her and she'd suffocated. I asked to see her body. But when I folded back the shawl, it wasn't Violet.'

'Are you sure?'

'Of course I'm sure! Apart from anything else the babe was too big. They said my brain had turned after the birth. After three weeks they told me I had to leave. I'd either have to work for Ma Cummings or be sent to Bedlam. But, Kitty, I know they drugged me and that Mrs Dove stole my Violet!'

'Mrs Dove?' Kitty rubbed her aching temples. 'Not Mrs Dove of Angel of Mercy House?'

'She's a devil woman!'

'But I know Mrs Dove.' Kitty frowned at Belle. The girl had lost her wits. 'She's a kind old lady. She takes in girls who get into trouble and looks after them.'

'She looks after them all right,' said Belle bitterly. 'She sends the best-looking girls to work in the brothels, to pay for their children's keep. And when they get pregnant again, she takes them back to Angel House and sells their babies.'

'I can't believe that! She's a friend of the mistress I used to work for.'

'But it's true. Jane, one of the other girls, whispered to me that I wasn't the first who'd been told their baby had died. She said the ugly children either die or else are apprenticed early. Mrs Dove keeps the pretty ones and either sells them when they're babes or brings them up and sells 'em to the highest bidder when they're older. Some go to the brothels. Others, as young as five or six, are bought by gentlemen for their pleasure.'

'But that's wicked!' Could she believe what Belle said or had Violet's death sent her barmy?

Belle gave a scornful laugh. 'You can't fight people like Mrs Dove, Ma Cummings or King Midas. Thick as thieves, they are, and powerful. But I tell you what, if I'd the chance to kill Mrs Dove, I'd go to the gallows happy.'

'Can you prove this?'

'Of course not! Although …'

'What?'

'She keeps a book of births and deaths and another of where children go to be apprenticed,' said Belle. 'The governors of Angel House look at them twice a year. She's particular about records. Jane said she'll keep private accounts of the children she's sold as well. If I could get into her personal sitting room I'd find out if she's kept a note of where Violet went.'

'You'd never get into the house.'

Belle's eyes shone feverishly. 'But, Kitty, imagine if I found out where my Violet is. I could steal her back again.'

Kitty hadn't the heart to say that, even if it were possible, it was going to be difficult enough for Belle to find work when they went to Kent, even without a baby in her arms.

'The river reeks,' said Belle, wrinkling her nose in disgust. 'Shall we go out and find something to eat?'

They left the Ship's Bell and walked away from the river, enjoying the sunshine.

Two sailors staggered out of an alehouse and one caught hold of Kitty's arm.

'Two pretty girls out for a good time,' he leered. 'Fancy coming down the alley with me?'

Kitty reeled back in disgust but Belle pushed him in the chest so that he fell over on to the cobbles.

'The trouble is, we look like whores,' said Belle after they'd run away. 'We need new clothes. I know a second-hand shop nearby.'

A while later Kitty had exchanged the shiny blue dress lent to her by Ma Cummings for a simple cotton print. Belle chose one in yellow and there was enough left to buy a shawl each and some serviceable shoes.

'I never thought I'd be happy to wear something so plain,' said Kitty. 'I don't want any man to look at me.'

A short distance away they found a pie stall and sat on a wall to eat slabs of beef and oyster pie out of newspaper.

'I've been thinking,' said Kitty, wiping a dribble of gravy off her chin. 'What you said about Mrs Dove ...'

Belle put her pie down. 'I can't bear to think of her, except to hope she'll be run down by a coach.'

'If she really does those terrible things ...'

'She does!'

'Then I must let Miss Venetia know. Her ma is Mrs Dove's friend. I'm going to warn her.'

When they arrived at Cheapside, they gawped at the burned out buildings and the boarded up windows. Shopkeepers were still sweeping up broken glass and there was blood spilled in the gutter.

'What happened here?' asked Belle.

'Looks like the work of King Midas to me,' said Kitty.

'Shhh!' said Belle, glancing around. 'Someone'll hear. His people are everywhere.'

'It's not as if the shopkeepers don't know what has happened, Belle.'

'But it's bad luck to mention his name.'

Kitty felt strange going in to Lovell and Chamberlaine again; so much had happened to her since the opening party. And now a glazier was busy fixing new glass in the windows so there must have been more trouble for the Lovells.

Mrs Lovell snatched open the door. 'Oh, Kitty, it's you! I'd hoped it was Venetia,' she said, smoothing her hair distractedly. 'So Mr Scott rescued you from that awful place?'

'He did. And Belle, too.'

'My daughter will be delighted. She's been very anxious about you.'

'We came hoping to have a word with Miss Venetia. It's important.'

'But she isn't here. Kitty, I'm so worried! She should have returned *hours* ago.' Tears welled in Mrs Lovell's eyes. 'And after what happened last night, I'm so afraid King Midas might have taken her in retaliation.'

Major Chamberlaine hurried out from the back of the shop and his face fell when he saw Kitty and Belle.

'Jack, it's not Venetia,' said Mrs Lovell.

'Perhaps she had some errands and she's been delayed?' said Kitty.

'She had an appointment,' said Major Chamberlaine, 'but she should have come straight back in a hackney after she delivered Mrs Dove's sewing table. Her brother has gone to see if she's still at Angel of Mercy House.'

Belle tugged at Kitty's sleeve. 'We'll have to tell them,' she whispered.

Kitty nodded. 'This is Belle,' she said. 'She told me something about Mrs Dove and I thought you should know, Mrs Lovell.'

Mrs Lovell and Major Chamberlaine listened to Belle's story with disbelief on their faces.

'You've made a mistake,' Mrs Lovell said, shaking her head when the tale was finished. 'I'm too worried about Venetia to listen to such scurrilous nonsense.'

'Stolen babies? Mrs Dove?' said Major Chamberlaine. 'She's an old lady who does good works. You must have misunderstood the situation.'

'No mistake,' said Belle, jutting out her chin. 'Not about something like that.'

Kitty knew they didn't believe Belle but she'd done her duty. It was out of her hands now.

'Mrs Lovell, you know Mrs Dove,' said Belle. 'You could get into her private sitting room and look for the records of stolen babies ...'

'I couldn't possibly!' Mrs Lovell looked shocked. 'But maybe I could speak to her about this.'

'She'd only lie,' said Belle. 'I'd hoped, after we helped Florence, that you'd help me.'

'You're asking too much.'

'Do you think so? She *stole* my baby. You got Florence back unharmed.' Belle stood up. 'Come on then, Kitty.'

She followed Belle out of the office, glancing back over her shoulder at Mrs Lovell's troubled face.

By the time they reached the Ship's Bell, Kitty was drooping with exhaustion. Upstairs in their room, she took off her shoes and stockings and lay down on the bed.

Belle had hardly spoken at all on the way back and took a seat by the window in silence.

Kitty was just drifting into a doze when Belle said her name.

'Kitty!'

'What?' She opened one eye to see Belle staring at her feet in horror. 'What is it?' She sat up.

'Kitty, have you any sore places?'

'My throat hurts.'

'Anywhere else?'

Kitty coloured and looked away. 'There's a sore patch down there, between my legs. But you can't help getting sore when there are so many men, can you?'

'Let me see!'

'I can't ...'

'This isn't the time to be shy. Let me see!' Belle pulled up Kitty's skirt, pushed her knees apart and peered between her legs. 'Dear God! You've got an ulcer.'

'I told you I was sore,' said Kitty, bewildered. She pulled down her skirt.

'Look at the soles of your feet!'

Kitty pulled one of her feet up on to her knee. 'It's blotchy. How strange!'

'And your hands?'

Obediently Kitty turned over her hands and inspected her palms. 'There's a rash on my hands, too. What is it?' The distress on Belle's face made her suddenly frightened. 'Not the spotted fever.'

Belle shook her head. 'Worse. You've got the pox.'

'The pox?' Terror engulfed her and she leaped to her feet. 'But I can't have! It makes your nose drop off and you go mad and then you die.'

'It was probably that bastard who bought your "virginity",' said Belle. 'Some men think if they lie with a virgin it cures their pox. God rot him!'

'What can I do?' wailed Kitty. All at once she could hardly breathe for the panic that gripped her.

'You can go to the Lock hospital,' said Belle. 'But the mercury baths are worse than the disease. They make your hair and teeth fall out and often they don't work.'

'So I'm going to die?' Kitty slumped on to the bed, shaking with shock.

'You might have a few years,' said Belle unhappily. 'The symptoms go away but they always come back. You can't lie with any men or they'll catch it, too. That's why Ma Cummings has a doctor examine her girls regularly. She needs the reputation of being a clean house or men won't visit.'

Kitty curled up into a ball, overcome by a fit of the shivers. She felt dirty. Tom wouldn't want her now. Between them, King Midas and Ma Cummings had taken away everything that mattered to her. There was nothing left to live for.

366

Chapter 37

Kitty sat with Belle and Tom in the taproom of the Ship's Bell, where the men had gathered to eat their dinner and talk about the day's discoveries. It was strange to see the fishermen's familiar faces and, except for the stench of the river instead of the briny sea air, she could almost imagine that she was back in the Admiral's Arms on the Kent coast.

'Still feeling poorly?' asked Tom. His big, callused hand was warm on Kitty's shoulder and she rested her cheek against it.

'Much better,' she said, summoning up a smile. He'd been so kind to her but she could never tell him the truth. She'd made Belle swear on Violet's life not to tell anyone about the pox, especially Tom.

The barmaid brought them plates of roast chicken and buttered carrots and Tom fell on his as if he hadn't eaten for a week.

Kitty was picking at a chicken wing when she saw Master Raffie and Major Chamberlaine in the doorway, scanning the crowd. They pushed their way through the crowded taproom.

'Thank God we've found you,' said Master Raffie. His face was pale. 'And is this Belle?'

'Who's asking?' she said with a suspicious frown.

'This is Miss Venetia's brother,' said Kitty. She thought Major Chamberlaine looked tired and ill.

'Might you be Tom Scott?' asked Major Chamberlaine.

'I am, sir,' said Tom.

'Then may we discuss a matter of extreme urgency?'

Tom moved along the bench to make way for them.

Major Chamberlaine rubbed his hand over his face. 'We believe Miss Lovell has been kidnapped.'

'Oh, no!' Kitty's hand flew to her breast.

'After you both came to the shop this morning,' said Major Chamberlaine, 'and told us that extraordinary story about Mrs Dove, I'm afraid we didn't believe you.'

'We could see that,' said Belle scornfully. 'But it's true.'

'But then …'

'I went to see Mrs Dove,' interrupted Master Raffie. 'She told me that Venetia had a headache and she'd returned to the shop in a hackney.'

'But she failed to arrive,' said Major Chamberlaine. His knuckles were white as he gripped the edge of the table. 'You're sure Mrs Dove is associated with King Midas?'

'They're in league, all right,' said Belle. 'Her and all the bawds, thieves, cutpurses, card sharps, pickpockets and fences in the city.'

'Tom,' said Major Chamberlaine, 'you've been looking for King Midas's headquarters?'

He nodded. 'We haven't seen him. He's as slippery as a wet fish. No one will talk about him, not even for money. Scared, I reckon.'

'But now I know where he lives,' said Master Raffie. 'As I was leaving Angel of Mercy House, a dark green carriage nearly ran me over. I could hardly believe it when I recognised the passenger as King Midas. So I ran after the coach to see where it went.'

'Well, I'll be buggered!' Tom scratched his head. 'So where are his headquarters?'

'Addle Street,' said Major Chamberlaine. 'But here's the interesting thing. The mews behind the house where his coach and horses are stabled adjoins a property on the corner of Love Lane and Wood Street.'

'Angel of Mercy House,' said Master Raffie triumphantly.

'After Belle said she thought Mrs Dove had a connection with King Midas, I put two and two together.' Major Chamberlaine's eyes glittered. 'I fear Miss Lovell never left Angel of Mercy House at all.'

'So you believe me now?' asked Belle.

'We'll need proof of a connection if Mrs Dove is to be brought to justice,' Major Chamberlaine said. 'Meanwhile, the magistrate has given me a warrant for King Midas's arrest, together with as many of his gang as we can capture. If we find that Miss Lovell is being held in Angel of Mercy House, that will include Mrs Dove, too.'

'Then you must find her!' said Belle. 'Perhaps then I'll discover where the old bitch sent my Violet.'

'I've spent the last few weeks in consultations with the magistrates,' continued Major Chamberlaine. 'The situation with King Midas is out of control but they've been too fearful of reprisals to act. So I've brought together a secret militia of ex-soldiers with the express purpose of ridding the city of this scourge.'

'And you want us to help you, Major Chamberlaine, sir?' said Tom.

'If you and your men join forces with us, our numbers should be sufficient to raid King Midas's headquarters and Angel of Mercy House all at the same time.' Major Chamberlaine cracked his knuckles as if he couldn't wait to get started. 'We must surround them and catch them like rats in a trap.'

Kitty closed her eyes. How she wanted that bastard brought to justice!

'What do you want me to do?' asked Belle.

'I'm extremely concerned for Miss Lovell's welfare and time is

369

of the essence. Belle, where would they keep her? You know the inside of Angel of Mercy House.'

Her chin quivered. 'There's the Coop in the attic and the Hole in the basement. Mrs Dove uses them for punishments. She put me in the Hole until I was sent to Ma Cummings's.' She shuddered.

'Will you take us there?'

'There are rats bigger'n cats down there and I don't never want to go back!'

'We'll protect you.'

Belle chewed at a fingernail and glanced at Kitty. 'Will you come with me? It's my only chance to find if there's a record of where she sent my Violet.'

Kitty nodded and reached out for Belle's hand. Her own safety didn't matter any more.

'I'll not leave your side until you're safe again, Belle,' said Raffie.

Major Chamberlaine turned to Tom. 'Let me explain my plan of action,' he said, 'and then you can rally your men.'

❦

Something hard dug into Venetia's hip. Her head throbbed. She licked dry lips with a swollen tongue. She stretched out her cramped limbs and consciousness began to creep back. Her eyes fluttered open on inky black darkness so thick it was suffocating.

Staring into the dark, she tried to remember. A mouse gnawed under the floorboards, the sound grating on her nerves. She reached out and winced as splinters from the rough boarding beneath her stabbed into her palm. Why was she here? She thought of nothing for a while until the spinning mist in her head began to drift away.

'Think!' Her voice sounded as if it had come from far away. Screwing her eyes shut, she let images flitter in and out of her mind. Taking tea with Mrs Dove. A black coach in the mews. A pair of stork-headed scissors. Swirling a headache powder into a glass of water. King Midas ...

She sat bolt upright and cracked her head. Pain exploded like a flash of lightning in her skull. Rocking back and forth, her fingers buried in her hair, she felt the stickiness of blood. Sudden panic rose like a trapped bird, fluttering against her ribcage. Must get out! Too dark to see. Breathe! In. Out. In again. At last the waves of pain subsided and she sat motionless, forcing herself to breathe steadily.

Blinking in the darkness, she became aware of a tiny glimmer of light from above. Reaching up, she touched a cold, sloping surface. Her fumbling fingertips discovered timber battens set in even rows. Working her fingers into cracks and crevices around the light, she pushed and pulled. She thumped with the heel of her hand and there was a slithering sound and then she was blinking in a sudden shaft of daylight.

She was in what appeared to be an empty cupboard, wedged in under the eaves. Above her, glimpsed through the hole she'd made in the roof, was sky. Scrabbling at the opening, she dislodged more roof slates. Shuffling forwards until there was sufficient headroom, she pushed herself into a crouching position.

She poked her head out of the hole and looked down on the same view she'd seen earlier from Mrs Dove's sitting room, except that now she was at the very top of the house. One of King Midas's black horses was being groomed in the stable yard and two men lounged against the gate to the big townhouse, chatting and smoking.

Withdrawing her head, Venetia looked around. She was crouching on a small island of boarded floor resting on timber rafters. The sloping ceiling was so low she couldn't stand upright. There was a little door in the wall but it had no handle. She must get out! All at once it was hard for her to breathe again. Pressing a hand to her chest while she tried to keep calm, she felt the notebook, still safely tucked inside her stays. She must get out of this place and show the book to Jack!

She shuffled back to the roof hole again and gulped in the fresh air. Grey clouds scudded overhead and the sun had dropped in the misty sky. Mama would be worried about her. King Midas had said he'd make her family sweat before he made his demands. Would Jack come to ask Mrs Dove where she was? Closing her eyes, she conjured up his face. She was lonely and afraid and she wanted him to come and save her.

But Jack wasn't here and she must find her own means of escape. She peered out at the stable courtyard again, so far below. King Midas's horse looked small enough to belong to a child's toy farmyard. It was impossible to climb down the sheer side of a house four storeys high. Despair at the thought of spending the night in this place until King Midas came to cut off her nose made her want to weep.

A man drove a cart into the stable courtyard. He went to speak to the lad grooming the black horse. It happened so quickly that Venetia blinked. Suddenly the stable lad was on the ground and the carter was kneeling on his legs and tying his arms behind his back.

The tarpaulin on the cart was thrown back and eight men jumped down and slunk across the yard, surprising the guards standing by the townhouse gate. A moment later, gagged and bound, they were thrown into the cart.

What was happening? The men ran into the stables and Venetia held her breath, waiting. A few minutes later another four men were frog-marched into the yard. One of the intruders prodded them with a musket while the others swiftly tied them up. They were lifted unceremoniously into the cart and the tarpaulin dragged over their heads. The carter drove the cart away.

Venetia gripped the edge of the hole in the roof. Could these men have come to rescue her? Or was this something else entirely? Two men stationed themselves along the alley leading to the stables, while the others forced open the gate and ran into the townhouse garden.

Surely, if Jack had come to save her, he'd have brought the

shopkeepers' militia with him? What if these men were another gang attempting to take over King Midas's territory?

She picked at the splinters in her palm while her thoughts raced. What was she to do?

The church clock struck seven as Kitty shifted from foot to foot while she waited with Belle and Master Raffie outside the Castle Inn. She wished she hadn't promised Belle that she'd go with her to find Miss Venetia. All she wanted was to curl up in bed with the sheet over her head and ignore the outside world while she decided what to do next. She could never go home to Kent with Tom now.

Belle, her arms wrapped tightly about her, stood beside Kitty, lost in her own fearful thoughts. Every now and again a shudder ran through her thin frame.

'Not long,' said Raffie, his gaze flicking up and down the street.

'Are you afraid?' asked Kitty. He looked jittery and it made her nervous that he kept patting the pocket where he'd hidden his pistol. He didn't look old enough to be in charge of something so dangerous.

'Of course not,' he said, a nerve twitching at the side of his eye. 'I just want to fetch my sister home and see an end to King Midas's reign of terror.'

Then Kitty saw Major Chamberlaine limping purposefully along the street towards them.

'All set?' he asked Master Raffie. 'The shopkeepers' militia and the fishermen are in position now,' he said in an undertone. 'Angel of Mercy House, the mews and King Midas's house are surrounded. My men will go into the Addle Street house and endeavour to arrest King Midas. Meanwhile, Sergeant Norreys will accompany you.' He turned to Belle. 'Once inside, lead the men to where you believe Miss Lovell might be held.'

Belle nodded, her fair hair falling in a curtain across her face.

Major Chamberlaine turned to Master Raffie. 'Take Venetia straight home. Stay with her until I arrive. Is that clear?'

'Perfectly. Where's Sergeant Norreys?'

'Waiting in the stable yard.' Major Chamberlaine rubbed his face. 'I'd come with you like a shot if I didn't need to arrest King Midas. Tell Venetia ...'

'Tell her what?' asked Master Raffie.

Major Chamberlaine sighed. 'Tell her I'll come as soon as I can.' He glanced at his pocket watch. 'I must hurry. Good luck!' He set off down the street.

'Let's go!' said Master Raffie. His face was so pale it was almost green.

They walked in silence up Wood Street. At the corner of Love Lane, Belle stopped outside the looming bulk of Angel of Mercy House. 'I hope to God Mrs Dove isn't watching us.'

'Keep moving!' said Master Raffie.

A group of men were gathered at the entrance to the lane behind Angel of Mercy House and a number of others loitered further along the street. Kitty recognised Peter Dennis and James Hitchins, fishermen she'd known nearly all her life. They nodded at her as she passed.

Sergeant Norreys came to greet them as they entered the stable courtyard.

'No time to lose,' he said. 'I'll lead us inside and you'll bring up the rear, Master Raffie. Ladies, stay close at all times and please do as you're told. Once we're in we'll need to disable the kitchen staff to give us clear access to the cellars. Any questions?'

Kitty shook her head and Belle caught hold of her hand in a fierce grip.

Keeping close to the wall, they sprinted through the garden towards Angel of Mercy House.

Already nervous, Kitty nearly screamed when something caught her by the hair, yanking her head back.

Master Raffie roughly untangled a stem of climbing rose from her curls and they set off again. Somewhere in the distance a man shouted.

The back door was unlocked and they crept into the rear passage.

Despite the comfortingly ordinary smell of cabbage soup and the clatter of dishes being washed in the scullery, Kitty wanted to turn tail and run away. Then a kitchen maid scurried into the passage carrying a pile of plates. Her mouth opened in an O of surprise.

Sergeant Norreys wasted no time. He clapped a hand over the girl's mouth and held her against his chest. 'Tear a piece off the bottom of her apron,' he whispered.

Master Raffie did as he was bid and Sergeant Norreys gagged the scullery maid. He bundled her, kicking and silently screaming, into a store cupboard and bolted it.

There wasn't time for Kitty to do more than feel sorry for the girl before Sergeant Norreys whispered to her and Belle to stay put in the passage. Then he flung back the kitchen door.

Inside, half a dozen girls in blue dresses were busy tidying the kitchen. The fat cook, eyes like currants in her lardy face, was sitting at the table reading the paper. She looked up and squealed at the sight of two men striding towards her with pistols in their hands. One of the girls dropped a pan with a crash.

Within moments they were herded into the pantry and the great pine table shoved in front of the door to prevent their escape. The cook, gagged to prevent a stream of vile language, was trussed up like one of her own fowls ready for roasting and locked into the coal store.

A few minutes later Sergeant Norreys had located the laundry and locked all the laundry maids inside.

'Right, Belle,' he said, 'take us to the Hole.'

She led them down the passage, past the coal and potato stores and then they descended a ladder leading to a dim and stinking chamber lit only by a small grate set under the ceiling.

Master Raffie retched and put a hand over his nose.

'Cess pit's underneath,' said Belle. 'Mind where you put your feet. It floods.' She pointed to a corner of the room. 'There!' she said.

Kitty peered into the gloom and saw the outline of a studded wooden door set into the brickwork. Iron bolts were fixed at top and bottom and a padlocked chain secured the centre.

Sergeant Norreys took a jemmy from inside his coat, levered off the padlock and scraped the door open. Inside, the Hole was in total darkness.

Kitty reached out for Belle's hand.

'Venetia?' said Master Raffie.

Silence. Then a rustle of straw and a clank of chains.

Belle stepped back, teeth chattering in fear. 'There's rats in there,' she said. 'They bite your toes if you sleep.'

A muffled sob came from within.

'Thank God!' said Master Raffie. 'It's me, Venetia.' He entered the Hole, arms outstretched into the darkness.

Kitty peered after him but could only see his back as he bent down and lifted someone up. He turned back to the door carrying his burden, a chain with a heavy metal weight on the end thumping along behind them. As they came from the blackness into the gloom Kitty gasped, 'But that's not Miss Venetia!'

A young woman, her dress filthy and her face bruised, blinked up at them in terror from Master Raffie's arms.

He stared at her in shock and carefully put her down.

Belle ran towards her. 'Susie?' She stroked a strand of hair off the young woman's face. 'What's she done to you, Susie?'

She fell into Belle's arms. 'Mrs Dove took my baby away and said he was dead! Just like you said she took your Violet. And she wants me to go and work for Ma Cummings again and I don't never want to go back there,' she wailed.

Belle rocked the other girl in her arms until her tears subsided into sobs. 'So you know now I wasn't going mad.'

Sergeant Norreys jemmied the metal weight off the chain. 'We'll saw the manacle off later,' he said. 'Susie, go out through the garden to the mews and tell one of the men there that Sergeant Norreys sent you. But now we must find Miss Lovell.'

'If she's not here,' said Belle, 'then she must be in the Coop.'

Chapter 38

Venetia kicked furiously at the lath and plaster between the floor joists. She was damned if she was going to wait meekly for King Midas to come and cut off her nose! Peering down through the ragged opening, she glimpsed a dormitory below. She slithered between the joists and gasped as a nail tore her sleeve and sliced into her forearm. Her legs dangled above the steep drop. She broke her fall by landing on the bed underneath.

She coughed as she brushed plaster dust off her clothes. Sucking the jagged wound on her arm, she hurried out of the dormitory and crept stealthily down the stairs.

Children were chanting their catechism in one of the rooms as she crept past. Then heavy footsteps crossed the hall below and began mounting the staircase. Was King Midas still here in the house? Venetia's breathing was quick and shallow as she sprinted across the second-floor landing looking for somewhere to hide. Mrs Dove's sitting-room door was ajar and it took all Venetia's courage to creep past and conceal herself behind the curtains at the landing window.

Heart thudding, she peeped through a tiny gap and saw a girl carry a tea tray into Mrs Dove's domain. Quickly, Venetia slipped out of her hiding place and ran downstairs to the entrance lobby. Nothing would stop her now! She grasped the great brass door handle and twisted it. The door was locked. She looked about wildly for a key. Nothing.

She scurried across the hall and into the kitchen passage. The kitchen was empty and the back door open. Laughing in relief, she ran outside into the garden. She'd done it! But, after only a few steps, a man carrying a cudgel leaped out of the shrubbery behind her. He clapped a rough hand over her mouth before she could scream and pulled her behind a rhododendron bush.

'Miss Lovell! Are you all right? You're bleeding.' Tom Scott removed his hand. His own cheek was grazed and bruised.

'You gave me such a fright, Tom!' His expression was so anxious that she glanced down at her filthy dress, all covered in spider's webs, plaster dust and smears of blood. She gave it a perfunctory brush with the back of her hand.

'Your brother and Sergeant Norreys, together with Kitty and Belle, are in the house searching for you. I'm worried for Kitty.'

'Oh!' So Jack hadn't cared enough to come and rescue her after all. 'But we must let them know I've escaped.' The thought of having to go back into the house again to find them made her quake.

Tom glanced over his shoulder. 'There's a right battle going on at King Midas's headquarters. We've two down and several injured and about the same to the other side. He's gone to earth somewhere but the place is crawling with his men.'

'But King Midas was in Angel of Mercy House earlier.'

'Was he now? I must report that back to the others. Major Chamberlaine's brought in a militia of ex-soldiers armed with swords and pistols. Together with my crew and the shopkeepers, I'd say we're an even match for King Midas's men.'

Venetia frowned. Where did Jack find a militia to help them at such short notice?

'You'll recognise them by their scarlet sashes.' Tom ran his hand down a wide ribbon tied diagonally over his shoulder and across his chest. 'Us fishermen have blue ones and the shopkeepers wear green.' He grinned.' Major Chamberlaine's thought of everything. Apart from King Midas's bodyguards, who wear black, the rest of his men are a ragbag of thieves and murderers dragged out of the gutter as reinforcements. They fight dirty, though.' He fingered the bruise on his cheekbone. 'I'll fetch men here to dig him out.'

'Fighting? Here?' Venetia looked at Tom in consternation. 'But what about the children?'

'What?'

'This is a children's home! You can't risk their lives in a battle-ground.'

Tom scratched his head. 'I suppose not.'

'I must find my brother.' Venetia's head jerked up as she heard a pistol shot in the distance, 'but first you must help me take the children to safety.'

'Quickly then,' said Tom. He hurried inside.

Venetia paused on the threshold, queasy with fear. What if King Midas caught her? But there were the children to consider. And Raffie ... She followed Tom.

At the end of the passage, he peered around the corner and beck-oned to her to follow him up the stairs.

She stopped on the landing outside the room where she'd heard the children chanting, took a deep breath and opened the door.

A sea of young faces looked up at her.

A stern-faced woman stood at the front of the class with a birch switch in her hand.

'Mrs Dove asked me to fetch the children,' said Venetia. She hoped she sounded authoritative. 'Come along, children, I want you to walk quickly and quietly downstairs.'

For one long moment they remained motionless.

'Stand up!' Venetia clapped her hands.

One by one the children rose to their feet.

'Sit down!' said the teacher, raising her switch.

Tom, who'd remained behind the door, strode into the classroom. 'No time to squabble.' He picked up the struggling woman, bundled her into the stationery cupboard and locked her in. She screeched and rattled the door. Tom kicked the cupboard and she went quiet.

'Children,' Venetia said, 'this is Tom. He's come to play a game of soldiers with us.'

One of the boys glanced at the stationery cupboard and laughed uncertainly.

Venetia bent down to speak to him. 'Are all of you in this room?'

He shook his head to indicate they were not.

'Is there a back staircase?'

The boy nodded. 'Children, please show Tom the back stairs and walk in silence to the garden.' She smiled reassuringly at them and then whispered, 'We don't want Boney to hear us, do we?'

A little girl squealed.

'Come on then, soldiers!' said Tom. 'Quietly now!'

Venetia bent down to the boy. 'Will you show me where the other children are?'

A short while later all the children were huddled together in the shrubbery, together with a dozen young women in various stages of late pregnancy. All the babies and toddlers had been scooped up from the nursery and handed into the care of the pregnant women.

'Take them out through the stable yard,' said Tom. 'One of the shopkeepers in the outer cordon can take them to safety but I must let Major Chamberlaine know that King Midas might be here.'

'When you find him,' said Venetia, 'tell him that I've discovered Mrs Dove is King Midas's mother.'

'Christ almighty!' Tom's jaw dropped.

'Go!' said Venetia. The sun disappeared behind a cloud and a fitful wind lifted her hair as she hurried to the children.

Mr Benson, a green sash across his chest, ran to shake her hand. 'Miss Lovell, we've been so worried about you!'

'I escaped,' she said, 'but will you take these women and children back to Cheapside while I find my brother?'

He glanced up at the darkening sky. 'I'll try and get them there before it rains.'

'Have you seen Major Chamberlaine?'

Mr Benson shook his head. 'No, but we've taken away the injured.'

Venetia returned to the garden. She stared up at the windows of the house but nothing moved inside. Raffie was searching for her in there and she must find him. She broke out in a cold sweat as she entered by the back door again. Creeping along the passage, she came to the hall.

Footsteps began to descend the stairs.

Venetia snatched open a door and slipped inside. She waited, scarcely breathing, until the echoing footsteps faded away. Just as she'd plucked up the courage to return to the hall she heard a noise behind her.

She whirled around to see King Midas sitting in a red velvet armchair holding a glass of brandy in his hand.

She shrank back, shock rendering her speechless.

He sighed heavily. 'You really are the most troublesome female I've ever been acquainted with.'

She jumped as a sudden volley of gunfire came from outside, followed by an explosion.

'Just listen to that!' King Midas shook his head. 'It's all your doing. The fighting and the burnings. The deaths. The shopkeepers were perfectly happy paying us a small percentage of their earnings until you came along, stirring up trouble.'

Rage seethed up in Venetia, boiling and red, like molten lava, evaporating her fear in a hiss of fury. 'Please do tell me,' she said, her hands on her hips, 'what it is that makes you dedicate your energies to destroying hard-working people and their live-lihoods.'

He threw back his head and laughed.

Venetia waited, consumed by anger. If she could understand what drove him to cause such misery there might be a way to stop it.

'My mother always told me that that although it's desirable to be rich, what really matters is power.' His eyes glittered. 'An astute and clever woman, my mother. Cheated and swindled, lonely and frightened, she worked her fingers to the bone to make a good life for me. Even now she never stops looking for new ways to increase our empire, long after we've gained all the riches we could ever need. And one day she'll hand over control of it to me.'

'I wonder,' said Venetia tartly, 'if she's so clever, how you'll manage without her.'

King Midas raised one eyebrow. 'Implying that I am not clever? How very impolite you are, Miss Lovell. Still, Mother has the will to live to a hundred so perhaps you need not worry.'

'I find it extraordinary,' she said, 'that it's possible one of my own sex can be so two-faced and wicked as to prey on children and their unfortunate mothers.'

'How can you say that? Mother provides the dregs of humanity with a safe haven when their need is greatest. Children who would otherwise perish in the gutter are found good homes.'

Venetia stared at him. His expression was hurt, as if he truly believed his mother was a saint.

Curiosity overcame her. 'Why the name King Midas?'

'Because everything I touch turns to gold, of course.' He smiled. 'Besides, my given name of Percy Dove hardly inspires terror and awe, does it?'

A kind of giddy recklessness overcame Venetia then and she laughed. 'Percy? It certainly doesn't.' She took a step back to the door. 'Percy! I wonder you're brave enough to tell me.'

His smile disappeared and he slid his hand into his pocket. 'It's the name my mother chose for me.'

'Still, *Percy*!'

His jaw clenched. 'Of course, I only let you in on my little secret because you'll not live long enough to tell. This whole farce of a rebellion will now be brought to a swift conclusion. My men are more than enough to deal with a few pathetic shopkeepers.'

'You haven't been very successful so far.'

'Enough! My patience is at an end. You do understand that one of us has to die, don't you?' His thin lips stretched into a smile. 'And it isn't going to be me.' He drew a pistol out of his pocket.

Upstairs, a shot rang out and a woman screamed.

King Midas glanced away.

Venetia spun on her heel and lunged through the door into the hall.

* * *

Kitty stayed close to Sergeant Norreys as he led them along the kitchen passage, across the stone floor of the hall and up the stairs. They heard and saw no one.

On the second floor Belle grabbed hold of his sleeve and nodded at a door. 'Mrs Dove's sitting room,' she whispered.

They tip-toed past and then ran up the stairs to the next floor.

On the fourth-floor landing Belle clung tightly to Kitty's hand. 'I'm so frightened,' she whispered. 'What if Mrs Dove catches us?'

'We can't leave Miss Venetia in the Coop,' hissed Kitty.

'For my sister's sake, Belle!' said Master Raffie, gripping her wrist.

Slowly, Belle nodded.

They entered a shadowy attic crammed with dust-sheeted furniture and boxes. The window was grimed with dust and the ceiling sloped. Belle pushed her way between the boxes until she came to a small door low in the wall.

Master Raffie pushed his way past her, dragged back the bolts and crouched down to look inside. 'She's not here!'

Kitty peered over his shoulder. 'Look!' A ray of light shone from above, illuminating a jagged hole between the floor joists.

Sergeant Norreys crouched down and went into the Coop. He pulled a scrap of black cloth from a projecting nail. 'Miss Lovell must have been here. And the lath and plaster has been broken through to the room beneath.'

Master Raffie caught hold of Kitty's arm and grinned. 'I do believe Venetia has managed to escape all by herself.'

'But where is she now?' asked Sergeant Norreys.

They ran down to the dormitory below. Lumps of plaster were scattered under the hole in the ceiling and dusty footprints and a thin trail of blood led to the door.

'She's hurt herself!' said Kitty, then nearly jumped out of her skin as a loud volley of gunfire and an explosion echoed outside.

Sergeant Norreys hurried to peer from the window. 'The militia's coming this way,' he said, taking out his pistol.

Master Raffie spun around as a shot reverberated downstairs and then a man screamed.

'Hurry!' said Norreys. 'They're inside!' He sprinted on to the landing and then stopped dead. Swiftly, he raised his pistol.

Kitty ran into the back of him and gasped. Mrs Dove was elegantly dressed in black, as usual, with her gold cross glinting on her breast. What was unusual was the small mother-of-pearl pistol she pointed at Sergeant Norreys.

'We have an impasse,' she said.

Belle peered around Kitty's shoulder. 'You!' she said. 'Well, I'm not on my own now, you miserable old bitch!' She thrust Kitty aside and stood beside Sergeant Norreys. 'What have you done with my Violet?' she demanded.

'Move aside, Belle!' barked Norreys.

Belle grabbed Mrs Dove by the shoulders and shook her like a terrier with a rat. 'Where's my Violet, you old hag?'

Sergeant Norreys reached for Belle just as Mrs Dove fired.

Kitty screamed.

Belle shuddered. A scarlet stain spread across her back. She sagged against Mrs Dove. 'You've done for me!' she whispered.

And then, before anyone could stop her, she bent Mrs Dove backwards over the banisters. They teetered over the handrail for a heartbeat.

Mrs Dove let out a terrible screech, so full of rage that Kitty screamed and put her hands over her ears.

Then, locked together in a deadly embrace, Belle and Mrs Dove plummeted down the stairwell towards the stone floor below.

A terrible, discordant banshee shriek came from the top of the stairs, a screech so full of rage that Venetia came skidding to a halt in the hall.

A monstrous, thrashing black shadow momentarily blocked out the light as it plunged and spun down the stairwell towards her from four floors above.

King Midas stopped abruptly beside her, the hand that held the pistol slack by his side as he stared upwards.

Then, with a sickening thud, the intertwined women smacked on to the stone floor of the hall.

Upstairs a woman screamed and screamed, the sound as jagged as broken glass.

King Midas let out a bellow and ran towards the bleeding tangle of twisted arms and legs. The two women looked like nothing more than a pile of bloody rags.

Shaking and sick, Venetia saw Kitty flying down the stairs with Raffie and Sergeant Norreys bounding behind her.

386

King Midas fell to his knees and gathered Mrs Dove's broken body into his arms, rocking her and kissing her face while he crooned words of love. Her head lolled backwards, blue eyes unseeing. A trickle of blood trailed from her nose.

Venetia stood frozen to the spot, staring at the puddle of blood spreading over the floor.

Raffie and Sergeant Norreys ran across the hall, shouting for assistance.

Keening, Kitty ran over to Belle. She crouched over her, stroking her bloodied hair and pulling down her skirt to cover her shattered legs. She kicked at Mrs Dove's body to free Belle's arm, caught underneath.

'Don't touch my mother!' snarled King Midas, tears running down his face.

Kitty tugged frantically at Belle's arm.

'I'm warning you, get away!' King Midas lifted his hand, the pistol still clenched in his fist.

Kitty lifted her chin and spat in his face.

He fired.

Kitty's eyes opened wide with surprise. She looked down at the blood pumping from her breast before she sank down on to Belle's body.

Venetia was jolted into action. She ran to Kitty and pressed her hand over the wound but the river of blood still bubbled up through her fingers. 'Kitty, don't die!'

Men shouted orders and booted footsteps marched towards them.

Kitty smiled and murmured, 'Nat!'

Venetia glanced up and saw Tom and Jack come to a standstill as they took in the terrible scene.

Kitty gave a long sigh and closed her eyes. She was gone.

Venetia turned to King Midas. 'You despicable bastard!'

Jack, a scarlet sash over his coat, limped forward and stood before King Midas. 'By the authority invested in me I arrest you ...'

King Midas raised his pistol again with murder in his eyes.

A jolt of ice-cold terror engulfed Venetia. Time stood still as she stared at the pistol in King Midas's blood-stained hand. Without Jack, her life would have no meaning.

King Midas took aim at Jack's heart.

Covered in Kitty's blood, Venetia reared up and screamed, '*No!*' She launched herself at King Midas, knocking him sideways and pinning him to the ground. A shot roared in her ear. Then another. And another. Her body jerked. Blood splattered her face. The sharp, sulphurous smell of gunpowder was in her nose.

King Midas convulsed beneath her and lay still.

And then they were lying inches apart, face to face on the cold stone floor.

His hooded eyes were hazed by pain. 'I told you one of us had to die,' he whispered, blood frothing from his lips. 'It seems you were a worthy opponent after all, Miss Lovell.' And then his eyes closed for the last time.

A man yelled, 'King Midas is dead! King Midas is dead!'

Venetia felt herself being pulled to her feet and then she was crushed against Jack's chest. His lips were on her hair, on her face and kissing her eyelids.

'My God, Venetia, I thought I'd lost you! You stupid, stupid, headstrong girl! You might have been killed and I couldn't have borne it.'

She clung to him. There didn't seem to be anything she could usefully say, so instead she kissed him. As their lips touched it was as if a bolt of lightning coursed through her, leaving her blood fizzing in her veins.

There was a shout and then a volley of gunfire and Jack looked over her shoulder and released her. 'Raffie,' he shouted, 'for God's sake, get your sister out of here!'

He grasped hold of her. 'Come on, Venetia!'

All at once, the hall was thronged with yelling men. Swords clashed, pistols fired and men shouted as they scuffled and fought, crashing into walls and knocking a table flying.

As Raffie pulled her away, she glanced back to see Jack, sword drawn, engaged in combat with a great brute armed with a pike. Her heart turned over. 'Raffie!' She caught his sleeve. 'Jack'll be hurt!'

'Jack can take care of himself but he'll never forgive me if anything happens to you.' Her brother snatched hold of her wrist and dragged her away.

In the kitchen passage a one-armed man wearing a red sash circled together with a bruiser in black, knives flashing as they parried and feinted.

Venetia and Raffie skirted around them and dashed for the back door. It was dusk and the garden was full of brawling men. There was a hint of bonfire in the air.

Venetia winced as she saw a man dressed all in black receive a sword slash to his shoulder. He moaned and fell to the ground.

The other combatant, a scarlet sash across his chest and wearing an eye patch, wiped the blood off his sword on the fallen man's breeches.

Venetia and Raffie ran, hand in hand, into the yard. Black smoke plumed from the stables. Orange flames licked the roof and illuminated the yard. Terrified horses snorted and pawed the ground, rearing up as men fought all around them.

'I must help the horses, Venetia,' said Raffie. 'Go and ask one of the shopkeepers to take you home.'

'But ...'

'Don't argue!' He raced to grasp the mane of one of the great black horses.

Venetia watched helplessly but then Raffie was joined by one of the stable lads and they worked together to lead the animals out of harm's way.

Behind them, the carriage house doors were wide open and King Midas's great black coach crackled and burned inside, the gold crown on the coach door blistering in the fierce heat. Eventually, the paint melted and then disappeared entirely.

Chapter 39

It had begun to spit with rain when Venetia emerged from the alley behind Angel of Mercy House. The casualties had been laid at the side of Wood Street, including three whose faces had been covered with coats. The shopkeepers were keeping curious pedestrians away and redirecting passing coaches around the scene. A doctor tended the wounded.

'Miss Lovell!'

Dazed, she saw Charles Murchison coming towards her through the gathering dark with his hands outstretched.

'My dear Miss Lovell! You're bleeding!'

'I'm not hurt,' she said. 'But King Midas is dead.' It was an effort for her to speak.

He grasped her hand and lifted it to his lips. 'Heavens be praised! And thank the Good Lord you're safe! Edwin and I have been worried sick, hearing all the fighting and knowing you were in such danger. And then Mr Benson told us you went back in the house *after* you escaped, to retrieve the children.'

Venetia began to tremble, hardly able to think of the horror she'd left behind her. And Jack was still in that place, fighting for his life.

Edwin Murchison appeared beside them, a smear of blood on his cheek. He kissed her other hand, tears in his eyes. 'How very brave you've been, my dear! And you're shaking. We'll take you home to your mama at once.'

'But we should do something to help the injured.' She shivered and her teeth chattered. The rain, heavier now, soaked her torn and dirty dress.

'Far better to leave that to the doctor,' said Charles. 'I shall procure a hackney to take you home.'

She shook her head. 'I must go to Cheapside to see if the children are all right.'

A short while later the hackney drew up outside Lovell and Chamberlaine. The shops were all closed and rain bounced up from the pavement, soaking her shoes and the hem of her dress.

Mama peeped out from behind the curtains and her face lit up with joy when she saw Venetia.

'My dearest, dearest child!' She enfolded Venetia in her arms and cried tears of relief as she stroked her daughter's hair and kissed her face. 'But you're covered in blood!'

'Not mine,' she said.

'Thank goodness! Come in out of the rain. And Raffie? Is he safe?'

'When I saw him last he was rescuing King Midas's horses from a fire.'

'But that's dangerous ... he's only a boy!'

Venetia shook her head. 'Not any more. I wish you'd seen him, you'd have been so proud of him. But Mama, King Midas is dead!'

Mama gasped. 'It may be un-Christian of me but I have never been more thankful for anything in all my life.'

Venetia glanced up as she heard running footsteps on the floor above and then children singing. 'They're here?'

'Mrs Benson and some of the other wives are looking after them,' said Mama. 'We've all those empty rooms upstairs and it seemed like the best place for them until they can return to Angel of Mercy House.'

A few moments later Venetia sat shivering in the office with a sample length of brocade wrapped around her shoulders and a cup of sweet tea beside her.

'Tell me what happened,' said Mama as she tied a strip of muslin around the wound on Venetia's arm. 'I've been in a terrible fret about Grace. Jack said she kidnapped you?'

'I'm afraid so. And there's worse,' said Venetia. 'She was King Midas's mother. Not only that, she was the mastermind behind the whole of his empire.'

Mama sank down on a chair. 'It can't be true! All those times we sat drinking tea together and she commiserated with me over our plight, she was orchestrating our downfall?'

'She was.'

'No wonder she encouraged us to give in to King Midas's demands. I was never so taken in by anybody!' She frowned. 'Did you say *was* King Midas's mother?'

Venetia nodded. 'She fell over the banisters.'

'She was my friend.' Mama's mouth quivered. 'And I shall miss her. At least, I shall miss the person I thought she was.'

'Let me tell you what happened.'

Venetia's eyelids were drooping with exhaustion by the time she'd finished. 'What I don't understand,' she said, 'is where the militia came from.'

'All those times that Jack disappeared off we knew not where,' said Mama, 'he was secretly persuading the magistrates to give him the authority to raise a body of men to crush King Midas.'

'But the shopkeepers had no money to pay for it.'

'A great number of soldiers have returned home from the wars and been unable to find work, especially those who were injured.'

'Like Sergeant Norreys?'

Mama nodded. 'Jack encouraged them to give their time with

the suggestion that, if they were successful, it was an opportunity to demonstrate they still had a value to society. It should afford them a better chance of employment. And the magistrate promised them a share of any spoils if King Midas were defeated.'

A banging came at the door and Mama hurried to open it. She returned a moment later with Raffie. 'Thank God,' she said, 'both my children are safe.'

Raffie, eyes shining in his soot-smeared face, reeked of smoke and the stable. 'We've done it!' Jubilantly, he hugged Venetia. 'King Midas's men have turned tail and run. The fishermen are rummaging through his coffers and taking their share of the gold.'

'What about Jack?' Venetia hardly dared to ask. What if he'd been injured? Or worse.

'Don't worry about Jack, he's in fine fettle,' said Raffie. 'The magistrate's arrived and the bodies have been taken away.' His face sobered. 'Poor Kitty!' He sighed. 'Jack said to tell you he'll be back as soon as the wounded are tended to.'

'Thank God!' said Venetia. She yawned.

'Why don't you have a rest?' said Mama. 'I'm going upstairs to see what I can do for the children.'

'And I'm returning to Angel of Mercy House to help Jack. You know,' said Raffie, 'he really is a decent fellow, Venetia. I didn't think so at first but I was wrong.'

Venetia curled up in the office armchair. King Midas was dead! It was hardly possible to believe that the vile blight on all their lives had gone. The businesses were free to flourish and grow.

She closed her eyes. Raffie was right; Jack was a decent fellow and she loved him. In fact, she loved him so much it hurt. She pictured the fear in his eyes when he'd pulled her into his arms after King Midas had died. His words still rang in her ears. *My God, Venetia, I thought I'd lost you! You might have been killed and I couldn't have borne it.* He hadn't ever said he loved her but he certainly hadn't wanted to lose her. Perhaps there was a nugget of comfort in that?

She yawned, exhausted by all that had happened. Sleep was what she needed. Upstairs children laughed and their little feet thundered over the floor. Smiling, she drifted into the arms of Morpheus.

Loud, masculine laughter and voices woke her. Someone started to play a lively tune on a fiddle. She sat up, confused. Every bone in her body ached and the wounds on her arm and head throbbed. But then she remembered: there was nothing to fear from King Midas any more!

Following the sounds of merriment, she went into the showroom to discover it was packed with the shopkeepers, fishermen and a number of men in red sashes. Mama, Raffie and Mrs Bernstein stood behind the counter, now a makeshift bar, dispensing ale.

Mrs Benson pushed her way through the crowd holding a tray above her head, heaped with custard tarts, bread and pies. Children descended upon her, screaming with delight and cramming the delicacies into their mouths. Three of the fishermen jumped up on to the counter and began to sing sea shanties.

Venetia felt a touch on her arm and Sergeant Norreys was beside her, a wide smile on his ravaged face.

'What's happening?' She had to shout over the noise.

'A party to celebrate freedom from oppression,' he said.

'So it's really over?'

He leaned closer so that she could hear. 'I was worried I'd be taken up after King Midas was shot,' he said, 'but the magistrate told Major Chamberlaine that there was no case to answer. Bullets from three different pistols killed him so it was a case of "death by person or persons unknown".'

'I should think the magistrate would be grateful King Midas isn't causing mayhem any longer.'

'The trouble is,' said Sergeant Norreys, 'now that that he's dead, other ne'er-do-wells will be looking to take over his patch.'

Venetia opened her eyes wide with horror. 'We cannot go through all this again.'

'You won't have to,' said Sergeant Norreys. 'It's been agreed that Major Chamberlaine's new militia will remain on standby, to be sent wherever they're needed to keep the peace. They'll be partly supported by the parish and also by businesses in need of guards.'

'What a marvellous idea!' Venetia leaned closer to him. 'Truthfully, most of the shopkeepers are totally unsuited to fighting off serious criminals.'

Sergeant Norreys's eyes twinkled. 'I agree, much better to leave it to the professionals. But there won't be enough to keep the men fully occupied so I've another plan.'

'What's that?'

'I'm going into partnership with Mr Marsden at the furniture factory. My father was a joiner and I learned the skills at his knee. Some of the ex-soldiers will join us to learn the trade.'

Venetia was delighted for him and shook his hand. 'Congratulations! I always liked Mr Marsden. He said he couldn't find apprentices worth their salt.'

The fishermen stopped their rowdy singing and Jacob Bernstein put down his fiddle. Someone called for quiet and then Jack held up his hand until there was silence.

Venetia drank in the sight of him, safe and unharmed, relief making her tremble again.

'What a day this has been!' Jack began.

A chorus of cheers went up.

'King Midas and his evil mother are dead and will trouble us no more. The misery they've caused is incalculable. There have been terrible losses and I'd like you all to close your eyes for a moment while we remember those who are no longer with us.'

Venetia saw Tom Scott wipe away tears as the assembly bowed their heads and folded their hands. She closed her eyes and thought of her father's smiling eyes. She pictured him cantering along the beach towards her, his cloak flying in the wind. And then there were poor Kitty and Belle, Mr Elliot and Mr Johnson's mother. King Midas and Mrs Dove had left a terrible trail of misery behind them that could never be forgotten.

Jack cleared his throat. 'The shopkeepers' militia, the fishermen and the new law and order militia have all played their part in the war against King Midas. We've emerged battered and bruised but survivors.'

A resounding cheer ricocheted around the showroom.

'None of this would have happened but for one person who was brave enough to defy King Midas. Her father had already lost his life in the same attempt. Despite her terror at King Midas's threats she *still* refused to give in to his gross and unlawful demands. She forced us all to strive for justice.'

Venetia stared at Jack and a lump rose in her throat. He was talking about her.

'Without this one brave young woman,' he continued, 'we'd all still be suffering at King Midas's hand. Her father would be so very proud of her today. Ladies and gentlemen, please raise your glasses to Miss Venetia Lovell!'

A great cheer went up and suddenly Venetia felt herself being lifted up and then was standing on the counter.

'Speech!'

Covered in confusion, she looked at all the upturned faces, waiting for her to speak. She smoothed down the front of her dress, stiff with dirt and bloodstains, and willed herself not to cry. 'As you can see,' she said, 'I've put on my best dress to come to this party.'

There were shouts of laughter and whistles but all she cared about was that Jack was smiling at her. 'None of you will know how tormented I've been by fears that I'd interfered and made everything worse. But this day would not have come if we hadn't *all* stood firm in the face of the enemy and refused to give way. I'm so thankful to every one of you that now we can rebuild our businesses and carry on with our lives without fear.'

'Huzzah!'

Sergeant Norreys lifted Venetia down to the ground and the men began to sing again.

Jack, on the other side of the showroom surrounded by ex-soldiers, caught her eye for a few long seconds but then Raffie brought her a drink and she was claimed by Mrs Bernstein.

One by one the shopkeepers came to say goodbye and it was a relief when at last she watched Jack lock the door behind the last guest.

'The children are asleep upstairs,' said Mama, 'all curled up together like puppies.'

'In the morning I'll call a committee meeting at Angel of Mercy House,' said Jack. 'King Midas had a vast store of treasure and some of it will be used to provide for the children.'

Raffie yawned. 'Let's go home.'

'My head is spinning,' said Venetia. 'Shall we walk?'

The air was sweet after the rain. The stars had come out and there was enough moonlight for them to be able to avoid the puddles.

Jack linked his arm through Venetia's and they followed behind Mama and Raffie.

Venetia kept thinking about Kitty and Belle. They'd both been good girls, victims of circumstance, despite what anyone else might think.

'Venetia,' said Jack. 'There's something I want to discuss with you.'

She caught her breath. 'Yes, Jack?'

'I have a plan for Lovell and Chamberlaine.'

She sighed in disappointment. Just for a minute she'd hoped he was going to tell her he loved her.

'I have ambitions to make it the most talked-about shop in

Cheapside,' he continued, his voice bubbling with enthusiasm. 'I want us to bring a whole new way of shopping to our customers.'

'I'm not sure I understand.'

'I'd like us to sell a wide variety of luxury goods, the very best available, to entice the public to buy.'

'But we can't afford expensive stock, Jack.'

'I know,' he said, 'but the Bernsteins have lost their premises. Supposing they opened up a department in the rooms above our showroom, to sell their furs? Then there's the haberdasher's and Johnson's stationery. We could rent out space to carefully selected businesses: jewellers, silversmiths, milliners, glove makers and the like. Customers would have to walk through our showroom on their way to purchase luxury items in other departments.'

'And so they'd discover our goods and services, too?' said Venetia slowly.

'Exactly!'

She turned the idea over in her mind. 'Perhaps we might serve refreshments also? Ladies could meet their friends and then spend a whole morning shopping with us.' Despite her exhaustion excitement stirred inside her. This could be the beginning of a much greater dream. 'Jack, it's a wonderful idea!'

'We're too weary to talk about it now,' he said, 'but I couldn't wait to share the thought with you.'

They arrived in Quill Court and Annunziata opened the door for them, exclaiming in horror at the state of Venetia's dress.

'It's been an eventful day, Annunziata,' said Mama.

Tired but too restless to go to bed, they sat quietly in the drawing room discussing the day's events.

'It's so very good to be home,' said Jack, as he sank wearily on to the sofa between Venetia and Mama.

Home. Venetia looked around the elegant room. The voices of her family murmured in the background as she studied the beautiful patterns in the French rug on the polished floor; the painting of Venice at sunset which hung over the marble fireplace was one of her favourites. Father's loving influence was present wherever she looked in this house where he'd dreamed of uniting his two families. She felt almost at peace for the first time in months.

'I never imagined,' she said, 'when we arrived here from Spindrift Cottage, grieving and apprehensive, we'd ever feel at home in Quill Court. But I've grown to love it.'

'Theo's idea of bringing all his family together was right after all,' said Mama. 'But I will always miss him terribly.' Her mouth quivered.

Jack put his arm around her. 'We all will,' he said.

'But now I have another son and daughter to love.' Mama patted his hand. 'I can't keep my eyes open another minute,' she said. 'I'm off to bed.'

Me too,' said Raffie, yawning.

The door closed behind them.

'We'll bring Florence home tomorrow,' said Venetia. 'I can hardly believe it's safe now.'

'There are still plenty of villains out there,' said Jack.

'But you've brought together a militia to keep them under control,' said Venetia. 'I wondered where you were when you kept slipping away from the shop. It's a wonderful idea to give work to injured ex-soldiers.'

'But also a selfish one,' said Jack. 'I needed to raise the militia to give myself a new purpose. I fell into the depths of despair when my leg was injured. I'd been a good soldier with every expectation of a long and successful military career. All of a sudden I was useless, thrown on the scrapheap.'

'Never that!'

'And then I met you. Bright, beautiful and clever ... you shone like a star.'

'You said I was a gold-digger!'

'I was harsh because I wanted you so much. But how could you possibly love a useless cripple with no career and no idea what he wanted from life? I had to find a new purpose, to be worthy of you.'

She touched his cheek. 'I never thought of you as useless! Besides, as a child of an illicit union, what did I have to offer you?'

He pressed her hand to his cheek. 'I loved my mother very much but she and your father were totally unsuited to each other. I can quite see why he fell so absolutely in love with your mama.' Then he kissed the inside of Venetia's wrist in a way that made her shiver with longing. 'Just as I have fallen in love with you,' he said.

'Oh, Jack!' A sob of happiness caught in her throat. He'd finally said the words she'd longed to hear; he loved her after all.

'Venetia, do you think, one day, you might love me?'

'But you must know I already do!'

He kissed her, holding her so tightly she felt his heart beating rapidly against hers.

At last he drew back and cupped her chin tenderly in his hands while he looked deep into her eyes. 'Miss Venetia Lovell,' he said, 'you are the most infuriating and enchanting female I have ever met. And I beg you, the day after you come out of mourning, please will you marry me?'

She frowned but in her mind she heard the joyful music of trumpets and cymbals. 'Bearing in mind my father's lack of propriety in matters matrimonial, I'm sure he wouldn't have minded if we don't wait that long.'

Jack shouted with laughter and gathered her into his arms.

She tipped up her face and he wound his fingers through her hair, dropping soft kisses on her eyelids and whispering words of love. His kisses grew more passionate until she was soft and melting inside, full of the tingling promise of what was to come.

Encircled safely in Jack's arms in the house in Quill Court, Venetia knew she had truly come home at last.

Historical Note

For most of my adult life I have been involved with designing the interiors of hotels and private residences. The Georgian period, especially the part of it known as the Regency, has always been my favourite for its grace, sophistication, and, sometimes, the extravagant flamboyance of its architecture and interiors.

Once I had decided to set this novel in the Regency era I began to research what it was like to live in London at that time. Very soon I became fascinated by the contrast between the elegant drawing rooms of the newly built townhouses, set around peaceful garden squares, and the gin shops and brothels in the warrens of squalid rookeries surrounding the city, where the underworld was based. Two completely different societies co-existed in the city.

Crime had reached epidemic proportions and there seemed to be no way of controlling the criminal underworld. Burglary was so common many householders were unable to leave their homes for any period of time without taking elaborate precautions. In the streets you were likely to be jostled by a predatory group of prostitutes or set upon by footpads and cutpurses.

While I was still deciding on the subject of this novel, I was astonished to discover that there was no centralised police force until 1829. Before that provision of law enforcement was patchy and corrupt, to say the least, and organised crime was growing out of control.

In the mid-eighteenth century Henry Fielding had established a centre for law enforcement in Bow Street and over the years the number of people it employed increased. Experienced thief-takers who were fleet of foot became known as Bow Street Runners and could be employed by private citizens. By the end of the century some of the Runners, who didn't receive a salary, were acting as middlemen, negotiating the return of stolen goods in exchange for a fee paid to the criminal. Sometimes the law enforcers took bribes or framed petty thieves in order to claim a reward.

In 1792 seven new Public Offices, managed along the same lines as Bow Street and manned by stipendiary magistrates appointed by the Crown, were opened. Each had six law enforcement officers but these men often owed their appointment to highly placed acquaintances rather than any special or appropriate skills of their own.

This sometimes corrupt, and often ineffective, force was reformed by Sir Robert Peel in his Metropolitan Police Act of 1829. From then on the Metropolitan Police employed salaried officers, and attempts to contain criminal activities became centralised within the city.

In 1814, however, when *The House in Quill Court* is set, the power and arrogance of the underworld gang leaders went virtually unchallenged and a co-ordinated attempt to administer justice was still a distant dream.

Further Reading

While researching for this novel I studied innumerable books but the following three were especially helpful to me:

Eavesdropping on Jane Austen's England by Roy and Lesley Adkins;
The Secret History of Georgian London by Dan Cruickshank;
Thieves' Kitchen by Donald A. Low.

Reading Group questions

- How did you experience the book? What emotions did the story evoke in you?

- Who was your favourite character and why?

- Justice is a strong theme throughout the story. There was no co-ordinated police force during the Regency era. Do you think this was the cause of the growth of organised crime or were there other reasons?

- How did the choices made by Venetia and Kitty affect their lives and what choices would you have made in those circumstances?

- Did you see Kitty as a victim or a heroine?

- Compare and contrast Jack Chamberlaine and Nat Griggs. Which was the greater hero?

- The Regency era was a time of great contrast in the way the rich and the poor lived. Did you feel the rich were portrayed as 'superior' and the poor as 'feckless'?

- What aspect of the novel did you enjoy most?

- Have you learned something from the novel? Did anything surprise you?

- If you don't usually read historical fiction, did you find the story engaging enough to want to read more in this genre?